I0602884

Vectors of Vengeance: A Military Women's Fiction

Mahoney & Squire Series, Book 4

Mike Krentz

Purple Papaya LLC

Dedication

A respectful salute to the committed physicians, nurses, medical service officers, and corpsmen who staff US Navy ships at the tip of the spear.

Note to Readers

I PREVIOUSLY PUBLISHED THIS story in 2016 as VECTORS, by Mike J. Krentz. This extensively revised and upgraded second edition bears a more relevant title.

Like many organizations, the US Navy and the medical profession have a plethora of acronyms, abbreviations, and slang phrases that might confuse some readers. A glossary appears after the last chapter.

Contents

Chapter 1

March, 2014. Pyongyang, Democratic People's Republic of Korea (DPRK)

V ICE MARSHAL SEONG CHUNGHEE, second in command to the Supreme Leader of the Democratic People's Republic of Korea (DPRK), advanced like a raging bear on General Jin Dongsun, Minister of People's Security.

"If you lie, the Supreme Leader will cut out your tongue and feed it to his dogs."

General Jin stepped back and bowed from the waist. His hand hovered over the pistol holstered at his hip, but his superior's hostile glare caused him to move the hand. Jin knew better than to threaten the Supreme Leader's most trusted adviser. This man could stand between Jin and sure death at the whim of their self-proclaimed "Dear Leader."

"Comrade Vice Marshal," Jin said. "I regret the truth. The American pilot escaped."

He bowed again and retreated another step. "Her comrades infiltrated the gulag and took her."

The vice marshal's face tensed, and his eyes narrowed. "Where was Colonel Chul Boo Ju when this happened?"

"Colonel Chul is dead, Comrade Vice Marshal. Shot before the American woman fled."

The vice marshal's explosive retort showered spittle over the general's face. "Shot? How did the prisoner get a gun?"

Jin squared his stance and returned his hand to the pistol holster. "The American did not kill Boo Ju. Lee Yeong Nae shot him. She enabled the woman's escape."

The vice marshal's face turned purple. He advanced on General Jin; piercing eyes and tense mouth a few centimeters from his subordinate's face.

"Tell me, Comrade General, how one of our most trusted operatives shot a respected comrade and helped an American spy to escape." He closed his own hand over the general's on the holstered pistol. "Tell me the whole truth in the next minute or I will destroy you with your own gun." He squeezed the general's hand. "Or shall I let the Dear Leader decide your fate?"

General Jin let go of the holster. Vice Marshal Seong withdrew the general's pistol and held it by his side.

Jin's words came in a rush. "Lee Yeong Nae betrayed the true Korean people and whored herself to the American intelligence agency. She wore the uniform of the Korean People's Army, infiltrated the camp, killed Comrade Chul Boo Ju, and extracted the prisoner. An American Navy helicopter retrieved the fugitive before our soldiers caught up to them."

He shrank backward. "This occurred soon after the American Navy jets destroyed our biological lab. That action distracted our defense forces."

The vice marshal pressed the gun's muzzle against General Jin's forehead. "You are dead, Jin Dongsun. But first you tell me if the traitor Lee Yeong Nae also fled."

Jin stared into the vice marshal's eyes and spoke in a defiant voice. "Lee Yeong Nae is dead. The American fugitive kicked her off the helicopter as it lifted. Then our soldiers demolished that traitor with gunfire."

"The Supreme Leader does not tolerate failure." Seong pressed the muzzle hard against the general's forehead and pulled the trigger. The man's head burst into a shower of flesh and bone and blood and brain.

At the sound of the gunshot, guards rushed into the vice marshal's office.

Vice Marshal Seong pivoted toward the door. "Clean up this mess before I return."

***

Thirty minutes later, in a secure location deep in the bowels of the DPRK headquarters building in Pyongyang, Vice Marshal Seong conferred with a handful of trusted confidants on the National Defense Commission.

"The Supreme Leader will demand retribution." Seong gestured toward General Jin's empty seat. "We must retaliate, or we will see more empty chairs at this table."

General Hwang, minister of the People's Armed Forces, spoke. "Our Special Purpose Operations Reconnaissance Bureau may have the solution." He cast a haughty look around the room. "Soon, the American military and their ROK bastards will conduct their annual military exercise out of Seoul and Busan. On that stage, we will rain down the Supreme Leader's revenge for the affront to our people by the American spy and her leaders."

"Tell us."

"The true Korea will behead the invading American naval force and wreak mass destruction on the puppet ROK." He offered a sinister smile. "We have a more trusted agent, a cousin of Lee Yeong Nae..."

Chapter 2

Lee Myung Suk gasped when Colonel Hong Dong Jon told her the news. Her cousin dead? She betrayed the state?

"How can this be?"

Across the table, Colonel Hong's cratered face repulsed Myung Suk. The scar running from his left ear to his left cheek rendered an angry purple line through the sallow pockmarks.

Myung constrained herself from a violent urge to lash out at the bearer of such unexpected, terrible news. But she knew better than to rile the infamous deputy head of the Korean People's Army's Special Purpose Operations Reconnaissance Bureau. This man killed at will. With impunity, and with pleasure.

Hong Dong Jon sneered. His stern voice evoked gravel pouring through a spout. "Lee Yeong Nae turned against the true Korean people and sabotaged her mission. Your weak cousin lacked the heart to resist capitalist evils. She debauched herself with an American woman and then betrayed the Supreme Leader's trust by becoming a counterspy. She killed a loyal KPA comrade and enabled the American's escape."

Lee Myung Suk buried her face in her hands. She and her cousin had grown up together like sisters after the state's internal security forces hauled Yeong Nae's parents and brother to a prison camp. At age ten, Lee Yeong Nae had reported her own parents to the state for Western-leaning tendencies. In reward for her loyalty, the authorities had allowed her to live with Lee Myung Suk's family.

"My cousin proved her loyalty to the state twenty years ago. She could not do what you say. If I may talk to her..."

"No one can talk to your treacherous cousin. The whore for whom she betrayed us pushed her off the rescue helicopter. KPA forces finished her."

Myung Suk rose from the chair. "You lie!"

Dong Jon rose, leaned forward. Myung Suk thought he would strike her. He sneered and pulled a photo from a file folder on the table and pushed it in front of Myung.

"Proof."

In the photo, a woman in KPA uniform lay dead in a green field, a bloody body riddled with bullet wounds. Vacant eyes stared at the sky. Lee Myung Suk sobbed as she recognized her cousin, Lee Yeong Nae.

The sobs soon turned to rage. She glowered at the emotionless colonel. "Tell me more. Tell me everything."

Dong Jon pulled another photo from the folder. It showed the Supreme Leader orating before a crowd assembled in the great square in front of the presidential palace in Pyongyang. Foreign television cameras on one side of the stage suggested an international audience. Behind the Supreme Leader stood a woman with cropped blond hair and fair skin, wearing a US Navy olive-green flight suit. Her hands were bound behind her back, but her eyes stared straight at the crowd as if to defy the Supreme Leader.

Colonel Hong pointed at the photo. "KPA Special Forces captured this pilot after she crashed a US Navy spy plane into the West Sea. She is Lieutenant Commander Jessica Squire, but her American colleagues call her 'Cricket.' She and your cousin were lovers." Dong Jon spat out the last word as if it were bile.

He pointed to another prominent figure in the photo, a uniformed KPA colonel standing on the other side of the Supreme Leader. "Colonel Chul Boo Ju delivered the American prisoner to the Dear Leader. After denouncing the spy in front of the entire world, the Dear Leader gave the woman to Comrade Boo as his concubine."

Myung Suk pointed to a person in the photo's background. "That's my cousin." In the picture, Lee Yeong Nae wore a KPA uniform and stood among a group of officers behind the Supreme Leader and the American prisoner.

"Yes," Colonel Hong said. "None of us knew then the treachery in her heart."

His gaze penetrated to Lee Myung's soul. "After the speech, Colonel Boo took the American to his private quarters near Prison Camp Eight, where he kept her locked in a bedroom. On the same day that American Navy bombers destroyed our biological weapons laboratory, Lee Yeong Nae gained entrance to that private room while Colonel Boo was taking his pleasure. Yeong Nae shot Colonel Boo and then escaped with the American to a clearing where a US Navy helicopter picked her up under heavy fire from our soldiers in pursuit. An American jet came out of nowhere to fire a missile at our forces, driving them back and allowing the helicopter to take off."

The colonel's eyes narrowed. "As it lifted, Yeong Nae tried to climb aboard, but the harlot she had just rescued kicked her. When she fell to the ground, well, you see in the photo what KPA soldiers did."

Lee Myung Suk stared at Colonel Hong. "This American pilot killed my cousin?"

Dong Jon crossed his arms and scowled. "Yes."

Mixed tears of sadness and rage streamed down Myung Suk's face. Colonel Hong cast her a dispassionate look.

Sensing the conversation had not ended, she wiped her eyes and regarded the colonel with a hardened face. "What do you want from me?"

"I have a message from Vice Marshal Seong Chunghee. The Supreme Leader gives you, Comrade Major Lee Myung Suk of KPA Special Forces, the honor of atoning for Lee Yeong Nae's treachery. You will be the Supreme Leader's personal instrument of death to Lieutenant Commander Squire, the despicable US Navy forces, and their ROK puppets."

Suicide mission.

Lee Myung Suk did not hesitate. "With gratitude to the Supreme Leader, I accept this honor in deep humility. I vow to execute the mission to the best of my ability." She paused and then added, "Even to my own glorious death in the service of the true Korean people."

A trace of a smile crossed Colonel Hong's face. "Very well. We begin at once to plan."

He pushed the file folder across the table to her. "First, you must learn everything about this 'Cricket' insect."

Chapter 3

Five months later. August, 2014. Novosibirsk, Siberia, Russia

NIKOLAI ORLOV REGARDED WITH dismay his daughter's shaved cranium and gaunt stature. As if she had a ninety-year-old's head on a five-year-old body. At age nine, Lora should have been home in Koltsovo, playing kickball with friends. Instead, she faced major brain surgery in the chilly confines of Novosibirsk State Medical University. He squeezed his little girl's hand and looked across the gurney. Svetlana stroked their daughter's cheek, her face wet with tears.

Nikolai swallowed hard. The gesture caught Svetlana's attention. "I am sorry," he mouthed.

An orderly with a clipboard emerged through the doors from the operating suite. The young man checked Lora's wristband against a paper on the clipboard. "Lora Nikolaevna Orlov, for sub-occipital craniotomy and resection of medulloblastoma," he said, as if reading a newspaper. "You are both the parents?" He eyed Nikolai with suspicion. At age sixty-three, Nikolai could be the girl's grandfather instead of co-parent with the young, photogenic dark-haired woman next to him.

Nikolai did not hide his annoyance. "Both parents."

The orderly shrugged. "You will find the waiting room down the hall to the left."

The man pushed the gurney toward the operating suite doors, but neither Nikolai nor Svetlana let go of Lora's hands.

Nikolai glared at the young man. "A minute, please."

The orderly stepped back. "Only a minute."

Svetlana squeezed Lora's hand so hard that the girl winced through the heavy sedation.

Nikolai leaned over and spoke into his daughter's ear. "Be brave, my little sun. Mama and I will be here when you come out." He looked at Svetlana, the woman who had brought unexpected joy and sunshine into his life.

"We will beat this."

***

Ten hours later, Nikolai and Svetlana hugged each other in the austere hospital waiting room. The anguish in his wife's voice and eyes carved a hole in Nikolai's heart.

"Is there no hope?" she asked.

"Never lose hope," Nikolai said. "The surgeons could not remove the entire tumor. Other treatments exist."

"But no cure."

"The doctor never said that."

"Lora still has a brain tumor. She will never be normal. The doctor said..."

"Doctors don't know everything."

Svetlana pushed away. "And you do? What does a genetic virologist understand about brain tumors?"

Other people in the room stared at them. Nikolai steered Svetlana out the door.

Downstairs in the hospital coffee shop, they sipped coffee at a small table. Svetlana calmed. Nikolai had slipped a shot of vodka from a pocket flask into his coffee. He looked at his wife. "I have studied the literature on Lora's disease. With radiation and chemotherapy, she can survive and live a normal life. The idiot doctors in this town are not competent enough for her. This hospital cannot provide what she needs."

Svetlana stared into her cup. "No cure. No hope."

Nikolai took his wife's hand. "My position provides me with, uh, international connections."

Some of which I cannot divulge.

"I know an American physician at the Boston Children's Hospital, part of the Harvard Medical School. They have an entire center for treating brain tumors in children. They are running a new clinical trial…"

"America? You are delusional, Nikolai Petrovich. Why not Moscow?"

"Our health system is broken. Hospitals overcrowded. People wait months for critical therapy. By the time Lora can get into treatment, it will be too late."

Svetlana pulled her hand away. "Don't do this, Nikolai. Americans pay dearly for their health care. We cannot afford it."

"We don't need to afford the treatment. They do not charge for the clinical trial because it's a scientific study to prove the treatment works."

"Lora can barely travel to the doctor's office, much less to America. Do they pay for transportation?"

Nikolai shook his head. "Lora would need medical air transport. Private companies exist for that. Very good care, I am told." His eyes dropped. "Very expensive."

Svetlana's eyes and voice hardened. "You offer nothing, Nikolai Petrovich. Do not taunt me with false hopes. Even in your 'position', we cannot afford such a dream."

She stood.

"There may be a way," Nikolai said.

Svetlana had already left the room.

Chapter 4

A WEEK LATER, NIKOLAI and Svetlana brought Lora home from the hospital. The doctors had refused Nikolai's ardent pleas to keep the girl a few more days.

"We need the bed," the uncaring surgeon had said.

After getting Lora settled and asleep in her own room, both parents tiptoed out in near exhaustion. Nikolai had not mentioned the American treatment option since their blow-up in the hospital coffee shop after Lora's surgery. Outside Lora's bedroom door, Nikolai whispered to Svetlana. "We must talk. I made inquiries about getting Lora to the United States for treatment."

Svetlana lashed out like a poked viper. "Do not talk fantasy to me."

"Even the doctors here say it is the best course."

"Will the doctors pay for the transport? Go with her to a strange country? Hold her hand when she pukes after the therapy?"

Nikolai stayed silent.

"I didn't think so." Svetlana stroked his cheek. "Come back to the real world, Nikolai Petrovich. We cannot afford to take Lora to Moscow for treatment, let alone America. She will wait her turn for therapy in Novosibirsk, and we will pray for the best."

"Lora deserves better!"

"She will get what we can afford. Please, no more nonsense talk. I can't take it. And do not dare to fill Lora's head with it."

Svetlana turned on her heel, walked into their bedroom across the hall from Lora's, and shut the door.

Exhausted though he was, Nikolai could not go to bed. He had managed only short snoozes in the previous week, but sleep would elude him now. In the kitchen, he pulled a bottle of vodka from the back of the cupboard, poured a full glass, and sat at the small table. He emptied the glass in minutes, but the liquor did nothing to quell the agony in his heart and soul.

Nikolai refilled the glass. Twice. Staring into middle space, he saw nothing but the tempest in his mind.

My life for Lora's. I die so my baby can live. Easy trade.

He buried his head in his hands and sifted through every grain of his intellect for a different solution, but found none.

The Korean man offered the only rational course. At what cost? Nikolai would not only lose his family but also betray his career, his life's work, and Mother Russia—maybe endanger the population of an entire country, if not the world. Would he want Lora to live in such a world? What would she think of her father if the truth came out?

And Svetlana...?

My life for Lora's. But how many other lives?

Nikolai tiptoed to Lora's room. At the sight of her, his heart plunged. She looked so tiny in the bed, so skinny and pale. Thin stubble as fine as baby hair dotted a scalp from which auburn locks had once hung in natural curls. The girl's breathing came in starts, perhaps from a nightmare.

He could not remember a healthy Lora. She had always been sick, dying in bits every day. Now his little sun's light waned dimmer with each breath. Could the clinical trial in America turn the impossible tide?

Too late?

Nikolai shook his head, never taking his eyes off Lora.

This is not a science study. This is my only child. Even if only a one percent chance...

Nikolai stared at Lora for many minutes, frozen in time. His heart and soul entwined in rhythm with Lora's labored breathing. Tears streamed down his face as he leaned over and pressed his lips to her forehead.

"Live, my angel. You must live."

Back in the kitchen, Nikolai poured another glass of vodka. Dawn peeked through the thin curtains over the kitchen window. He downed the vodka in one gulp and stepped out of the house. Even in late July, the brisk Siberian air sent a shiver through his body. Nikolai pulled a cell phone from his pocket, scrolled to a number, and stared at it for a full minute before punching the call button.

A man answered as soon as the phone rang. He spoke in English with a Korean accent, his voice coarse as gravel.

"Nikolai, I trust you have made the right choice."

Nikolai responded in English. "I will do this thing for my daughter." He swallowed hard. "I will do it tonight."

The other man hung up.

Chapter 5

Koltsovo, Russia: State Research Center of Virology and Biotechnology VECTOR

Two decades ago, Dr. Nikolai Orlov, Deputy Director General for Scientific and Methodical Work and International Cooperation at the Vector Institute, would never have imagined what he was about to do now. The best punishment he could expect for this imminent action would be life imprisonment. His scientific prominence might forestall the death penalty. Or assure it.

Nikolai shook the thought from his head as he undressed to don biohazard protection gear. To his benefit, security at the institute had degraded in pace with the Russian health-care system and academia. The vault no longer required two keys held by two different people. Nikolai controlled both keys. Armed guards worked daytime hours only. They trusted the institute's perimeter security to keep out nighttime intruders, and the closed-circuit video surveillance to monitor all activity within the vault. Nikolai made a mental note to erase the videotape after he finished.

As if anyone ever looks at it.

Soon after midnight, Nikolai approached the vault. Clad in a full bio-protective suit, he resembled a moonwalking astronaut instead of a world-renowned scientist. Sweat ran down his back despite the filtered cool air circulating inside the suit. He paused at the vault door. Should he have awakened Svetlana before leaving the house early that morning?

To say or do what?

He had choked on tears when he'd kissed Lora, but the sleepy nine-year-old had sensed no change in her father's mood and demeanor. She was too sick to notice.

Svetlana, in contrast, would have felt his angst as soon as he entered the bedroom. Maybe she already suspected something. Her voice had sounded frigid when he called in the late afternoon to say he had to work into the night. "To catch up from the prolonged absence from Lora's surgery."

Not too late to turn back...

Nikolai shrugged and moved forward.

At the outer airlock door to the Biosafety Safety Level 4 (BSL 4) laboratory, he stopped to catch his breath and calm his nerves.

"For Lora." His voice rasped inside the suit. With a last sigh, he used both keys to unlock the door and stepped into the chamber. Inside the small lab, he surveyed the area. No one else there. Satisfied, he moved to a second secure door. He steadied himself, turned the lock, and stepped inside.

Nikolai's eyes took a minute to adapt to the azure cast of the room. Once his vision adjusted, he organized the workspace under the laminar flow hood, then heated a water bath on the countertop. He needed to work quickly for this venture to succeed. When the water bath stabilized at thirty-seven degrees Celsius, Nikolai stepped to the liquid nitrogen cryogenic freezer—a waist-high stainless-steel vat a meter in diameter. A thin sheen of frost glistened on its surface. Over the bio-protective rubber gloves he already wore, Nikolai donned a second thermo-protective pair, then opened the pressure lid.

A cloud of vapor rose from the liquid bath inside the ice-encrusted interior. Nikolai lifted a vertical rack that contained twenty-four individual vials. He removed vial number eight—the one on which he'd completed the biogenetic modification a month earlier—and plunged it into a container of dry ice. He replaced the rack into its container, slid the container back into the liquid nitrogen, and shut the freezer.

He doffed the thermal gloves before carrying the extracted vial to his workspace. There he swirled the vial in the water bath for fifty-eight seconds by the clock.

When he removed the vial from the bath, Nikolai noted with satisfaction a single bit of ice at the bottom. Under the laminar flow hood, he teased open the stopper on the vial. Using a calibrated pipette, he dripped a pre-warmed diluent into the vial, then closed the vial and gently agitated it until the liquid turned clear.

The virus was now suspended throughout the diluent. Nikolai placed the vial in a test tube rack. He stepped back, gazed at the vial, squeezed his eyes, and sighed.

Point of no return.

In slow, deliberate motions, Nikolai removed the rubber gloves and released the hood of the bio-protective suit. The hiss of escaping positive pressure at first rattled him, but he steadied himself. As he reached for the vial, a sudden surge of fear caused him to freeze in mid-reach.

Cannot do this.

What would the Korean do if Nikolai did not keep their rendezvous? Could Nikolai gather his family and run? He knew better. If he didn't do as promised, Lora would die. So would Svetlana—and Nikolai.

Must do this.

He picked up the vial in his right hand, shook it, popped open the stopper, and held the vial inside the hood near his face. He closed his eyes, snorted the liquid deep into his nose, and held his breath. He forced himself not to blow the liquid back out of his nostrils.

Ten times, he sucked the liquid into his nasal passages until the vial was empty and his head spun. Once confident that he'd inhaled most of the virus-laden liquid, Nikolai resumed normal breaths and resealed the hood on the bio-protective suit. He passed his hands over the suit. No air escaped. The barrier between man and environment was again intact. Nikolai refilled vial number eight with diluent and reversed the earlier procedure to return it to the cryogenic freezer. Then he policed the work area so that it looked undisturbed.

Satisfied, he left the vault.

In a daze, Nikolai transitioned from high-intensity Biosafety Level 4 to the bland world of a Russian scientist-bureaucrat: first the chemical decontamination shower of the suit, then removing the suit and lab-supplied underwear before a final standard body shower. When he emerged into the nonsterile changing room, his watch read 1:03 AM.

Ten minutes later, dressed in his own clothes, Dr. Nikolai Orlov left the Vector Institute. On the way home, he thought about the impossibility of removing even a single virus-laden vial from the secured inner sanctum while keeping the contents viable.

A sardonic smile crossed his face.

The vials themselves have no value. The contents will change the world.

Chapter 6

August, 2014. Yokosuka, Japan. US Naval Forces Base. USS Shenandoah (LCC 21)

J ESSICA "CRICKET" SQUIRE STIFLED a scream as piercing pain roused her from nightmare terror. Chisels driven by powerful, uncaring hands ripped into her ankle bones. She bore the agony in silence, a dominance over suffering that she had learned under the most vicious attacks of her North Korean torturers.

Not six months ago.

Still as stone, Cricket dissociated mind from body, as if her soul hovered over a corpse freed from agony. She had taught herself many such defenses while curled up naked in the hell-black hold of the torture boat, waiting for the next assault. The psychic armor had kept her alive, and almost sane.

The stabbing ankle pain settled into a deep throbbing ache, a welcome reprieve from the horrific nightmares.

Cricket's eyes opened to the familiar confines of her new home, a small gray windowless stateroom aft on the second deck of USS *Shenandoah,* flagship of the United States Seventh Fleet, moored in home port, Yokosuka, Japan. As her eyes accommodated to the dim ambient light, she twisted in the narrow rack to check the time. The chisels returned with a vengeance, gouging into the bones, forcing Cricket to squeal in pain. She bit her lip to hush herself, lest her captors hear her cry.

But no stinking commandos loomed in the darkness. Relieved, Cricket looked at the clock's illuminated numbers: 4:00 AM. Three hours since the last Vicodin.

Tolerance. As the doc predicted. Dare not take another pill so soon.

She must remain alert for the morning report, to generate the operations plans and prepare to fight an imaginary war that could never compare to the ongoing fracas within her own body and soul. Cricket worried that the narcotics and sedatives made the nightmares more vivid, but she needed to control the pain. The doctors who had treated her at Tripler Medical Center in Hawaii had tried to put her on another six months of limited duty, or LIMDU, thinking that she was not yet well enough in mind or body to return to the operational environment.

I would have died on LIMDU. Here I am alive.

The more she ached, the more alive she felt, and the more committed she was to survival—and vengeance.

"Failure is not in falling down but in staying down." Or something like that. I get up, or I die.

The worst nightmares often caused Cricket to awaken mummified in nightclothes and bedsheets, whereupon she would thrash about in panic to get free. She'd resorted to sleeping naked on top of her rack. Even when the ship's environment was too cold for most sailors, Cricket slept better with the air cooling her skin against the heat raging inside her body.

She slept better, but never well. Restful sleep had become as elusive a dream as flying again. The Navy flight surgeons had dashed the latter dream by permanently grounding Cricket from flying duty. The North Korean tormentors had forever robbed her of restful sleep.

Cricket switched on the light over her rack and wiped the spectral image of Colonel Boo's last climactic grimace from her vision. She took a deep breath, braced for the expected pain, and swung her legs out of the narrow rack. As soon as she did, a brutal hammer pounded the traumatized left ankle. She sat on the rack's edge and panted like a wounded puppy. Gravity aided blood flow to her crippled limb. After a minute, the hammering stopped, and the pain regressed to its usual chronic ache.

She could not recall a time when her ankle did not hurt. Cricket remembered little of her life before she plunged the wounded P-8 *Poseidon* reconnaissance jet into a controlled crash into the West Sea and nearly drowned. She had emerged to the surface gasping for life, with only the painful shattered ankle to prove she was alive and not in heaven.

If only she had known then that she'd plunged into actual hell…

Across the small room, Lee Young's image smiled from a photograph taped to the bulkhead. A reminder of happier days together when Cricket thought her lover was Korean American, not North Korean; a time before hell, before the betrayal, the rescue, and…

Cricket looked away. Lee had given her the framed photo just before Cricket deployed to the Western Pacific for a routine six-month tour that had turned into catastrophe.

"An engagement present," Lee had said. In the photo, she wore the black leather dress she'd bought for the engagement celebration; postponed when Cricket received orders to Okinawa.

Lee's beguiling face and penetrating eyes in the photo held Cricket's gaze. A warm flush coursed through her body. Then the specter of Lee's abject surprise as she plummeted from the rescue helo cut into Cricket's reverie. The warm glow gave way to a shiver. She stared at the steel beams in the overhead above her rack. Every day after her escape, she wondered in vain why she had hurled the one love of her life to certain death.

She looked back at the photo. "Who the hell were you? Did you love me, or was that also a lie?"

Cricket sat on the edge of the rack for another five minutes before she could push off and stand on her good leg. Leaning against the bulkhead for support, she transferred half her weight to the gimpy ankle and sucked wind as the bones screamed out against the added burden. She took tiny ginger steps until the acute pain released and she could pad around with a slight limp. With the flagship moored to the pier, at least Cricket did not have to brace against the unpredictable rolls of the flat-bottomed ship bobbing like a cork in open water.

In front of a full-length mirror on the stateroom door, Cricket examined her body. Maybe she'd gained a little weight, although her once muscular arms looked thin. Her breasts drooped, and the skin hung loose on her abdomen. She ignored the scars and old bruises on her torso and extremities. They had become as much a part of her as the thin blond hair.

Today I will make time to work out.

Of course, she lied. Once she left her stateroom, the operational tempo would be unrelenting. No Seventh Fleet Deputy for Current Operations (N3B) had leisure time to shit or piss, let alone pump iron—especially preparing for a major military exercise of the non-aerobic sort.

Cricket donned a terry bathrobe, slipped into shower sandals, slid her stateroom key card into a pocket, and limped out the door and down the passageway to the female officers' head and shower.

Twenty minutes later, she returned and donned loose-fitting underwear and a royal-blue tee-shirt. She climbed into an olive-green flight suit and sat on the rack to put on thick socks and her aviator boots. She laced the left boot tight to brace the weak ankle. Then she stuffed a PowerBar into a breast pocket and walked as erect as possible from her stateroom.

Once again the confident naval aviator, Commander Jessica "Cricket" Squire went to work. She left the pain and the nightmares and the faces of Colonel Boo and Lee Young back in the stateroom.

Chapter 7

"**R**ATS WHERE?"

Lieutenant Commander Troy Pearson, USS *Shenandoah* medical officer, scowled at the pallid woman sitting on the edge of the exam table in his cramped office. Her flight suit hung loose on a body it had once fit. Wary green eyes suggested a tiger hidden under the suit, ready to spring at the first inkling of a threat.

Commander "Cricket" Squire smirked and glanced at her crotch. "You heard me, Doc. Bowels too." She rubbed a hand through stringy blond hair. A veil of weary sadness banished the light from her eyes. "Not really, but at the time..." Her voice cracked. "It seemed real."

"Tell me more," Troy said.

The woman dropped her gaze. He tried to reassure her. "Just what's comfortable. Save the rest for another day."

Commander Squire sighed. She stared at something far beyond the exam room. "There were real rats," she said in a flat voice. "The men kept me naked in a dark hold. I couldn't see the rats, but I heard them skitter. When they came near, I shooed them away. That got harder as I grew weaker. One rat chewed..."

Her voice trailed off as she looked at the floor. "Then my mind played tricks, and I imagined the rats had crawled inside me."

She shrugged. "I had menstrual cramps and dysentery, not rats." Her shoulders drooped, her head bowed, and a shiver coursed through her body.

Troy handed her a water bottle. She drank in small sips.

"Your captors," he said. "They were rats too?"

At once she stood, the tiger rampant, eyes fierce. "Look, Doc. I went through that psych shit at Tripler. I've got PTSD, okay? Flashbacks, nightmares, panic attacks, the whole syndrome. Textbook. I didn't come to you for psychotherapy. I need something to help me sleep at night so I can do my job."

With taut muscles and pinched face, she advanced into his personal space. "You want to hear how those North Korean animals abused me before you give me medicine, I'll tell you. You want to concoct a Freudian connection between what they did and my hallucinations of rats in my snatch and ass? Go ahead. Whatever gets you jollied up, so long as I walk out of here with Ambien."

She stepped back. "But if you want to play amateur shrink, I'm gone." She folded her arms. "Here's the thing, Doc. No amount of reliving that nightmare will get me past it. Ever. I'm done with that psych crap."

Troy raised his hands. "No jollies here, ma'am, honest. I appreciate your trauma, and I don't mean to open wounds." He tried a reassuring look. "I can help you."

The commander did not respond.

"I can give you Ambien for now," Troy said. "Work with me and we can get to where you don't need it." He paused, wondering how far to push her. "Or the Vicodin."

Commander Squire's red-hot stare bored into his forehead.

Why is this woman on this ship? She needs intense psychotherapy, not a demanding operational job. Who the hell approved her orders?

Troy knew the answer. The drama of her rescue, soon after Kim Jong Un paraded her in front of the entire world as his puppet, had titillated the American media. They made the attractive naval aviator a national hero. When she announced her resolve to return to the Seventh Fleet and reengage the North Korean threat, no doctor or flag officer in the Navy dared to deter her.

His patient held the threatening pose for almost a full minute before drawing back and speaking in a softer tone. "Tell you what, Doc. Give me the Ambien now, and I promise to return for another talk when I'm rested."

"I don't believe you. Once you get meds, you won't come back until you need a refill. We both know where that road leads."

Squire's face and voice turned hard again. "Fine. Cold turkey. Won't be the first time." She pointed a finger between Troy's eyes. "If I cannot do my job and someone gets killed, that's on you, Doc."

She started toward the door. Troy stood and blocked her path.

Squire glared at him. "Don't mess with me, Doc. You're out of your league."

"You can't do your job with a mind dulled by narcotics and sedatives. You want to be here? Crave revenge? I will help you do that. All of it. But you must cooperate. Otherwise, you end up back at Tripler talking to shrinks every day."

"Out of my way, Doc."

Troy did not move. "You're the one out of your league here, Commander. You can choose to walk out without Ambien." He looked her in the eye. "People consider you a hero for coming back. How about being a proper hero? You have monsters inside you bigger and scarier than rats in your lady parts. Face them or they will devour you."

He touched her shoulder. "I can help you."

Commander Squire pushed past him. "Go shrink yourself, Doc."

Chapter 8

A S SOON AS HE finished morning sick-call clinic, Troy climbed to the flag deck to find the Seventh Fleet surgeon. He stopped at the stateroom door that featured the Seventh Fleet logo over the words, *Captain Rosalie Deckert, MC, USN. Fleet Surgeon*.

A short, fit, fortyish woman answered Troy's knock. She wore the prescribed navy-blue and gray working uniform, or "aquaflage," as sailors called it, without the uniform blouse. A tight-fitting, dark blue standard-issue tee-shirt clung to the woman's chest. Ample trousers draped a lower body well with the limits of US Navy body-fat standards.

Troy wore a similar uniform, tailored to his athletic build—which the woman admired at the same time that Troy glanced at her breasts.

The captain smiled. "Hey, Troy. What brings you to the flag deck?"

"I need to chat with you about a member of the Seventh Fleet staff."

Captain Deckert sighed and opened the door wider. "Come in." She ushered Troy into a stateroom larger than his own exam room, with a full-size desk, a faux leather couch that converted into a rack for sleep, and a private head.

Rank does have its privileges.

The captain motioned Troy to the couch. She sat in the desk chair across from him. Various medical certificates decorated the bulkhead. Neither the desk nor the bulkhead contained any personal photos.

The two physicians had collaborated in the past, when Troy was the medical officer at the Navy's branch medical clinic in Chinhae, South Korea. Captain Deckert's expertise in infectious disease had supported Troy's investigation into botulism outbreaks at both the US Navy base in Chinhae, and the Korean counterpart in Busan—outbreaks engineered by North Korea special forces. That had led to the Seventh Fleet-directed destruction of a North Korean bioweapons facility, and the rescue of Cricket Squire from a North Korean prison camp.

Rose Deckert gave Troy a knowing smile. "You're here to discuss our national hero, Commander Squire." A statement, not a question.

Troy nodded. "Yes."

"She came by here earlier this morning."

Troy tensed. "Did she ask for medication?"

"She did. Commander Squire suffers from PTSD and horrific nightmares. I gave her a prescription for Ambien."

"Damn," Troy said. "Anything else?"

"Vicodin for her chronic ankle pain." She frowned. "Are you saying...?"

Troy nodded. "She came to you right after I denied her request for Ambien."

Captain Deckert stiffened. "Who wouldn't need pharmaceutical support after what she endured?"

"She can't function in her job if she's on drugs."

"Seemed functional to me. She described how the North Koreans used narcotics to control her, weaken her resolve, and enslave her. She never succumbed."

"So she believes. She's carrying a pile of crap under the surface that she won't face. Narcs and sedatives won't help that."

Deckert folded her arms. "She's here in a seagoing high-tempo operational billet. Responsible medical authority cleared her for full duty."

"Captain, we both know the overseas medical screening process is a joke, especially when higher line authority meddles with it. As you said, Commander Squire became a national hero after what she endured in North Korea. The brass would have cleared her for full duty even if she were a quadruple amputee. No one who wants to move up the Navy medical career ladder would dare to block her return to the tip of the spear."

"I might disagree with you on that, but I get the point. Regardless of how she got here, or whether she should be, Commander Squire is our responsibility—my responsibility first, since she's assigned to Seventh Fleet." She scowled. "I appreciate the heads up. Maybe she bamboozled me this morning, but it won't happen again."

"We should collaborate," Troy said.

Deckert nodded. "Yep. From now on, we are a coordinated medical team. No more getting played against each other."

Troy shook his head. "She shouldn't be here. At all. She's not fit for sea duty, let alone a high-level staff job."

"Will you send her home, Commander?"

Troy did not respond.

"Didn't think so," the captain said. "We will have to do our damnedest to keep her sane and healthy." She took a breath. "The cost of failure is unthinkable."

Chapter 9

August, 2014. City of Changjon, Southeast Coast of North Korea

B Y NORTH KOREAN STANDARDS, the Kumgangsan Hotel on the outskirts of Changjon near the border with South Korea epitomized luxury. Built during a time of more harmonious relations between North and South, the mid-rise hotel had hosted many South Korean tourists. But in 2008, after North Korean soldiers shot and killed an innocent South Korean woman who wandered into a military zone, the Republic of Korea (ROK) government had ceased to support cross-border travel by its South Korean citizens.

Now the hotel hosted a smaller clientele of Chinese and other foreign tourists, plus the rare North Korean civilian privileged to stay there. The hotel made the ideal base for Lee Myung Suk to wait for her mission to launch.

Myung traveled light. A tattered rolling duffel bag with a false bottom carried clothing that a South Korean businesswoman would wear on vacation. She'd hung the black leather dress in the hotel room's small closet. The duffel's hidden compartment contained the tools of her actual occupation as a North Korean Special Forces operative. These included the disassembled Type 88 Chinese-made semi-automatic assault rifle she hoped not to use.

A woman has better weapons.

After three days in the hotel, Myung had grown restless. Waiting to launch had always been the most difficult phase of a mission. As the evening of the fourth day turned to night, she lay on top of the bedcovers wearing faded military camouflage. Combat boots stood ready on the floor. Myung dozed on and off, but remained in touch with the surroundings.

She had always slept that way, the nature of a household where your family lived under constant suspicion. They never knew when the police or government officials might raid the house to haul the family away; for a just reason, or not. Memory of the night the government seized Lee Yeong Nae's parents and brother still burned in Myung's memory. She had saved the rest of the family by her offer to serve the Supreme Leader in whatever way he desired.

Her hand touched the handle of the North Korean homegrown Type 70 pistol underneath the pillow. A constant companion, the weapon had eliminated several threats to Myung's life over the years.

The burner cell phone's buzz woke her from light sleep. She answered before the vibration stopped.

Dong Jon's gravelly voice. "Begin Operation Vector." He hung up without waiting for a response.

Myung clicked off, then punched a speed-dial button. "We go now."

She jumped off the bed and donned the combat boots. Then she removed the SIM card from the phone, ripped it between her fingers, and flushed the pieces down the toilet. She destroyed the battery and crushed the phone's remaining carcass under the heel of her boot. She removed the black leather dress from the closet hanger, zipped up the bodice, folded the garment with extra care, and placed it on top of the duffel's contents.

Myung expected to travel for several weeks before completing her mission. She had no illusions about a return to the homeland, nor did she care. She had long ago sold herself. Now, in honor and glory, she would sacrifice her life for the Supreme Leader and the true Korea.

Lee Myung Suk slung the duffel bag over her shoulder and left the room without looking back.

Chapter 10
Near Sokcho, Northeast Coast of South Korea

A s soon as the rigid hull inflatable boat (RHIB) scraped sand, Lee Myung Suk jumped out and ran up the beach in a combat crouch. She swept the Type 88 rifle in an arc, ready to fire at the first sign of interdiction. Her comrades unloaded the duffel onto the beach, and then the RHIB pushed off from the shore. They would be back in the DPRK before Myung reached tactical position.

Once she confirmed the beach was safe from threats, she retrieved the duffel, slung it over her back, and reached the thin tree line on the deserted beach. There she crouched in the underbrush and waited, her finger resting on the rifle's trigger.

In less than a minute, Myung sensed a presence behind her. She wheeled and pointed her weapon toward the sound. A Korean man about sixty years old, dressed in farming attire, pushed the muzzle away from his chest. He held a finger to his lips.

"Shh. I am Shin Koh. Come."

He turned and walked away. Myung Suk had to hurry not to lose him in the predawn darkness.

Within fifty yards, the tree line broke onto a road. Shin Koh directed Myung to a canvas-covered truck with lights doused. He helped her into the back of the truck, then flicked on a penlight to illuminate a large backpack in the corner.

"You change."

The light flicked off, and Shin Koh closed and tied the curtain covering the rear of the truck. She heard him enter the driver's side. Several seconds later, the truck lumbered down the road.

Myung figured a twenty minutes' drive to Sokcho. She extracted a penlight from the blouse of her camouflage and held it unlit in her mouth. In the darkness, she doffed her combat gear and arranged it in a neat bundle beside her. She flicked on the penlight in spurts, just enough to open the backpack and don the peasant clothing and simple shoes provided. She stuffed her combat attire and tools into the backpack, dismantling the Type 88 to make it fit. If the mission went as planned, Myung would not need combat gear. She transferred the other contents from the duffel and placed the leather dress on top. She tucked the pistol into an outside pocket she could reach with ease.

Transformed from soldier to farm girl, Lee Myung Suk closed the backpack and used it as a pillow where she lay back to rest.

Long days ahead.

The twenty-minute journey took more than an hour as Shin Koh drove a circuitous route through the South Korean city of Sokcho. This city had belonged to North Korea until the American invaders and their ROK pawns redrew the boundaries after the armistice. The ROKs had turned the city into a tourist attraction, but many of its residents had relatives in North Korea and remained loyal to the DPRK. The man who called himself Shin Koh was probably not a DPRK sympathizer but a member of the North Korean Special Operations Forces that maintained a presence in the South, indistinguishable from the locals.

When the truck slowed, the pungent odor of fresh-killed fish told Myung that they had arrived at Taepo Harbor south of the city.

The vehicle stopped. She climbed out into an early morning melee of fishermen and customers conducting chaotic business at rows of open stalls. Recent catches hung from each stall, mostly squid drying in the sunlight.

Shin Koh pushed Myung along the street between the fish markets on the shore and a single row of two- and three-story buildings across the street. Those housed small businesses on the ground floor and apartments above ground. Shin Koh and Myung Suk did not rush, but made intermittent stops to shop and haggle with the fishmongers. At one stall, Shin Koh made a purchase, paying South Korean won for a plastic bag containing a large squid.

He smiled at Myung. "Dinner."

They walked another half block before Shin Koh guided Myung into an alley. Halfway down the narrow passage, he stopped at a door, scrutinized the alley in both directions, and then looked upward. Satisfied that no one had observed them, he turned the lock and guided Myung through the door. They climbed a narrow flight of stairs to one of two apartments on the landing. A man sat on a wooden chair in the alcove between the two apartments, reading a newspaper.

Armed guard.

The one-room apartment contained a single bed, a small wooden table with two chairs, and a tiny kitchen with a two-burner ovenless stove, a single dish cabinet, half refrigerator, and sink. The other end of the room featured a bathroom smaller than the kitchen, with a commode, sink, and shower stall.

Shin Koh motioned to the bed. "You are safe here, but double lock the door. Rest. This evening I will make dinner. We move out at dark." He turned and left the apartment.

Lee Myung Suk peeked out the window shade to the street below, more packed now as tourists joined the commercial fray.

All are worthless fish.

She left the window and stretched out on the bed. The thin mattress was more comfortable than the one she and Yeong Nae had shared as children. With the tension of the insertion into South Korea now passed, Myung drifted into sleep. She dreamed that she and Yeong were children playing soldier, their favorite game. Together, they fought off the ROK scum and the American villains.

They never lost.

Chapter 11
Koltsovo, Novosibirsk Oblast, Russia

N IKOLAI GOT HOME FROM the institute just before 2:00 AM. At the front door, the full impact of his actions in the virology lab assaulted his mind, as if the disease had run its entire course during the half-hour commute. He felt lightheaded, his pulse raced, his head pounded, and he needed to vomit.

Nerves. Too soon for symptoms.

Nikolai paused in the entry to steel himself, then went straight to Lora's room. Even knowing that he was not yet contagious, he stood at a distance with his hand over his mouth.

The little girl slept in quiet peace. The irrational fear of contamination succumbed to a father's genuine passion, and Nikolai stepped up to the bed to kiss his daughter's forehead.

Lora stirred but did not wake.

"I love you, little sun."

Nikolai did not want to disturb Svetlana in the bedroom, so he stretched out on the living room sofa. Over the next four hours, between fleeting catnaps, he stared at the ceiling. The enormity of his action, and what remained to be done, overwhelmed his fragile soul.

When the morning sun peeked through the window, he could not face Svetlana or Lora awake. He tidied up as best he could in the bathroom, then crept out of the house.

Forever.

***

When Nikolai returned to his office at the Vector Institute that morning, the woman who had managed his professional life for thirty years eyed him askance over the top of her computer screen.

"You look pale, Doctor. Have you been eating well? Do you get enough sleep?"

Nikolai shrugged. "The doctors sent Lora home too soon. Svetlana and I stay up with her most of the night."

The secretary frowned. "I am so sorry, sir. Why not take the day off?"

"The work must get done, Olga. I can do little for Lora at home."

Olga shook her head and turned back to the computer. "Whatever you say, Doctor."

The next six hours seemed like a century as Nikolai sat in the office and conducted mind-numbing routine business. He skipped lunch. By mid-afternoon, he could no longer pretend to concentrate. At 2:00 PM., he did his usual routine of tidying the desk where he had labored and prospered for decades; from which he had climbed to the pinnacle of scientific art and achieved world renown. Nikolai Orlov had given mind and soul to Mother Russia. Yet that mother had failed her son in a time of most dire need and had forced him to turn to foreigners to save the life of his only child.

He would never return to this place.

As reality set its hooks, Nikolai vacillated anew. The Korean's stern words reverberated in his mind: "I watch you always." Nikolai let out a long sigh of resignation and defeat. His die was cast, his fate no longer in his hands.

In the outer office, he spoke to Olga. "I do not feel well. You were right. I must take off the rest of the day." He paused. "And tomorrow too."

The old lady forced a smile. "Please take care, Doctor. You cannot help your family if you get ill."

Nikolai looked back with a blank face that hid his silent response.

Yes, I can.

Chapter 12

NIKOLAI DID NOT GO home. He walked as planned to the transit station, where he boarded a bus for the twenty-kilometer trip from the bucolic science town of Koltsovo to Novosibirsk, the third-largest city in Russia. He sat in the back of the bus, keeping a distance from the other passengers.

Just in case.

He got off the bus at the prescribed station and found the designated locker. With the cipher code the Korean had provided, Nikolai opened the locker and removed a leather briefcase identical to the one he had carried from Koltsovo. He looked around with furtive eyes, but no one in the bustling crowd paid him any mind. Nikolai switched the briefcases, shut the locker, and went to the men's room. Sitting in a stall, he opened the briefcase and examined the contents that included two phony passports.

With the new briefcase in hand and the first passport stuffed into a shirt pocket, he left the station. A fifteen-minute walk brought him to the Azimut Hotel Siberia, where he registered using the phony passport under the name Yuri Andreevich Pavlov.

Locked inside his hotel room, Nikolai opened the briefcase and extracted the second passport, a pair of scissors, and a bottle of hair dye. In the bathroom, he used the new passport photo as a guide to cut his long silver-gray hair to a half inch all over his scalp. He applied the black hair dye and watched himself turn into Semyon Molotov, the younger man in the passport photo. Satisfied with the likeness, he cleaned up the bathroom and disposed of the clipped hair and remaining dye in the toilet. He ripped the first phony passport to small shreds and flushed those down the toilet in small batches.

Back in the bedroom, he peeked out the curtain. The sun had not yet set. Semyon Molotov, nee Yuri Pavlov, nee Dr. Nikolai Orlov, needed fortification.

At a bar across the street, Nikolai paid cash for a bottle of vodka and hurried back to the hotel. Illogical though it was, he steered clear of any people who might cross his path. Back in the room, he sat on a wooden chair by the window, sipped the vodka from a bathroom glass, and watched the lights of the city come up as dusk fell.

In the waning light, Nikolai Orlov considered the sundown of his tumultuous life. Born in a Moscow ghetto, orphaned and raised into adulthood by uncaring relatives at the height of the Soviet regime, Nikolai's gritty determination had sustained him through the nadir and compelled him to become one of the most respected scientists of his day. His academic prowess as a leading-edge genetic virologist culminated in a prestigious faculty appointment at the Novosibirsk State Medical University—a convenient cover for his actual work in biological warfare development at the Vector Institute.

Nikolai's academic privilege had crashed with the fall of the Soviet Union and the demise of the patrons who had enabled his ascension to the top. On the rebound, he had sought love to fill the void too long ignored in his soul. After a series of sordid affairs, he had married Svetlana late in life because he needed stability, and a reason to stay in Siberia. The couple had enjoyed several years of relative marital harmony before Lora arrived, a welcome accident in Nikolai's mind. Less so in Svetlana's.

"You will be a doddering old dolt before she grows up," Svetlana had said. Nikolai never knew if she was kidding.

By the time of Lora's birth, Nikolai had reentered the world of investigative science where his earlier clandestine experience in biological warfare made him a desirable asset to the emerging Russian leadership. His academic cover restored, Nikolai resumed the role of lead scientist in the top secret business of researching genetic mutations to weaponise deadly viruses. The Soviets had searched for a biological weapon of global proportions, second in its potential for mass destruction to a nuclear bomb. Residual distrust of the West and fear of America's potential for world domination had kept the program intact, albeit more clan-destine and not so well funded. Nikolai may have been the lead scientist, but his salary barely exceeded that of a government administrator. However prestigious his position in the scientific world, Dr. Nikolai Orlov had struggled to support his family.

By the time dusk turned to night, Nikolai had finished half the bottle of vodka. Eight o'clock, and he could delay the inevitable no longer. Svetlana had accepted his working late hours at the institute, but tonight she would expect him home. He opened his cell phone and punched the speed dial for his home number. Svetlana answered on the second ring.

"Sorry, but I must stay the night in the lab. I have much catch-up yet. I will make this up to you, I promise."

The silence on the other end of the line made his heart skip. He spoke again. "How is Lora?"

Svetlana spoke with the now familiar edge of anger. "Same. She misses her daddy."

He remained silent, not from anger but from dismay. Seconds passed before he could speak. "I am so sorry. It will be better soon. I know it. Please kiss Lora for me." He fought off a choking wave of emotion. "Goodbye, my love."

Nikolai clicked the phone off before Svetlana could answer.

Chapter 13

Nikolai awoke the next morning sprawled across the bed, still in the previous day's clothes. His mind felt sharp, despite the empty vodka bottle on the floor beneath his hand. The time was 7:00 AM, later than planned. He rushed through a quick shower, but kept his hair out of the stream in case the dye had not fully set. He did not bother to shave.

For what purpose?

He dressed in the same clothes and left the hotel after paying with the phony credit card.

Outside the hotel, Nikolai circled the block twice to be sure no one followed him. He found the white Volga Siber, a rebranded American Chrysler Sebring, parked in the designated spot, but he walked past the vehicle and took another turn around the block.

To be doubly sure.

In truth, he needed the walk to calm rattled nerves.

Next time around, he opened the unlocked driver's-side door and looked under the seat. The keys and a large brown envelope appeared, as expected. He popped the trunk of the car and found a plain black roller suitcase packed with fresh clothing, toiletries, and sundries. Everything the Korean had promised.

Strapped into the driver's seat, he opened the brown envelope and found a map with a highlighted route tracing the Trans-Siberian Highway from Novosibirsk to Vladivostok, 5,800 kilometers east. The trip should take seventy hours of driving, three days. Sleep breaks would increase the time to five days.

Nikolai started the engine, noted the full gas tank, put the car in gear, and drove. He maneuvered through the city in heavy morning traffic to the P384 highway and headed east. Once on the highway, he thought of Lora and Svetlana. By the time anyone realized that Dr. Nikolai Orlov would not come home, Mr. Semyon Molotov would sip vodka in Krasnoyarsk, 779 kilometers away.

Would they ever know the sacrifice Nikolai had made for them? Deep inside, he hoped not.

"*Na zdorovye*," Nikolai said aloud. A watery film covered his eyes, and he feared he might crash the car.

Chapter 14

August, 2014. US Naval Base, Yokosuka, Japan. USS Shenandoah (LCC 21)

O N THE LAST DAY before the flagship would get under way for the annual joint exercise with the Republic of Korea, a magnified image of Kim Jong Un in full rant greeted the staff members as they filed into *Shenandoah's* Flag Conference Room (FCR) for the morning brief. The boyish leader of the world's most reclusive and repressive nation harangued from the billboard-sized center video screen at the front of the room.

Shaped like a small theater, the FCR contained eight rows of seats behind a continuous semicircular counter in front. Nine senior staff leaders occupied the front counter, upon which were computer stations and microphones. The rest of the staff filled the theater seats behind.

The official US/ROK communications plan described the imminent *Ulchi Freedom Guardian* (UFG) exercise as a two-week joint military simulation to rehearse a "customized deterrence plan against Pyongyang's nuclear threats and weapons of mass destruction."

The Democratic People's Republic of Korea (DPRK) wasted no time in spinning the allies' official media message to suit its own agenda. Kim Jong Un shook his fist at the camera. The larger-than-life video amplified the spittle that spewed with his words. A voice-over translated in halting English:

"The UFG is dangerous nuclear war drills aimed to mount a surprise preemptive strike at the Democratic People's Republic of Korea under the deceptive signboard of 'tailored deterrence' and adventurous ones to be staged under the simulated conditions of an actual war designed to ignite a local and total war under the pretext of nonexistent 'provocation' of someone.

"Now that the US imperialists and the South Korean puppet forces have declared a war against the DPRK by announcing their plan to apply the 'tailored deterrence strategy' to an actual war, we reclarify that the Korean-style most powerful and advanced merciless preemptive strike will start any time chosen by us.

"The US imperialists and the South Korean puppet forces will pay a dear price for their acts of going against the nation, reunification, and peace, as they reacted to all the peace initiatives and proposals made by the DPRK with good faith and magnanimity with extremely dangerous war maneuvers."

The side door at the front of the conference room swung open, and the booming voice of the command master chief diverted the staff's attention from the DPRK Supreme Leader.

"Attention on deck!"

The assembled men and women jumped to their feet as Vice Admiral Louise Lassiter, Commander US Seventh Fleet, entered the room for her first operational brief since relieving Vice Admiral Darnell Lewis a fortnight earlier.

Just returned from strategy conferences at the Pentagon and Pacific Command headquarters, the first woman to command the forward-deployed naval force in the Western Pacific strode to her seat at the center of the front counter but did not sit. Behind her, the assembled staff remained at attention as the admiral glared at the screen that showed KJU continuing his harangue.

"Get that baby fat ass out of my sight." Her voice rang with a distinct Southern accent.

The screen went blank, and the sound silenced. Admiral Lassiter took her seat in the padded executive chair and looked at the briefer, Captain Eric Mikleson, Seventh Fleet intelligence officer (N2), standing at the podium. Eric looked askance at Captain José Santiago, the new Seventh Fleet chief of staff, who sat next to Vice Admiral Lassiter.

Taking the cue, Captain Santiago leaned across and whispered in the admiral's ear.

"Christ on a cracker," she said as she turned in her seat to face the assembled staff, still standing at attention. "Be seated, please. From now on, don't wait for permission. If I sit, y'all sit. We got stuff to do here more important than protocol."

She smiled and turned back to Eric Mikleson. "Now if we could please begin the brief; and I do mean 'brief.'"

"Aye, aye, ma'am," Eric said. "I'll dispense with the routine material that you can read at your convenience from the briefing book in front of you."

"Done it. Go on, please."

"I would like to share intelligence learned this morning after we prepared the briefing book."

"Go on, please."

"We expect provocation from the North Koreans in response to UFG."

The admiral crossed her arms and rotated her seat from side to side. "Well, golly gee, ain't that a surprise? Tell me something I don't know."

"We assess that the North Koreans plan a provocation larger in scale than in prior years. More dramatic, a tangible threat to the South."

The admiral stopped spinning her chair and stared at Eric. He realized he'd captured her full attention. "Our sources suggest they may conduct an actual strike, one that could kill or injure a large population of ROKs."

"I call that an act of war, not a provocation," the admiral said.

Uncertain whether to respond, Eric continued his brief. "KJU's speech this morning, part of which you just saw, seems consistent with our assessment that he plans a preemptive strike to shore up support within his own regime. He lost face among his leadership after we destroyed his biological weapons capability."

Eric glanced at Commander Jessica "Cricket" Squire seated in the second row. He paused and bit his lower lip. "And, uh, he is reported to be in a constant rage over losing his leverage on the international stage."

Multiple sets of eyes in the room turned toward Cricket Squire. The dauntless woman stared straight ahead, impassive except for a slight facial flush. Her escape and rescue from North Korean custody less than a year earlier had embarrassed

KJU throughout the world. The DPRK knew that Commander Squire had returned to *Shenandoah* to play a key role in conducting UFG.

Eric's face flushed. Cricket Squire looked toward him, and for a second their eyes locked.

You may be a target, he thought.

Admiral Lassiter turned in her seat for a quick smile at Cricket, then back to Eric, her face and voice stern as steel.

"I don't give a rat's ass about KJU's rage. We do what we must to support our ROK allies, and I won't hesitate to take the fight to him if he provokes it. I will use our best people and resources to do it. Clear?"

Eric nodded.

"Now, what threat do we know exists? I'm not interested in speculation, Captain."

Eric returned his attention to his briefing notes. "We believe that the DPRK's attempt last year to spread botulism to US and ROK naval bases on the lower peninsula was a successful field test of their biological weapons capability. We eliminated that threat with the strike on their laboratory. We have no information to suggest that any other similar facilities exist. If they intend to cause extensive damage to a large population, it means a chemical or nuclear attack. However, they lack a reliable delivery system for chemical weapons."

He turned to the video monitor that showed a satellite imagery photo. "Then we have this. The North Korean Sinpo South Shipyard. On the next slide is a *Sinpo*-class submarine we identified yesterday in a secure boat basin. On the next slide, we zoom in to see an opening on the sub that appears to house two vertical launch tubes capable of firing either ballistic or cruise missiles."

The admiral scowled. "Are you saying they have a submarine that could launch missiles with nuclear warheads?"

"From under water, more difficult to detect and deter than land-based missile launchers."

The silence lasted a full minute before the admiral broke it. She spoke in a deeper and more serious tone.

"Well, we can't let that happen, can we?"

Chapter 15

L ATE THAT AFTERNOON, CRICKET pressed the button outside the cipher-locked door of the Joint Intelligence Center (JIC). The female petty officer who opened the door looked no older than nineteen. Pleasant surprise flashed across her face when she recognized Cricket.

"How can I help you, ma'am?"

Cricket had never aspired to celebrity status, but she was getting used to it. She gave the young sailor a genuine smile. "I'm here to see Captain Mikleson."

She glanced at the name band on the woman's aquaflage uniform. *Bennett.*

"Aye, ma'am. His office is—"

"Got it. Thanks, Petty Officer Bennett."

The sailor stood at attention as Cricket passed through the door. Two steps toward the N2's office, she turned back to the young lady, who remained at attention. "Thank you for choosing to serve your country."

I actually meant that.

The young woman blushed. "Thank you, ma'am. It's my honor." She hesitated for a second. "If I may say so, I am especially honored to serve here with you."

Embarrassed by the compliment, Cricket forced a response. "Thank you. The honor is mutual." Another smile, maybe less genuine. "We all do important work here."

The petty officer beamed. "Yes, ma'am."

Cricket nodded and turned toward Eric's office.

She found him behind a large desk, staring at three computer monitors connected to three different classified networks.

When he saw Cricket, Eric stood. "Commander Squire."

Cricket came to attention. "Captain Mikleson." A smile broke across her face. "Naval custom does not require a captain to stand for an officer of lower rank." She stood at ease. "And please call me 'Cricket' when it's just the two of us."

Eric returned to his chair. "Where I grew up, a gentleman always stands when a lady enters the room... Cricket." He smiled. "You may call me 'sir' or 'Captain,' Always." Then he laughed. "What the hell, just call me 'Eric.' We're shipmates here. Formality gets in the way."

Cricket sat in a chair across from his desk. "One reason I came back to the flagship. Needed to escape from uptight shore commands."

Eric snorted. "Got that. But don't underestimate the reach of PACOM and PacFleet. Those shore commands may not have us on a physical leash, but the flagship's antennae tether us to them twenty-four/seven. They can haul us into a face-to-face video teleconference whenever they want. Convenient to their 'aloha time,' of course. Their staffs tweak our work at will, no matter if they understand our battle space. Think of it as a four-thousand-mile-long screwdriver."

Cricket chuckled. "Strong feelings about that higher authority, Captain?"

Both laughed. Cricket shifted in the chair. "Speaking of PACOM, do you hear much from Kate? I mean, Captain..." She corrected herself. "I mean, Rear Admiral Mahoney?"

Kate Mahoney had been Seventh Fleet chief of staff during Cricket's ordeal in North Korea. She had directed the rescue mission, flown the F/A-18 air support, and later overseen Cricket's repatriation, debriefing, and rehabilitation at Tripler Army Medical Center in Honolulu. Fast-tracked for promotion to flag rank, Rear Admiral Mahoney now served as director for operations at US Pacific Command (PACOM) under Admiral Darnell Lewis, the former Seventh Fleet commander and Kate's mentor.

"She's the one sane mind in that cast of idiots called the PACOM senior staff," Eric said. "We talk little, but I've got a direct line anytime I need it. She has Admiral Lewis's ear." He squinted across the desk at Cricket. "I thought you and Kate were friends. Have you not stayed in touch?"

"Kate wasn't thrilled about my return to the fleet, although she didn't resist it. Didn't think I was ready. We've sort of drifted apart since she made flag and moved to Hawaii."

Eric grimaced. "Kate's not alone in that opinion about your readiness to return to the tip of the spear."

Cricket's face hardened. "I was dying in Hawaii. Plus, I have a score to settle with a certain evil regime in this region."

Eric blew out a long breath. "You mean a job to do on the Seventh Fleet staff, neh?"

"Why I came to see you, sir. To learn more about this *Sinpo* threat, and anything else that might help me do that job."

"Roger. Maybe we can make it mutual. If you'd be willing, I'd like to learn more about your experience in North Korea. You may have heard or seen something that could help us figure out KJU's next move."

"I'm willing to share whatever will help," Cricket said. "But I remember little of it. They kept me drugged most of that time." She sighed. "And my mind flat out blocks the worst of it."

"I'm not prying," Eric said. "Just thought you might..."

Cricket raised a hand. "I get it. You're an intel guy. You're curious." She smiled. "I trust you. If I know or remember anything that will help bring those assholes down, I'll damned sure share."

***

For the next thirty minutes, Eric and Cricket discussed the classified intelligence about the *Sinpo*-class submarine and its potential threat to South Korea and the upcoming UFG exercise.

When they finished, Cricket leaned back in her chair. "Something's missing."

Eric cocked his head. "Such as?"

"For sure, Kim Jong Un is pissed. But launch a nuke on South Korea in front of the entire world?"

Eric nodded. "I share your pessimism. But the one predictable thing about the DPRK is unpredictability."

"KJU knows we would retaliate against an overt strike."

"With massive force," he said. "A war the DPRK cannot hope to win. Plus, I don't see the Chinese supporting an unprovoked nuclear attack. The North Koreans would be on their own against the world."

Eric stroked his chin. "You saw the KJU show this morning. 'Massive preemptive strike' suggests more than ground troops trickling across the DMZ. If not nukes, what? We need to broaden our scope, but I don't know where. Hoped you might help with that."

Cricket looked at her watch. "Just past 1730. We get under way early tomorrow, which means we go dry until Busan. Can we continue this discussion at the O Club?"

"I'm supposed to meet Melody, my wife, there at 1830. Would you like to join us?"

"I'd love to meet your wife, Eric." Cricket paused. "Uh, will our being together at the O Club cause her to suspect—you know, anything inappropriate? We're about to deploy for three months. She knows I'm safe, right?"

"Melody will trust us together because she knows me, and she understands we are professional colleagues."

Cricket sighed. "I feel foolish for asking, but as a female officer, I've endured my share of mistrust from threatened Navy wives."

She waved her hand in a dismissive gesture. "Let's go. I'm not getting less thirsty."

Chapter 16

MELODY MIKLESON HAD NOT yet arrived when Cricket finished her second draft IPA at the Yokosuka Officers' Club. She described her ordeal in North Korea to Eric. "Colonel Boo rescued me from the sadistic rapists on the North Korean special-ops ship that captured me from the West Sea. When Boo took me from them, I was in shock and near death—but not close enough. I wanted to die. Boo saved my life."

A chill ran through Cricket as she visualized the torture boat. She forced her mind back to the present and ordered another beer.

"I remember little from the period after Colonel Boo took me off the boat. They had me in a wretched hospital and loaded me with narcotics. They did surgery on the broken ankle, but the doctors—if they were doctors—didn't align the bones. Just screwed them together so I could stand without support next to KJU when he denounced me to the world as a spy."

Cricket took a deep quaff of beer. "My mind was so messed up, I considered Boo my personal savior. He killed the men who had tortured me, and he killed my pain with drugs. He treated me with kindness, like a father."

Eric swallowed hard. "Stockholm Syndrome."

"Yeah." Consumed by a wave of emotion, Cricket took another swig. "I learned Boo's true nature after KJU gifted me to him for wicked pleasure. He turned out to be the worst of the animals."

She forced back a tear. "I was sorry when Lee shot him in the head. He deserved a slower death—with terrible pain."

Cricket stared into space; her mind blank, at once oblivious to the surroundings.

The shuffle of Eric's chair broke Cricket's reverie and signaled Melody's arrival.

Cricket had seen Eric's spouse once before, and she admired her poised beauty. Vivacious and friendly, Melody hugged Eric and Cricket and then stood back to regard Cricket at arm's length. "You're looking good, Commander."

"Thanks, ma'am," Cricket said. "Every day is a little better."

The three sat, and Melody ordered a Viognier. Cricket figured her to be about thirty-five to Eric's forty-three years old.

"Time for one quick drink," Melody said to Eric. "You need to say goodbye to our girls tonight, because they're going to a sleepover at the Drummonds' house." Her eyes turned soft, and she stroked Eric's hand. "And we need to get you ready to deploy tomorrow."

Eric glanced at Cricket and blushed.

"You two go ahead," Cricket said. "One advantage of living on the ship, I don't have to pack to get underway."

When the drinks came, Eric and Melody downed theirs in gulps and took their leave. Melody hugged Cricket again. "I hope you have an uneventful float. You've earned one." She turned and took Eric's hand. "All of you."

In a flurry, the couple departed, leaving Cricket with a half mug of IPA and a mind full of disconnected thoughts and runaway feelings.

At the nearby bar, a trio of young naval officers gazed in her direction and talked in low tones among themselves. Annoyed, Cricket wondered again if she would ever get used to quasi-celebrity status. She carried the beer to the pool deck and found a secluded table, apart from the few outside patrons braving the sultry August heat.

Without warning, tears filled her eyes. Talking about her personal trauma in North Korea had opened the mental compartment where she had locked those memories away from consciousness. Her mind jumped to the scene when Lee Young had burst into the sleazy bedroom that Colonel Boo had made into Cricket's prison. Lee's arrival in a KPA uniform had interrupted Cricket's planned vengeance on Boo. She had gained a top position in the bed, pinned Boo to the mattress, and tried to strangle him. Lee pulled Cricket off the monster. Free and gasping for air, Boo ordered Lee to kill her.

Cricket could still feel the pistol muzzle pressing against her temple.

"I so wanted to make love to you one more time," Lee had said in her ear. Then she pivoted and fired a round into Boo's forehead.

Cricket's thoughts drifted to an earlier time, when she and Lee first met and fell in love. Life had seemed full then. Cricket was living the dream as a Navy pilot at the naval air station in Kaneohe Bay, Hawaii. Within the first month of the assignment, she had met Lee Young at Wang Chung's in Waikiki. The two had connected at once and spent the first of many nights together.

Each woman had maintained a separate apartment, but they slept apart only when Cricket deployed. Then the Hawaii legislature legalized same-sex marriage after two decades of debate. Cricket and Lee decided, without need for discussion, to change their living arrangement and marry. While Cricket deployed to Okinawa, Japan, Lee bought them a house. They set a wedding date for Cricket's scheduled return.

On the last day of that deployment, the Navy extended Cricket's tour. The squadron commanding officer assigned her, his best pilot, to fly the new P-8 *Poseidon* on a critical reconnaissance flight over the troubled South China Sea. Cricket's last phone conversation with Lee had turned acrid when her fiancée had demanded an explanation that Cricket could not give her.

"It's classified."

Lee's furious reaction had ended the engagement—throwing Cricket into bitter depression.

But Lee had already known how the reconnaissance mission would end, with the Chinese People's Liberation Army Air Force commandeering the P-8 and trading it to North Korea. Unbeknown to Cricket, Lee was a CIA double agent; a North Korean agent who had targeted the US Navy through Cricket, but later flipped. Knowing that the P-8 would fly to North Korea, Lee's strident demand that Cricket come home instead of flying the mission had been an effort to save her lover from certain captivity and probable death.

Truly, she loved me.

Cricket stared at the bottom of the empty beer mug. A soft buzz filled her head, but her ankle was pain-free. She debated ordering another beer, but as the evening air cooled, more O-Club patrons crowded the pool deck. When Cricket saw the earlier trio of young naval officers approaching, she dropped cash on the table, got up, and walked past them.

"Enjoy the evening, gents."

The walk from the Officers' Club to *Shenandoah* traversed a small hill. Cricket paused at the summit and gazed at the lights of the base and of Monkey Island out in Sagami Bay. Her thoughts turned back to Lee Young. Cricket pictured her former lover's exotic face, sensuous skin, and alluring eyes.

She spoke in a whisper. "I so wanted to make love to you one more time, too."

Chapter 17
Vladivostok, Russia

N IGHT HAD FALLEN ON the fifth day of his journey by the time Nikolai
Orlov, exhausted and covered with road grime, stepped into a musty
room on the third floor of the Versailles Hotel in central Vladivostok, Russia. He
forced open a window sealed by multiple layers of paint, then breathed in fresh
air from the nearby waterfront. A welcome wisp of salty aroma rode on the slight
breeze that wafted into the confined space.

Nikolai sucked the air deep into his lungs and then studied his surroundings.
A European-style bedroom with a double bed, side table, single sitting chair, and
armoire. A worn door led into a closet-sized bathroom with a sink, commode,
and pedestal tub.

In an earlier life, Nikolai would have thought it splendid.

The Versailles might be a tired old hotel now, but in the glory days of Russia
it had hosted socialites and VIPs of the highest order. Perhaps the tsar himself
had sipped vodka in the ornate piano bar before dining in the once sumptuous
restaurant off the gilded lobby. More recent guests might have included senior
officers and defense officials during the era when Vladivostok hosted the Pacific
arm of the powerful Soviet Navy's Red Fleet.

The few military ships in the harbor now were mere vestiges of a once mighty
global force.

Nikolai poked his head out the open window and scrutinized the street. As
ordered, he had parked the Volga Siber in a predesignated spot and left the keys
in the ignition. Already, someone had moved the vehicle; a subtle reminder that
shadows followed his every move. He pulled his head back into the room, and the
now familiar pall of gloom robbed the freshness from the cool night air.

He recalled the Korean's parting words to him. "You are always in sight."

Nikolai considered phoning Svetlana, but the Korean had given explicit instructions. "Stay in the hotel. Do not venture beyond the bar or restaurant. Avoid people. Make no phone calls. Someone will come to you."

Would they know when to come? Now five days past exposure, Nikolai reckoned that the window of contagiousness would open in two more days and stay open for another ten. If it were up to him, he would time the transmission for day twelve, the peak probability of infection. That assumed a normal course for the typical strain of this virus.

If his life's work in the lab had succeeded, Nikolai's body hosted a genetically mutated microbe that should be more virulent and more resistant to innate or acquired antibodies. In that case, the peak could be sooner than twelve days.

He shrugged. Not for him to say now.

Nikolai wondered where and how the virus exchange would happen. He was just a vector, a carrier, an inconspicuous agent of doom—a potential weapon of mass destruction.

Who are the intended victims? And where?

Too many questions. Nikolai's brain, of all the scientific intellects in the world, had produced the optimal design for the disease's progression and fatal outcome. But he had sold his right to independent thought and decision-making the instant he'd agreed to earn his daughter's cure by betraying his integrity, his career, his country, and by attacking someone unknown. Perhaps a city population or an entire nation.

Would the victims include Lora? Svetlana? The Korean had promised to keep Nikolai's family safe. "No pandemic," he had said. "Why fight the body of the beast when we can simply behead it?"

What beast? And why Vladivostok? The city had been in decline since the Red Fleet had disintegrated after the fall of the Soviet Union. What "beast" would Nikolai meet in Vladivostok?

No more time on speculation.

He was hungry and needed a drink. He yearned for female companionship but could not risk contact with another human. Close physical contact? Oral contact? Out of the question.

I have some integrity left.

Nikolai took a quick bath and put on clean clothes. Even if he could not bring a woman to his bed, at least in the downstairs bar the piano man, food, and drink might free him from morose introspection. He closed the window before leaving the room, thought better, reopened it, and took a deep breath. Despite the cool salt air wafting into his lungs, Nikolai Petrovich Orlov choked. He steadied himself, took deep breaths, left the window ajar, and hurried to the bar.

Chapter 18

THE NEXT MORNING, NIKOLAI awakened to sunlight streaming through the open window, sounds of people walking and talking on the street below, and a crushing headache. He'd consumed too much vodka the previous night while the piano man's melancholy strains drowned him in deep introspection about his life and the fate he'd thrown into motion.

He tried to lie still in the bed, to catch another hour of sleep, but his body felt restless. After a vigorous forehead massage failed to relieve the headache, he got himself up and bathed in the rustic tub. Dried off and feeling somewhat better, he dressed in casual attire and combed his hair. Again, he did not bother to shave.

In the lobby, Nikolai found the hotel's business center and a computer with Internet access. With trembling fingers, he logged in to the joint bank account he shared with Svetlana. Numbers on the screen jolted the remains of the hangover from Nikolai's head. The balance showed more rubles than he'd ever imagined earning.

The Korean had delivered. Lora and Svetlana would soon be on their way to America.

Now Nikolai must complete his part.

Or not?

With his family safe, and the payment for Lora's treatment in hand, why not disappear? Perhaps he had erred in his calculations. He might not have infected himself. Maybe the virus was not as virulent as he'd planned. He might get sick but survive. Escape to a different life. Someday reunite with Svetlana and Lora. Even if fatally infected, he could die alone, isolated in a remote place, his diseased brain not burdened with remorse over becoming a vector of death. To whom and how many?

Nikolai worked that notion in his mind as he left the business center, but then he noticed two burly Russian men sitting in the lobby watching him. He'd seen one of them before, in a hotel lobby in Irkutsk on the second day of his journey. They looked rough, but were too well dressed to be street thugs.

Bratva?

If the powerful Russian organized crime group played a role in this affair, then the Federal Security Service of the Russian Federation backed whatever operation had Nikolai in its clutches. How did Bratva relate to the Korean? Nikolai sensed a conspiracy at the highest levels of government.

You are always in sight.

For Nikolai Orlov, escape was no option.

He tried to ignore the men as he headed toward the elevator to return to his room. The huskier one intercepted him in the lobby.

The man growled. "You come with me."

"My luggage..."

"Leave it." A meaty hand surrounded Nikolai's arm and steered him toward the front of the hotel.

The second man pushed open the door and gripped Nikolai's other arm, pulling and pushing him out to the sidewalk. They guided Nikolai to an automobile with its engine running. A rear door swung open, and Nikolai spotted a third man in the backseat. One assailant pushed Nikolai into the backseat and then got in beside him and slammed the door. Nikolai found himself pinned in the middle while the other abductor got into the driver's seat.

The three men donned surgical face masks. One forced Nikolai to do the same. The car moved into the street, not speeding but keeping pace with the traffic.

"What?" Nikolai pointed to the mask. "I am not yet infectious."

"Silence," said the man to his right. The one on his left pressed the muzzle of a handgun into Nikolai's side. He donned the mask. No one spoke for the duration of the ride. Nikolai stared straight ahead, immobile.

After a few minutes, the car pulled off the main street and meandered through various side alleyways before stopping at the rear door of a warehouse. The abductors pulled Nikolai from the car and ushered him through a large metal door that opened when the group approached.

Once they were inside, the door slammed shut behind them. Nikolai blinked to let his eyes accommodate to the near darkness. He was in a large utility room, lit by a single bulb and abandoned save for his captors and another figure whose face was obscured by the shadows.

"Good morning, Igor."

Nikolai recognized the raspy voice that spoke English with a Korean accent.

Igor?

Nikolai did not answer.

The Korean man stepped into the light. He wore a surgical mask, but around the edges Nikolai noticed facial pockmarks and a gash-like scar running from ear to temple.

"For what remains of your miserable life, you are no longer Nikolai Orlov," the man said. "You are Igor Kartashkin, a Russian shipping executive. You will soon travel on vacation." He gestured to the thug standing next to Nikolai.

The man handed Nikolai a shopping bag. "Change clothes."

"Here?"

The enforcer showed the pistol under his coat. Nikolai stripped to his underwear and donned the clothing from the bag; modest casual slacks with a shirt and blazer that a businessman might wear on holiday. When Nikolai doffed his original clothing, one man removed his wallet from the inside jacket pocket. Once Nikolai had changed clothes, the man handed him a different wallet containing rubles, Korean won, and a credit card in the name of Igor Ivanovich Kartashkin. With the wallet came a new passport with the same name. The photo showed Nikolai with a bald head.

As if on cue, one thug pushed Nikolai into a chair while the other produced a razor and shaved what remained of Nikolai's hair.

When the task was done, the Korean approached him. "You heed what I tell you now, or your wretched life will end sooner than expected. Understood?"

Nikolai nodded.

The crater-faced man pulled an envelope from his pocket and handed it to Nikolai. It contained an economy-class ticket for the *Eastern Dream* ferry from Vladivostok to Donghae, Republic of Korea.

"You will walk from here to the terminal and board this ferry that departs at 1400. Once aboard, you will go straight to your stateroom, and you will stay there until the ferry lands in Donghae. Speak to no one. Congregate with no one. Contact no one."

He glared into Nikolai's eyes as if to test his comprehension.

Nikolai nodded in silence.

"When the ferry arrives in Donghae tomorrow, you wait until all other passengers leave, then you disembark. You will hail a taxi and go straight to the Eastern Tourist Hotel, where you will check in, go to your room, and wait for instructions." He moved closer, his eyes like lead bullets. "Are you clear on what we expect from you, Igor Ivanovich?"

Nikolai looked down. "Yes."

"We will watch you the entire time, Igor. If you stray from the plan so much as a centimeter, your life will end. Your daughter, Lora, will not get the treatment she needs. Your wife, Svetlana, will meet a most undignified and painful death."

He sneered. "Any questions, Igor?"

Nikolai shook his head. One man hauled him out of the chair while another produced a rolling suitcase and thrust it at him.

The Korean spoke. "You must walk at a brisk pace to make it on time." He gestured at the two burly men. "Dimitri will lead the way and Sergei will follow to be sure you don't get lost. Now go."

The man named Sergei grabbed Nikolai, ripped the mask off his face, and shoved him out the door.

Forty minutes later, a man named Igor Kartashkin sat alone in a windowless stateroom on board the *Eastern Dream*.

Nikolai Petrovich Orlov broke down and sobbed.

Chapter 19

US Navy Base, Yokosuka, Japan. USS Shenandoah (LCC 21)

"UNDER WAY. SHIFT COLORS." Tugboats pushed *Shenandoah* away from the pier and into Truman Bay to begin the three-day sail around the southern shores of Japan to Busan, Republic of Korea.

By the time the flagship reached the mouth of Tokyo Bay, the men and women of the embarked Seventh Fleet staff had settled into final preparations for *Ulchi Freedom Guardian* (UFG). The two-week exercise would begin the following Monday. While in Busan for the weekend preceding UFG, the staff would conduct initial briefs and embarkation of ROK Navy (ROKN) members to work on the ship alongside their American counterparts during the exercise.

Monday morning, the flagship would get back under way and transit to the East Sea (known by the rest of the world as the Sea of Japan). They would conduct the first week of UFG en route to Donghae, on the northeast coast of South Korea, then make a weekend port visit and conduct networking with the ROKN First Fleet. The second week of the exercise would return the flagship to Busan for a final weekend in Korea, debriefs, and disembarking of their ROKN guests.

Then the ship would return to sea for the rest of the three-month patrol, conducting "diplomacy ops" to Hong Kong, Vietnam, Singapore, Malaysia, Thailand, and Manila, before returning to home port in Yokosuka, Japan. As self-rewards for the grueling work of UFG, many of the staff had booked hotel rooms and five-star restaurant reservations in the more glamorous future ports.

Cricket cared about none of that as she entered the Flag Conference Room for the morning brief. She took a seat behind her immediate boss, the director of operations (N3), and watched Eric Mikleson prepare his intel presentation on UFG. He looked nervous, an unusual demeanor for the man whom she considered a professional colleague, friend, and potential liberty buddy—assuming she had time for or interest in liberty during any future port visit.

Maybe Eric was nervous because Admiral Lassiter had embarked in the flagship for the transit to Busan. Usually, the Seventh Fleet commander did not spend the three days at sea but took a three-hour flight on a military transport jet from Atsugi Naval Air Station to Seoul for high-level Combined Forces Command (CFC) meetings. Then she would join the flagship in Busan for UFG.

What did the admiral's presence on board now suggest? Cricket figured that Eric wondered the same thing.

"Attention on deck." The staff jumped to their feet and stood as the admiral entered. She took her seat and nodded at Eric to start the brief.

"Good morning, Admiral, staff."

A map of the Korean Operations Area appeared on the giant video screen behind Eric. "As expected, the DPRK has ramped up the anti-US and anti-ROK rhetoric ahead of UFG. Besides the usual government propaganda and news clips from the central government, we've seen a steady barrage of hostile broadcasts from loudspeakers across the DMZ. The ROKs responded in kind, generating heightened tension across the demilitarized zone. We have reports of shots fired from both sides across the DMZ in the more remote areas.

"Yesterday, an incident occurred at the Joint Security Area in Panmunjom. A US Navy reservist medical admiral and several of his staff in Seoul for UFG took a tour of the JSA with the Eighth Army surgeon. Because it was an official VIP visit, these officers wore service dress uniforms. When the group entered the conference room where the armistice was signed..."

He looked at Admiral Lassiter. "That conference room straddles the line between North Korea and South..."

"Been there, Captain. Please continue."

"Aye, ma'am. The tour allows visitors to step across the white borderline inside the building and stand in North Korea, guarded by ROK sentries. When the medical VIPs crossed the white line, North Korean soldiers made a show of storming the building. They pounded on the north-side door and windows and shouted threats against the Americans. ROK sentries responded with weapons drawn. They evacuated the VIPs from the room. The situation de-escalated, but later the DPRK issued formal statements condemning the uniformed US military officers for 'provoking' North Korea."

Vice Admiral Lassiter laughed. "I would have liked a whiff of those docs' skivvies after that one. Who the hell takes a DMZ tour in dress uniform when tensions are high?" She stared at the fleet surgeon. "No one on this staff, I hope."

All eyes shifted to Captain Rose Deckert at the end of the front row of senior staff. Startled by the sudden attention, the doctor offered a smile to her boss. "No, ma'am."

The admiral turned back to Eric. "Thanks for the comic relief. You got anything substantive?"

"Afraid so, ma'am," Eric said. "Yesterday, the South Korean *Yonhap News* characterized the upcoming UFG as an opportunity for the US/ROK alliance to test its deterrence plan against Pyongyang's 'weapons of mass destruction.' This provoked a response from Kim Jong Un himself. He charged that the United States and ROK have declared war against the DPRK. I quote, 'Our revolutionary force is ready to respond to any kind of war the American imperialists want. Through the line of Songun politics, our Korean People's Army has become the world's strongest revolutionary force, and our country has become an impenetrable fortress and a global military power.' For the benefit of anyone in the room unfamiliar with the term, Songun refers to military-first politics. Guns before rice, so to speak."

"Words cheap as a ten-dollar hooker," Admiral Lassiter said. "Tell me about that *Sinpo* submarine."

Eric frowned. "We've seen no movement since yesterday. It may be a decoy to mask a different planned provocation."

"Decoy or not, stay on it," the admiral said. She looked around the room and then back at Eric. "Let's talk WMD. What weapons of mass destruction do they own right now?"

"Nuclear weapons remain the primary threat," Eric said. "We believe they can strike the US homeland, let alone South Korea. But we see a nuclear attack on either as a last resort. KJU won't risk another international embarrassment after..."

He glanced at Cricket and continued. "Further, with winter on the horizon, even the use of tactical nuclear weapons could cause international sanctions that would cut off food donations." He motioned to the screen behind him. "That's another reason we believe the *Sinpo* threat may not be real. Same with conventional weaponry. An overt attack will cause dire consequences downrange for the Kim regime."

"Well, shit fire and save matches," the admiral said. "We can all go to Busan and Donghae and tie one on, because the North Koreans pose no serious threat."

She turned to the staff seated behind her. "Last one to Haeundae Beach gets extra mess duty for the rest of the float."

Amid the ensuing nervous laughter, she turned back to Eric; her face grim, her voice stern. "Except that bastard is a psychotic megalomaniac, and we have no frigging clue what he might do. Am I right, Captain Mikleson?"

Eric had turned red at the joke and now waxed crimson under the frontal attack. He sighed. "We have clues, ma'am. But the North Koreans are unpredictable."

"Humor me, Captain. Declare yourself for once. Predict the unpredictable."

Eric straightened. "I assess, I mean I predict, that they plan a provocation, revenge for the humiliation suffered earlier this year. It will be covert yet dramatic, difficult to trace to the North Korean leadership—unless or until they choose to take credit."

The admiral stroked her chin. "You mean WMD other than nukes?"

"Yes, ma'am," Eric said. "But we don't know what they have."

Admiral Lassiter thought before speaking. "Can we assume they no longer produce biologicals after we destroyed their lab last year?"

"With reasonable certainty, we believe they no longer have biological weapons production capability." He paused, weighing his words. "We have no reliable information about acquisition."

"Who the hell would sell biological weapons to that psycho?"

"No legitimate government," Eric said. "Even those not friendly to us or the ROKs."

"Black market? Rogue nations?"

"I don't know, ma'am."

Admiral Lassiter snorted and turned to the fleet surgeon. "Doc, assuming the bastards could get hold of biological weapons, what's the threat and how do we detect it?"

Dr. Deckert leaned forward and keyed the microphone on the desk in front of her. "Uh, the most dangerous would be anthrax. Or smallpox. Both are highly contagious airborne pathogens that need extreme handling precautions to prevent self-infection. Doesn't seem possible, even if they could get them."

She un-keyed the microphone and sipped from her coffee mug. The admiral stared at her, expecting more, so the surgeon re-keyed the mike. "Something like the botulinum toxin they released in our DoD school in Chinhae and the ROK Navy base in Busan last year might be more workable."

Admiral Lassiter stared at the doctor. "Suppose they figured out a way to transport the bad stuff? How do we detect a biological attack?"

Captain Deckert swallowed hard. "We can't. Not till people get sick."

"You're telling me we can't detect that shit before it kills folks?"

"Sensors exist, but they are not reliable—and it takes time to process results. We can't depend on them like chemical weapons detectors." She took another sip of coffee. "Infectious diseases have to incubate in the human host after exposure. It can take one to two weeks before someone infected shows any symptoms. By then..."

Admiral Lassiter waved her off. "Got it, Doc."

She stared straight ahead for a minute and then turned back to Eric. "So, for chemicals, we have sensors, but they don't stop the actual attack. For biologicals, we must depend on deterrence because we can't detect an attack. And for nukes, we hope the Kim regime will act smarter than they talk. Great brief, Captain. I wish I could say 'enlightening brief,' but not even close."

Eric turned red. "Ma'am, I..."

The admiral held up her hand. "It's not your fault, Captain. Sane people have difficulty guessing what a nut bag will do."

Eric recovered his poise. "In light of the setback at our hands last year, and the flavor of the current rhetoric, we should expect an attack on US personnel and ROKs. We don't know where, when, or how."

"We might should conduct a preemptive strike after all," the admiral said. "Not that the National Command Authorities will consider a course of action that involves actual balls."

She turned to the staff. "Folks, every military instinct within me says we are up against a serious threat. We cannot let down our guard. I need everyone focused on task until UFG is over. I won't suspend what little liberty y'all get in Korea, but I damn well expect that no one will step off this ship, even for a beer on the pier, until you've dotted your respective i's are and crossed those t's. We need constant vigilance. Expect the unexpected and plan for it."

She folded her arms. "Questions?"

No one dared raise a hand.

"Very well," she said. "Carry on."

All hands jumped to their feet as the admiral departed. Instead of the usual post-brief chatter, the room remained somber as the staff members filtered out. Now Cricket understood why the admiral had embarked in the flagship for the UFG preparations. She had taken the helm in a time of impending crisis.

Cricket admired and respected such leadership, including the older woman's salty exterior. The Pentagon had held up Admiral Lassiter's selection for a third star and appointment as Seventh Fleet commander because some male officials objected to her frequent use of crusty language. Cricket's own experience in North Korea told her that Louise Lassiter had exactly the right mind-set for this volatile region.

She waited until the room emptied before she approached Eric as he gathered his briefing papers. Despite the air-conditioned chill in the room, sweat soaked through his khaki uniform.

"Rough one," she said.

"Worst ever. Not for the grilling—been through plenty of those." He shook his head. "We're supposed to know what might happen, but I don't have a clue. Our most elaborate intelligence network in the world has come up empty. I get this enormous sense of impending crisis, but I can't figure it."

"I hope you're wrong."

"I'm not wrong."

Cricket pursed her lips. "How can I help?"

Eric shook his head. "You can come get a cup of coffee with me."

They walked out together in silence.

Chapter 20

USS Shenandoah (LCC 21). Transiting Sagami Bay, Japan.

C RICKET WAITED UNTIL 1000 to visit the medical department. She'd spent enough time around Navy ships' medical facilities to know that on the first underway day a steady line of sailors would inundate the place. They either sought attention from illness or injury ignored in the hectic last days before deployment, or hoped for an excuse to get light duty. At the least, time spent in medical kept them away from the workplace. The heaviest load came at mid-morning after most of the ship's departments had completed morning musters, physical fitness activities, and daily briefings.

When Cricket walked through the door, waiting sailors lined both sides of the athwartships passageway.

Well timed.

With any luck, she could get what she needed and not draw unwanted attention. Her hopes plummeted when Cricket bumped into Lieutenant Commander Pearson coming out of his office.

"Commander Squire," the ship's doctor said. "What brings you to medical this morning?"

Cricket noted the tangy edge of sarcasm in his voice.

"Didn't intend to bother you, Doc. I'm here to see the independent duty corpsman for a refill."

"Step into the office and I'll take care of that. I expect you need to get back to work."

He opened the door and ushered Cricket into his office. She sat on the edge of the exam table as Dr. Pearson closed the door and faced her. "Which medication did you need refilled?"

Cricket tried an icy stare. "I need a supply of Vicodin and Ambien. Now, before UFG starts."

"Didn't you just get a prescription from the fleet surgeon?"

"I did, but I was hoping for a supply to last through UFG. It's nearly impossible to get down here once the ops tempo heats up."

Doc Pearson smiled. "Tell you what, Commander. If you run low during the exercise, call me and I'll be happy to deliver what you need."

Cricket scoffed. "Not giving me any refills today, are you?"

The doctor crossed his arms. "That would not be in your best interest, Commander."

Cricket hopped off the exam table, exaggerating the near fall when her gimpy ankle struck the deck. "Thanks for your time, Doc." She opened the door and left.

***

Ten minutes later, Cricket knocked on the fleet surgeon's stateroom door, which stood ajar.

Captain Deckert spoke through the opening. "Come in, please."

Cricket entered the room just as the doctor hung up the phone. She turned to Cricket with a pleasant smile. "Commander Squire. What can I do for you?"

"I wanted to get a refill on my medications before UFG ramps up to full ops tempo."

"Didn't we just give you a refill?"

Cricket made a point of looking at the telephone on the doctor's desk. "I get it, Doc. No prescription from you today either, right?"

The fleet surgeon crossed her arms in the same gesture that Cricket had seen from Doc Pearson.

Must be a doc thing.

"If you run short on medications during the exercise, just call me or tell me in the morning brief. I'll be happy to get it for you."

Cricket folded her arms in imitation of the doctor. "Docs in cahoots. Must be fun to play God." She turned and left.

Without thinking about it, Cricket made her way to Eric Mikleson's office. She sat in the chair across from his desk, having expressed frustration at "the Navy medicine blockade" she'd just encountered. She calmed under Eric's gaze, an unfamiliar mix of gravitas and compassion not seen in either of the physicians.

Eric spread his hands. "I can't give medication refills, but I can promise to look out for you during UFG and the rest of the patrol."

Cricket scowled. "I don't need protection."

"Didn't mean it that the way. I'll be around and available whenever you need. Even if just to talk."

Cricket relaxed. "I came straight here when I was upset. Guess I sensed that support. I appreciate it, Eric."

Eric leaned forward and spoke in a serious tone. "I've never been tortured or physically harmed. I hope to God never to suffer what you did. I have a deep and abiding respect for you, as does this entire staff. That includes the doctors, who are just trying to do right by you. We all admire your courage in returning to the fleet. You can count on any support I can give, any time you need it. That is a promise."

Cricket squirmed. "Thank you, Eric." She bit her lip. "When I came back, I didn't think about making ties or friendships. I feel pretty fortunate right now."

Eric gazed away for a second, and when he looked back, his tone carried an edge. "You know I'm uneasy about this UFG, and I fear what may lie ahead. Because of your history with the North, you may play an undesirable role. I hope my premonition is wrong. Whatever comes, we will get through it. And when we get to Hong Kong, I know a great restaurant where we can celebrate."

"I'll take that as a promise, Captain."

"You'd best believe it, Commander."

Cricket smiled, shook Eric's hand, and left. Walking down the passageway and up the ladder to the flag deck, she stepped livelier than any time since her return to Seventh Fleet.

Chapter 21
Donghae, Republic of Korea (South Korea)

NIKOLAI STAYED IN THE windowless stateroom for over an hour while the other passengers disembarked. After twenty hours of isolation during the transit from Vladivostok to Donghae, he yearned for fresh air and vodka. Waves of nausea washed through him, no doubt the effects of the sea journey combined with the meager sustenance his handlers had provided.

At first Nikolai had resisted the dried apricots, half-rotting apple, overaged cheese, and stale bread. By midnight, hunger drove him to eat. Now he wished he'd abstained. In the wee morning hours, belly cramps had forced him to risk leaving the stateroom for a surreptitious visit to the communal bathroom halfway down the passageway. He knew that hidden eyes watched, but he needed to retch, pee, and shit.

After returning to his stateroom, he'd managed a few hours of sleep in a narrow bed with a thin mattress that made his back ache. By mid-morning, the nausea had returned, but he dared not risk another trip to the bathroom. Instead, he rolled into a fetal position and whimpered.

Visions of Svetlana and Lora needled his brain. Had they accepted that Nikolai was not coming home? Had the Russian scientific community heard about the disappearance of the prominent Dr. Orlov? Nikolai shook his head. Soon he would be old news, except to his family. Lora might be too sick to understand her father's absence, but Svetlana would get it. She would connect Nikolai's disappearance with the sudden monetary windfall in the family bank account. His wife would understand but say nothing. Even if interrogated, Svetlana would say nothing. Nikolai hoped that the understanding of his sacrifice might yield forgiveness—someday.

Nikolai would never know if Svetlana forgave him. He ached deep inside, with both a longing and an anger that engulfed his soul. Why had fate made his dear Lora the victim? Why had God forced Nikolai to save his daughter's life by sacrificing his own?

There is no God.

Nikolai had waited long enough. He needed to get out of that narrow space. He needed to pee and shit again, and the nausea was getting worse. He closed the small suitcase, lifted it, and left the stateroom.

Burdened with fatigue from the journeys of the previous week, Igor Kartashkin walked down the ramp of the Eastern Dream and set foot on the pier at Donghae, Republic of Korea.

Nikolai Orlov is dead.

Chapter 22

ON THE MORNING OF the second day of isolation in the Eastern Tourist Hotel in Donghae, Nikolai lay naked on the bed with a washcloth over his forehead. He had left the lights off and the curtain closed to assuage the headache that mushroomed behind his eyes. The pain ground into his brain and stoked the nausea that had remained constant since the ferry trip. The handlers had not included a thermometer in the few supplies they provided.

Not that the exact reading mattered. Nikolai had a fever.

As the discomfort deepened, Nikolai admitted the symptom cluster was not the fault of a rotten apple or overripe cheese. Each fresh sign confirmed his ultimate destiny. Now he had no options but to await whatever irrevocable step the Korean had arranged. When he'd embarked on the *Eastern Dream* ferry, Nikolai had spotted Dimitri and Sergei, the two Bratva thugs, walking up the gangplank behind him. He did not see them again, but he sensed their presence in this hotel.

He forced himself up and stood woozy by the bed until his legs steadied. He opened the window to let in a breeze. The action left him just enough energy to fall back onto the bed. The fresh air cooled his body, and he slept.

For the next two days, Nikolai slept in fits, getting up only to go to the bathroom and sip water.

Midway through the fourth night, he awoke with severe throat pain, as if someone had jammed a burning torch into his mouth. He gagged, which made the flame roar against his palate. Unable to swallow, barely able to draw in a breath, Nikolai thought he might die right then from suffocation. He stumbled to the bathroom for a drink of cool water, which made the pain flare as if he'd thrown gasoline onto the fire. He crawled on hands and knees back to bed. As soon as his body hit the sheets, he passed out.

When Nikolai awoke on the morning of his fifth day in Donghae, his throat felt full of smoldering charcoal. The other symptoms had subsided, the headache dulled to a nagging discomfort, and the fever broken. His body felt cooler, and not so weak. Wet sheets beneath him showed that he'd sweated out the fever during sleep. Could he be getting better?

Cannot be. Disease will be fatal. No cure for this Igor.

Nikolai padded to the bathroom. He winced at the sickly bald old man staring at him from the mirror. Struggling to ignore the throat pain, he took a cool shower, where he examined his body from torso to legs.

Nothing.

As he dried off, Nikolai scrutinized his back in the mirror. So far as he could see, nothing. He avoided the anatomy he most needed to inspect and got dressed first. Then he would look.

He took time dressing. He fought the muscle aches in his arms and legs, which gladly delayed his return to the bathroom. The headache felt worse, but no signs of the fever and nausea that had wracked him for days. Hot coals still burned in his throat.

"Don't be stupid, Nikolai Petrovich," he said aloud. "You think not looking makes it not be?"

Nikolai shrugged and grabbed the small flashlight from the bag. Back in the bathroom, he leaned into the mirror, reflected the light into his open mouth, and stuck out his tongue.

Even seeing what he expected, Nikolai shuddered. A fine rash of small, bright red bumps covered his tongue and palate. All the spots looked alike.

He reeled away from the mirror. Waves of heat and chill and nausea and pain crashed over him. He dropped the flashlight into the sink, pulled away, and slumped to the cool tile floor. He buried his head in his hands. His body shook—not from fever, but from sheer terror as the last wisp of denial departed his brain. He stuck his head in the toilet and dry-retched, which enraged the flame in his throat.

In time, Nikolai calmed himself. He stood and investigated the small room, scrutinized the mirror, the walls, and the overhead light. He did the same in the bedroom. Everything looked normal, but Nikolai sensed watchful eyes and attentive ears monitoring his every move.

Igor Katarshkin, nee Nikolai Orlov, stood in the center of the room and spoke in a steady voice. "I have the enanthem. It is time."

Chapter 23

ANOTHER DAY PASSED. NIKOLAI wondered if his handlers had aborted the operation. Had they left him to die alone in this place, far removed from those he loved, in a strange country that bore no resemblance to his homeland?

Nikolai's body temperature felt normal, and the headache had waned to a vague discomfort. His muscles still ached, but the severity had diminished. His throat burned less. Or he had grown used to the pain. No longer emotional about his fate, he'd resorted to scientific curiosity in examining his throat every few hours. The red spots had tripled in size and turned into fluid-filled blisters. Along both sides of his neck, Nikolai felt lumps the size and shape of lima beans. Enlarged lymph nodes, the body's immune system fighting a pitched battle against a viral invasion—a battle it could not win.

Meanwhile, Nikolai waited in growing angst for the next step in this terrible journey.

By late evening, he'd had enough of waiting. An external circumstance or event must have derailed the plan. Was the Korean still alive? Had the Bratva men returned to Russia? Died?

Nikolai Orlov must take charge of his own destiny. The thought that he might reunite with Svetlana and Lora filled him with a new longing, a fresh hope. He must leave this room, this hotel, this country. Get back to Russia, to the best medical care he could afford. With vigorous treatment, Nikolai might survive this virus.

Better to hope on the move than languish alone in despair. He threw clothes into the suitcase.

A firm knock on the door interrupted Nikolai's packing and filled him with dread. He tiptoed to the door and stood sideways to look through the peephole. A Korean woman raised a hand to knock again.

Nikolai cracked the door open to the most sensuous woman he'd ever seen. She wore a tight black leather dress with a plunging neckline that exposed a bulging cleavage. An erotic aroma assaulted his olfactory nerve. Stupefied, he blinked and stared at the woman.

His unexpected guest pushed into the room and shut the door. She stepped to the window and closed the blinds, then stood close enough to Nikolai that he smelled her sweet breath. She tilted her head, eyes inviting.

"You are Igor?"

Nikolai shook his head, but then nodded, not sure what else to do.

"You are sick?"

Puzzled, Nikolai nodded again.

"Dong Jon sent me."

Nikolai raised an eyebrow. "I don't know that person."

"Dong Jon brought you to Korea. He regrets you are ill. Dong Jon sent me to give pleasure, to take your mind off the illness."

"You are a...?"

"Dong Jon's favorite whore. Call me Suk."

In a slow, erotic motion, she slid the zipper down to her waist, revealing almond breasts with erect brown nipples.

Despite the involuntary arousal, Nikolai stepped back.

"You cannot... I have..."

Before he finished his sentence, the woman advanced on him, grabbed the back of his head, pulled his mouth onto hers, and thrust her tongue deep into his throat.

Nikolai yanked away.

"No, no, you must not..."

He tried to push her away, but she stood firm. The woman's strength both surprised and enticed Nikolai. He forced a step back.

"I must not expose you..."

A sudden mouth and tongue re-attack silenced him as the woman drove him backward until they both fell onto the bed. She continued plunging her tongue deep into his throat until Nikolai needed air. He pulled away and gasped.

In an instant, the woman stood and dropped the leather dress to the floor. In another instant, she climbed naked on top of him and planted her mouth on his while she undid his pants and reached inside his undershorts.

Overcome, Nikolai surrendered.

She is a whore, and it is too late to spare her now.

***

The woman called Suk stayed the night with Nikolai, treating him to waves of pleasure that made him forget his illness, and from which he slept the soundest he had in weeks.

When the first light of day peeked through the window, she roused him with her tongue thrust deep into his mouth. Overcome with lust, Nikolai no longer cared about the fate to which he condemned this woman, this unfortunate Korean prostitute.

After they finished, Nikolai went to the bathroom to clean himself and urinate. He reexamined his tongue and throat in the mirror. The blistered lesions had ruptured, no doubt spewing live virus into the saliva he had swapped with Suk, the prostitute sentenced to die. No longer in the throes of passion, Nikolai's heart sank. The Korean man had promised no collateral damage. Why did Dong Jon send this woman to Nikolai?

She's a person. She has value.

Now Nikolai had to detain her—kill her. How could he let her live to infect her next innocent customer or a fellow passenger on a crowded bus?

Nikolai Orlov had never taken another person's life. He could not fathom destroying that of the woman who had given unexpected pleasure to his waning time on earth. A torrent of regret stormed through his mind. She didn't deserve what he'd just given her.

What should I do?

He sat on the commode and thought. He must tell her the truth, advise her to seek immediate medical care. Maybe an immunization would forestall the infection. Good supportive care might help her survive. Nikolai had heard positive reports about the South Korean health-care system. Even if she got sick, they could quarantine her in a hospital where she would not infect others.

He must force Suk to go to the hospital, to get care, maybe to live.

When he returned to the bedroom, Suk sprawled naked on the covers and beckoned him to join her.

Remorse succumbed to reignited lust. *One more time. Then I will send her to the hospital.*

He climbed on top of her, but Suk rolled him onto his back and straddled him. She leaned forward as if to kiss him. Then, in a sudden move, she pinned him to the bed and covered his face with a pillow. Nikolai tried to twist away, but she was so strong, and he was ill and weak. Vise-like elbows squeezed his head like pincers, while powerful hands wedged the pillow harder over his nose and mouth.

Nikolai tried to squirm out from under the attacker, but her legs pressed harder and immobilized him. Desperate for air, he tried to buck her off, but her body pushed him into the mattress. The struggle made him more air-hungry against the unyielding pillow. His vision dimmed.

As the world faded to black, a flash of insight enlightened his oxygen-starved brain.

So this is how it happens. Brilliant.

He quit struggling. A few seconds later, Dr. Nikolai Petrovich Orlov died with a stupid smile on his face.

Chapter 24

LEE MYUNG SUK HELD position for a full minute after the Russian stopped struggling. When she removed the pillow from his face, the deep purple cast of his skin confirmed death.

A twinge of regret surged through her. Not for the murder—she had killed other men—but for treating herself to a night in his bed. She should have taken his life after the first deadly soul kiss, but his vulnerability had aroused her. Her government did not appreciate an agent taking personal advantage on a mission. But the state would never know. The state would never see Lee Myung Suk again. Guilty pleasure in her last mission seemed a just reward—a small reward, all things considered.

Myung left the bed, went to the window, and opened the blinds. A prearranged signal. She threw her clothes into the bathroom, along with the large handbag she'd carried to the hotel. Then she unlocked the hotel room's outer door.

Back in the bathroom, she bolted the door and started the shower.

Thirty minutes later, Myung Suk emerged from the bathroom dressed in casual attire, with the leather dress rolled up inside the handbag. The bedroom was empty. Someone had removed the body, made up the bed with fresh linen, and locked the door. Dimitri and Sergei had performed as advertised.

Myung stared at the bed for a few seconds and then left the room. Outside the hotel, she watched her back as she strolled the half block to the Meridian Hotel. That hotel's staff knew her as Min Kyung-Soon, a businesswoman from Seoul registered there for an extended vacation in Donghae. Instead of entering the hotel, Myung took a casual turn around the full block, as she had done daily since arrival, scrutinizing every building and alleyway, thinking and planning.

Back at the hotel, she went straight to the ground-floor restaurant. Hungry and spent from the night's activities, she indulged in a full Korean breakfast of grilled short ribs, bean sprout rice, a spicy seafood salad, stewed fish, cold cucumber soup, seasoned kelp, and radish strip kimchi. She took her time eating, to the point of picking up single grains of rice in the tips of the metal chopsticks and relishing the texture in her mouth.

Perhaps Dong Jon always ate such a sumptuous breakfast. Despite her continuous service to the state since childhood, Lee Myung Suk had not risen to that level of privilege in her homeland.

When she finished eating, she paid the bill with won and took a surveillance stroll around the hotel lobby and first floor. She noted the relative locations of the bar lounge near the hotel entrance, the restaurant where she'd just eaten, and the private dining rooms off a separate alcove. Restrooms were at the juncture of the alcove and the main lobby. Standing in that location, Myung had a direct line of sight to the bar lounge.

She stepped into the women's restroom. It was small but clean, with two stalls—ideal for the plan developing in her mind.

Back in her room, Myung Suk reviewed again the dossier she had brought with her from Pyongyang, even though she'd long since memorized it. She reread every word of text and studied every square millimeter of the photographs. She lingered on the picture of the young American woman with cropped blond hair staring in defiance at the Supreme Leader and the crowd in the square below her—the same photo that showed Myung's beloved cousin, Yeong Nae, in the background.

Myung stroked a finger back and forth over the American woman's image.

She spoke to the image. "Little Cricket, soon you will meet in person Lee Myung Suk, the instrument of the Dear Leader's justice upon you, and the avenger of Lee Yeong Nae."

Chapter 25

USS Shenandoah. On Approach to Busan, Republic of Korea

C RICKET WATCHED FROM USS *Shenandoah*'s exterior bridge wing as the hills and high-rises of Busan grew closer on the horizon. Her first sight of the Korean Peninsula since the rescue almost a year earlier. The ship's slowing passage through the water generated a slight breeze on a hot and muggy August day. Cricket wore the prescribed port-arrival summer white uniform. The polyester fabric seemed to melt in the heat, and she perspired despite the air circulating around her.

As the landscape moved closer, Cricket touched the rack of ribbons in rows of three over her uniform's left breast pocket. A finger lingered on the top row, three mounted cloth strips 1¼ by ⅜ inches. They represented the Navy and Marine Corps Medal, the Purple Heart, and the Air Medal with an attached bronze *V* for valor. Thus had the National Command Authorities and the US Navy rewarded and thanked Lieutenant Commander Jessica Squire for her courage and suffering in North Korea.

Cricket recalled the political controversy over the medals. Vice Admiral Lewis had recommended and advocated for higher awards: the Silver Cross, Prisoner of War Medal, and Distinguished Flying Cross. The Secretary of Defense declined to endorse those medals, citing Department of Defense regulations that reserved them "for valor while engaged in action against an enemy of the United States or in conflict with an opposing force." SecDef had refused to characterize the events in North Korea as either. He feared that awarding combat-related medals to Cricket might escalate the strained relationship between the two nations.

Reward for Cricket's valor took the backseat to the two governments' wishes to obfuscate the recent skirmish.

Pieces of cloth.

Eric Mikleson appeared beside her. He wore a summer white uniform, tailored to his muscular physique. Cricket's uniform hung loosely on her body. She'd had to cinch the belt around her waifish waist, causing the waistband to fold over itself in two places. She studied Eric's athletic figure.

How does this guy find time to work out?

"I've heard a nasty rumor about you," Eric said.

Cricket turned. "What now?"

Eric smiled. "That you won't go to the hail and farewell at Haeundae Beach tonight."

"Not up for it, Eric."

"Because it's Korea?"

Cricket lied. "No. Navy parties are not my thing." Only the latter was true. The thought of setting foot on Korean soil again did disturb her.

"You're on the 'hail' list."

"All the more reason not to go. I don't like attention."

Eric did not reply. They both looked over the rail as *Shenandoah* entered the turning basin at the ROK Navy base. On the pier where the flagship would soon moor, a band played martial music. Dignitaries in business suits stood beside ROK sailors in white uniforms. All had gathered to welcome the Seventh Fleet commander and her staff and flagship to the Republic of Korea. In front of the crowd, a group of South Korean children dressed in traditional garb prepared to sing and dance for the American visitors.

Eric motioned toward the crowd. "You are a hero, Cricket, to this nation and to your own colleagues and shipmates. It would be rude to stand them up."

Cricket's eyes flashed. "I'm not going to the hail and farewell, Eric."

He stepped back. "Got it. But just so you know, I talked to Nick Juel. We've appointed ourselves your liberty buddies whenever you step off ship in Korea."

"I appreciate the gesture, Captain. Although I would enjoy your company on liberty, I don't need personal bodyguards."

"Fine," Eric said. "We would enjoy your company as well. And there's a reason it's called 'liberty.' You can't work all the time."

"Not going."

Cricket turned away to view the show on the pier.

Chapter 26

CRICKET AWAKENED THE NEXT morning with a giant headache that made her usual morning ankle pain dull in comparison. She pressed a hand to her forehead.

I told those guys I didn't want to go.

Cricket had attended the hail and farewell. An hour before they were to leave for the party, Eric and Nick had circled back together to persuade her to change her mind. She held fast, but wavered when she noted the meager dinner offering in the flag mess: cold cuts, wilted lettuce, dried-up bread, and thin tomato soup.

Nick closed the deal when he informed Cricket that the traditional "beer on the pier" availability would not happen. A new directive from United States Forces Korea (USFK) banned consumption of alcohol by any *Ulchi Freedom Guardian* (UFG) joint participants within forty-eight hours of STARTEX, the beginning of the exercise. Fear that an alcohol-related incident might undermine the US relationship with the ROK hierarchy had reached a higher level of sensitivity. In the past, the US military authority in Korea had ordered that UFG participants stay dry from STARTEX to FINEX, the end of the exercise. Now it appeared they didn't want to risk even a pre-exercise embarrassment.

The one exception allowed supervised official events to serve alcohol. To get a beer, Cricket had to attend the hail and farewell.

"I thought we were adult warriors," she said. "Why treat us like rowdy juveniles?"

"We adult leaders get to set the example for the rowdy juveniles," Nick said with a wink.

Despite earlier misgivings, Cricket enjoyed the social event at Sharky's Bar and Grill, an American-style beachfront eatery in the Haeundae Beach resort area. The Seventh Fleet officers had the entire outdoor patio to themselves. The warm weather, American comfort food, and ample libations favored a relaxed evening of socializing and camaraderie. Just what the staff needed before they gave up their lives to the grueling operational tempo of UFG.

Vice Admiral Lassiter showed up for the official "hails" to new arrivals on the staff, and "farewells" to those departing the flagship during the first phase of the deployment. The admiral's adulation of Cricket's "heroism" in North Korea, and the boisterous standing ovation from her new colleagues, had unnerved her. After that, she'd lost track of how many beers she consumed.

Eric Mikleson and Nick Juel turned out to be ideal liberty buddies. "What happens on deployment stays on deployment" had become an unofficial mantra for a small cadre of single or estranged sailors seeking companionship. In the past, Cricket had suffered amorous advances from both sexes. But she felt safe with Eric, as happy a married man as one could hope to find, and Nick, whose ongoing relationship with Kate Mahoney was the worst-kept secret in the Navy. Rumor had it the two planned to marry once Nick executed his new orders to Pacific Fleet and joined Rear Admiral Kate in Hawaii.

When the formal event ended and the staff members dispersed to return to the ship or enjoy a dry night on the town, Cricket, Eric, and Nick lingered at Sharky's. An aficionado of single malt scotch, Nick insisted on introducing Cricket to his favorite brand.

As relaxed as she'd been in months, Cricket enjoyed her new friends and their stories. She laughed with them when they recalled helping an inebriated Captain Kate Mahoney back onto the ship in Manila after a social event with the Philippine Navy. Kate had over-celebrated a diplomatic victory with her chief-of-staff counterpart over a stratagem in the South China Sea.

Through the fog in her buzzed brain, Cricket had a vague awareness that it was the same South China Sea crisis that had led to her flying the P-8 reconnaissance flight—the mission that started the chain of events leading to her captivity in North Korea.

Cricket's mind returned to the present as the headache drove nails into her brain. She wondered if her mentor, Kate Mahoney, had felt this hungover the morning after her Manila celebration. She suffered through her usual morning routine of getting out of bed in careful, orchestrated stages to reduce the impact on the gimpy ankle. When she opened the medicine cabinet over the sink, she discovered she was out of Vicodin.

Shit. I need to go back to the quack.

The medical department had just begun its workday when Cricket arrived. With much of the crew on liberty ashore, only a few sailors waited to be seen in sick call. A corpsman ushered Cricket into Lieutenant Commander Troy Pearson's office.

To her surprise, the ship's doctor empathized.

"I understand that the ops tempo will speed up starting tomorrow," he said. "And you did not overuse your last supply. I will give you ten more Vicodin to get you past the headache and into the UFG routine. If you need more later in the week, call me."

Cricket thanked the doctor and went straight to the pharmacy. A few minutes later, she carried the precious bag of ten pills back through the sick call area, and ran into Captain José Santiago, the Seventh Fleet chief of staff. He stopped in front of Cricket.

"How is he?"

Cricket's forehead wrinkled. "How is who?"

"I thought you came to see your boss, the N3. He's a patient here. Didn't you know?"

"No, sir. I didn't know."

"He left the hail and farewell early, complained of a stomachache. I learned this morning that they admitted him to the medical ward."

"Is he okay?"

"I came to find out. Let's go see."

They found Captain Mark Gunderson, the Seventh Fleet director of operations (N3), receiving IV fluid on the medical ward. He appeared ill. The fleet surgeon, Captain Rosalie Deckert, attended him. The doctor turned to them with concern on her face. Cricket pocketed the plastic envelope containing the Vicodin, but the fleet surgeon was not scrutinizing her.

Dr. Deckert addressed the chief of staff. "He has appendicitis. We need to take him to the hospital in Busan."

"You can't take care of him here?" Captain Santiago asked.

"He may need surgery. We don't do that on this ship."

The chief of staff furrowed his brow. "You're a surgeon, but you don't do surgery?"

"Fleet surgeon is just my title—a holdover from British Navy customs. Even if I were a surgeon, there's no operating room on this ship. The South Koreans have a world-class health-care system. He will be in excellent hands. I trust them to treat any of our staff, including me."

Captain Santiago appeared skeptical. "Gotta trust your judgment on this, Doc. Just don't be wrong."

Captain Deckert glanced at Cricket and then turned to the chief of staff. "Captain Gunderson will miss UFG. If things go as expected, we can pick him up in two weeks on our return through Busan after the exercise."

"Very well," the chief of staff said. "Do what you must, Doc."

He turned to Cricket. "Looks like you're the acting N3 for the duration of UFG, Commander Squire." A pitying look crossed his face. "Congratulations."

Chapter 27

USS Shenandoah (LCC 21). East Sea (Sea of Japan)

N EAR THE END OF the first week of the *Ulchi Freedom Guardian* (UFG) joint exercise, USS *Shenandoah* plowed circles in the East Sea. The Seventh Fleet staff crowded into the confined spaces of the Operations Department (N3) for the early morning "real-world" brief.

The UFG exercise had taken over the larger Flag Conference Room, where simulated briefs and teleconferences occurred throughout the day. Because their ROK Navy guests had free access to that room, the fleet's NOFORN (no foreigners) actual operational business had moved to the N3 spaces.

Looking around the room, Eric Mikleson noted the combined stress of the exercise and the real-world uncertainty reflected in the fatigue on the faces of the staff officers.

Cricket Squire's empty seat worried him. The acting director of operations needed to be in her place and ready to brief before the admiral arrived, or...

"Attention on deck!" Most of the fifty officers jammed into the room were already standing when the admiral entered from the starboard passageway. The few who occupied seats also stood, and everyone came to attention.

"As you were." The admiral took her seat and looked at Eric. "Proceed."

Eric saw Cricket in her seat next to the chief of staff. She must have entered from the port passageway when the admiral came in from the opposite side. Cricket looked weary, thinner than usual. The toll of being thrust into a key lead role in both real-world and exercise operations showed in her sunken eyes.

He turned his attention to the admiral. "Good morning, Admiral and Staff."

Eric pointed to a video screen next to him, an update of his earlier slide showing the North Korean submarine base at Sinpo. "As you can tell from this morning's satellite image, the modified *Sinpo* submarine is no longer moored. We assess it got under way overnight."

"You didn't see that when it happened?" The admiral frowned.

"Cloud cover obscured our view, ma'am."

"Where is it now?"

"We don't know, ma'am." Embarrassed, Eric looked down at his notes.

Cricket came to his rescue. "We've sortied a P-8 from Okinawa to the East Sea, and USS *Key West*, a Los Angeles–class submarine, is patrolling the most likely location. We'll find it, ma'am."

The admiral smiled at Cricket. "Nice save, Commander. Please find it. Soon would be good." She looked back at Eric. "Continue."

Eric reiterated his assessment of low potential for nuclear attack from a missile-launching submarine. "No new information to suggest an attack is imminent. We expected it to get underway, probably as a decoy. We continue to hear chatter that the DPRK plans a serious provocation, if not an actual strike, against the ROK or our own forces. We have reports of increased North Korean Special Forces activity in the South." He directed his gaze at Admiral Lassiter. "In my five years in this area of responsibility, DPRK threats against UFG never panned out. This one seems different. I can't put my finger on why."

Admiral Lassiter leaned back and folded her arms. "Well, Captain, maybe when you get your finger out of your behind, you will give us information we can use. I find nothing actionable in your entire brief."

Eric stiffened. "I understand, ma'am. We have no hard intelligence, but sometimes we must trust our instincts. The unique pattern of DPRK actions and rhetoric over the past two weeks suggests they are planning something different and dramatic."

The admiral leaned forward. "Can your instincts tell me what to do with the cream puff information you just presented? Shall I cancel the Donghae port visit? Ask PacFleet for another carrier battle group? Order a higher force protection posture?"

Eric's face turned scarlet. He did not reply.

"What do you suggest I do about this weekend's engagement with the First ROK Fleet leadership, Captain? Do I put my entire senior staff at risk by going ashore to socialize with our counterparts in one of our nation's most important alliances? Or should I tell my people to cower on board this ship instead?"

She half-stood and glowered. "Until you can give me something definite, something on which I can make a data-driven decision, please don't pollute the air with instincts. Am I clear?"

"Yes, ma'am."

A pall of silence permeated the room. Admiral Lassiter swung her chair in a circle to peruse the assembled staff sitting behind her.

"Let me be clear. I pick on the N2 because I can. Just as I like to pick on the doc and the chaps. But even though I ripped the Two a new orifice just now, he may not be wrong. Y'all must understand we are in a danger zone here. Up the road lives a megalomaniac numb-nut despot of marginal sanity. Because he exists and because we bloodied his nose in public not long ago, we cannot drop our guard. Without solid intelligence of a clear and present threat, we must continue normal operations. The most powerful navy in the world does not duck heads to threats and innuendo. This forward-deployed naval force does not kowtow to a baby-ass dictator."

She paused for dramatic effect. "However, let's not make ourselves vulnerable to a sucker punch. Instruct your people to stay alert at all times."

Lassiter turned back to Eric. "Sorry if I came on strong there, Captain. I wouldn't trade jobs with you for all the kimchi in Korea. Please produce something tangible so we can make informed tactical decisions."

"We're working it hard, ma'am."

"Thank you, Captain. I know you are." She stood, signaling the end of the briefing session.

The petty officer at the door called out, "Attention on deck."

"Carry on, please," the admiral said.

She remained at her place and motioned for Eric and Cricket to join her. She leaned forward and spoke in a low voice. "Trust your instincts, Eric. I have the same feeling. But I can't sell pre-emptive action to the pussies up the chain based on instincts. Find me something I can take to our leadership before that ass hat up north starts a full-out war."

"We'll do our best," Eric said.

"Do better than that." The admiral stood and left the room.

Chapter 28
USS Shenandoah (LCC 21). East Sea (Sea of Japan)

M ID-WAY THROUGH THE FIRST week of the UFG exercise, Cricket limped down the passageway to the fleet surgeon's stateroom. She had used up the most recent Vicodin supply, and a frantic yet fruitless search for the emergency stash in her sock drawer had made her almost late for the morning brief.

The operations' tempo had forced her to work twenty-hour days as she carried a dual load as acting N3 for both real-world and exercise contingencies. A nagging headache from stress and sleep deprivation compounded the ankle pain that had worsened every day, despite taking Vicodin every four hours.

Now she had less than a half-hour before the next UFG video teleconference (VTC) with Combined Forces Command, the headquarters of the dual US and ROK leadership on the Korean peninsula. The VTC would include all the US and ROK military leaders taking part in UFG. Cricket could not stomach another two hours of bilingual parley and posturing without something to dull the pain in her ankle and head.

Captain Deckert's face showed alarm when she invited Cricket into her stateroom/office. "What can I do for you, Commander?"

"I'm in pain. I'm out of Vicodin. I have a brief in less than thirty minutes. May I please get a prescription?"

"When did you get the last prescription?"

Cricket sighed, failing to hide her impatience. "Doc Pearson gave me ten just before UFG. I took the last one yesterday."

Captain Deckert thought about it, then rummaged in a desk drawer. She withdrew a prescription pad. "Another ten seems reasonable. That should last you until the weekend exercise pause. Our medical computer network is down, so I need to write a script. Haven't done this in forever, but I think I remember how to do it."

"Thank you, ma'am. I really appreciate it."

With written prescription in hand, Cricket headed down the ladder to the second deck. She stepped into her stateroom before going to medical. The headache throbbed behind her eyes, but she stared at the handwritten prescription. Written in black ink, the figure *#10* showed the number of pills to dispense, but the surgeon had neglected to confirm that number with the written word *ten*. Cricket thought for a minute, then took a black ink pen and overwrote the *1* to make a *4*. The prescribed number of pills now looked like *#40*.

Cricket hurried to the medical department and entered through an aft door to avoid the main passageway where she might run into Doc Pearson. At the small room that served as pharmacy, she smiled to see a junior hospital corpsman at the window. Cricket handed the prescription to the young man.

"Could you please expedite this? I have an important brief in fifteen minutes."

The corpsman raised an eyebrow. "Forty? That's a lot of pills, ma'am."

"I know," Cricket said. "The fleet surgeon wrote for a month's supply because the operational schedule often keeps me from coming down here."

The corpsman hesitated. "I should clear this with Doctor Pearson."

Cricket pleaded. "I don't have time to wait. You recognize the fleet surgeon's signature, right? When I get back upstairs to the brief, I can have her call you to verify it. Right now, I'm in a lot of pain and I need medication." She looked at her watch. "I can't be late for that brief."

The corpsman nodded. "Okay, ma'am. Just ask Captain Deckert to call when she gets a chance."

Minutes later, Cricket returned to her stateroom, swallowed two of the pills, and hid the rest in the sock drawer. She arrived in the Flag Conference Room just as the Combined Forces Command brief started.

The ops tempo would cause her to "forget" to pass the message to Captain Deckert. She reckoned a 50/50 chance the medical department's workload would have the same effect on the corpsman.

Chapter 29
Donghae, Republic of Korea

NINE DAYS AFTER THE seduction and murder of the Russian scientist, Lee Myung Suk perused Donghae Harbor from a nearby hillside. She ignored the fever and headache as she watched tugboats push the US Navy ship toward the pier at the ROK Navy base.

Target in sight.

She would attack in thirty hours. "Revenge and honor," she said in a proud whisper. "Honor and vengeance in the name of the Dear Leader."

Myung watched until the tugs eased the ship next to the pier. Then she headed back down the hill toward her hotel. Early symptoms weakened her. She needed to rest and revitalize before executing the crucial mission.

Her room in the Meridian Hotel had annoyed her when she checked in as Min Kyung-Soon. The space allotted to a single occupant could accommodate an entire family in North Korea. Her comrades would think the furnishings opulent, although most South Koreans would find them nondescript. But in the short time she'd stayed there, Myung had grown more accustomed to the place. She enjoyed surfing the channels on the large-screen digital television mounted to the wall, fascinated by the well-dressed, active South Koreans enjoying shopping and nightlife in Seoul. Such an opulent lifestyle would be disgraceful in her own country. She stretched out to relax on the double bed and found an American news channel on the TV. The decadence of that society disgusted her, and now she understood how it had seduced Yeong Nae.

No excuse, cousin, for betraying your family and the Supreme Leader.

A hot flush chased by a spiking shiver ran through Myung's body. The sensation dissipated as swiftly as it had arrived. She closed her eyes and tried to rest, but a new pain in her throat sounded an alarm in her brain. In the bathroom, she leaned into the mirror and stuck out her tongue. Red spots, all the same size, covered it.

Back in the bedroom, Myung extracted a burner cell phone from her purse and connected to the familiar gravelly voice of Dong Jon.

"We are in position. Timing is perfect."

"Site and time confirmed as briefed," he said. "Unknown if the target will attend. Prepare your backup plan. Obtain visual contact and signal me before you engage. Repeat."

Myung parroted the instructions back to Dong Jon. He hung up without replying. Myung felt feverish. The headache had returned. Her throat burned. She should rest, maybe skip dinner. She stripped to her underwear and reclined on the bed with a wet washcloth across her forehead.

As she closed her eyes, she whispered, "Soon, dear Yeong Nae, I will avenge your death—and your treason."

Chapter 30

E ARLY THE FOLLOWING EVENING, Lee Myung Suk took position in the Meridian Hotel lobby bar.

Although her throat still ached, a night of uninterrupted sleep followed by a day of rest had dulled the pain in her back and head. The fever had subsided. A long, luxurious tub bath had relaxed her to the point of listlessness. Putting on makeup, perfuming her body, and sliding into the sexy leather dress re-energized her. A soldier donning battle gear. Examining her throat before leaving the hotel room, she'd noted that the red spots had turned to small blisters.

The semi-automatic pistol in her purse became the backup weapon.

A quicker death. For both of us.

Myung chose a location that afforded a view of both the hotel entrance and the alcove to the private dining room where the ROK Navy First Fleet leaders planned to entertain their American counterparts. Satisfied that she had a full view of the battlefield, she ordered a shot of whiskey, turned her chair toward the hotel entrance, and waited. The first sip of the whiskey burned her sore throat, but a few more sips numbed the pain just enough.

The ROK Navy puppets arrived first, dressed in business suits or dress slacks and sports coats. Did they think that aping Western dress styles dignified them in front of the imperialists?

They should move to the USA. Leave this peninsula to the true Koreans.

The ROK Navy entourage included men only, ideal for Myung's planned attack.

Thirty minutes passed before the American devils arrived.

Late as always. As if the world should expect to wait for them.

The Americans also wore business attire, except for the leader of the filthy flock. The serious-looking woman with bobbed gray hair wore a tailored white top over black slacks. A single strand of pearls adorned what little skin showed above the modest top. To Lee Myung Suk, the first woman to command the US Navy's Seventh Fleet looked nothing like a warrior.

No match for a true soldier.

Lee's heart skipped when she saw no other women among the female admiral's sheep. Mindful of her growing physical discomfort, she doubted she could repeat this scenario over the next two days.

Must happen now.

Then a wisp of blond hair at the rear of the entourage caught her eye. A skinny woman walked with a slight limp between two taller, larger men.

Bodyguards?

Dressed in white slacks too big for her frame and a loose-fitting blue blouse, the woman looked frail. Yet she carried herself with an upright, confident posture that suggested a hardened warrior, alert and dangerous. As the woman passed the lobby bar, she glanced in Myung's direction. A surprised expression flitted across her face, and her gait faltered for a second. Then she looked away and continued on with her comrades.

Myung stayed impassive as her eyes followed the woman into the alcove.

At last we meet.

When the dining-room door closed behind the leaders of her homeland's two most despised enemies, Myung Suk finished the whiskey and beckoned the server. She ordered ice water. Her mind must stay sharp while the decrepit South Koreans kept their glasses and those of the American sots flowing with whiskey and beer.

Whenever her quarry emerged, Myung would need but a few minutes for the attack. The wanton drunkenness inside that room would work to her advantage. If not... She reached into her purse and touched the loaded pistol.

The server delivered a tall glass of ice water. Lee Myung Suk settled back in her chair with her eyes fixed on the alcove.

The cobra, ready to strike.

Chapter 31

CRICKET ENTERED THE MERIDIAN Hotel flanked by Eric Mikleson and Nick Juel. The Vicodin tablets she'd taken before leaving the ship had kicked in, and she walked with little pain and just a slight limp.

"For all my visits to Korea, first time in Donghae," Nick said. "I'm impressed. Great bike ride through the hills this morning."

"Just over a hundred miles from North Korea," Eric said. He seemed nervous.

"Seoul is closer to the DMZ," Cricket said. She turned toward Eric. "That never bothers you."

She did not hear Eric's reply. From a table in the bar, wearing a familiar black leather dress, Lee Young looked straight at her. Cricket's breathing quickened and her step faltered.

Lee Young, here? How?

Could she have lived? Cricket glanced again at the woman. A close resemblance, but Lee Young would show emotion at the sight of her former lover. This woman's stony face didn't flinch, not a glimmer of recognition.

Not Lee.

The exchange had taken but an instant. Cricket refocused on Eric. "You don't have to be nervous, Eric. We're in a public place. Nothing will happen here."

"Combined leadership of US and ROK fleets in a public place makes for soft targets."

"We got security all over the place," Nick said. "I, for one, intend to do my part to foster international relationships in the finest traditions of the Seventh Fleet. That means have a good time and keep up with our Korean counterparts in the alcohol department."

Their hosts greeted them in the alcove for a brief reception before proceeding to the private dining room. Cricket put the woman in the lobby from her mind as she transitioned to diplomacy mode. With a posing smile on her face, she exchanged halting pleasantries with men who spoke limited English.

She spoke nothing of their language. In earlier, healthier days, she'd escaped polite conversation with high-level foreign dignitaries. Senior officers had little to gain from befriending one as junior as Cricket. Junior officers with whom she'd interacted showed more interest in her fit and fertile body than in conversation, never suspecting that she preferred women.

The woman in the bar. Could she...?

Cricket forced her mind back to the dining room and turned to the ROK Navy officer talking to her. "Sorry," she said. "I didn't catch your name."

"I am Captain Park Yun-Pai, Director of Operations for First ROK Fleet. Same job as you."

Not in your wildest dreams, mister.

"Pleased to meet you, sir. I am Commander Jessica Squire, Seventh Fleet Deputy for Operations. But you knew that." She sipped whiskey from the glass that a hostess had placed in her hand. "My colleagues call me Cricket."

"Cricket? Like the bug?"

Cricket took another sip of whiskey. "It's my call sign. I'm a US Navy pilot."

Park Yun-Pai held out his hand. "I am pleased to meet you, Commander Cricket." As they shook hands, his furtive gaze shot to her breasts.

Men.

"Likewise," she said. She chugged the rest of the whiskey in her glass, which Captain Park refilled at once.

***

As they entered the private dining room, the party of allies removed their shoes at the entrance. They sat on the floor at two long low tables loaded with Korean delicacies on small plates, including three different varieties of kimchi, pickled vegetables, fresh lettuce, and several plates of unidentifiable fare—no doubt from the sea. Each table contained three charcoal grills on which the participants cooked thin slices of meats and vegetables in the traditional style of Korean barbecue. Bottles of beer and whiskey stood at the ready for the participants to fill each other's small glasses.

In East Asia, one never poured one's own drink, and one never let a companion's glass get empty.

By the time the servers brought the second round of meat for the barbecue, Cricket felt light-headed. She had switched from whiskey to beer, which she tried to sip in small drafts. The attentive Korean officer, who seemed to consider himself her date for the night, filled the glass whenever it reached half empty. Cricket lost count of how many glasses of whiskey and beer she'd consumed. A look around the room assured her that the others had kept pace. Her dinner companion's ruddy complexion and slurred speech showed that he had charged well ahead of her on the inebriation pathway. His words had become unintelligible, so Cricket just nodded and smiled without understanding.

The man did not notice. His gazes at her chest had become less furtive as the evening continue.

Cricket had sat on the floor with legs folded underneath her for over an hour. Her ankle throbbed, and the libations had distended her bladder to the point of discomfort. The party showed no signs of winding down. When her Korean companion planted his hand on her thigh, a wave of dizziness and nausea passed through her.

Time for a tactical retreat.

Cricket turned to her ROK host. "If you will excuse me, Captain, I'm going to powder my nose."

The Korean man looked puzzled. "Your nose looks okay."

"Sorry. American expression. I have to pee."

Before the man could react, Cricket got up, stepped to the dining room entryway, and donned house slippers for the excursion to the ladies' room.

Both Eric and Nick moved to get up and follow her. Cricket waved them off. "Ladies' room. You can't come."

She glanced toward the bar on her way. The same Korean woman sipped a clear liquid. Their eyes met for a second, and Cricket thought she saw a hint of recognition in the other's eyes before she looked away.

Pain shot through Cricket's ankle during the short walk from the dining room through the alcove to the restroom. She limped into a small room that contained a sink and two stalls. She stopped at the sink, took a Vicodin from her slacks pocket, and thrust it into her mouth. Thinking better of drinking tap water, she swallowed the pill dry and headed to the nearest stall. To her dismay, both stalls contained East Asia–style squat toilets—porcelain troughs at floor level. Cricket sighed and blinked away the fuzziness that clouded her brain.

Of course I wore slacks and pantyhose.

To use the toilet without soiling her white slacks, she stepped out of one leg of both the slacks and pantyhose and hiked them up in a wad to her thigh. Standing on one leg, she lost her balance and stumbled against the wall.

Another wave of dizziness and nausea washed over her, but she recovered and squatted over the hole in the floor. As she urinated, she heard the bathroom door open, followed by footsteps.

An electrical warning of imminent danger coursed through her, but she was in no position to move. Cricket remained in the squat until the other woman used the stall next to hers. With her body balanced over her feet, pain shot through Cricket's ankle, and she feared it would give way. She sprang from the squat, lost her balance, and fell backward onto her butt. The slacks and panty hose now lay clumped on the floor beneath her.

The toilet flushed in the next stall. The door opened and footsteps moved toward the sink, followed by the sound of a faucet running and then shutting off. The footsteps retreated toward the bathroom door, which opened and closed.

Silence.

Cricket was alone again, thankful that the other woman (no doubt a Korean aware of Americans in the hotel) had been too polite to embarrass Cricket by investigating the sound of a crash from the next stall. In the confined space, Cricket struggled onto her hands and knees to get up from where she'd fallen. As she stood, another wave of dizziness hit her, and the room twirled around her head. In a near faint, she braced herself against the stall partition until the wave passed. With great effort, she got her bare leg back into the panty hose and slacks and pulled them up. A grungy stain adorned the right rear panel of her white pants.

"Damn."

Cricket leaned against the stall partition to catch her breath. She was so woozy she could not think straight. She sank into a half-awake stage of confusion. A dense fog invaded her mind, and she wondered where she was.

Korea. Somewhere in Korea. With a stain on my pants, and a party...

With great effort, she forced herself alert and blinked her eyes hard until the room became clear again.

Dirty pants or not, she had to return to the party, to Eric and Nick, and...

Her mind blurred.

That woman?

Cricket weaved, about to pass out.

Must get back.

The room darkened, and then she heard the click of a door locking.

What the...?

Cricket's mind drifted to the edge of consciousness. Her legs gave way, but she caught herself against the door to the stall. The walls closed around her. Desperate to escape, she fumbled with the door latch, but the stall twirled upside down.

Just as she lost her balance, the door swung out and Cricket tumbled through the gap. Straight into the arms of Lee Young.

"Whaad?" Cricket leaned her head back but could not focus her eyes. "You dead woman."

"I live for you, Jess."

Cricket closed her eyes, but the room spun, with Lee and her at the center of the vortex. Lee and Cricket descending, floating through space, together. But she was so dizzy, she had to lie down. She had to sleep. If she could just sleep next to Lee...

In one smooth motion, Lee lowered them both to the floor and cradled Cricket's head to her bosom, rocking her in a slow rhythm. She stroked Cricket's cheek with a sensuous gentleness that at once stopped the spinning and made Cricket's body tingle.

With eyes closed, Cricket turned her head up and parted her lips. In an instant, Lee's mouth was on hers. Their tongues massaged each other as their mouths and bodies locked together.

When they broke apart, Cricket floated into a still darkness that enveloped her in warmth and comfort. Her mind released from her body, from the sound of retreating footsteps, a door unlocking, opening, closing.

Immersed in the cozy euphoria of finding and loving Lee again, Jess Squire hugged herself, curled into a fetal ball, and slept.

The faint sound of male voices shouting and someone pounding on a distant door did not disturb the ecstasy within her soul.

Chapter 32

L EE MYUNG SUK RELEASED from the kiss.

The American woman had passed out in her arms. Myung cradled the tousled-blond head as she lowered it to the tiled floor. Standing, she regarded the face of her victim, a woman warrior tortured in body, mind, and soul. In a different world order, they might have been comrades in arms.

Myung Suk almost pitied her prey. Almost.

We are both dead.

Myung looked into the other woman's vapid face and smiled, a wicked victory smirk. She paused in front of a mirror long enough to check her appearance, glanced back at the flaccid woman snoring on the floor, and left the room.

As Myung passed the private dining room where the US and ROK Navy leaders drank and dined, two American men hurried out the door. She recognized the two naval officers who had flanked Miss Jessica Squire, the doomed "cricket," when the US Navy entourage had entered the Meridian Hotel hours earlier. Their anxious, glassy eyes randomly searched the hallway and alcove.

One spoke to Myung in slurred English. "Can you tell us where the ladies' room is?"

Myung put on her most clueless face. "No Engrish."

The man frowned and walked away without a word.

Rude pigs.

The Americans would find the unconscious victim in less than a minute. Myung crossed the lobby at a brisk walk, bypassed the elevators, and sprinted up the stairs to her third-floor room. Inside, she wiggled out of the black leather seductress dress, now damp with sweat.

Perfect.

She left the dress on the bed. In the bathroom, she sponged and toweled her body, and left the linens piled on the floor. Then she dressed in loose cotton underwear and nondescript casual clothes.

From the closet, she retrieved the duffel bag already packed to conceal the disassembled Type 88 rifle at the bottom. She transferred the Type 70 pistol from her purse to the bag. Hefting the bag over her shoulder, she left the hotel via an employee entrance and hurried away.

The dress!

She had left it on the bed. Did she dare go back to retrieve it? She shook her head. Too risky. The hotel staff would remove it.

Myung felt at once very ill. She had studied the disease. Little time remained to spread it before the telltale rash would force her into isolated exile. She covered the short distance to the Donghae Bus Terminal and bought a ticket for the next ride to Seoul. In short order, she boarded, stashed her duffel in an overhead rack, and sat in the middle of the vehicle. She hoped to expose as many South Koreans and tourists as possible during the three-hour trip to Seoul.

She would arrive at her apartment in the early morning hours, with enough time to rest up and get into character before her evening date.

Chapter 33

USS Shenandoah (LCC 21). East Sea (Sea of Japan)

"YOU PROMISED TO LOOK out for me!" Cricket Squire's face glowed hot and her eyes flashed.

Eric Mikleson retreated a step from his shipmate's fury. He leaned against the closed door to the medical department's quiet room, hoping to attenuate his shipmate's trumpet-like tirade. Not good for the corpsmen on duty to overhear a senior officer's uncontrolled rant.

Eric opened his mouth to speak, but Cricket yelled over him.

"You and Nick knew I didn't want to set foot in Korea again. You talked me into that party by saying you'd protect me." She folded her arms and glowered. "Guess your new best ROK friends were more important."

She scowled. "I should never have trusted you guys." Her voice switched from angry to wistful. "I should've never left this ship."

Eric sat down in a chair next to the bed where Cricket had spent the night sleeping off the combination of alcohol and narcotics that had caused her to pass out in the restroom at the Meridian Hotel. He spoke in a gentle voice. "When you left your table, we got up from ours. You said you were going to the ladies' room and that we couldn't follow you."

Her eyes flared, and her skin flushed. "That's it? That's your pathetic excuse, Mr. All-Chivalrous? Lady has to piss, so you leave her on her own recon, behind enemy lines?"

"C'mon, Cricket. That's harsh."

"You wanna talk harsh? You and Nick the Magnificent abandoned me from the git-go. You left me to fend for myself with that horny ROK captain—whatever his name was. The creep groped me with his eyes the whole damned night."

"I'm sorry," Eric said. "You seemed to have a good time."

She snorted. Then her face softened, and the glare turned to mortification. "How bad was it?"

Eric looked down at the deck. "What do you remember?"

"Not much. The ROK captain was drunk before the first round of barbecue." She raised her hand. "Not that I was sober, I know. By dessert, he groped me for real. I felt ill. I had to get out of there."

She bit her lip. "Okay, I waved you two off. You should've followed me, anyway."

"You're right," Eric said. "Again, sorry."

Cricket sighed. "The, uh, head was, you know, tight. Asian style. I struggled to, uh, get it done, and I slipped and fell. Passed out. I don't remember."

"You fell in the stall? That's the last thing you remember?"

She thought for a second, then tilted her head and forced a confused smile. "Yeah, that's it."

"When you didn't come right back, Nick and I worried. We went searching for you. We found you passed out on the floor of the women's head."

Cricket squeezed her eyes to quell the tears. "Shit. The admiral?"

"Not happy."

Cricket's expression resembled that of a little girl caught in wet pants. "Tell me."

"Nick and I got you to your feet. You were out of it, but we didn't find any injuries. I stayed with you while Nick went back to the dining room to tell the chief of staff. By then, the party was winding down. The ROK captain asked for you, but Nick told him you were ill and that I had taken you back to the ship in a taxi. The COS told us to hide you in the head until the ROKs left.

"That turned difficult because they insisted on seeing everyone off. Nick orchestrated a show of leaving. The COS and the rest of the staff took the bus while the admiral and Nick left in her car. The driver circled the block and parked a short distance away. After the ROKs had all left, the admiral and Nick came back for you and me. We rode back in her car."

"I don't remember any of that."

Eric averted his eyes. "Good thing."

"What?"

"You threw up." He drew a long breath. "To be blunt, you puked in the admiral's lap."

Cricket turned ashen. "Oh, God, no."

"Yeah, you did."

"How angry was she?"

"Hard to figure. She can be stoic when she wants to be. When we returned on board, she just said, 'Get her down to medical.'"

Cricket rocked back and forth with her faced buried in her hands. Eric wanted to reach out and touch her, comfort her, but he feared how she would react. She looked up, eyes terrified.

"I'm trying to remember, but I can't."

"You should rest," he said. "Whatever happened is over now. Don't flog yourself."

Cricket flopped her head onto the pillow.

Eric touched her hand. "If you need anything at all, ask the corpsmen to call me."

She nodded.

He rose and started for the door.

"Eric."

He turned.

She raised her head, a puzzled frown on her face. "Did I kiss that Korean guy?"

Chapter 34

A FIRM KNOCK AWAKENED Cricket from a fitful sleep. Before she could reply, the door opened to admit Vice Admiral Louise Lassiter. The one visitor Cricket dreaded.

Cricket made a move to stand, but got tangled in the IV tubing.

The admiral raised her hand. "Don't get up, Commander." She entered the room and closed the door. Pulling up a chair, she spoke in her classic Southern drawl. "I want to chat with you a bit."

Cricket untangled herself and sat up in the bed. She must face whatever was in store with her head high. She took a deep breath. "I've been expecting you, ma'am. I want to say straight up that I'm sorry for what happened last night."

The admiral shook her head. "Sorry ain't gonna cut it, sweetheart." Her voice was at once gentle yet stern. "You need to give me one damned good reason not to boot you off this ship on the next helo."

Cricket pursed her lips. The admiral stared at her, eyes sharp but tinged with compassion.

"Yes, ma'am," Cricket said. Her mind raced to nowhere good.

"It's your ass on the line," the admiral said. "You might should think real hard about what you say next."

Cricket rubbed her eyes. "I am sorry, ma'am. I'm especially sorry for throwing up on you."

The admiral waved her arm in a dismissive gesture. "You think that's the first time I've held someone's head who got too liquored up? I have three younger siblings, plus I've visited plenty of liberty ports in my Navy career. I was a junior officer once. You can wash or replace clothes. Naval officers are harder to fix."

"Send me home," Cricket blurted. "I'm a disgrace to the Seventh Fleet and the United States Navy."

The admiral bristled. "You got one gnat's breath to shit-can the self-deprecating talk, missy. That dog don't hunt with me."

Cricket's head buzzed. "I don't know what you want from me, ma'am."

"I told you. Give me one good reason not to fly your ass away from here." She leaned toward Cricket. "Do I have to spell it out for you?"

She wants me to stay?

Cricket dared not look the admiral in the eye. "For one thing, you're without an ops officer until we pick up Captain Gunderson back in Busan. You need me for at least another week."

The admiral stared at her, face impassive.

"Two," Cricket said, "I can still contribute. No one understands the North Korean devils better than I do."

The admiral continued to stare in silence.

Her nerves prickling, Cricket said, "Three, I let you down last night. I need to make it right. It won't happen again, ever."

"You sure?"

"As sure as I can be. I'm embarrassed and humiliated. I could have ruined our relationship with the ROK Navy."

Vice Admiral Lassiter burst into laughter. "Don't give yourself so much credit, girl. Those guys were shit faced well before your little escapade. None of them had a clue, not even the jackass who felt you up with his eyes all night."

Cricket chuckled, despite her nervousness. "I appreciate your words, Admiral, but I don't get what you're asking of me."

"Fine. I'll spell it out. I don't give a rat's ass if you get drunk on liberty. We've all been there, except for the Bible thumpers, and they could stand a good loosening up."

She moved closer to Cricket, her tone serious. "I care a hell of a lot about what you've been doing to yourself since you returned from rehab. Not for nothing, last night was a major alarm."

Cricket shrugged. "I don't..."

"Did they put stupid-juice in that IV bottle? Or are you that deep in denial? I'll ask you straight. Did you take any pills before we went to that soiree, or while we were there?"

Cricket stared at the overhead. "Yes, ma'am. I took Vicodin because my ankle hurt."

"May I assume that, as an officer in the United States Navy, you've received training, at some point in your career, about the dangers of mixing narcotics with alcohol?" Vice Admiral Lassiter's tone had turned grim.

"Yes, ma'am."

"Did you take narcotics last weekend before we went to the hail and farewell?"

"Yes, ma'am."

"And?"

"That's all, ma'am. I don't..."

The admiral interrupted. "Here's the deal, Commander. I don't give a crap if you get drunk once in a while. I don't care if you take pain pills. Lord knows you got enough pain to kill. I do care, and I will boot your ass out of here, if you ever again do stupid shit like mix narcs with booze—especially on a diplomatic engagement with one of our closest allies."

She let her words sink in. "Do you feel me now, Commander Squire?"

Cricket nodded. "Aye, ma'am."

The admiral shook her head. "I don't think so. Not yet."

Cricket looked up, puzzled.

"You know some flag officers tried to block your return to the fleet, right?"

Cricket nodded.

"My three stars trumped their twos, so you got to come. I wanted you on my staff because you are a woman of courage, spunk, and intellect, and you know those North Korean bastards in a way that no one else does. You've been close enough to sniff them."

She looked Cricket in the eyes. "I still want you on my staff, Commander Squire, now more than ever, because I think we face a threat beyond anything imagined. We need your help to figure it out so we can stop those ass wipes from starting a war."

Cricket pursed her lips. "Ma'am, I want to do that. It's all I've wanted since I escaped from that prison."

"Then show me, damn it. You're no good to anyone on this self-destructive course. Least of all yourself. Get it together and clean up your act, or I will kick your butt all the way back to Tripler, where you can rot in Shrinksville. Am I clear?"

"Yes, ma'am. Crystal."

"So, what's the one good reason I shouldn't fly you off on the next helo?"

"Because I will do whatever it takes to support the mission, ma'am, and to take down the enemy if it comes to that. You can count on that."

"Good." The admiral rose from her chair. "Thank you, Commander. You get well now, hear?"

"Thank you, ma'am. I will."

Without another word, the admiral was out the door.

Chapter 35

Seoul, Republic of Korea

"**I** AM VERY TIRED."

Myung Suk did not lie. The victory thrill from her attack on the American naval officer had long since given way to progressive fatigue. The operations tempo of planning and executing the mission, added to her body's battle against the invading disease, had left her drained. The fever and nausea had abated by the time she woke from her nap, but the aching in her head and back, and the fire in her throat, had almost driven her back to bed.

Only the prospect of striking another blow to the enemy had motivated Myung to bathe, slither into tight slacks and a provocative blouse, and move out to keep her date.

Because she took longer than usual getting ready, she had arrived late at the restaurant in Seoul's Itaewon district. Her mark had been on his second beer when he saw her, and the worry that had clouded his face gave way to rays of unabashed affection.

Fully in character, Myung responded in kind, almost giddy. She often felt such delight when she got close to a victim, not from romantic anticipation but from the thrill of her impending attack.

As they dined, Myung's appetite waned with her strength. The fever must have returned, because her sheer blouse clung immodestly to clammy skin. She pushed the food around the plate and limited herself to tiny sips of beer from a small glass. Only halfway through the meal, Myung wondered if she could complete this last mission in the service of the Dear Leader.

Cannot fail now!

Resolute, she forced a smile.

Across the table, the muscular South Korean Army soldier had been staring at Myung's moist cleavage while vigorously sucking up noodles from the bowl in front of him.

Practicing for later?

At the word *tired*, he stopped staring and sucking, crestfallen.

Concern for her welfare? Or that his plans for the rest of the night might not materialize?

Myung reached out and stroked the young man's hand. "I will be okay. I had a tedious business trip to Donghae. I returned to Seoul on the bus early this morning."

She leaned forward to expose more cleavage. "I took a good nap, and I promise to perk up." As if to prove it, she took a quaff of beer. "You said you had news. A new assignment?"

Her companion beamed. "You are looking at the newly assigned translator for the Combined Forces commander."

Myung's face broke into a genuine smile. Far better news than she had hoped. She had chosen her prey with care months ago during a recon sortie into the ROK. Corporal Gi Kwang-Hee was a rising junior officer in the ROK Army community known as KATUSA, meaning "Korean Augmentation to the United States Army." Selected for English fluency and military aptitude, KATUSA were young ROK officers assigned to US Forces Korea to serve as translators, drivers, and other support staff throughout the command's infrastructure.

At the time she met him, Myung did not know in what way the soldier would become useful to her, but she trusted he would. She ignited the relationship during two torrid nights in the Seoul apartment that she rented under an alias. Afterward, she maintained the contact from a distance by claiming to be on constant travel for her business. She had arranged the current dinner date as a joyful "reunion" upon her return "home."

Lee Myung Suk was now poised to reap multifold returns on her meager investment in developing this naïve ROK contact. In his new position supporting the combined US and ROK commands, Corporal Gi had direct contact not only with the highest US military leadership on the Korean Peninsula, but with their ROK counterparts as well.

"That is wonderful news," she said with genuine liveliness. "We must celebrate." She stroked his hand again. "I feel much better, and I have a bottle of fine champagne back in my apartment." Myung flitted her eyelids. "As you know, it's a short walk from here."

Corporal Gi beckoned the server for the bill.

Lee Myung Suk glowed.

Wonderful news, indeed.

Chapter 36
USS Shenandoah (LCC 21). East Sea (Sea of Japan)

DISCHARGED AFTER REFUSING TO spend another night in the medical department, Cricket returned to her stateroom just after lights-out. In the relative quiet, Vice Admiral Lassiter's stern words reverberated in her brain. Cricket had not experienced such a dressing-down since early in her career as a cocky ensign, and it was even more upsetting now to the golden girl with hero status. She'd begun to relish the adulation, no matter how much she denied it.

Cricket closed the stateroom door behind her but left the light off. The slight red glow seeping under the door from the passageway night-lights created an otherworldly environment, as if she'd descended into a surrealistic cave—or the entrance to hell. The thought matched her mood.

Sitting on the edge of the rack, Cricket buried her face in her hands. Deep fatigue and a sense of abysmal failure penetrated to her core. Alone in the dim light, she recalled the worst days of her capture and captivity in North Korea. The torture she suffered in the blackened hold of the spy ship. The rescue by Colonel Boo. His initial kindness and subsequent betrayal. The emotional abuse far more vicious and painful than what she'd endured at the hands of the commandos. Finally, the soul-gutting vision of Boo's blood and brains spattered on the wall of the bedroom after Lee Young destroyed the monster.

Cricket felt nothing while she reminisced, as if she were watching an awful movie so outlandish that it had to be fiction. Her body went numb, her mind blank, her heart and soul empty. She thought about her last flight, that fated P-8 mission that had entered a storm of events that would steal everything dear to her: her flying career, her lover, her health, her reason to live.

What did I expect to prove by coming back here?

Sitting with legs hanging over the bed made her injured ankle swell and ache. Cricket hobbled to the sink, retrieved the bottle of Vicodin from the medicine cabinet, and dispensed two tablets into her left hand.

Raising that hand to her mouth, she glanced into the mirror. The gaunt, distressed face looking back at her forced the hand to halt in mid-reach. A heartsick surge of emotion rose from deep inside her. At the corner of one bloodshot eye, a single teardrop emerged. She blinked, and the drop rolled partway down her cheek, its place taken by another drip, while yet another appeared in the other eye. As she continued to blink, both eyes filled with sheets of tears that blurred the mirrored image.

With no further warning, a crashing wave of hopelessness overwhelmed Cricket, and she cried full out, sobbing, racked with agony. Torrents of tears flooded her face. She braced herself on the sink as tears and snot dripped into the bowl.

Angry, she commanded herself to stop crying. To no avail.

Cricket dropped the two Vicodin tablets into the sink, then retreated and stumbled into the rack. She buried her face in the pillow to both soak up the tears and stifle the sobs, lest they be heard by shipmates traversing the passageway outside her door. In short order, her body convulsed with despair.

In all her life, even as a tortured captive in the hold of that dark vessel, Jessica Squire had never felt more alone.

***

She awoke in the pitch darkness of the floating prison boat. Muffled voices warned her that men came to hurt and violate her. She rolled herself into a tight ball, cringed against the bulkhead, and shivered, more from fright than cold.

Footsteps and other voices, American and loud. Beneath her naked body she felt not the cold, wet steel of the hold, but the thin mattress of her own rack on *Shenandoah*.

She opened her eyes. The red night-lights glowed under her door. In the throes of despondence, she had fallen asleep.

How long?

Cricket looked at her watch: 0400. She had slept for almost six hours, a record even in her healthy and fit days. As she uncoiled from the fetal position in which she'd slept, she yelped when the chiseling pain re-attacked her ankle. Then she remembered: the pills, the mirror, the tears, the despair. She rolled onto her back and stared up into the darkness of the overhead. The ankle pain could wait—as it had throughout the ordeal on the torture boat.

The admiral's scolding resounded in Cricket's head. Without a doubt, Louise Lassiter would follow through on her promise and threat. Cricket had to choose. Sobriety or Shrinksville. She knew well the torment of narcotic withdrawal, because Colonel Boo had forced it upon her.

Only one way he controlled me.

As much as she had suffered and beat that agony, she also hated the sessions with the military psychiatrists at Tripler. Cricket had no need or desire to bare her soul to the clueless men who aimed to know her deepest secrets, a more terrible personal violation than Boo's physical assaults. She had neutralized Boo and the commandos by shutting down her feelings and blocking any glimmer of emotion. But the shrinks never quit. They probed and pried, deceptive and relentless in their pursuit of her psyche, delving into parts of her she never wanted to see.

Sobriety over Shrinksville? A simple choice.

Especially since the shrinks would also demand sobriety.

Cricket flipped on the light over her rack. She knew what must happen next, yet she hesitated. As if on cue to test her resolve, the ankle pain intensified into a withering fusion of fire on her skin and icy chisels piercing the bones. She took several deep breaths, scrunched up her face, and heaved herself out of the rack, deliberately letting the injured ankle strike the deck first without support. Shock waves coursed up her leg.

Let it come. Embrace the pain. Own the agony. Get hold of your life!

An unchecked screech escaped her throat. Cricket sat on the rack's edge and panted like a wounded puppy. The pain abated by only ten percent. Taking another deep breath, she stood and put her full weight on the tortured ankle. Lightning bolts exploded there, and her leg almost buckled.

"Eat it, Jess," she said. "You'll soon wish it was only this bad."

She hobbled to her closet. Each step punished her body with galvanic bolts. She donned her terry robe over her naked self and stepped to the sink for a long drink of cool water. Then she ran the water until the discarded tablets dissolved into the drain. With gritted teeth, she placed the bottles of Vicodin and Ambien into her pocket. One last look in the mirror, where she grimaced through a mixed mask of agony and determination. Then Cricket was out the door and hobbling down the passageway to the women's head.

No one was in the bathroom at that hour of the morning. In the first stall, Cricket sat on the commode, took a pill bottle from her robe, opened it, and dropped the contents between her legs into the toilet. The second bottle's contents followed. Without pause, she flushed the toilet three times, then replaced the empty bottles in her pocket. She would destroy those back in her room.

When she stood up, the ankle pain recoiled with a vengeance, as if the devil punished her for the act she'd just committed. Immediate misgiving seized her. Could she get more pills from the doctors? Possibly. She sat back on the cool porcelain and buried her face in her hands.

"What the fuck do I do now?"

Vice Admiral Lassiter appeared in Cricket's imagination. Except it wasn't Louise Lassiter, it was Anna Squire, Cricket's mother, forcing a confident face through her own mask of agony, dying from cancer ten years earlier.

"You must be strong, Jess," her mother said. "For both of us."

Cricket hobbled to the shower, set the water to warm, and indulged herself in a prolonged "Hollywood" shower, not so much for the soothing warmth of the water, which she relished, but because it took her that long to stop crying.

Fifteen minutes later, Cricket returned to her stateroom. The ankle pain had become integral to her being, but it paled against the torment in her heart.

Chapter 37

A s *SHENANDOAH* NAVIGATED THE East Sea on Monday of the second week of the *Ulchi Freedom Guardian* exercise, the Seventh Fleet staff crowded into the N3 operations spaces for the morning real-world brief. Eric had not seen Cricket since the tense conversation in medical the previous day. He watched her take position at her station, well ahead of the admiral's arrival. She appeared detached.

Drugs?

Eric knew that Vice Admiral Lassiter had spoken to her acting operations officer about the Meridian Hotel episode. He surmised that the salty Southern lady had minced no words. She'd no doubt put Cricket on some sort of probation, a penalty more humiliating to her than a public flogging.

Cricket nodded or spoke politely to anyone who approached her, but she did not engage colleagues on her own. Eric felt an unsettling pang in his own exile outside Cricket's personal shell. She never once looked at him.

"Attention on deck!"

The room silenced, and heads turned to the starboard entry as Vice Admiral Lassiter swooped into the room, followed by the chief of staff and flag aide. Eric saw her glance in Cricket's direction with the bare trace of a smile.

"Sit down, those of you who can," the admiral said. "I trust y'all had a relaxing port visit and are ready to get back to work." She nodded at Eric. "What's our favorite megalomaniac up to today, Captain?"

"More rhetoric, ma'am," Eric said. "This morning the DPRK news agency released a statement from Kim Jong Un, his typical word storm decrying this UFG exercise as a threat to his people." He paused for effect. "Then he said something unusual, and I quote: 'We have planted the seed of total victory over the invading US forces and their ROK puppets.'"

"Any clue what that means?"

"Not sure, ma'am. It is the first time the North Koreans have spoken of something in progress, as opposed to their usual threats of future destruction." He shrugged. "We may be reading too much into it."

"I doubt that," Lassiter said. "That goofball has something cooking, and it ain't kimchi."

"We agree, ma'am," Eric said. "We assess a high probability of an imminent North Korean provocation."

Lassiter smiled and tilted her head. "You don't have a clue what it's gonna be, do you?"

Eric shook his head. "No, ma'am."

"What about the *Sinpo*?"

"Still loitering in international waters in the East Sea." He looked at Cricket. "Our units continue to shadow it."

Cricket took to the cue. "No change over the weekend, ma'am. We're working on a plan to neutralize it if we see an imminent threat."

The admiral frowned. "Working? *Worked* is the word I want, Commander. I need a plan now to neutralize it without hesitation, *before* it puts a nuke into the heart of Seoul. I'd rather answer for averting an attack than try to explain how we never saw it coming."

Lassiter scowled at Cricket. "Get it done, Cricket. And consider yourself authorized to take swift, decisive action if needed."

Cricket pursed her lips. "Aye, ma'am."

The admiral turned in her chair to face the group behind her. "Does anyone in this room believe that KJU's statement has anything to do with that sub?"

No one raised a hand.

She smiled. "Good. Does anyone have the slightest clue what, if anything, that maniac may be up to?"

Again, no hands rose.

Vice Admiral Lassiter frowned, shook her head, and turned back to Eric. "Still nothing along the DMZ?"

"Nothing, ma'am."

"Northwest Islands?"

"No, ma'am."

"Special forces activity?"

Eric glanced at his notes. "We have unconfirmed HUMINT reports of North Korean Army special forces activity along the northeast coast of South Korea; before our arrival in Donghae." He shook his head. "Not unexpected, given the high visibility of our visit there, but we saw nothing of interest over the weekend."

"Doesn't mean nothing happened." The admiral turned back to the group. "You all canvass your sailors. Did anyone observe any unusual activity in Donghae? Y'all know what I mean. Unusual contacts, overly curious foreign nationals, attempted sexual seduction, all that information security stuff we get fed till it leaks out of our pores. I want reports from all department heads by this evening's brief. That includes the *Shenandoah* ship's company. Chief of Staff, you get with the ship's CO and get it done. I wanna know if any of our sailors had even the slightest brush with a potential North Korean agent. Clear?"

Heads nodded around the room.

The admiral turned back to Eric. "Okay, Captain, you can proceed with your canned brief, and I do mean 'brief.'"

As he spoke, Eric noticed that Cricket had a far-off, puzzled look on her face.

Chapter 38

E XCEPT FOR THE PERPETUAL black night in the torture ship's hold, this day was turning out to be the longest in Cricket's life. Suffering at once from her ignominious failure in Donghae, the admiral's conspicuous displeasure, the unrelenting fire in her ankle, and the pangs of her body's rebellion at the sudden absence of narcotics and sedatives, Cricket would have welcomed the isolation of that dark hold—without the torture and rape.

The onetime fit triathlete for whom tenacity was virtue now struggled for survival against the onslaught of fatigue, depression, and withdrawal. In the rare gaps between meetings, briefs, and one-on-one conversations required of the acting N3, Cricket hurried to the nearest women's head—sometimes a trek, depending on her location in the ship—to throw up, release explosive diarrhea, or mop the sweat off her face and torso.

By mid-afternoon, she'd cleared most of her inbox and delegated routine tasks to subordinates. Exhausted in both mind and body, her spirit a complete vacuum, she rested her elbows on the desk and massaged an aching head. A mild pain dug into her lower back.

Lieutenant Commander Jake Morris, her primary subordinate, appeared beside her desk.

"Ma'am," he said in a tentative voice, "we all think you should get some rest. We can run the shop for a few hours. You could take a nap."

Cricket raised her hand to protest, but dropped it when she noticed a tremor. "I appreciate that, Jake. Please call me if anything at all comes up. If there's the slightest chance the admiral or chief of staff will ask me about something, you need to be sure I know it before they do. Understood?"

"Aye, ma'am," Morris said.

"Let me know the instant that submarine moves south or west, or if the nut jobs up north so much as burp in our direction."

The lieutenant commander smiled. "We got this, ma'am."

"Okay, thanks."

When she left the department, Cricket hoped none of her subordinates noticed her shakiness, or the near stumble as she limped through the doorway.

***

Cricket awoke with a start, drenched in sweat from a nightmare of Colonel Boo violating her body.

After the unsteady trek from the N3 office to her stateroom one deck below, she had thrown off her boots and flight suit and crashed on top of the rack, falling asleep at once.

Coming fully awake, she felt hungry. She looked at her watch: 1816. If she hurried, she could make it to the flag mess before it closed. Doing her best to ignore the unrelenting ankle pain, she filled her sink with water and sponged and dried herself as best she could. Then she donned a fresh tee-shirt and flight suit and hustled out the door without taking time to lace and tie her boots.

When Cricket entered the mess, the enlisted mess specialists had half-cleared the buffet. They stood aside and beckoned her to go through the line. Mindful of her earlier nausea and diarrhea, Cricket bypassed the dry chicken breasts and overcooked pasta. She took soup, bread, and a plate of steamed vegetables, plus two tall glasses of ice water.

At the tables, a few officers lingered over their meals. One was Eric Mikleson, by himself amid a jumble of used plates not yet cleared by the mess staff. A shudder of regret reminded her she had not talked to Eric since she'd berated him about what happened in Donghae.

She walked up to the table. "May I join you, Eric? Or are you about to leave?"

"For you, I stay."

He shoved aside the dirty plates next to him, but Cricket cleared the spot across from him instead.

"I'm sorry I haven't talked to you," she said. "Kinda overwhelmed today."

He shrugged. "No apology needed. I imagine it's been hell for you."

"Ya think?"

"It will pass."

Cricket wasn't sure if he meant the narcotic withdrawal or the aftermath of her Donghae calamity.

Probably both.

"I know," she said. "Been through worse." She regarded him over the brim of her soup spoon. "How are you doing?"

"Not bad. I'm almost used to being the admiral's favorite whipping boy."

"Hey, she only whups you 'cause she loves you." They both chuckled, a bit strained.

"I understand her frustration," Eric said. "I'm perplexed too. KJU's rants about a strike on the ROK and United States being 'already in motion' are not idle rhetoric. But what's the threat? I'm clueless."

Cricket smiled. "That sits well with you, eh, Captain?"

Eric raised his eyebrows.

"I haven't known you long," she said. "But I get you don't handle ambiguity well."

"You sound like my wife." Eric chuckled. "But, you're right. It drives me nuts to think I may be missing an imminent threat against our allies, or our own forces."

"Have you ruled out nukes? Kim has the capability, and he's talked loud and long about it."

"I haven't ruled out anything. My gut tells me that all the nuclear saber rattling is a diversion from something clandestine. I don't believe they would launch a nuke first. Frankly, I'm not convinced they have the capability, regardless of what they claim. But that 'we're gonna nuke you' rhetoric makes brilliant cover."

Cricket finished her dinner. She tented her fingers under her chin and looked Eric in the eye. "Maybe you should step out of your military mind and quit thinking like a rational human. If you want to understand the KJU mind-set, you gotta think crazy; and vindictive as hell."

Eric cocked his head. "KJU's revenge, you mean? How might that unfold?"

"Think that through and you may get a lead, but you gotta put aside the decent man and scheme like an amoral demon."

"That will be difficult."

The mess staff had cleared the tables. Cricket and Eric were the only officers still in the mess.

"Less arduous task," she said. "Get us both coffee before they shut down the machine. I'll take mine black."

"Of course." He rose from the table.

When he returned with two cups of coffee, Cricket thanked him. "We've got the place to ourselves. How about we chat about anything except the North Korean monster or current operations?"

Eric squirmed. "Such as?"

"Such as," Cricket said with a twinkle in her eye, "how's your family, shipmate? Jeez, Eric, two naval officers of different sexes can have a personal conversation without it being scandalous. Besides, I'm gay. Your flat chest and skinny ass do nothing for me."

Eric blushed a deep purple. "That's not what I..."

"That's exactly what you meant. I get it all the time. Belay the PC crap. We could both use some good old-fashioned friendship."

Eric relaxed. "Yeah, so, family... Doing okay. Deployments are harder on Melody now that the kids are older and need more from the 'single parent,' as she calls herself. I have less time now that I'm more senior."

He paused, pondering. "I used to call her every night when underway. Now I seldom stop working until she and the kids are in bed, or the time difference screws us up. When I get to call, she's often busy with a school or church thing." His eyes turned sad. "Sometimes I feel that we're growing apart, and I worry that whenever we get time together, we'll have lost what we had."

Without thinking about it, Cricket reached across the table and touched his hand. "I doubt that, but I know what you mean."

She thought about her final phone call with Lee Young, when Cricket had put duty over love. "If I could do my life over, I'd be living in Hawaii right now—married, maybe bored, but content."

"I question that," he said. "Let's be honest. We both relish the tip of the spear, the rush of the fight. Could you live without it?"

"I like to believe I could."

"Yeah, me too."

"Would never work," they said in unison, and laughed.

The mess staff started wiping down tables and swabbing the deck. "We need to go," Eric said. "They are politely telling us we're in the way."

"How about a walk topside?"

Eric looked at her ankle. "Can you?"

"I can do any damn thing I want, Captain. Once I get my mind around it."

Topside, they made slow circuits around *Shenandoah*'s main deck as the ship cut through the sea toward Busan. The air was warm, with just a slight breeze generated by the ship's movement. Under a clear, moonlit sky, the waters were calm and the ambience soothing. They talked about their respective lives, past and present, and futures. Eric described his marriage to his high school sweetheart, with whom he had two children who meant the world to him.

He stopped walking and said, "Melody wants me to leave the Navy and settle down, get stability into our lives by the time the kids reach high school. In four years, I'll have my twenty, retirement eligible. If I stay another ten, I could get more responsible positions: Pacific Fleet, major combatant command, Pentagon, maybe make admiral."

Eric looked out over the sea. "Despite what we laughed about earlier, and as much as the Navy is in my blood, I don't plan to stay a day beyond twenty. I want to spend the latter part of my life with my family, see my kids through college, watch them get married, and be a grandpa." He turned to look at Cricket. "Navy gets twenty years of my life, not a day more."

For the second time that evening, she touched his hand. "You stick to that plan, my friend. Don't blow it like I did."

She described her relationship and engagement to Lee Young and how she had postponed their Hawaii wedding to fly the first P-8 mission from Okinawa over the South China Sea—the mission that had resulted in the Chinese People's Liberation Army hijacking her plane and selling it, and her, to North Korea.

"The next time I saw Lee Young, she wore a KPA uniform and stood behind Kim Jong Un when he denounced me to the world. Later, she rescued me from Colonel Boo."

Cricket fought back tears. "In the end, I killed her."

Eric touched her shoulder, then withdrew it, embarrassed. They resumed their walk.

"I can't imagine how that feels," he said. "But you're too hard on yourself. Lee Yeong Nae, her real name, was a CIA double agent who used you to get to the North Koreans. She rescued you and killed Boo not for love, but to save her own ass."

He gauged whether to continue. "Your ideal marriage would have started with a lie. Never works."

Cricket stopped, stunned by his candor. "I guess that's why I pushed her off that helo."

"What I would have done. But your personal story doesn't end there. You will find someone else, someone you deserve."

"Sure as hell not on this hunk of metal. No viable candidates here." She gazed over the placid sea. "Not interested in a Navy relationship, anyway. I'm done with the fight, Eric. When we finish this tour, I'm going home. I qualify for a medical retirement. May get it forced on me, the way things are going. Either way, I'm done. Don't know where I'm going, or with whom. I'll figure it out."

Eric turned, and they faced each other. "No matter what," he said, "life goes on."

"Life goes on."

Chapter 39
Seoul, Republic of Korea

L EE MYUNG SUK AWOKE bathed in sweat, yet her body shivered as if naked in an ice storm. Her head pounded, her throat burned, and she craved water.

She was alone in the bed. Corporal Gi had left at dawn for his early muster. When she turned to look at the time, a sharp pain arced like lightning across her lower back. A sudden wave of nausea caused her to roll out of bed and scurry like a cockroach across the floor to the bathroom. She reached the commode just in time to vomit in spasmodic waves.

Gut emptied, Myung summoned a reserve of iron will to defy the backache and stand. Leaning on the sink, she looked at herself in the mirror. Her hair matted across her forehead, her skin appeared pallid, and...

She moved closer to the glass.

Crops of small red bumps adorned her chin and trailed down the front of her neck. Similar crops infested her hands and extended up her arms. Examining herself from head to toe, she saw crops of identical lesions on her legs and feet. A few also appeared on her chest and abdomen. She stepped back from the mirror and, despite the pain, rotated her back to examine her torso. The same rash had emerged across her lower back and buttocks, red bumps identical to those that appeared on her extremities. No pustules, at least not within her limited field of view. Her legs weakened under the exertion of self-examination, and another wave of shivering and nausea drove her back to the toilet.

After several waves of dry retching, the nausea subsided, but the weakness worsened. Myung lay on the bathroom floor, staring at the low ceiling.

My work is done, mission complete. I cannot leave this apartment. Here I give my life for my people and for the glory of the Supreme Leader.

Myung crawled across the floor into the bedroom. When she forced herself up into bed, a paroxysm of excruciating pain coursed through her body. She barely made the climb. Panting and grimacing, she lay on top of the sheets, eyes closed, mind fighting the agony.

Her thoughts drifted to a different time and place, to a long-ago event that started her down a life path that would end in this sordid apartment:

Two girls played a game with makeshift sock dolls on the bare concrete floor of a cramped apartment in Pyongyang. They hid the toys at the sound of a commotion in the outside hallway. Adults shouted. Myung recognized the shrill voices of her aunt and uncle, parents of her cousin and playmate, Lee Yeong Nae.

Myung's parents rushed into the main room just as the front door burst open. Soldiers held Yeong's parents, their arms bound behind them. One soldier pointed at the two girls and yelled at Yeong's mother, "Which brat is yours?"

Yeong Nae's mother looked at Myung Suk's father but did not speak. Tears ran down her face. The soldier struck her on the cheek. "Which of these brats sprang from the loins of a traitor?"

The two girls cowered together, hugging each other in terror.

The bound woman's eyes glanced at Yeong Nae, and the soldier yanked her away from Myung Suk.

"Stop," said a commanding male voice from the doorway. A senior officer entered the apartment. "Leave the girl. She stays with these people."

Yeong Nae's mother looked again at Myung Suk's father. "Please," she cried. "Take care of her."

The first soldier struck Yeong's mother. "Silence, traitor."

The soldiers dragged their prisoners out of the apartment.

Neither Lee Yeong Nae nor Lee Myung Suk ever saw them again.

***

In the present, Myung Suk lapsed in and out of awareness for the next two days, getting out of bed only to crawl to the bathroom to relieve herself and to slake her raging thirst. Sips of water rekindled the fire in her throat, so she gave up trying. As her febrile body's water loss exceeded intake, she required fewer trips to the bathroom.

On the third day, she awoke with her body ablaze from head to toe. She imagined the apartment had caught fire and that she would die from merciful, quick immolation, freed from the constant agony.

Myung opened her eyes to a dank, flameless apartment. The red bumps on her hands and arms had turned to blisters filled with milky fluid. She struggled out of bed to examine herself in the bathroom. The pus-filled rash had spread across her entire body, including her face and scalp. All the lesions looked the same: half-inch-diameter, blebs on the verge of bursting.

Her body stank like rotting flesh. She craved a shower, but dismissed the notion. If water on those blisters was going to cause the same fiery pain as it did in her mouth, she would prefer the fetid odor of her body as it died in increments.

Myung returned to the bed and crashed into it. The effort and reality of the self-exam had depleted her energy and will.

She slept. She dreamed. She remembered.

As young adults, Myung Suk and Yeong Nae entered state service as agents in the Korean Peoples' Army's Special Purpose Operations Reconnaissance Bureau. On the day they were to depart for indoctrination and training, Myung Suk's mother told her the rest of the story.

"You remember that Yeong Nae was not sent to prison camp with her parents?"

"I often wonder why," Myung said.

"Your cousin turned them in to the state," her mother said. "Yeong Nae heard them plotting to leave our country in defiance of the Great Leader, Kim Jung Il. She reported what she heard. That is why they spared her from prison camp, and why she—and you—got selected for state service."

"I understand," Myung said. She did not understand.

"There is more," her mother said. "Yeong Nae's father is not a traitor."

"What? I saw them take him."

"They did not take Yeong Nae's father, only her mother and the husband. Yeong's father and yours are the same man who raised and honored you both. You are not cousins, but sisters."

Myung Suk awoke to a dark room. She had no idea how long her consciousness had waxed and waned, little notion of what day it was, and less interest. The fire over her body had diminished, and the head and back pain had gone.

For the first time since coercing the Russian scientist into infecting her, Myung considered she might survive. Death was not inevitable with this disease.

The thought of surviving terrified her. Scarred for life, no longer a soldier? What would she do? She knew no life but the one she'd led since emerging into adulthood.

I cannot bear to live without the thrill of the fight.

Chapter 40

USS Shenandoah (LCC 21). East Sea (Sea of Japan). Approaching Busan, ROK.

O N THE LAST MORNING of the UFG exercise, Cricket awakened to severe pain, but not in her ankle. The expected bone chiseling took second place to the pickax hacking at her skull; both assaults savage and raw without Vicodin. The headache pounded in rhythm with *Shenandoah*'s bobbing approach to Busan through seas that had turned choppy. The dual pain and the bouncing caused a sudden wave of nausea.

Cricket bolted out of her rack, only to be dropped to the deck by a sudden spasm in her low back.

"What the hell?"

She rolled onto her side and lay immobile on the thin carpet that covered the steel deck. Three days had passed since she'd dumped the narcotics and sleeping pills.

This is some weird withdrawal.

She rolled onto her back with knees flexed in a futile effort to relax the spasm.

Suck it up, sailor.

Cricket stayed down for another five minutes while the nausea abated and the back spasm released. The hammer inside her head showed no signs of letting up. In slow micromotion, she got herself to a sitting position and braced her torso against the rack while also trying to guard her ankle. After a minute, she pulled herself erect. The room spun, and the nausea returned with fury. She lunged for the sink and retched. Only a few strands of mucus came up.

Leaning on the sink, Cricket saw in the mirror a frightful face twisted in agony. By habit, she reached into the medicine cabinet, but found only a half-full bottle of acetaminophen.

Lotta good that crap will do.

She swallowed two of the capsules and washed them down with water cupped in her hand from the sink. As soon as the liquid hit her stomach, another wave of nausea seized her and she regurgitated water, capsules, and stomach acid. She grabbed the pills out of the goo, stuffed them back into her mouth, and swallowed them without water.

This time, they stayed down. Cricket rinsed the sink and washed her face. She still felt ill.

Perhaps a shower...

She forced herself to put on her terry robe, each movement taking forever as she fought against the pain in her head, her back, her ankle, and a body unwilling to activate even the smallest muscle. When she reached to open her door, another wave of nausea and dizziness halted her. She stumbled back to the rack and sat on the edge, her head between her knees.

Without warning, Cricket burst into tears; not from the pain and nausea, but from an inner surge of despair and foreboding—like sulfur rising from hell.

She lay back on the rack. "I want to go home."

***

Cricket awoke thirty minutes later. The headache and nausea had left, but the low back pain nagged her to get out of bed. She felt flushed, but at least she could move without the need to retch. She looked at her clock.

The morning real-world brief would begin in ten minutes.

Shit!

With no time to shower, Cricket cleaned up at her sink, extra-brushed her teeth to get rid of the vomit smell, and plunged into underwear, tee-shirt, and flight suit. She had difficulty lacing her boots because bending over worsened the back pain. After a few futile attempts, she tied the laces one third from the top and then stumbled out the door, down the port passageway, up the ladder, and forward to arrive at her position in the N3 spaces a few seconds before Vice Admiral Lassiter entered from the opposite starboard passageway.

As Eric Mikleson began the intel brief, he glanced at Cricket. A furrow creased his brow. Over her left shoulder, Cricket's deputy handed her the operations brief.

"You okay, ma'am?"

Cricket did not look at him. "I'm fine, thanks."

She barely listened to Eric as she sped-read the operations brief. Nothing new or noteworthy since she'd last been at her desk.

The room seemed more crowded and warmer than usual. Stifling. A hot flush coursed through her body, followed by a shiver that she hoped no one would notice. Cricket focused on Eric's brief, to take her mind off her own discomfort.

After the usual give-and-take between Eric and Vice Admiral Lassiter over the intel brief, the admiral thanked Eric and turned to Cricket. Concern crossed the admiral's face.

When Cricket stood and propped herself against the desk to present her brief. She fought off a fresh wave of nausea and dizziness.

"Good morning, Admiral and Staff. Our defensive posture remains the same as yesterday, and we continue to shadow the *Sinpo*."

She paused and swallowed hard as another wave of nausea hit. Despite the heat in the room, her skin felt cold and clammy, her head fuzzy. She stumbled over the next few words in the brief and then stopped altogether to fight off another wave.

"Are you all right, Commander?" the admiral said.

Cricket stiffened. "I'm fine, ma'am. I may have caught a bug in Donghae."

A chortle from somewhere behind Cricket invoked an immediate dagger-like stare from the admiral.

"Proceed with your brief," Lassiter said.

Cricket toughed her way through the rest of the brief, skipping the routine boilerplate. By the time she finished, she'd broken into a sweat.

"Are there questions, ma'am?"

"None for now, but please see me after this meeting."

"Aye, aye, ma'am. That concludes my brief."

Cricket slumped into her chair and lowered her head to combat the dizziness and nausea. Clammy sweat covered her body. Self-conscious, she withdrew into herself.

I must reek of sick.

When the meeting ended, the admiral dismissed the staff and remained at her seat. She beckoned to Cricket.

Cricket approached the admiral, striving to walk straight and maintain erect posture despite the backache that had worsened when she stood.

"Yes, ma'am?"

The admiral waited until the room had cleared of all but her aide and the chief of staff, both of whom stood a respectful distance away.

"What the hell, Cricket? Are you withdrawing, or are you sick?"

"I don't know, ma'am. I've never felt like this. It may be the flu."

"Get someone to fill in, then get your butt to medical and find out."

"I'll be fine, ma'am. Really. I need to do my job."

The admiral's eyes flashed. "That was not a request, Commander. I'm taking you off duty until the doc tells me you're all right. Clear?"

The coup de grâce for my career?

Cricket nodded. "Aye, aye, ma'am. I'll go straight to medical."

"Tell the doc to report back directly to me, no one else."

"Yes, ma'am. By your leave, ma'am."

The admiral nodded, and Cricket left the room.

I am so hosed.

Chapter 41

D r. Troy Pearson emerged from his office to check on progress in the sick call room. He expected a larger-than-usual crowd as sailors came in for tune-ups before post-UFG liberty in Busan. As soon as the exercise ended, United States Forces Korea would lift the ban on alcohol. Busan's lively night scene would be waiting.

Turning a corner, Troy spotted Commander Squire sitting with other sailors waiting to be seen. The woman appeared thinner than he remembered, and she had that caged-animal look that Troy associated with drug seeking. Ordinarily, he would invite a field-grade officer such as her into his own office/exam room instead of making her wait to be seen in sick call. Remembering the prior contentious encounters with this officer, he let her be.

Troy nodded to her as he passed, a cursory gesture that she did not return.

She may not be on board much longer.

Troy had seen the admiral's livid expression, and he'd overheard the tenor if not the details of her tirade with Commander Squire after the younger officer's mishap in Donghae. Any other sailor who pulled a stunt like that would be escorted off the ship on arrival to Busan and put on a plane back to the US within twenty-four hours.

Troy spoke to Chief Anthony Martinez, the independent duty corpsman who supervised the two junior medics conducting sick call.

"Chief, I'd like you to see Commander Squire, who is waiting out there. She's the fleet deputy operations officer, has a history of substance abuse and drug-seeking behavior. In the past, she's tried to play us against the fleet surgeon to get her fix."

The chief petty officer raised his eyebrows. "See her and do what, sir?"

"Treat and street, Chief. No narcs. No sedatives."

The chief's blank stare challenged Troy.

Troy shuffled his feet. "My prior encounters with her turned a bit hostile. She'll do better with a fresh mind."

Chief Martinez shrugged. "Aye, sir."

"Thanks," Troy said. "I'll head back to my office. Inform me of anything unusual."

Chief Martinez nodded and returned to his business. Retracing the path to his office, Troy did not look at the commander when he passed her.

A half hour later, Chief Martinez entered Troy's office, holding a medical chart.

"Sir, I've seen Commander Squire. She didn't request drugs. She's sick. Headache, low back pain, nausea and vomiting, fever. Temp is 102. She looks dry. Pulse is 90, BP normal. My assessment is viral illness, maybe flu. I'd like to give her some IVs and put her SIQ, but I wanted to check with you first. I know she spent a night on the ward last weekend after some event in Donghae."

"She didn't ask for drugs?"

"No, sir."

Troy bit his lip. "I'll look at her. Thanks, Chief."

Commander Squire looked ill, worse than when he'd seen her after she passed out in Donghae. Her typical haughty posture and defiant attitude were nowhere in evidence. If anything, she seemed anxious and a bit scared.

"When did you get sick?"

She shrugged. "Never felt well after Donghae." Her voice was flat.

"Do you get sick often?"

A brief flash of anger crossed her eyes. "Never. Or I just ignore it."

"What's different this time that caused you to come to medical?"

"The admiral."

"Vice Admiral Lassiter sent you?"

She nodded. "Otherwise, I sure as hell wouldn't bother you."

Good thing the admiral made her come. She's for sure ill.

"Anything unusual happen in Donghae? Or in Busan the weekend before?"

Squire smirked. "You know as much as I do about Donghae. Nothing unusual in Busan." She swallowed hard. "I feel like shit."

Troy conducted a full history and physical, but found nothing diagnostic other than fever and moderate dehydration.

"I agree with Chief Martinez's assessment," he said to his patient. "You have an ILI, 'influenza-like illness,' probably a virus you picked up in Donghae or earlier in Busan."

"So?"

"You'll be sick for about a week, but you will recover. A couple of liters of IV fluid now will help you feel better. I'm ordering you sick-in-quarters, for two reasons. One, you need rest, not work; and two, you shouldn't expose the rest of the staff to your virus."

"I can't do SIQ, Doc. I'm the acting N3 until the real deal returns aboard in Busan. We don't have a deep bench."

Here comes the request for narcs so she can continue to work.

"I'll talk to the fleet surgeon," Troy said. "You all can work out something. Your health is more important than a military exercise."

Commander Squire frowned and shook her head. "Whatever, Doc. I've put up with far worse than the damned flu."

Troy was direct. "To be honest, Commander, I thought you would want medications."

She looked at him with steely eyes through narrowed lids. "I'm fine on that score, Doc."

"Okay," Troy said. "The corpsman will take you down to the ward and start the IV."

Commander Squire smiled, a mixed expression of both gratitude and cynicism.

"Thanks, Doc."

Troy watched her limp down the passageway toward the medical ward. She refused to let the corpsman support her.

She is one gutsy sailor.

Chapter 42

L ATE THAT AFTERNOON, RELEASED after six hours in medical, Cricket stepped into her stateroom. As expected, the fleet surgeon and ship's doc had conspired to keep her SIQ, with the admiral's blessing. She had no will to object.

The intravenous fluids had helped, but she still felt sick. The fever had broken during the infusion, leaving her wet and clammy. On top of the flu symptoms, her ankle throbbed in deep pain. Cricket shook off her boots, dropped the flight suit on the deck, donned her robe, and hobbled to the women's head. She treated herself to another "Hollywood" shower, turning the water as hot as she could bear.

Feeling somewhat better, Cricket returned to her stateroom and dressed in clean underwear, tee-shirt, and flight suit. The time was 1500. The exercise leaders had declared FINEX, the end of the exercise, an hour earlier. Despite the staff's misgivings, UFG had finished without overt provocation from the North Korean regime. Now *Shenandoah* meandered into Busan. Many of the ship's crew and fleet staff had already shifted colors to liberty mode, prepping for celebratory sorties to the "target-rich" nightlife environment of Haeundae Beach. At the height of the South Korean summer vacation season, the singles' clubs and discos would rock long and hard into the wee morning hours.

Cricket sat at her desk and turned on the computers. Then she called her office. The N3 operations staff would still be there to complete the UFG wrap-up and lessons learned. Perhaps she could support them from her stateroom.

To her surprise, Captain Mark Gunderson, the permanent N3, answered.

"Captain," Cricket said. "I didn't expect you back so soon. This is Commander Squire, by the way."

"I recognized your voice, Cricket," Gunderson said. "I hopped a ride on the logistics helo from Busan early this morning. They told me you were in medical. Are you okay?"

"Some kind of virus," she said. "I should be fine in a few days, but they made me SIQ. I'm happy to do what I can from here."

"I gotta say the South Koreans have excellent health care. I'm a full-up round just two weeks after my appendectomy."

"That's good news," Cricket said. "I'm not the first one to welcome you back, but I may be the most grateful."

The pause on the other end of the line seemed prolonged. "Cricket, thank you for the great work you did while I was away. Now I'm back in battery, so you can focus on getting well."

"I'm not sure what you mean."

"With UFG over, I can concentrate on current operations. If you feel like it later, you can write up your UFG after-action report in your stateroom. Otherwise, you're off the hook."

"I feel better. I can pull my load, sir."

Another pause, longer than the first. "The restriction is not from me," Gunderson said. "That's the admiral's direction."

Cricket bit her lip. "I get it." She inserted her own prolonged pause. "Did the admiral mention she would look to me for insight into what the North Koreans might do next?"

"She did," the captain said. "But for now, your health is the top priority."

Cricket fumed. "It's just the damned flu. I'll get over it in a couple of days." As if in retribution for losing her cool, her body shuddered with a sudden chill and a wave of nausea.

"I get it," Gunderson said, "but the admiral insisted."

Cricket was so angry and disappointed, she could not respond.

I might as well pack my bags.

Mark Gunderson's voice broke the silence. "When you feel up to it, and only if you feel up to it, I want to spend some time discussing your assessment of the North Korean threat. Eric Mikleson still suspects something afoot that we don't understand. I think he's right."

Cricket found her voice. "You can count on me anytime. I don't feel that bad." She took a deep breath to stifle the bile rising into her throat.

"We don't have to do it now. You can rest this afternoon and maybe we can chat this evening, or even tomorrow."

The nausea intensified, and Cricket feared she would vomit on the phone. "Okay. I'll get in touch with you this evening." She swallowed a bitter glob in her throat.

"Thanks, Cricket. I will talk to you later."

"Bye." Cricket threw down the receiver and ran to the sink to vomit.

Recovering, she tried to clean up the mess, but sudden lightheadedness forced her into her rack. Within minutes, she fell asleep.

Chapter 43
USS Shenandoah (LCC 21). Moored at Busan, ROK.

C RICKET DIDN'T CALL CAPTAIN Gunderson back as promised, because she slept through the evening and into a fitful night of tortured sleep and haunted dreams. Just before dawn, she fell into a deep slumber and never heard reveille.

Mid-morning, she awoke to the 1MC announcing "Liberty Call, Liberty Call."

Other than a mild sore throat, her flu symptoms seemed improved. She called Mark Gunderson, who was still working in the N3 office. They discussed potential scenarios regarding North Korea. Both wondered why the flood of hostile rhetoric from the DPRK had stopped right after the UFG FINEX.

"Maybe idle threats after all," Mark said.

"Never count on that," Cricket said.

Their talk lasted about thirty minutes, during which Cricket's sore throat worsened—more of an annoyance than the flu-like discomfort of the previous day. Still on informal probation under the admiral's apparently omniscient cognizance, Cricket had to keep her commitment to Doc Pearson. She washed up, got dressed, and headed forward in the starboard passageway to the medical department amidships on the same deck as her aft stateroom.

When she entered, the place seemed deserted. This being the first full day of liberty after UFG, most of the crew and fleet staff would have gone ashore early. That included the entire medical department, except for a pair of corpsmen on duty for emergencies. Cricket found them on the medical ward watching a movie on ship's TV.

"I can call Doc Pearson," the second-class petty officer said after Cricket explained her reason for being there. "They all went to Haeundae Beach, so it would take an hour for him to get back."

"That won't be necessary," Cricket said. "It's no emergency, and I'd hate to spoil his liberty. I feel better except for a sore throat. Maybe you could give me some Tylenol in the interim?"

"No problem, ma'am," the corpsman said. "Come with me." Cricket followed him to the sick call area, where he doled out twelve tablets of Tylenol into a small plastic bag. "Take two of these every six hours, ma'am."

Cricket took the bag and thanked the corpsman. He nodded politely, then hurried back to his movie.

Back in her stateroom, Cricket flipped off her flight boots and lay atop the rack. She stared into the overhead, and her thoughts and emotions wandered. As a pilot, she appreciated order and precision. Cricket had perfected the skills to maneuver a large jet like the P-8 through an array of challenges, honing her mind/hand coordination to maintain the right airspeed, angle of attack, throttle settings, and systems monitoring to fly an exact, predetermined path to meet the planned objective. At the same time, she had developed keen situational awareness, perspective, and insight to respond without hesitation to any emergency, any threat—as she had done when a missile struck her P-8 off the South Korea coast, forcing her to execute an emergency ditch into the West Sea.

She had survived that crash and her subsequent imprisonment and abuse in North Korea because she had never lost the ability to compartmentalize everything else in her life and focus on the most important outcome: survival. Now she felt disoriented and out of balance, as if she had lost control of her own body, and perhaps her mind. She closed her eyes and felt herself floating on the surface of the West Sea, wondering how long it would take to die there.

A bolt of anxiety ran through her. Cricket opened her eyes and stared hard at the overhead, concentrating, compartmentalizing, forcing her mind and body back to the reality of lying on top of a stationary rack in a stateroom on a ship moored to the pier, neither rocking nor sailing anywhere.

Going nowhere. All my life I've had somewhere to go. But now...

A rap on the door wrenched Cricket from her thoughts.

"Hello?" she said, and all at once her throat felt like two hot coals had replaced her tonsils.

"Chief of Staff," said the familiar voice on the other side of the door. "Just checking on you, Commander."

Cricket forced herself to speak over the burning embers on her palate. "Stand by, sir."

She eased off the rack and steadied herself against a wave of lightheadedness. At the sink, she splashed cold water on her face, ran a hand through her hair, and decided not to bother with her flight boots. She turned on the stateroom light and cracked open the door.

Captain José Santiago spoke through the partial opening. "Don't worry. I've had my flu shot. May I come in?"

Cricket opened the door and motioned him to the desk chair. She left the stateroom door ajar, as she always did with a male visitor, and sat on the rack.

"I'll be okay, sir."

They chatted for about twenty minutes. Because of the pain in her throat, Cricket let the chief of staff do most of the talking. He briefed her on the latest intel and operations activity, none of which was new.

"Tomorrow the admiral, N2, and N3 depart for Seoul for Combined Forces Command meetings and debriefs," he said. "We won't see them again till we get to Hong Kong."

Cricket hid her disappointment that Eric would not make the transit in the ship to Hong Kong.

"You will be my acting N3 here on the ship, SIQ or not," the chief of staff said. "If you feel up to it, I'll have update reports delivered to you here twice a day. The admiral, the N2, and the actual N3 will have point ashore, but I need... The entire staff needs your expertise and insight here, on the flagship. With due respect to the operations department, no one there can fill your shoes."

He leaned forward, his face close to hers. "But let me be clear. I will not, under any circumstances, jeopardize your health. We will do this only if you're up to it."

Cricket smiled. "It's only the flu, sir. I feel better except for this sore throat. It should run its course soon. I expect to be a full-up round in a day or two."

"Very well." He chuckled. "That's what the fleet surgeon told me before I came down here. But, I say again, do not overdo it, or Admiral Lassiter will have both our asses in a sling. Work here in your stateroom until you feel well enough and the docs think you're not contagious anymore."

She laughed. "The docs need some common sense. Contagious? I'm probably the only member of the entire Seventh Fleet staff who did not get a flu shot. You all are safe from me."

"That's how I see it." Captain Santiago stood. "Take the day to rest, and let me know tomorrow how you're feeling. You can call me anytime."

Cricket stood. "Thank you, sir. I appreciate you keeping me in the game. I would consider *seppuku* if I had to stay SIQ another day."

The COS smiled. "I know what you mean, Commander. We aviators don't handle grounding well. Stay in the fight or perish." He stepped through the door. "Take care of yourself."

Cricket closed the door and went straight to her sink to take two more Tylenol tablets. They felt like bricks when they passed through her inflamed throat. Instead of returning to her rack, she sat at her desk and turned on her computers.

Back in the game! Without my wingman, Eric—but only for a while.

Chapter 44

THE HARSH JANGLE OF her desk phone jolted Cricket awake in the dark, silent stateroom. Realizing the absence of nausea and headache, she stumbled out of her rack to reach the phone.

"Hello?" A rasping pain in her throat subdued her voice.

"It's Eric. I was worried about you."

Cricket rubbed her forehead. "What time is it?"

"It's 0900," Eric said. "I wanted to check on you before I head to Seoul with the admiral."

"Seoul?"

"For the UFG debrief and other meetings with Combined Forces Command?"

Cricket ran a hand through her hair, her memory jumbled. "Wait, what day is it?"

"Sunday. Sunday morning, 0900." A deep pause. "Are you all right?"

She blinked her eyes as if lifting a veil off her consciousness. "Yeah, yeah. Good. I must have slept since yesterday afternoon." She took a deep breath.

As the last trace of sleep left her mind, she noticed dampness in her underwear and flight suit. Old sweat. She sniffed. A stale reek of old vomit from the sink. She tried to clear her throat, but that felt like someone drilling her palate.

Cricket forced out the words. "Sorry, Eric. I was kind of out of it when I first answered. I must have run a fever during the night." She swallowed hard against the rawness in her throat. "Hang on a second."

She put down the phone, ran water into the sink, and swished it around the bowl. After the vomit residue swilled down the drain, she washed her face in cool water and filled a drinking glass, forcing herself to swallow over the pain. She returned to the phone.

"I'm back," she said. "Needed water."

When Eric did not respond, she continued. "I feel better now. Just a devil of a pain in my throat. Hard to talk."

"Fleet surgeon says you have the flu. I guess a sore throat goes with that."

"Bummer," Cricket said. Her spirits lifted, talking with her friend. "Can you stop by before you leave the ship?"

"Doc says you're in isolation."

"Bullshit. Doc's covering his butt like they all do. Besides, COS has been here. I want to see you off."

"Unlike some people, I got my flu shot this year. I imagine I'll be safe in your presence."

"Gimme fifteen minutes to tidy up?"

"I'll give you twenty. Like you aviators say, 'It always takes longer.'"

"Sometimes a good thing." Cricket's rising spirits quelled the flame in her throat. "See you in twenty, shipmate."

She hung up the phone, washed out the sink again, forced down two Tylenol with water, sprayed air freshener around the room, exchanged her flight suit for the terry robe, and headed to the shower. Aside from the sore throat, she felt well.

Might even get to the office today.

***

Twenty-five minutes later, Cricket sat on the edge of her rack holding a glass of ice water that Eric had brought from the flag mess. He sat across from her in the desk chair, his face lined with concern.

"You look like crap."

"Thanks, Eric. You sure know how to make a girl feel pretty." She tried to laugh, but the pain in her throat stifled the first giggle. "I'm okay. Really. Just the flu."

"Flu or not, you don't look well. You should see the doc again."

"Quack, quack. What else are they going to do?"

"Maybe more IVs, or a different diagnosis?"

"Like narcotic withdrawal?" Cricket surprised herself by saying that.

Eric's face reddened. "Not what I meant. You should know me better."

"I do. Sorry. Although I've wondered if that's a part of how I've felt since I chucked the pills."

"I wouldn't know about that."

"I withdrew before, in North Korea. When Boo stopped giving me narcs. It was different. This time, I'm clean for a week, and no craving or withdrawal."

"You should talk to the docs about this, not me."

She took a sip of ice water. "Okay, okay. I'll go to medical right after we talk." She took another sip. "Tell me about Seoul. What's going on there?"

Eric relaxed. "Admiral asked the N3 and me to go with her for the UFG debrief, but that's not the real reason. We still can't figure out KJU. All that ranting during the exercise, but no provocations, then silence. We think another shoe will drop, just don't know when, what, or where. We plan to meet with our counterparts at NATO and USFK to share intel and come up with a way ahead. Then we'll talk to the ROKs and Combined Forces Command."

"The COS wants me to run the ops shop while Gunderson is gone."

Eric forced a smile. "Not you, shipmate. You're SIQ, remember?"

"More like I'm in hack," she said. "How convenient for me to get sick. Spares the admiral from publicly downing me."

"I doubt that." Eric's vague expression suggested a modicum of truth in her statement.

"I may be done here, Eric."

He looked concerned, but did not speak.

Cricket took another sip of water. "I really screwed the pooch in Donghae. Don't know that I'll recover from that."

Eric shook his head. "Stop the crap talk. You've got the admiral and entire staff rooting for you. Most of all, me."

She looked him in the eye. "You don't know how much that means to me. But you know they would send any other officer home after what I did."

He reached out and touched her hand. "You, Commander Squire, are not any other officer. In the entire Navy, in all the world's navies, there is no officer like you. You exemplify courage and honor. Your voluntary return to this staff, when you could have rested on your fame, showed a commitment beyond what most officers would dare to consider. Have you not seen the other women on this ship beam when they pass you? You are the ultimate role model, not only for the women but for all of us. You are respected and loved beyond measure. Not one person on this staff would want you to quit now."

He drew a breath. "You're not in hack, Cricket. You're where we all need you to be so you can get well and get back to the job we all need you to do. I'm not talking ops. I mean leadership. What you do better than most. So stop with the self-flagellation, get yourself well, hold your head high, and return to the fight a full-up round."

Eric looked into her eyes. "You are loved. Clear?"

A torrent of emotion flooded Cricket's mind and soul. For an instant, she forgot the sore throat, the illness, the embarrassment of Donghae, her own inner struggles, and mourning over losing the love of her life. She felt a strange emotion for this man—not lust, not sexual, but not fraternal, either. Maybe love, but she didn't care what she called it. She wanted it, deeply. She needed it, badly.

Cricket leaned closer to Eric. "You are such a dear, dear friend. I would be adrift without you. I will miss you while you're gone." She gave him a sheepish smile. "I love you, Eric. Thank you for being my friend."

"That's mutual," Eric said. "We make quite the team. I'm sorry you can't come to Seoul. Concentrate on getting better so we can resume this partnership for the next phase of the deployment."

Eric stood to leave. Cricket stood and hugged him. "Thanks, friend. See you in Hong Kong. I'll be well. You can buy me a drink at the Four Seasons."

"Drink, hell," Eric said. "I'll buy you the whole five-course dinner."

They hugged again, and then he was gone.

Now that Cricket was alone in her stateroom, the sore throat and ennui returned, and with them a sense of impending doom. She washed her face, straightened her flight suit, and headed down to medical.

∗∗∗

As Cricket had expected, a different duty crew of corpsmen manned the medical department. The petty officer who examined her throat suggested some ibuprofen to go with the Tylenol.

"It's okay, Doc," she said. "That stuff tears up my stomach, and I'm feeling better anyway. Just a matter of waiting it out."

"Only time cures flu," the corpsman said. "You have inflammation and a slight rash in your throat. Ibuprofen will help that. Maybe take it with some milk?"

Cricket stared at the young corpsman. "No way, Doc, but thanks for your suggestion."

When she left the medical department, an announcement sounded over the 1MC.

"Seventh Fleet, departing."

That would be the admiral, Eric, and Mark Gunderson walking off the ship to the helipad across the pier, where a chopper waited to transport them to Seoul. Emptiness overcame Cricket, and she paused in the passageway.

I should be on that flight.

Instead of joining the admiral, Eric, and the rest of the joint military leadership on the peninsula, amid the fight, solving the North Korean enigma and planning an overwhelming response, she was relegated to her stateroom, accompanied only by the common virus that had attacked her body.

No stranger to captivity and imprisonment, Jessica "Cricket" Squire returned to her place.

Incarcerated once again.

With the ship moored to the pier, the late August heat on Korea's south coast had warmed the room to an uncomfortable level. Cricket heaved a sigh and doffed her flight boots (the constant ankle pain now just an annoyance) and the flight suit, leaving on the royal blue tee-shirt. She donned a pair of gym shorts, took a drink of water (less painful than before), switched on a portable fan, and stretched out on top of her rack.

Now it was late Sunday afternoon. The ship was nearly deserted as the crew and fleet staff took advantage of their last hours in port before getting underway for Hong Kong early the next morning.

Supine in the darkness, with the cooling air from the fan wafting over her body, Cricket thought about the earlier farewell with Eric. She felt neither surprise nor embarrassment about hugging him, and she sensed he had felt the same way. That spontaneous action expressed the new bond between them, a natural physical manifestation of unity in mind and spirit.

Natural or not, for Cricket it was new and exciting.

She'd had other male friends. In her questioning youth, she'd experimented with heterosexual activity; pleasurable enough but never reaching her. She'd relished friendships and intense love affairs with other women, most of all with Lee Young, to whom she'd surrendered not only her body but her essence.

Yet she'd never had a friend like Eric Mikleson. Eric got her, understood her better than she understood herself. Eric cared for her because of who she was, and he expected nothing in return. Eric filled a void in her life, touched a part of her she'd never known, never sensed how much it needed filling. Eric was a gift, to be cherished beyond any friend or lover.

Mixed tears of joy and pathos came to her eyes.

After all that Cricket Squire had achieved and endured in her life, here on the Seventh Fleet flagship, she'd found a soul mate.

Chapter 45

USS Shenandoah (LCC 21). Underway From Busan, ROK.

E ARLY THE NEXT MORNING, Cricket awakened in her stateroom with her face in a pool of saliva. Her pillow was soaked, and the sheets reeked.

Had she peed herself during the night? She checked, but no.

She must have sweated out another fever overnight. Exhausted from five days of illness, she'd slept hard with her face in its own drool.

"Yuk," she said aloud. She turned on the light above her rack and looked at her watch. 0430. Only the red glow of nightlights and silence in the passageway outside the door.

Cricket yawned and eased her legs over the side of the rack, the familiar ankle pain only a moderate annoyance. She'd slept in the same underwear and tee-shirt she had worn throughout the previous day, and maybe the day before that. Those days had all become a blur.

She sniffed herself. "Double yuk." She stood up, threw the soiled tee-shirt and underwear into her laundry bag, and studied her body in the full-length mirror on her stateroom door. Red spots had appeared overnight. They covered most of her body. Perhaps some had tiny clear blisters at their peaks, but Cricket could not be sure in the subdued light of her room. She grabbed a flashlight and examined her throat in the small mirror over her sink. A similar rash appeared on her palate, maybe some with blisters. She tried to drink water. It burned her throat, but less so than two days earlier. She took two Tylenol tablets and swallowed them with sips of water.

Despite the rash, Cricket felt better. The fever seemed less severe than the prior days.

I need a shower.

The other women in her part of the ship would sleep until reveille at 0600. The shower and head should be vacant. As she moved to her closet, the pungent odor of old sweat from the rack assaulted her nostrils.

Get rid of those sheets.

In a flurry of action that weakened her, Cricket donned her bathrobe and flip-flops, pulled the sheets and pillowcases off the rack, stuffed them into the laundry bag along with her dirty underwear and other clothing, and hung the bag on the hook outside her door as she left for the head and shower. She pitied the enlisted sailors who would be stuck doing her laundry, but for this one time, she could not do it herself.

One time will be okay. Most of the captains on this staff don't know where to find the self-service laundry rooms.

Fifteen minutes later, Cricket returned to her room, clean and refreshed, but also tired and weak. She actually looked forward to another day of sick-in-quarters away from her office. She would accomplish more in her room without the constant chatter and interruptions of the crowded operations spaces. Intermittent naps would help as well.

She opened the door and noted that someone had already picked up the laundry bag.

Those sailors don't get enough credit. They function as our maids and cooks, and they take such pride in their work.

Inside the room, she dressed, sat at her desk, and fired up both the classified and unclassified computers.

One hundred thirty unopened e-mails filled the classified inbox alone. Suddenly exhausted, Cricket shut off the computers and climbed into her rack, not bothering to undress or put on the clean sheets that the coop cleaner had left for her.

In less than a minute, she slept.

Chapter 46

USS Shenandoah (LCC 21). Underway, East China Sea.

O N THE FIRST AFTERNOON out from Busan, *Shenandoah* traversed the
East China Sea en route to Hong Kong. Most staff and crew had left
UFG in the wake. Only the leadership and the intel and operations staffs worried
whether the North Korean regime still had an attack or provocation up their
sleeve. The rest of the ship's occupants had turned their attention to routine
operations, and to preparing for one of the most popular liberty ports in the West
Pacific.

Fantastic sightseeing, sumptuous international cuisine, nonstop nightlife, and
shopping, both chic and cheap, awaited them. Many planned first-day visits to
shops that would custom-tailor and deliver fine suits, at a fraction of US prices,
before the flagship left port on the fourth day. The on-again/off-again tensions
between the United States and the People's Republic of China had, for the nonce,
resolved to cordial talk of collaboration, so some of the crew and staff booked day
trips to Guanzhou, the nearby PRC city formerly known as Canton.

One such sojourner would be Lieutenant Commander Troy Pearson, who
looked forward not only to his first trip to China but also to a potential professional relationship with the People's Liberation Army Navy (PLAN) physician
who would attend the first evening's diplomatic reception hosted on the flagship
by the Seventh Fleet commander (who would fly from Busan to Hong Kong to
rejoin the flagship) and her senior staff. Not so gregarious as Troy, Fleet Surgeon
Captain Rose Deckert had invited him to join her in hosting the PLAN medical
entourage. She had also agreed to take duty call for medical emergencies to enable
his trip to Guanzhou.

In his office, reviewing medical charts from the weekend and morning sick call, a particular record caught Troy's eye. Commander Squire had visited medical twice over the weekend for "flu-like symptoms," with her chief complaint listed as "sore throat."

The corpsman who had examined her on Sunday had written, *Rash consisting of small red papular lesions and ? vesicles on the palate and throat, without exudate or lymphadenopathy.*

The corpsman had entertained and ruled out the possibility of strep infection before writing his final diagnosis, "Viral pharyngitis." Commander Squire had not asked for narcotics, and the corpsman had offered her ibuprofen, which she had declined.

Troy carried the chart to the sick call area to find the corpsman. "Tell me more about Commander Squire. Describe her physical findings to me."

The corpsman looked puzzled. "Not much to describe, sir. At first I thought it was petechiae in her throat, maybe tiny blood vessel ruptures from coughing or retching, but on magnification it looked like a papular rash." He hesitated. "And something I've never seen, almost like tiny blisters, but I couldn't be sure."

"Nothing on her body? You undressed her and looked, right?"

The corpsman averted his eyes. "She refused a full exam. Said she knew it was just the flu, but her command had made her come. I asked about a rash, but she said she didn't have one."

"Did you get the chief petty officer to look at her?"

"No, sir," the corpsman said. "He was busy in the treatment room. The commander didn't want to wait."

"Let's bring her back down and take a look together," Troy said. "Just in case."

Twenty minutes later, Troy responded to a tentative knock on his door. The corpsman stood at semi-attention on the other side.

"Sir, I contacted Commander Squire as directed, but she said she doesn't have time to come back to medical now."

A flush of anger welled up inside Troy. "Doesn't have time? She's SIQ."

"She said she was too busy, sir, and that she's feeling better now."

Exasperated, Troy said, "Give me her number. I'll call her."

The corpsman looked chagrined. "I really thought it was viral pharyngitis,"

Troy forced a smile. "It probably is. Commander Squire is a difficult patient under the best circumstances. We need to be extra careful with her."

He touched the corpsman's shoulder. "You did nothing wrong. I know you and the others are well trained and you work hard. But when you're still new to this game, you don't have a fully developed clinical judgment, especially for dilemmas like her."

"Thank you, sir." The corpsman handed Troy a slip of paper with the phone number to Commander Squire's stateroom.

"Carry on," Troy said. "I've got this." As the corpsman walked away, Troy called after him. "Please pass the word to the others that no one is to release Commander Squire from sick call until either Chief Martinez or I have reviewed the case."

"Aye, sir." The corpsman turned down the passageway without looking back.

Troy dialed the number that the corpsman had given him, but no one answered.

She's either sleeping, showering, or defying orders and working.

He hung up the phone, then picked it up again and dialed the fleet surgeon. No answer. Troy shook his head. Perhaps he'd overreacted. The corpsman was probably right, just a viral pharyngitis. Nothing serious. But an enanthem with vesicles? An image in the cobwebs of his mind caused him concern, but he couldn't bring it into focus.

Not a medical emergency.

Troy locked his door and changed into workout clothes. An hour in the ship's gym might clear his head.

Chapter 47

W HEN TROY RETURNED TO the medical department the following morning, the same corpsman met him in the passageway.

"Sir, I have Commander Squire in the isolation room. I think she may have chickenpox."

Before they entered the isolation room, the corpsman handed Troy a surgical face mask and then donned one himself. "Chief said to put her under respiratory isolation until we're sure what she has."

Troy nodded, put on the surgical mask, and entered the room. He did a double take at the commander's appearance, which had deteriorated in the four days since he'd last seen her. Thinner than he remembered, unkempt and emotionless, she regarded Troy with glazed eyes, no trace of her signature haughtiness.

"Good morning, Commander," Troy said. "How are you feeling?"

A bitter half smile crossed the woman's face. "Ready to run a marathon, Doc. I came here on my own. How do you think I feel?"

Troy forced a smile. "I understand you came in a couple of times over the weekend."

"Yeah. Your corpsmen took good care of me. No complaints. Today I noticed this rash. I figured I might as well get it checked out, because for sure the admiral will make me come if she sees it." Her defiant look failed to cover a trace of uncertainty and a glimmer of fear.

Troy checked her chart. She had a low-grade fever of 100°F. Her pulse rate was 80 beats per minute, which would be fast for her. Given her baseline fitness, Troy figured her normal resting heart rate would be around 50 to 60. Her respiratory rate was above normal, which Troy attributed to the fever. Vital signs aside, he worried more about her general appearance. She looked toxic.

He crossed his arms and affected a stern tone. "Be honest, Commander. Tell me how you really feel."

"Better than a few days ago," she said. "My headache and backache are gone. Mild sore throat this morning, but not bad. Honestly, I'm here because the stupid rash will keep me from going back to work."

"Let's get you undressed and into a hospital gown so I can look at it," Troy said.

As he waited outside the room and donned latex gloves, a niggling uncertainty buzzed around his head, like an unseen, pesky fly. An omen, perhaps?

Troy Pearson, MD, did not believe in omens or premonitions. He shook off the sensation and, like a scientist, considered the holistic data about the patient now in his care: A national hero under a storm cloud of uncertainty after succumbing to drugs and alcohol to anesthetize herself against the inner demons she'd brought with her from imprisonment in North Korea.

What exposures had she experienced in captivity? When? A year ago? Too much time had passed for anything there to cause her current symptoms.

Too long ago for acute infections. But what about her immune system?

He felt anger that politics had sent this woman back to sea, under his care.

When Troy returned to the room, the wiry naval officer looked skeletal in the ample one-size patient gown.

He asked if she'd eaten anything since she took ill, and got a shrug in response. A careful head-to-toe physical examination yielded findings of questionable nutrition, moderate dehydration, and the rash. In her throat, a few small blisters on her palate; on her skin, raised red bumps of uniform size, about a half inch in diameter. The macular rash, as Troy would describe the bumps, adorned her face, arms, and legs, but not her torso.

He brushed two lesions with a cotton swab.

"Painful?" he asked.

"Not so much."

Troy thought for a minute and then said, "I need to ask some specific questions. Some may be personal, for which I apologize. I need you to answer truthfully."

"Get on with it, Doc."

"Did you ever have chickenpox, or did you get the vaccine as a child?"

Squire shook her head. "I don't recall having them. As for the vaccine, my parents didn't believe in them. Neither do I."

"You never had the recommended childhood immunizations?"

"I might have had some shots, but I don't know which ones."

Troy stroked his chin. "What about..." He swallowed hard. "Can you describe your sexual history for me, please?"

The commander laughed. "Geez, Doc. You're embarrassed. You know I'm a lesbian. I've had lesbian sex. With multiple partners. Would you like me to describe that to you?"

Troy blushed. "That won't be necessary, ma'am," he said. "Any heterosexual encounters?"

"What the hell does all that have to do with my rash?"

"I'm sorry," he said. "I have to be thorough. Consider any exposures that could be associated with a nonspecific rash."

Commander Squire looked down and spoke in a flat voice. "While in captivity, I was serially raped and sodomized by monster men who spewed me with body fluids."

When she looked up, her eyes had turned to steel. "You can ask directly, Doc. I am HIV-negative. I have been tested multiple times since repatriation. It's in my medical record if you'll take the time to look."

Troy raised a hand. "I'm sorry, ma'am. Perhaps we can move on."

"No 'perhaps' about it."

Troy sighed. "Since your return to the fleet, have you been anywhere unusual or had any exposures that would not be in common with others on the crew or fleet staff?"

"None whatsoever. I went ashore twice, but never without companions."

She paused, a puzzled look on her face. "Unless it's possible to pick up something in a ladies' bathroom in a hotel in South Korea."

"Not likely, if it was a reputable hotel."

"Meridian Hotel in Donghae. Good enough for the ROK and US Navy brass."

"No more risky than a major US hotel."

Troy shook his head. "To be honest, ma'am, your symptoms and rash are not typical, especially the small blisters in your throat. We see a lot of unusual rashes on Navy ships, most of them related to the industrial environment. At the worst, you may have chickenpox, although your presentation and the rash are not textbook for that. We need to take that possibility seriously, because chickenpox in an adult can be severe, even fatal. Especially if you never got the vaccine."

Commander Squire's brow furrowed. "You're doing a great job of obfuscating, Doc."

"Frankly, I don't think it's chickenpox. I mentioned that from an abundance of caution. More likely, it's a nonspecific viral exanthem, a medical term for a rash caused by a virus." He paused. "Most of the time, these go away once the viral illness runs its course. In the meantime, we'll hydrate you with some IV fluid and keep you here in isolation."

Her face hardened. "I'm not staying here, Doc. You've kept me isolated in my stateroom for four days. That should be good enough, especially since you don't think this is serious. I'm acting N3, and I can work from my stateroom. I can't do that here."

Troy thought hard about the pros and cons. At the least, not keeping the contentious commander in medical would make life easier for everyone. "We can work with that. But you shouldn't let anyone into your stateroom, not until we have a definitive diagnosis."

Commander Squire shrugged. "Not that anyone would want to do that, the way it smells."

"We have a deal, then," Troy said. "After we get that IV fluid into you, we'll release you to your stateroom, where you will remain SIQ. No visitors. I need to see you again in twenty-four to forty-eight hours. Sooner if you feel worse or develop new symptoms."

"Aye, aye, Doc."

"Do you want anything for your discomfort?"

"I'll take more Tylenol if you've got it."

"Roger that."

Troy left the room. Back in his office, he wrote notes on her chart and issued the order for IV fluids and a supply of Tylenol. He thought for a minute, then called Captain Deckert to fill her in on the commander's illness and plan.

"I'll be right down to look at her," the fleet surgeon said.

***

Twenty minutes later, Troy and Rose sat in his office after examining Commander Squire together.

"It's not chickenpox," Deckert said. "And I doubt a common viral exanthem."

"Any clues?" Troy hoped her expertise in infectious disease would finally shed a light on the clinical conundrum.

"Clues? Maybe." She frowned. "More of a differential than a clue."

Troy threw up his arms, frustrated. "Care to share your differential?"

She took a breath. "I hope I'm wrong. Let me do some research first. Meanwhile, let's take some photos and send them to a respected infectious disease guy I know at Tripler. He may have an idea."

Troy's eyes narrowed, and he cocked his head. "Out with it, Captain. What's your differential?"

She shook her head. "Think about the worst contagious disease that could happen on this ship."

A terrifying specter arose in Troy's mind. He reached into his desk drawer and pulled out a digital camera. "Let's go get those photos."

Chapter 48

CRICKET AWAKENED TO A polite knock on her stateroom door.

"Who is it?"

"Petty Officer Espiritu, ma'am. I brought you a lunch tray."

At the mention of food, Cricket felt famished. She got up, opened her door a crack, and recognized the young mess specialist who tended the female senior officers' rooms. Embarrassed that the woman had to smell her sickness, Cricket forced a smile.

"Thank you, MS3," she said. "I'm not supposed to let you in because the docs don't know if I'm contagious. You can leave it on the deck there and I'll get it after you leave."

The sailor nodded. "Aye, ma'am."

She set the tray down and stood at semi-attention. "Also, ma'am, I picked up your laundry this morning. I'll have it back to you tomorrow. Do you need anything else? Do you have enough sheets and towels?"

"Thank you, Ms. Espiritu," Cricket said. "I appreciate your taking the laundry. I would do it myself, but..."

"Not a problem, ma'am. We are honored to serve you."

Cricket wondered if the MS team gave her special attention over the other officers.

"I appreciate what you all do, MS3. Neither the Navy nor this ship can function without you. I'm fine for now. Thanks for bringing lunch."

The sailor came to sharp attention. "Aye, ma'am. By your leave, ma'am."

Cricket waved her hand. "Of course, and thanks again."

The petty officer turned on her heel and marched down the passageway.

The meal was typical Navy midday fare: a greasy hamburger on a dry bun, with lettuce, tomato, and onions on the side next to a pile of soggy fries. MS3 Espiritu had provided little cups of catsup and mustard, as well as packets of salt and pepper. A bowl of chicken noodle soup, crackers, and a slice of chocolate cake looked more palatable. A pair of tall, covered Styrofoam cups accompanied the food. The first contained ice water. When she opened the second one, Cricket squealed in delight at the vanilla milk shake—her favorite.

How do they know?

She sat at her desk and wolfed down the food. Days had passed since she'd eaten anything solid, let alone drank anything but painful sips of liquid by mouth. But now her throat did not hurt, and Cricket ate with a vengeance. She saved the milk shake for last, savoring every mouthful as if she'd acquired golden nectar.

When she finished, Cricket placed the empty dishes on the tray and set it outside the stateroom door. Then she returned to her desk and fired up her computers.

Maybe I'm getting better. Over the worst of it, at least.

Five minutes later, Cricket raced down the passageway to the women's head, arriving just in time to puke her entire lunch into the toilet.

When she had emptied her gut, she sat on the deck, leaned her back against the metal partition of the stall, and panted from the volatile retching. An odd sense of familiarity came over her, as if she'd been in this same predicament recently. Something about white slacks...

Then she remembered.

I fell in the ladies' room at the hotel in Donghae just before I passed out.

Eric and Nick had found her on the floor of that bathroom, near the sinks.

How did I get from the stall to the sinks?

Another wave of nausea knocked Cricket out of her thoughts. After two bouts of dry heaving, she got to her feet and—thankful that no one had entered the head—washed her face. The reflection in the mirror over the sink seized her attention. The same red bumps and blisters appeared, except the blisters had grown larger—and ugly. Cricket felt faint.

I will not—dammit—pass out on another bathroom floor. Least of all this one.

She steeled herself and hurried out of the head and back to her stateroom, looking down at the deck in case anyone passed.

Back in her room, Cricket pulled down the top of her flight suit and lifted the tee-shirt. The same red bumps with blisters she'd seen on her face also appeared on her chest and arms. She pulled down her bra. The rash covered her breasts.

"What the hell?" Then she saw the same rash on her hands, and on her legs and the tops of her feet.

Some goddamn virus this is.

Without bothering to turn off the computers, Cricket dove back into her rack, still without fresh sheets or pillowcases, and moaned.

***

In her dream, Cricket drifted on her back in the East Sea, so buoyant that she expended no effort to stay afloat. Her head reclined on a soft bubble of a pillow, and her legs rested on a cushion of air. No pain at all, anywhere. She had never felt so good as just now, floating in the calm sea without a care.

A harsh rap on the door startled her.

The hideous Colonel Boo!

Immediate fire seared her ankle, spear-like pain attacked her low back, and her head pounded. She turned away from the door and rolled herself into a tight ball. The demon would have to tear her limbs off before he could violate her again.

Another rap, followed by a familiar voice. "Commander Squire, Commander Squire. Are you awake?"

Still, she cowered.

This time, a familiar female voice. "Commander Squire. It's Captain Deckert and Doc Pearson. We need to see you."

Full consciousness exploded on her like a harsh blaze of light. She knew who and where she was—far away from that calm sea and painless drifting.

"Just a minute."

Her legs reacted like lead ingots, and when she raised her head, the room spun and nausea boiled in her gut. She dropped back onto the pillow.

"I'm afraid I can't get up right now."

Footsteps retreated from the door. A few minutes later, more footsteps returned. A key card clicked in the lock, and MS3 Espiritu swung it open. The fleet surgeon and Doc Pearson pushed past the petty officer into the dim room and shut it behind them, leaving Espiritu outside.

Both doctors wore full-length surgical gowns, head covers, and face masks. Latex gloves covered their hands. Captain Deckert carried a printed e-mail in her right hand.

Someone flipped on a light, and the two physicians stared at Cricket and then at each other. Their eyes gaped wide over the surgical masks.

Cricket could not tell which of them looked more terrified.

Chapter 49

WHEN TROY SAW COMMANDER Squire in the light, all the blood drained from his face.

The ill woman struggled in slow motion to sit up, as if her body was cast in hot wax. When she turned toward her visitors, the new eruptions on her face, neck, and hands jolted Troy's heart. He'd seen the telltale pox in textbooks and in a frantic Internet search before meeting up with the fleet surgeon. Identical to those pictures, raised red bumps dotted the commander's skin from head to toe. Many showed fluid-filled blisters in their centers.

Captain Deckert sighed. The two doctors exchanged solemn glances.

"You two all right?" the commander asked. "I'm not a ghost." Her tremulous tone reflected the alarm on the doctors' faces.

Rose Deckert found her voice first. "We need to examine you, Commander." She handed Cricket a surgical mask. "First, put this on, please."

Commander Squire hesitated as she reached for the mask. "Why are you all dressed like that?"

Troy found his voice. "You may be contagious. It's a precaution."

Squire frowned. "I wasn't contagious before now? You already isolated me in this room." Her eyes glazed over, like a little girl about to be disciplined.

Troy managed an embarrassed shrug. "It may be worse than I thought."

The warrior's eyes darted between the two physicians as she put on the mask. "Then you damned well better come clean." She spat out the last word like a chunk of spoiled food. "You've screwed around long enough with this...whatever it is."

Captain Deckert approached their patient, her voice calming. "We'll need you to undress, Commander, and we have a few questions as you do that."

With effort, Squire sat on the edge of the rack, unzipped her flight suit, and tried in vain to wiggle out of it. "I'll need some help."

While the captain assisted the commander with the flight suit, Troy leafed through the health record in his hand. "I don't see any documentation of a smallpox vaccination."

Squire stopped doffing the flight suit, an animal without an escape route. "Smallpox? Why do you care about that?"

Rose Deckert spoke in a calm but stern voice. "Did you get the mandatory smallpox vaccination, Commander Squire?"

The commander looked down at the deck. "Maybe I didn't." When she looked up, her eyes had gone blank.

"Let's proceed with the exam," Deckert said. "We'll be gentle and quick." She swallowed hard. "Then we'll talk."

With painful, methodical movements, Commander Squire dropped her flight suit to the deck and, with Deckert's help, lifted the royal blue tee-shirt over her head. The effort left her spent and panting.

The pox had infested her chest and abdomen. She looked at the fleet surgeon with a plaintive gaze as she reached behind her back. The captain nodded, and Squire removed her bra. Similar lesions covered her breasts. Then she slid to the edge of the rack and hooked her thumbs into her panties.

"You can keep those on," Troy said. "We see enough."

Both physicians moved in for closer looks at the lesions covering Squire's torso, arms, and legs, front and back. Most contained fluid-filled blisters like the ones on her face and hands. The rash became denser on her arms, legs, hands, and feet.

Using sterile swabs, Troy scraped some lesions to collect the fluid. Then he placed the swabs into a test tube.

Rose turned to Troy. "As you know, chickenpox tends to be more central and doesn't involve hands and feet."

Under the mask, Troy bit his lip.

I am a damn miserable excuse for a doctor.

He nodded, then turned to Commander Squire. "Does it hurt?"

"Like a mild sunburn, but all over. Not so bad." Her gaze pleaded. "Yet?"

Troy looked away, searching for a reassuring voice before he turned back to his patient. "Commander, this looks for all the world like smallpox."

Her face went ashen, but he raised his hand. "It doesn't make sense. As of now, we can't say for sure without definitive tests. Don't panic yet."

Squire clenched her fists. "Yeah, right. Trade places with me, Doc? Suppose you're me, and..." She motioned toward Captain Deckert. "...that doc tells you not to panic."

"I get it," Troy said. "But we must be objective. We don't know that it's smallpox." He could think of nothing else to say.

Deckert broke the tense silence. "Are you sure you didn't get the smallpox vaccine? I just found a misplaced entry in your health record that you received the vaccine in 2008."

Squire shook her head. "I didn't get it, ma'am."

"How did you...?"

"I gundecked it." Her voice turned mean. "Your medical records system is a farce. Stuff falls through the cracks during a move to a new station. I thought I might have HIV, and I knew better than to get the smallpox vaccine. I couldn't reveal my orientation back in the days before 'Don't ask, don't tell.' When I moved to Hawaii, I faked the entry in my record before I handed it in to the clinic. Later I went to a civilian free clinic, and my HIV test came back negative. I never followed up on the smallpox vaccine. Figured it was just BS, anyway."

She shivered. "Can I get dressed now, please?"

"Just a minute," Troy said. He produced a digital camera from his pocket. "We need to take more photos."

"Make it quick," Squire said. "I'm freezing."

"You may have a fever," Troy said.

She looked at him with a "duh" expression.

Troy took multiple photos of the rash, including close-ups. When he was done, Squire put on her bra and tee-shirt, and asked for the robe from her closet. Once she was covered, Troy asked the question foremost in both doctors' minds.

"Our biggest dilemma, Commander. If it is smallpox or a similar infectious disease, where did you get it? Working the timeline of your illness backward, the most likely period of infection would have been while we were in Donghae."

That startled Commander Squire. "Donghae?"

"Can you tell us where you went in Donghae?" the fleet surgeon asked.

"I left the ship only for the hail and farewell and that ROK Navy dinner."

"Other than the ROK Navy officers and our own staff, did you come in contact with anyone else?"

Squire shook her head. "No. Nick Juel and Eric Mikleson were with me both times." She caught her breath. "Please tell me they're not sick too."

Both doctors shook their heads. "No one is sick except you," Troy said. "That we know of."

He spoke to the fleet surgeon. "We should contact those two officers and tell them to remain in their staterooms until we can examine them."

Panic erupted in Squire's eyes. "You can't get Eric. He's gone to Seoul with the admiral and Captain Gunderson."

All three officers stared at each other. None could articulate the enormity that bored into their thoughts and imaginations.

Troy broke the silence. "We'll deal with that as we can. Right now, we need to get you down to medical where we can treat you."

Deckert touched his arm and pulled him aside. "Do you think that's wise? You risk contaminating your entire department."

"Good thought," he said. He turned to Commander Squire. "We'll let you stay here. You might be more comfortable. We can bring treatment to you."

Squire shrugged, her mind elsewhere. "Do what you must, docs."

Troy turned to Captain Deckert. "We have lots to do and think about. I'll start by turning this place into a medical isolation room, get her blood drawn, IVs going, and the like. Then we need a plan for the rest of the staff and crew."

He turned back to Squire. "Have you been in contact with anyone since you got sick?"

"Just Eric Mikleson and the chief of staff," she said. "And you two."

"We have to brief the COS anyway," Deckert said to Troy. "We can check him out at the same time."

"What about Mikleson?"

"I'll get word to him," Deckert said. "Advise him to let us know if he gets flu-like symptoms. If he is infected, we can intervene before he becomes contagious." She paused. "Even in the worst case, transmission is unlikely with only casual contact."

Troy turned back to Squire. "We'll take good care of you, ma'am. For now, we have to treat this as smallpox, to be prudent. We'll run those samples I just obtained through our PCR analyzer. That's a pretty definitive test. Until then, let's stay optimistic."

Squire rolled back onto her rack. "Sure thing, Doc." The familiar sarcasm dripped from her voice.

"I'll be back soon with some corpsmen to get your blood and start an IV to keep you hydrated. We'll turn this space into a hospital room." He paused. "And we'll bring you something for pain."

She turned on her side to face him. "Forget the pain medicine. Just answer me one last question."

"If I can."

"Smallpox," she said. Her eyes pierced through him. "That's fatal, right?"

He glanced away for an instant. "Not always," he said. "Not always."

Then he and the fleet surgeon left the room.

Chapter 50

TROY PEARSON AND ROSE Deckert fidgeted in their seats under the chief of staff's icy stare. They had come straight to his office after leaving Commander Squire with a pair of trusted corpsmen sworn to secrecy until further notice.

Captain Santiago folded his arms and leaned back in his chair. He stared at each physician in turn.

"It can't be smallpox."

The fleet surgeon responded. "Can and probably is."

"That's impossible. Why did we all get the damned vaccine? We're immune, right?"

Troy answered. "Commander Squire didn't get the smallpox immunization, sir."

Santiago turned livid. "How the hell not?"

"She altered her health record," Deckert said.

The COS rubbed his forehead. "We should court-martial her ass and put her off the ship in Hong Kong."

Both doctors looked at each other, and then Rose turned to the chief of staff. "Sir, she's contagious. Beyond that, in two days when we get to Hong Kong, she'll be too sick. Her condition will soon turn critical. She may die."

Santiago's anger deflated as the full import of the physicians' message pierced his outer shell. "You can't give her anything to…"

"No, sir," Troy said. "We have no treatment for smallpox, certainly not on this ship." He let the words resonate before he continued. "The best we can do is offer her supportive care and hope her own immune system fights off the disease."

Rose Deckert heaved a sigh. "Of everyone on the ship, she may have the worst compromised immune system because of what she's already endured."

The chief of staff looked away.

Rose continued. "Our primary concern must be protecting the rest of the staff and crew. Smallpox is contagious. We don't know how many others are already exposed. We need to mitigate the risk of more infections."

Those words snapped the chief of staff out of his mood. "The vaccine is mandatory for this area of operations, right? The rest of us who got the vaccine are immune, right?"

"We can't assume that," Troy said. He glanced sideways at the fleet surgeon. "We don't know where Commander Squire picked up the infection. We have to consider an attack with an altered virus."

"Attack?"

Deckert continued. "Naturally occurring smallpox was eradicated worldwide by 1977, a result of global immunization. The only known stores of smallpox left in the world are in two laboratories: our CDC in the US and the Vector Institute in Russia. The former Soviet Union conducted a program to alter smallpox as a biological weapon. In theory, terrorists or states that support them could have obtained a weaponized smallpox virus. That's the reason for the mandatory vaccinations of our military personnel.

"In short, sir, our standard smallpox vaccine today may or may not be effective against re-engineered smallpox virus. We cannot guarantee immunity, even among those who got the vaccine."

Captain Santiago rubbed his forehead. "You're describing a potential disaster of massive proportions."

"If it's not contained now, yes, sir," Troy said.

"What do you propose?"

"We've isolated Commander Squire in her stateroom starboard aft on the third deck where the female senior officers live. We recommend quarantining that section. Move the other women to another location in the ship. Close the watertight doors from forward of the women's head to the aft bulkhead, and close off the athwartships passageway.

"We've identified two corpsmen to care for her around the clock, plus the fleet surgeon and I will be in frequent attendance. No one else will be allowed in that area. If we can contain the infection in that small section of the ship, the rest of the crew and staff may continue to function."

"Why not take her to medical?"

"Last thing you want, sir, is to contaminate the medical department. That could take your entire health-care capability out of the fight. Plus, moving her could contaminate the passageway between her stateroom and medical."

"Someone would see her," Captain Deckert added. "She's not a pretty sight. We must not only contain the infection, but head off shipwide panic."

The chief of staff pondered. "Are you certain it's smallpox?"

"High probability, based on the clinical scenario," Troy said. "A time-honored medical adage says, 'If it has feathers like a duck, walks like a duck, and quacks like a duck, it's probably a duck.'"

The analogy elicited a steely-eyed glare from the COS and a look of reproach from the fleet surgeon.

"Sorry," Troy said. "Inappropriate metaphor."

"To continue," Deckert said, "we sent photos of the commander's rash yesterday to an infectious disease colleague at Tripler. Both he and a dermatologist suggested a high probability of smallpox. The rash progressed into today, so we're sending additional photos now."

She took a quick breath. "Also, and most important, we've taken samples to run through our LightCycler PCR instrument that can identify viral DNA. That will be the definitive test."

"How long will that take?"

"We'll get results today."

The COS thought in silence for another minute before speaking. "You got any of those photos with you?"

Troy showed him the digital photos in his camera.

"Holy Christ," Santiago said. "Who else has seen her? Who else on the ship knows about this?"

"Just us and two corpsmen, sir."

"That's already too many," Santiago said.

He picked up his phone and punched in a number. "Officer of the deck, this is the chief of staff. Set River City now." He listened to someone speaking on the other end of the line.

Troy tried to wave him off. "River City" was the Navy code word for the operational security process of turning off all non-secure communications from or to the ship. Sailors would lose all contact with the outside world, including Internet access and the ability to email families and loved ones.

"Sir, that may cause undue concern."

The COS covered the mouthpiece with his hand. "I have no choice, Doc. If word of this gets out before we've briefed the admiral or the chain of command..."

He spoke back into the phone. "I can't give you a reason right now, Lieutenant. Just do it."

He hung up the phone and addressed the two doctors. "You need to make sure that whomever you consult understands that this is highest classification. They must not divulge to anyone without a proper clearance and need to know."

Troy and Rose nodded.

"Under threat of court-martial," COS Santiago added.

A few seconds later, the announcement blared over the 1MC, "Now set River City. I say again, now set River City."

The phone on the chief of staff's desk rang.

"That will be the ship's captain." He picked up the phone.

"Skipper. I know. Didn't want to call you on the phone. Come to my office now, please."

He put down the phone. "So it begins. You docs damned well better be right, because we'll all be looking for new jobs if you're wrong."

He dialed another number. "FLAGSEC, I need to get hold of the admiral now. En route to where? Shit. Okay, I need to talk to her when she's available. We'll need a secure line."

He hung up the phone. "Admiral's in the air with the ROKs. When she's available, I'll need one or both of you with me to brief her."

Both doctors nodded.

"To be sure I understand," the COS went on, "we're not certain what we've got, right? So, the immediate plan is to isolate Squire and to keep the deck-plate rumor mill off topic. We won't do another damn thing, and that includes moving female officers out of their staterooms, until you have irrevocable proof that we're dealing with smallpox." He glared at both physicians. "I still don't believe it."

"Aye, sir," the doctors said in unison.

"I mean, for one thing," the COS said, "where the hell would she get it? Back in that prison camp?"

The fleet surgeon answered. "That's the puzzlement, sir. She's too far out from captivity to have acquired it in North Korea. She would have been exposed in the last two weeks."

"That's too strange to be true," the COS said. "How could that have happened?"

A knock on the door was followed by the entrance of the ship's captain.

"Captain," the COS said, "have a seat. The docs here have disturbing news."

Chapter 51

ALONE FOR THE FIRST time since the doctors had entered her stateroom and spun her already tumultuous life farther out of control, Cricket lay in the rack with eyes closed. The small room had become claustrophobic with the addition of medical supplies that included a metal pole from which hung a bag of fluid with tubing connected to an intravenous catheter in her arm. A resuscitation "crash cart," cardiac monitor, and a mechanical ventilator stood at the ready against the bulkheads.

For what?

The IV tube in her right forearm caused only mild discomfort compared to her burning skin. The slight sunburn sensation she'd described earlier now felt like she'd come too close to an open fire but could not retreat.

Doc Pearson had offered her narcotics to ease the pain, but she'd refused.

"They may think I won't recover, but I'm not buying that," she said.

Doc Deckert had given her the odds. "Thirty-five percent mortality, if it's really smallpox, and if it behaves like the naturally occurring strain. At worst, 50/50."

That's a 50 to 65 percent survival rate. Better odds than I had in North Korea or in that shit-hole torture ship. I beat those monsters. I can damn sure beat a stupid bug.

A wave of exhaustion—worse than any she remembered from captivity—coursed through her. Tears filled her eyes. At first in trickles and then in pools.

I could stare down those North Korean ogres, see the cowardice in their eyes. All I see of this enemy is what it's done to my skin.

Cricket opened her eyes, visualizing an unseen attacker.

How did I get infected?

She succumbed to the flood of tears, feeling alone, abandoned, empty, powerless. How could she fight such an invisible, potent enemy? And what if she won the fight? What if she got into that sixty-five percent survival column? What then?

What life would I have?

She had thought about calling or e-mailing Eric, but River City had removed those options. She could not contact Eric or anyone outside the ship. Heartsick that she might have infected him, she longed to call him, warn him, tell him to get checked.

How? For what?

In truth, Cricket wanted to share her own fear and dread with Eric, her new trusted friend.

How would that be fair to him, especially if he's not infected?

No matter. River City had isolated her more than the docs had.

The phantom flames licked Cricket's skin, and she wondered if she wanted to live or die. Even if she survived, the disease would leave her disfigured for the rest of her life. Could she live with that? Cricket had never considered herself vain, but she had been proud of her fit and toned athletic body—which she sometimes flaunted for a potential companion or lover.

Not vanity, but reality. A life lived alone, repulsive to other humans. I would become a recluse.

Cricket closed her eyes. She allowed darkness to envelop her as if it were death itself. Imagining herself dead, compared to the current reality and prospect of future suffering, calmed her.

"To die, to sleep," she muttered. Her eyes flipped open.

Shakespeare? Really, Jess?

"'Tis a consummation devoutly to be wished, to die, to sleep."

Exhausted from the pain and morning activity, Cricket welcomed drowsiness. She mouthed the next words in silence. "For in that sleep of death what dreams may come?"

Jessica Squire and Caroline Ford, one blond, the other brunette, skipped hand in hand along the wooded path in Golden Gate Park. The thirteen-year-olds quickened their pace on approach to their secret sanctuary. Like two birds in synchronized flight, they veered off the path and ran into the woods. Fifty yards in, they broke into a clearing where unmowed grass stood eight inches high.

The young maidens tumbled to the ground and rolled together in the soft thickness of the grass, rolling and rolling until their momentum stopped, with Jessica on top as always. She nudged Caroline's dark locks off her face and kissed her, hard and long. Caroline returned the kiss, and they rolled again, mouths locked, tongues caressing each other.

The sudden roar of a gas-powered engine disrupted their pubescent passion. Jess looked up in time to see a riding mower, driven by a Korean man, bearing down on them. She jumped up, pulled Caroline to her feet, and pushed her toward the woods. The rumbling sound of the mower surged toward them. Then the piston-driven roar became the thumping of a huge fan beating the air.

A gust of wind almost blew them over. Jessica peeked into the clearing. A haze-gray helicopter landed just as the woods on the opposite side erupted into flames. From the helicopter, men in military battle gear beckoned for the two girls to get aboard. Jess grabbed her friend's hand, but it was not Caroline.

Lee Young stared back at Jess, her face etched in fright. Jess pulled on her arm, and they ran together, hand in hand, to the waiting aircraft.

The flames now engulfed the woods all around the clearing. North Korean soldiers in black battle dress chased the two girls and sprayed withering fire from automatic weapons. The girls reached the helo just before the meadow grass erupted in flames. As soon as Jess hit the helo's deck, the aircraft lifted off. Jess squeezed Lee's hand as hard as she could to pull her aboard, but the slight Korean woman got heavier by the second.

Now the firm hand gripping Jess's was no longer Lee's. Eric Mikleson hung from her grasp, the meadow beneath him a sea of fire. Her strength was his only rescue from certain death. The soldiers stood in the blaze, unburned, and aimed their weapons at the lifting helicopter.

The aircraft struggled to gain altitude. A crewman shouted at her, "Let go. He's too heavy. We're taking fire."

She tightened her grip. *This time, I don't let go.*

The helo lurched and banked, and then a crushing explosion rocked the airframe. The aircraft rotated and spun in slow motion, descending into the flames. She held tight to Eric's arm and did not let go.

Cricket awakened in agony. The fire consumed her skin, scorched her eyeballs, charred her throat, sucked out her breath. She screamed, but no one heard. The heat penetrated her skin and muscles and bones and inner organs. Flames lapped around her heart, consumed it, and left behind a smoldering lump of charcoal.

She screamed again, but made no sound because the fire had taken her breath, her life, her soul.

Her eyelids opened. Intact, unmelted eyeballs took in the dim stateroom and medical equipment around her. Her breath came in rapid, shallow gasps, and her heart raced through the pain and the fear and the final despair within her soul.

Over this, I choose death.

Chapter 52

V ice Admiral Louise Lassiter's distressed face appeared larger than life on the monitor screen in the top secret Joint Worldwide Intelligence Communications System (JWICS) conference room on board USS *Shenandoah*. On her right, Captain Eric Mikleson looked outright stricken, while Captain Mark Gunderson, seated to her left, stared zombie-like into the camera.

The Seventh Fleet chief of staff had just finished a synopsis of the reason for the urgent secure video teleconference. He looked to the fleet surgeon to begin her portion of the brief.

"Good morning, Admiral and Captains," Rose Deckert said. "The instrument is called a LightCycler PCR. It assays specimens to detect specific viral infections, using genetic probes to detect and identify DNA in the specimen." She paused. "These instruments were placed on high-profile US Navy ships about ten years ago for detecting biological attacks." She turned to Troy.

Troy looked into the camera. "Commander Squire's rash resembles smallpox, especially the blisters that appeared yesterday. We processed samples of the blister fluid from three different lesions through the LightCycler." He stopped speaking. His next words would throw the Seventh Fleet, the US Navy, his country, and perhaps the world, into uncharted chaos.

"Well?" the admiral said.

Troy pursed his lips. "The results confirm our clinical impression that Commander Squire suffers from smallpox."

A pall of silence descended on the room. On the monitor, the admiral looked down and rubbed her eyes. When she looked into the video camera, her face became stone-like. "How certain? Can you get another opinion?"

"As soon as possible, we will send specimens off the ship to the Naval Health Research Command in San Diego for confirmation," Troy said. "But that will take at least a week. Based on all available information, the LightCycler PCR is very reliable."

Captain Deckert rescued him. "It's smallpox, ma'am. The evidence is overwhelming."

On the monitor, Captain Mikleson asked, "Do you have any idea where she got it?"

"Not exactly where, but a good idea of when," Troy said. "Based on the historical epidemiology, the pathogenesis of smallpox, and the timing of her symptoms, the exposure occurred while the flagship was in Donghae."

He watched as the admiral and her intelligence officer exchanged looks. Captain Mikleson asked, "Is anyone else sick?"

Troy shook his head. "No one, sir. But it may be too early. The incubation period for smallpox is broad, seven to seventeen days, with an average of twelve days. We're collecting a list of her contacts; anyone she was with from Donghae to now."

More silence as the participants fathomed the enormity of the situation. "That includes everyone on this brief," Captain Mikleson said.

"Aye, sir," Rose said. "But the risk would be low for casual contact. The virus can be airborne, but would likely require closer contact than, say, just being in a room with her." She took a breath. "However, our information comes from the history of naturally occurring smallpox, which no longer travels the world. Until we know for certain otherwise, we must assume that the commander's illness results from a biological attack with a weaponized form of the virus. If it was genetically altered, we know nothing for sure about its characteristics."

The admiral turned to Captain Mikleson. "How the hell would anyone in this region have weaponized smallpox?"

"I won't speculate, ma'am," Mikleson said. "The possibilities are ominous."

"I got that," the admiral said. She leaned into the camera. "Chief of Staff, put out an immediate OPREP PINNACLE message." (*OPREP* referred to an operations report, and *PINNACLE* meant a highest priority threat to national security.) "We'll take this straight to the National Command Authority and Joint Military Operations Center rather than wait for the news to filter through our chain of command. If this turns out other than y'all have said, I'll take the heat. Write that USS *Shenandoah*, command ship of the US Seventh Fleet, has smallpox—probable weapons grade—on board, confined to one sailor, at present." She pursed her lips. "For Christ's sake, don't identify her. Say that we can continue operations and respond to national tasking until further notice."

She stopped and turned her gaze into the camera at Troy and the fleet surgeon. "Please tell me you can control this, docs."

"We have a plan, ma'am," Captain Deckert said. "Surveillance and containment. The surveillance piece is to look for other cases. For containment, we've isolated the commander in her stateroom, cleared out the other staterooms in the vicinity, and quarantined that section of the ship by closing it off at the watertight doors. For the next step, we will administer smallpox vaccine to her contacts and then to the contacts of those contacts. We have some smallpox vaccine on board, and we will begin vaccinating the commander's immediate contacts today."

"Wait," the admiral said. "Aren't they already vaccinated?"

"Commander Squire did not get the vaccine," Troy said. He paused a second for that news to sink in to his audience. "As for the others, there's some thought, not definitive, that early post-exposure vaccination can prevent the illness in contacts." He explained that even though most of the ship's crew had been vaccinated, they had no guarantee of protection against genetically altered weaponized smallpox.

"In short, ma'am, the vaccine is the only weapon we have right now. We believe the risks of giving it early outweigh the risk of ineffectiveness if given too late."

"So we really don't know the enemy," the admiral said. "Chief of Staff, in your message request all assistance to deal with this imminent threat to Seventh Fleet command and control."

The chief of staff had been writing on a notepad. He looked up. "Yes, ma'am."

"I know you've set River City. Is the public affairs officer in the room?"

"No, ma'am," Captain Santiago said. "Just the docs and me. At present, we're the only ones read into this situation."

"Read in the PAO. As soon as that PINNACLE hits, the shit will fly like bats out of a cesspool. We need a communications plan."

"Aye, ma'am," the COS said. "As soon as we're done here."

"Read him in before you send that message, COS. But don't take all day. I don't want to explain why the Seventh Fleet commander sat on this."

"Will do, ma'am." Captain Santiago looked like a whipped puppy.

The admiral spoke again. "You docs been in contact with anyone who can help you? PACOM Medical? BUMED? CDC?"

Captain Deckert said, "Not yet, ma'am. We thought we should brief you first." She paused. "We did, uh, send some photos of her rash for verification by infectious disease and dermatology colleagues at Tripler, but they are sworn to secrecy."

The admiral leaned into the camera with a face turned vermilion. She pointed her finger at the center of the lens. "Get this straight right now. We're riding a bow wave into an international calamity, and you two are on the point. You are the strike leaders for an all-out assault. I know y'all docs aren't used to that, but all the bombs and missiles in the fleet can't help us in this fight. You do your jobs, take action, get what help you need, and move out with confidence that you'll defeat the enemy. You don't ask, 'Mother, may I?' every whipstitch. Got that?"

"Yes, ma'am," the two said in unison.

The admiral waved her hands as if to encompass her entire audience. "And y'all don't ever again wait for me to get off a chopper before you take action."

No one spoke, but the three heads in the room all nodded north to south.

"You got anything else for me?" the admiral asked.

The COS said, "We haven't discussed your plans, ma'am. We urge you to stay put rather than rejoin the ship. You too, Captains."

"I'll let you know about that," the admiral said. "Another thing, y'all won't make that Hong Kong port visit, so we need a different plan."

She looked at Captain Mikleson. "For the immediate future, we'll brief the US commands here on the peninsula. I'll wait for the National Command Authority before I share anything with the ROKs. I'm sure I'll get plenty of advice once POTUS and SecDef and the joint chiefs see the PINNACLE message."

Troy spoke up. "Ma'am, we urge you and the two captains there to get smallpox vaccinations soonest. We know you had contact with Commander Squire. Ideally, she was not yet contagious, but we can't assume so."

"How do you suppose we do that, Doc? Without creating a stir here?"

Captain Deckert said, "I'll contact the USFK surgeon, ma'am. It will be discreet."

"From what y'all are saying, it may not do any good. I'd rather forgo it than maybe cause a ruckus on the Korean peninsula. Not that it won't happen, anyway."

Captain Mikleson broke in. "Excuse me, ma'am." He looked into the camera. "Have there been any indications of a similar illness here in Korea? Do you have a way of finding that out from the ROK medical folks?"

"I have a contact I can try," Troy said. "I can be vague enough to not tell him anything about our problem."

"Do it, please," Mikleson said. He turned to the admiral. "Besides all the medical stuff, we need to track down the source. ROKs might help."

Vice Admiral Lassiter leaned back in her chair, pursed her lips, and nodded. "Okay," she said. "Now if you folks have nothing else, we need to get to gettin'. COS, you send out that PINNACLE, and then brace for the shit storm."

Her face turned soft, sad. "Good luck to you, docs. You got the lead, with all the support we can muster for you. Whatever you need, we will damn well get it. I don't envy your positions, but I'm glad we've got you there." Her voice broke. "God help Cricket. God help us all."

Then the screen went blank.

Chapter 53

THE "SHIT STORM" THAT Vice Admiral Lassiter predicted turned out to be a full-blown fecal typhoon. As soon as the OPREP PINNACLE reached higher authority, said authority—at multiple levels up and down the chain of command—assumed immediate self-mandates to micromanage events aboard *Shenandoah*. As expected, the four-star Pacific commander, Admiral Darnell Lewis, a former Seventh Fleet commander, canceled the flagship's port visit to Hong Kong and the remaining ports on its diplomatic deployment schedule. The US Pacific Fleet commander ordered *Shenandoah* to return at "best speed" to its forward-deployed home in Yokosuka, Japan.

What would happen with the ship, its crew, and its smallpox patient became the subject of intense conversations, from the flagship's senior leadership, through higher military and civilian Department of Defense authorities, all the way to the White House. Action officers and other staff at headquarters from South Korea to Japan to Hawaii to DC worked nonstop to craft hypotheses, scenarios, and solutions—all reduced to point papers, full-length briefs, and PowerPoint presentations—around three major objectives:

(1) Controlling the outbreak, if indeed it was an outbreak and not an isolated case;

(2) Responding to the threat of biological attack, to include identifying and neutralizing those responsible;

(3) Controlling the strategic message, especially regarding US allies in the Western Pacific.

Despite the mayhem of operational frenzy, plausible, executable solutions proved elusive.

One plan favored by higher authorities in the United States would remove Commander Squire from the flagship once it reached Japan and transport her to the National Institutes of Health Clinical Center in Bethesda, Maryland.

A similar strategy had worked for removing victims of the 2014 Ebola epidemic in Africa to US hospitals such as Emory University Hospital in Atlanta. Since this case involved a military patient, the NIH Clinical Center became the logical choice because of its location across Wisconsin Avenue from the Walter Reed National Military Medical Center. Per the plan, civilian and military infectious disease experts would collaborate in treating Commander Squire and in diagnosing whatever additional threats this virus might pose.

Japanese authorities begged to disagree on the plan to return the flagship to its home port. When the US ambassador to Japan presented the plan to the Japanese minister of foreign affairs, she was told, with much bowing, sucking of teeth, and saddened expressions, that "it would be very difficult" for Japan to accept the risk to its citizens. Similar parley between the commander of US Forces Japan and his Japanese Self Defense Force counterpart to execute a revised plan as a joint military operation resulted in a similar polite but firm refusal.

By the end of the first day of *Shenandoah*'s transit back to Japan, word came down that Japanese authorities had "regretfully" denied diplomatic clearance for the flagship to enter Japanese territorial waters.

Anticipating similar rebuffs from the other major US allies in the Western Pacific, the planners, action officers, and gofers returned to their respective computer terminals and conference rooms to hash out more point papers, briefs, and PowerPoint slideshows.

In due time, all eyes turned to the US territory of Guam. Higher authorities directed PACOM, PacFleet, and Seventh Fleet operations staffs to develop a plan to transfer the stricken commander from *Shenandoah* to Anderson Air Force Base in Guam, thence to Andrews Air Force Base in northern Virginia, and from there to the NIH Clinical Center in Bethesda. Once the patient left the flagship, *Shenandoah* would make port at the US naval base on Apra Harbor on the southern tip of Guam to undergo decontamination—the details of which were vague, since no one had ever dealt with such a scenario.

The planners' primary concern, beyond the familiar operational logistics, would be assuring safe transport of the patient from point to point to point without risking further contamination and disease along the way. Somewhere in the national capital area's complex and competitive upper stratosphere of strategy, politics, and policy, a decision was made to treat this new biological threat with the same combined military and civilian forces that had managed the Ebola crisis.

"We can replicate the process in this case," one expert said. "Send a go-team to Guam, along with the disposable portable isolation unit and bioprotective gear, to manage the transport from Anderson."

"How soon can we get our infectious disease experts onto that ship?" said another. "I doubt whatever medical staff they have is up to a challenge of this magnitude."

The medical team on board the flagship had already received more than enough help. Medical leaders at Pacific Fleet; US Pacific Command; the Navy Bureau of Medicine and Surgery; the Navy and Marine Corps Public Health Center in Portsmouth, Virginia; the Navy Environmental Protection Unit 6 in Honolulu; the Army Medical Research Institute of Infectious Diseases in Fort Detrick, Maryland; the Defense Health Agency in Arlington, Virginia; and the civilian Assistant Secretary of Defense for Health Affairs all provided unsolicited counsel and advice, uncoordinated and often contradictory, very little helpful.

Overwhelmed with advice, their time monopolized by phone calls and demands for teleconferences, Troy and Rosalie Deckert divided responsibilities. Troy would focus on the medical care for Commander Squire (besides his regular duties as the ship's medical officer), and Deckert would work the surveillance and containment operations as well as become the primary point of contact for external communications.

Troy and Rose found the best advice from the Centers for Disease Control, including insights into the potential nature of weaponized smallpox. The CDC had dealt with its own crisis in 2014 when forgotten vials of smallpox virus had been discovered in an unused warehouse at the NIH.

Shenandoah sailed northwest of Taiwan, en route to Hong Kong, when it altered course toward Japan. Then the new order to proceed to Guam resulted in a vector that brought the flagship within helicopter distance of Okinawa and its regional US Naval Hospital. Troy and Rose persuaded the operators to loiter in that area long enough to get needed medical supplies. Besides Okinawa's considerable stock of smallpox vaccine, Troy requested and received supplies of IV fluids, biocontainment suits, dressings, and other disposables in anticipation that the outbreak might spread beyond the one ill officer.

With the requested supplies on board, the ship turned southeast for the three-day transit to Guam.

The medical team completed the containment strategy of vaccinating the commander's immediate contacts, and also a second wave of vaccinations for their contacts. Anyone known to have had even casual contact with Commander Squire received a mandatory smallpox vaccination, under threat of nonjudicial punishment if they refused. For the medics and leaders on board the flagship, the scenario had become a waiting game: waiting to see if anyone else developed symptoms, waiting for more information from their expert consultants, waiting to see what course the disease would take in Commander Squire's tormented body.

***

Cricket languished between severe agony and drug-induced sleep. The blisters now contained putrid, foul-smelling pus, but the sensation of being burned alive had not diminished. Since she'd made the choice to die rather than fight this most recent and monstrous torturer, she had welcomed the doctors' offer of a self-controlled morphine IV drip.

Sometimes, when just emerging from narcosis, she would feel almost normal—until the stench of the pustules attacking her flesh and the searing pain all over her body forced her to pump the machine for more drug, even if she were locked out for the programmed waiting period between doses.

On one such awakening, a biocontainment-clad corpsman held the receiver of her desk phone toward her ear.

"Ma'am," the sailor said. "Comms has patched a secure satellite call to your phone."

Cricket tried to reach for the handset, but the movement inflamed her arm, and she withdrew. The corpsman held the receiver to her ear and mouth.

"Hello?" Her voice sounded ghost-like, even to her.

"Cricket?" Eric's voice.

She could only mumble. "Eric, sorry. Can't talk loud. Sore throat." She panted for a few seconds. "Where you?"

"Admiral and I are still in Seoul. Figuring out the options. I wanted to talk to you, to let you know we're thinking of you and supporting you all the way."

She coughed, causing more severe pain in her throat. "No use. Dying here."

"I refuse to believe that. The best medical experts in the world are busting butts to get you through this."

"No cure. Accepting it."

"We don't know that. You can fight this, Cricket."

"Too hard." Tears filled her eyes and dripped down her pox-ridden cheeks. "I'm done, Eric." Then she remembered something. "You? How you?"

"I'm fine."

"You. We." Cricket could not find the words. "You know we…"

A bit of a pause and then he said, "No worry. I had my vaccine. I'm fine."

"Don't lie."

"I'm not. Don't worry about me, please. Concentrate on beating this. You and I both know you can."

"Can't. So much pain." She felt the rush of the next morphine dose flooding her bloodstream, slurring her speech all the more. "Gotta rest now. You get care, Eric."

"Don't you give up, Cricket!"

She'd already lapsed into narcosis and didn't hear him.

Chapter 54
Seoul, Republic of Korea

"SIR, SHE'S FALLEN ASLEEP," the corpsman said.

"Thank you," Eric said. "Can you give me an update on her condition?"

"She's very sick, sir. The rash is all over her body, and it's becoming pustular. She's in constant pain, taking a lot of morphine for that. Vitals remain stable, but..." The young man's voice broke. "We've never seen this disease. We don't know what will happen next."

Eric seethed with unfamiliar emotion. "Listen, Petty Officer. You take good care of her, you hear me? You care for her as if she were your own sister."

"I will, sir."

"She is your sister. She's our sister. All of us. You take good care of her."

"Aye, sir. Doing our best here, sir."

"I know you are. Thanks, Petty Officer."

Eric switched off the satellite phone and wiped tears from his eyes. He had researched smallpox on the Internet. When he'd come across old photos of actual victims, his heart had seized. Cricket, the intrepid Navy pilot and tenacious war fighter, the national hero who had thwarted the evil North Korean regime, did not belong in one of those pox-ridden bodies.

Of all the people in the world, she least deserves this.

The roughest cut of all was hearing her express defeat. This was not the Cricket Squire whom those close to her respected and loved. Eric staggered under the weight of the possible, the most plausible explanation for the turn of events that had robbed his friend of her strength, passion, and dignity. In time, it would all become clear, but in his soul Eric knew the perpetrator of this evil.

"This cannot happen," he said aloud. "That devil doesn't get to win."

Eric had placed the satellite call to *Shenandoah* from a secure sensitive compartmented information facility, or SCIF, deep inside the USFK headquarters. All at once, he hungered for air. He replaced the phone, left the SCIF, and headed out the door of the pristine white building in the center of Yongsan Garrison. Without picking a direction or destination, he set off walking. Anger and fear stormed inside of him.

In his mind, Eric justified his lie to Cricket. She didn't need to know that he'd forgone the original smallpox vaccination because at the time of the mass military inoculations Melody was pregnant with their second child—a known risk and official contraindication to the vaccine, including those living in the same household. After that first frenzied wave of vaccinations, when more reliable intel rendered the threat of smallpox less likely, he'd forgotten, or neglected, to get it. Even when assigned to the Seventh Fleet staff, he'd not received the vaccine. By then, the safety profile of the vaccine had been questioned. Deaths had been reported. As a senior naval intelligence officer, Eric knew with reasonable certainty that neither of the potential enemies in the region, China and North Korea, possessed the virus. Avoiding exposure to a risky inoculation in the face of minimal actual threat seemed a reasonable judgment at the time—one that he kept to himself.

How the hell did they get to Cricket?

Should he, Vice Admiral Lassiter, and Mark Gunderson get the vaccine now? They had not followed the docs' initial advice, for fear of alerting ROK and other US authorities. The risk of political fallout had seemed too great. But now...?

Almost a week had passed since Eric had been close to Cricket. He felt fine. He needed to concentrate on validating the source of the attack, knowing full well where the trail would lead. The old photos entered his mind, and he visualized Cricket suffering. He could worry about himself later. For now, he must figure out the key question. Who had masterminded and executed this heinous attack? What consequences should they face?

His meanderings had taken him to the Dragon Hill Lodge, the military hotel on Yongsan Garrison, where he and Vice Admiral Lassiter were staying. He was supposed to meet the admiral for dinner in her suite in thirty minutes.

She would be eager to hear about his conversation with Cricket.

Chapter 55

LESS THAN TWO MILES from the Dragon Hill Lodge, in her small hillside apartment in Yongsan-gu (*Yongsan* in Korean means "Dragon Hill"), Lee Myung Suk lay abed, toxic, dehydrated, dying. No more stench of rotting flesh. Had she gotten used to the foul odor? Or did it fade away as the pustular lesions turned to scabs? The question mattered only as an intellectual exercise to distract her waning consciousness from the fresh pain attacking her defeated body like a pillaging enemy. Flames no longer licked her skin. In their place, deep aches penetrated her knees, ankles, elbows, and wrists; so debilitating that she no longer got out of bed to take the little nourishment left in the small refrigerator or to drink the fluids she'd stored there. Without food or drink, she no longer needed the bathroom.

Death by starvation. How unfitting for a warrior of the Korean People's Army.

She groaned as she shifted position in bed and reminded herself that the manner of death did not matter. Her mission was done, her fight complete. Glory lay ahead of her.

Myung had lost track of the days since she'd seduced the young KATUSA officer in this bed—maybe a week, maybe longer. By now, the soldier might have early symptoms. In typical male fashion, he would shrug off the headache, backache, and low-grade fever as flu. Myung counted on her prey's dedication and commitment to duty. Even with the inevitable sore throat, he would endure the symptoms in silence while he worked for the Americans and their puppets; clueless that he was killing them. With luck, the soldier might unknowingly attack the four-star commanding general himself.

Justice!

A paroxysm of coughing and knife-like chest pain caused Myung to double over. Another wave came hard after the first. The heavy racking raised thick sputum into her throat, which was so dry that she almost gagged on the gooey blob. She spat it onto her pillow, a thick yellow-green clump that stank like putrid flesh.

When the coughing fit ended, Myung rolled over onto her back, too weak to clean up the mess. As if by instinct to stave off the stabbing pain of deeper breathing, her breaths came in rapid, shallow spurts. As her respirations leveled out, her thoughts turned to the American woman she'd attacked in Donghae. That victim would now have the rash. Would she know that the Dear Leader had exacted his revenge upon her in a most masterful and ingenious way? Would the arrogant Americans have a clue about their impending defeat?

Myung felt confident that she'd destroyed the target, as sure as if she'd blown the vile woman's head off with a single shot from her assault rifle. That filthy female would soon die, haunted by the knowledge that her perversion had launched a mass attack on the US Navy and ROK and opened the path of ultimate victory for the Dear Leader.

She closed her eyes and thought of her half-sister Lee Yeong Nae and the familial love the two had once shared—a love that Yeong Nae had betrayed and Myung Suk had avenged.

Three glorious victories for the price of my life.

A full-body flush of pleasant warmth infused her. In a voice so soft that she did not hear herself, she cursed the Americans, cursed her treacherous sister, and praised the Dear Leader. The warmth became a glow.

It is time.

Lee Myung Suk reached under her pillow and extracted the loaded Type 70 semi-automatic pistol. In one slow, painful, but deliberate motion, she thrust the barrel deep into her mouth, aimed it upward, took a last breath, and pulled the trigger.

Chapter 56

USS Shenandoah (LCC 21), Philippine Sea, Underway Toward Guam

"SO MUCH PAIN, ERIC." Cricket awakened to fire consuming her body.

Am I in hell?

"Commander, are you awake?" Not Eric's voice, Doc Pearson's.

Not in hell, but close to it.

Cricket opened her eyes. The Navy doctor stood over her, like a marshmallow man in his bioprotective suit.

"Still alive here." Her voice croaked.

The doctor sat down to address her at face level. "Are you awake enough to listen to me?"

Cricket nodded.

"Still in a lot of pain?"

Another nod.

"I'd like to try something different that might help. For your information, the ship just turned southeast from near Okinawa, heading to Guam. The transit should take three days, but there's a storm developing to the southeast of the island. That might delay us."

Cricket shrugged. Days had become irrelevant.

"We've obtained additional supplies from the Naval Hospital in Okinawa." Doc Pearson showed her a medicine vial with a red top. "This is ketamine. It's a type of anesthetic."

Cricket blinked herself alert. She had trouble focusing, as if a thin veil covered her eyes.

"Your pain is breaking through the morphine," the doctor said. "We can't raise the dose for risk of depressing or even stopping your respirations."

She waved her hand. "No problem with that, Doc. Get this dying shit done."

Dr. Pearson stiffened. "Don't give me that, Commander. We don't expect you to die. We're giving you the best possible supportive care while the disease runs its course, which it will do. We can keep you physiologically stable, meaning IVs to maintain hydration, and keep your cardiovascular system functioning normally, protect your lungs from infection, and so forth. Within a day of our arrival in Guam, you'll be at the NIH getting the best possible care. You will recover."

"Recover for what?"

"For whatever lies ahead of you. You don't get to quit, Commander. I, for one, won't let you."

"Who elected you God?"

"Just give us...give yourself a chance. At the very least, we can make you more comfortable."

"Shoot, Doc."

"This ketamine will put you to sleep. Free of pain, your body will have more reserve to fight the infection, to heal itself. Unlike the morphine, this drug won't affect your respiratory drive."

"Sleep? How long?"

"We'll keep you down for as long as it's safe, based on your vital signs and other physiologic parameters. We'll have to wake you up eventually, but we plan to give you a good time-out from the pain."

"Do it, Doc."

"One precaution. This drug can cause vivid dreams, even nightmares or hallucinations. Most patients don't remember them, but they can be disruptive. If you get agitated to the point of affecting your breathing or vital signs, we'll have to wake you up."

Cricket shrugged. The conversation had become annoying. "Whatever. Just wanna sleep. Don't give a shit about nightmares. Get them all the time."

"Okay," the doctor said. "We'll start with a mild sedative." His voice projected in a different direction. "Please push two milligrams of midazolam."

***

Cricket plummeted through dark sky. Above her, a P-8 hurtled downward, flames and smoke spewing from its starboard engine, lighting up the sea that rushed upward at dizzying speed. Her body would break apart when she hit the water...

No parachute!

As she plunged within a few meters of the surface, the water rose in soft waves, like feathers that caught her and lowered her gently onto a cloud-like bed. The feathers tickled her cheeks and stroked her naked body in soft, slow arcs, making her skin tingle. Lee Young, dressed in flowing white, wielded the feathers—an angel whose aura emanated an ethereal glow. At once soothed and aroused, Cricket writhed in the soft bed. Lee kissed her lips and cheeks and whispered into her ear. "I will never leave you, Jess."

The bed rotated, dumping Cricket out of the softness, away from the glow. Again she fell, accelerating in a spiraling plunge into a dark, bottomless well. The blackness swallowed her, but she was not alone. Lee fell past her, out of reach. She disappeared into the black pitch beneath Cricket.

Now Cricket descended alone, inexorably alone.

Diabolical laughter arose from the darkness—wicked laughter that pierced her soul like molten daggers.

I am going to hell.

She descended through a sea of grotesque, pox-ridden faces, cackling, deriding, demonic masks that mocked her; first the tormentors from the torture boat, then Colonel Boo in his death grimace, and, larger than all, Kim Jong Un cackling and pointing at her as his face turned to hot crimson.

"Worthless whore. The Great Leader sentences you to horrible, agonizing death."

Cricket's skin burst into flames. She screamed.

A sudden cooling wind came over her, and her descent slowed into a velvety smooth deceleration. The voices, the faces, all gone.

Cricket drifted deeper into the well and made a sudden, unexpected hard landing on the bottom. Here, the well was close and narrow. Standing, she felt the walls close around her. Her head swam, dizzy. She braced herself against the wall to get her pants down. She slipped and fell onto a damp floor, soiling her white slacks. What would Eric and Nick think of her with stained pants? She struggled into a standing position, steadied herself against the wall of the well. But the wall gave way, and again she fell downward, downward toward oblivion.

Someone caught her. Gentle, caring arms cradled her head. Her eyelids opened and she looked straight into Lee Young's alluring face. She lifted her head and parted her lips. In an instant, Lee's lips were on hers. Their mouths locked and their bodies pressed together.

When they broke apart, Cricket gazed deep into the eyes of the woman—the woman who was not Lee!

Cricket gasped and fought to break free from the embrace, but she could not move.

The woman smirked, lowered Cricket to the floor, and disappeared. At once euphoric and distressed, Cricket slumbered on the cool tile floor.

Rough hands and crude male voices shook her awake.

"I'm sorry, Commander," Dr. Pearson said. "We had to stop the ketamine drip for your own safety because you became agitated. It sometimes happens. Sorry."

Awake, Cricket grabbed the doctor's arm.

"I want to live."

Chapter 57
USS Shenandoah (LCC 21). Philippine Sea

T ROY AND ROSE DECKERT sat next to each other in the top-secret communications room in the flagship's JWICS spaces. They had confirmed that
their consultant spoke by phone from a secure location and that he understood
the mandate for absolute secrecy.

"I am Doctor Vishwamitra Menon, head virologist here at the Centers for
Disease Control. I know about your very disturbing crisis, and I am authorized
to offer you the full support and assistance of the CDC."

Rose responded. "This is Captain Rosalie Deckert, United States Seventh Fleet
surgeon. With me is Lieutenant Commander Troy Pearson, medical officer for
USS Shenandoah, the Seventh Fleet flagship. We are speaking to you from the
ship."

"I am honored to meet you, Doctor Menon," Troy said. "You have an impres-
sive international reputation."

"Please, call me Vish," said the voice. "I suspect we will become quite familiar
with each other over the next several days."

"And we are Rose and Troy," Deckert said. "If I may add, sir, I had the honor
of meeting you during my infectious disease fellowship rotation to the CDC."

"I remember you," Dr. Menon said. "I regret our reacquaintance comes under
such stressful circumstances." He cleared his throat. "Perhaps we should get to
the heart of it. You have a patient with symptoms and positive PCR for smallpox
infection?"

Troy answered. "Yes, sir. If you would provide a secure e-mail address, we can
forward photos of the rash. It confused us in its early stages, but now seems

pathognomonic. We've repeated the PCR assay twice more. We now have three results positive for the smallpox virus."

Menon gave them a secure e-mail address.

Troy had loaded the images onto the top-secret computer in front of him. He drafted a quick e-mail to the virologist and pushed *Send*. A few minutes passed as the transmission cleared firewalls and encrypted nodes before the message arrived on Dr. Menon's secure computer.

"Looking at them now." His voice sounded strained. "Like you, I have never seen an active smallpox infection. But I must agree that these photos show the expected progression through the macular, papular, vesicular, and pustular stages. At each stage, the lesions all resemble each other. Without doubt, this is smallpox. What have you done so far, for treatment and containment?"

Rose explained how they had turned the female officers' berthing section into a quarantine area, vaccinated Squire's contacts and their contacts, and maintained strict infection control procedures throughout the ship.

Troy described their supportive patient care, and mentioned that they had administered the smallpox vaccine to Squire early in the course, after they discovered she'd not been vaccinated.

"Unfortunately," Menon said, "the vaccine may be effective in preventing infection in contacts, but it has no proven benefit in the post-lesional phase of the disease. Based on the extent of the rash before you made the definitive diagnosis, I doubt the vaccine will do much good for your patient."

"That seems to be the case," Troy said. "If anything, her course has advanced faster than expected."

"We're hoping for another option," Rose said. "In my research, I came across reports on an antiviral drug, tecovirimat, showed promising results in animal models of orthopox, which is related to smallpox. Primates infected with orthopox still got the disease," she said. "But all survived, and most experienced only minor symptoms, including less severe rash, reduced oropharyngeal virus shedding, and less toxic effect."

"Excellent," Menon said. "For obvious reasons, controlled clinical trials on humans with smallpox don't exist, but early safety trials indicate the drug is safe in humans. The FDA recently approved a clinical trial at the US Army Medical Research and Materiel Command. That study will include DoD personnel exposed to or infected by orthopox viruses or who have experienced serious complications from vaccinia inoculation."

Rose cut to the chase. "Can we get that drug here in the next twenty-four hours?"

Menon sighed. "I am painfully aware of the bureaucracy surrounding approval and use of experimental drugs. It is a long shot, but possible if you—we—can get the right people energized."

"Still a long shot," Troy said.

"One other consideration," Menon said. "How long has your patient been sick?"

"Depends on the definition," Troy said. "The prodromal flu-like symptoms started a week to nine days ago. This is day four of the rash, and it's already pustular." He frowned. "We thought at first it was chickenpox."

"Understandable, Doctor. Common things are common," Menon said. "The trials of which I spoke all introduced the tecovirimat within two to four days of clinical infection. We can't infer effectiveness beyond that window."

"All the more reason to go to general quarters," Deckert said, looking at Troy. "What other choice do we have, except to wait for the transport window from Guam?"

"Transport window?" Menon said.

"Sorry, we assumed you knew," she said. "Higher authority directed us to transfer the patient off the ship in Guam, from where she will be transported to the NIH Clinical Center in Bethesda. To be honest, I have serious concerns about that plan, but it came about way above my pay grade."

"When would that transfer occur?" Menon asked.

"At best, in two to three days," Deckert said. "Although a storm brewing to the southeast of Guam could affect the timing. Our ship is en route there as we speak."

After a long pause, Menon spoke in a firm voice. "That is a foolish plan."

Troy and Rose looked at each other, unable to hide their smiles at what they'd just heard.

"Not our plan," Troy said. "Dictated by higher authorities in Health and Human Services and DoD, maybe even the White House. We assumed the CDC played a role in the decision."

"Would it surprise you to learn that DHHS and the CDC are as bureaucratic and stovepiped as the DoD?" Menon said.

"Can you help us articulate why it's a foolish plan?" Rose asked.

"First," Menon said, "at this stage of the disease, what is NIH going to do that you are not doing already? Second, by the time you execute the plan, your patient's fate will be determined. She will either survive or she won't, regardless of where she's treated. Third, when—not if but when—the news breaks, the American people may have, uh, difficulty accepting this deadly disease into their country."

Troy smirked. "We agree, Doctor, but the decision was handed to us as a done deal. Perhaps those factors were considered and dismissed in favor of higher priorities?"

Another long pause preceded Dr. Menon's next statement, words that struck a resounding chord in Troy's heart. "What priority could be higher than your patient's survival? Or the survival of others who may be infected but are not yet symptomatic?"

"You just articulated our own thoughts," Troy said. "To take it one step further, this new drug could alter not only her course, but that of other potential victims?"

"In my judgment, yes."

Troy looked at Rose. Her eyes reflected the brashness of what he was about to propose and inferred her assent. "Then we will keep her on board and treat her here. Vish, can we count on your help?"

"Mine and that of many others in the CDC. This is a national crisis, not just a military problem."

"Then we are decided," Troy said. "Persuading higher authorities in both our organizations will be difficult, but we must do it."

"Indeed, we must," Vish said. A pause. "Another issue: do you have any perspective on the source of your patient's infection?"

"None," Troy said. "Biological attack tops the list of possibilities."

"As you know," Menon said, "only two known stockpiles of smallpox virus exist. The infecting agent came not from the CDC. I am sure of that."

"Probably not from Russia," Deckert said. "North Korea is the most likely culprit, but we don't know how they could do it."

Vish responded, "Do you know about the 2014 incident, when forgotten vials of smallpox virus were discovered in an unsecured vault at the NIH? No harm came of it because the vials were unopened, but the embarrassment resulted in more stringent security."

"Your point?" Troy asked.

"We can't assume that the Russians' standards are up to our own. Perhaps...?"

"The virus got into North Korean hands from Russia? Seems far-fetched," Troy said.

"You have the first human anywhere in the world in almost thirty years with active smallpox infection. It didn't materialize from the atmosphere."

"Suggestions, Vish?" Deckert said.

"I have a counterpart at the Vector Institute, a Doctor Nikolai Orlov. I do not know him well, but we have met at scientific meetings. Perhaps he can shed some light. I will contact him."

"Most appreciated," Troy said. "Thank you, Vish. If there's nothing else to discuss, we need to get moving on this tecovirimat clearance."

"I wish you best fortune," Menon said. "Please call me anytime you need my help, day or night."

"You've already helped a great deal," Deckert said. "Good night."

Troy switched off the secure phone and turned to Rose Deckert. "Well," he said, "are you ready to take on the highest military and health authorities in the land?"

She smiled. "Beats sitting on our hands watching Cricket Squire die."

Chapter 58

USS Shenandoah (LCC 21). Underway, Philippine
Sea, East of Okinawa, Japan.

A FORMER MENTOR HAD once told Troy, "When in conflict, advocate for
the patient and you usually prevail. Win or lose, you will sleep better
knowing you did right."

In this conflict, the flagship medical team got a fortuitous assist from the
weather. The storm southeast of Guam intensified and became a threat to the
island. Although most meteorological models forecast a storm track veering to
the east, some variants predicted a Category 3 typhoon striking the US territory's
gut about the time *Shenandoah* would arrive. To avoid that eventuality—however
low the probability—and to steer clear of serious weather that could damage the
ship, *Shenandoah* would alter course due south, remain well west of the storm,
and then follow it into Guam. That maneuver would add two to three days to the
transit.

Troy Pearson and Rosalie Deckert took advantage of the predicament to suggest an alternative course of action to the various agencies that had either direct
authority over them or played influential national security roles.

"In the best interests of our patient and anyone else who may harbor the
infection but not yet show symptoms," Troy said, "instead of transporting Commander Squire from Guam to Bethesda for treatment, bring the treatment,
tecovirimat, to the flagship through Okinawa."

In short order, the *Shenandoah* medical team got support from the chief of
staff and Vice Admiral Lassiter, who recommended the change to the Pacific Fleet
commander. There, the process met a roadblock in the person of the Pacific Fleet
surgeon, a Navy captain, protégé and confidant of the Navy surgeon general. As
Rose Deckert's superior on the medical side, The PacFleet surgeon refused to

deviate from the original plan favored by experts at the Bureau of Medicine and Surgery (BUMED) and approved by the surgeon general.

Deckert stood firm. "This is not like treating Ebola in a third-world country. With proper support, we can provide US-quality care here on the flagship without bringing the virus across our nation's borders."

When the haughty surgeon summarily dismissed her argument, she arced around him to the higher-ranking Pacific Command surgeon, Rear Admiral Miles Matteson. On the strength of Dr. Vish Menon's endorsement, the medical two-star admiral recommended approval of the plan to Rear Admiral Kate Mahoney, the PACOM operations officer, a former Seventh Fleet chief of staff, mentor and friend of Cricket Squire. She forwarded it to her boss, Admiral Darnell Lewis, the "supported" combatant commander in the Pacific. All other military commands, including PacFleet and BUMED, were cast as "supporting" PACOM.

Rose Deckert's end run effectively nullified any further pushback from Pacific Fleet.

Their medical plan encountered vigorous resistance at higher levels of military medical authority in the national capital area. Vish Menon encountered similar resistance on the civilian side. Much of the opposition seemed self-serving by clinicians and scientists who saw the opportunity to enhance their own reputations.

Disingenuous or not, the naysayers had strong political and personal connections at high levels of government and military hierarchy whom they could call into the fray. The ensuing debate would scuttle any chance of success by delaying action until it was too late.

Vish Menon won the battle on the civilian side on the strength of his unparalleled scientific prowess and fierce patient advocacy. The flagship team's CDC ally won the day when proponents of the NIH-transfer plan failed to establish credible or definitive scientific or clinical evidence that moving the patient 8,000 miles through the air in a portable isolation bag would give her any better chance of survival than establishing the same or similar level of care in her current location. Those in favor of transfer had to admit to low odds of survival under either scenario, but that the transfer option would be far more expensive, not to mention risky.

The added requirement to prepare for and treat any additional victims from the flagship, and the threat of inadvertent release of the smallpox virus into the US population, clinched the decision in favor of the *Shenandoah* team.

Navy medicine leadership, however, continued to resist. When the Navy surgeon general—the epitome of pomposity—demanded that the PACOM surgeon support the original plan, Rear Admiral Matteson declined. The bombastic three-star surgeon general then ordered the two-star PACOM surgeon to comply under threat of removal from office.

"I don't work for you, sir," Rear Admiral Matteson said to the highest-ranking physician in the Navy. "We are in combat status here, and I work for Admiral Lewis, the four-star PACOM commander. We neither require nor recognize your direction right now."

Rumor had it that after Rear Admiral Matteson hung up on him, the BUMED staff heard the Navy SG howl 100 yards down the corridor from his secluded office. Admiral Darnell Lewis, himself no fan of Navy medicine officialdom, supported his PACOM surgeon all the way to the Oval Office and his longtime friend, the commander-in-chief.

Once the opposition and roadblocks fell away, Troy Pearson and Rosalie Deckert witnessed firsthand the effect of the tip of the spear of the world's most potent military.

Within hours, and with the help of their new best friend at the CDC, their request to obtain the experimental, non-FDA-approved, proprietary drug, tecovirimat, for emergency administration to history's newest smallpox victim ascended through the chains of command of both the US Departments of Defense and State to the president's desk. By executive order, the commander-in-chief authorized the immediate procurement and most rapid transfer of the medication from the US Army Medical Research and Materiel Command at Fort Detrick,

Maryland, to USS *Shenandoah* in international waters off the Japanese island of Okinawa; in supply sufficient to treat all current and potential victims on board the flagship.

The order read, "To counter a known biological attack on the United States Navy that also endangers the health and welfare of citizens of the United States of America."

Five hours after the President signed the order, said citizens in the continental USA would awaken from their night's rest and begin their morning routines, oblivious to the life-and-death drama taking place on a haze-gray Navy ship half a world away.

Twenty-four hours after Troy and Rose's initial conversation with Vish Menon, a US military transport jet carrying enough tecovirimat to treat two dozen patients landed at Kadena Air Force Base, in Okinawa. The boxes of medication were rushed onto a waiting olive-green-painted HH-60 helicopter bearing the three-star logo of Commander US Seventh Fleet. The helo lifted off immediately for the short transit to USS *Shenandoah*.

Troy and two hospital corpsmen retrieved the package on the flight deck before the helicopter's rotors stopped turning.

In the ship's medical department, Troy and Rose opened the package, took out one of the several bottles of pills, and scrutinized the enclosed instructions. After securing the remaining medication bottles in a locked vault, they hurried down the passageway to the makeshift quarantine area, donned bioprotective gear, and entered Commander Squire's stateroom.

"We have the medication that we discussed," Troy said, out of breath.

She held out her arm. "Shoot away, Doc."

"It's oral medication. Do you think you can swallow these pills?" In his hand, he held three 200-milligram capsules of tecovirimat.

"One at a time, I can." She took each pill separately, swallowing with small sips of water. She pointed to her throat. "Burns like hell."

"We'll work to get you better pain relief," Troy said.

After she had swallowed all three pills, Commander Squire looked from one doctor to the other. "Now what?"

"We wait," Rose Deckert said. "And we hope."

Squire nodded, laid her head back on the pillow, punched the morphine release button, and closed her eyes.

***

Cricket came suddenly awake and raised her head. A startled corpsman approached her.

"Ma'am, are you okay?"

Cricket looked around. Her stateroom, not the filthy bathroom she'd seen in her most recent dream. "Get the docs."

The corpsman made a call, and within minutes, both Doc Pearson and the fleet surgeon entered the room, still donning their bioprotective gear.

Cricket half-sat up in her bed. "I know who did this to me."

Chapter 59
Seoul, Republic of Korea

I N THE JWICS CONFERENCE room at US Forces Korea headquarters, Eric
Mikleson and Mark Gunderson listened to one side of Vice Admiral Lassiter's
top-secret conversation with Admiral Darnell Lewis, PACOM commander.

"Nothing new here, sir," the admiral said. "The docs got their gear from Oki,
and *Shenandoah* made the turn south to stay west of Guam. Monitoring that
weather picture." She paused, listening. "We're about to get a medical report from
the ship."

Another pause. "Yes, sir, I will let you know as soon as we know. I will tell them
that, sir. I'm sure she'll appreciate it. Aye, sir. Good day, Admiral."

She switched off the phone as the secure video monitor screen came to life. In
seconds, the chief of staff, fleet surgeon, and ship's doctor all appeared.

"Good morning, ma'am, Captains," the COS said.

"Good morning, y'all," the admiral said. "Before you get to your brief, I just
talked to Admiral Lewis. He asked me to pass on his personal warm regards to
Commander Squire."

"Will do," the fleet surgeon said.

"How's our patient doing?" the admiral said. "And is anyone else on the ship
sick?"

The fleet surgeon answered, "No one else is sick, but it may be too early. I'll let
Doctor Pearson brief you, since he's the one who requested this meeting."

"Commander Squire appears stable," the ship's doctor said, "although that's a
relative term. She's suffering from the smallpox rash, which is quite painful. No
signs of secondary organ involvement. If we can keep her physiologically stable,
she's got a decent shot at surviving this."

The admiral frowned. "Does she want to survive? Given the handicaps she'll have for the rest of her life? Last we talked, you said she'd about given up."

"She wants to live now, ma'am." He paused, then leaned forward. "That leads into the main reason for this brief, and why we wanted it in person, verbal only, instead of risking messages that others might see."

"Go on." The admiral spoke in a concerned voice.

"Commander Squire remembered a Korean woman in the bathroom at the US/ROK function in Donghae. The woman resembled a former lover." He paused. "They, uh, swapped spit."

Silence filled the room as the group digested what the physician had just said. Admiral Lassiter broke the silence. "From a medical standpoint, could that have been the source of Squire's infection?"

"If the woman had active smallpox, yes, ma'am," Captain Deckert said.

"How would that woman have the infection?"

"We don't know, ma'am," Doc Pearson said. "We've seen no evidence of smallpox in Korea; North or South. But it's the most plausible explanation so far."

Eric felt as if he'd just been told that a nuclear warhead careened toward the Seventh Fleet flagship. On the periphery of his mind, he saw a shadowy image, unidentified but dangerous.

"Confirm for us," he said, "that the only known repositories of smallpox virus are in the United States and Russia."

"That's correct," the fleet surgeon said. "Specific to North Korea, after our destruction of their biological weapons lab, we see no credible chance that they could possess smallpox, much less the means to weaponize, transport, and disseminate it." She paused, hesitant. "Unless one used a human vector. A carrier. The woman who kissed Cricket Squire in the bathroom may have been a vector." She paused. "That still begs the question of how that vector got infected."

The shadow on Eric's peripheral consciousness burst into light: the *Eastern Dream* ferry moored in Donghae when *Shenandoah* arrived for the port visit. He turned to the admiral.

"Russia," he said. "They got it from Russia."

"Sonofabitch," the admiral said. "A deliberate, premeditated attack on the flagship with a biological weapon. That's what KJU was yammering about!"

"Except we can't prove any of it," Mark Gunderson said.

The admiral glared at Eric, her eyes on fire. "You get that evidence, Eric. You get it good, and soon."

Then she turned to Mark. "You work out a plan to nail that devil once and for all. I want to see him roast on a spit like the hog that he is."

Louise Lassiter's gaze pierced each of the other officers, including the faces on the monitor. "Hear this, y'all, and hear it good. This thing does not happen."

She slammed her fist on the table. "The forward-deployed naval force does not suffer bioterrorism. Not on my watch. Never." She stood. "Questions?"

The Seventh Fleet commander didn't wait for an answer. She turned and stormed out of the room.

Chapter 60
Seoul, Republic of Korea

"WE SHOULD MOVE INTO this conference room," Vice Admiral Lassiter said. "Look at all the time we'd save from walking back and forth to the lodge."

Eric ignored a mild headache as he and Mark Gunderson chuckled on cue at the admiral's attempted wit. At least her temper had settled since the news implicating North Korea's potential role in the crisis.

The three waited in the US Forces Korea JWICS conference room for another impromptu video teleconference connection to *Shenandoah*. The admiral appeared tired and wan, but as engaged as ever.

She regarded Eric. "You feelin' okay, Eric? You look a little peaked."

"Nothing that two solid days of sleep couldn't cure, ma'am. The walks back and forth are the only exercise we get, so I'd just as soon keep doing them." He hoped he sounded more convincing to her than he did to himself.

A few minutes later, the video teleconference started without the usual greetings. Captain Rose Deckert got straight to the point. "Admiral, we have another disturbing issue. A half hour ago, I received a secure message from the Eighth Army surgeon in Seoul. A KATUSA officer assigned to the USFK staff has taken ill with a flu-like illness. This morning he presented to the Army hospital in Yongsan Garrison with an unusual rash, for which they quarantined him. At my request, the surgeon sent photos. The rash resembles what we saw on Commander Squire early in her illness."

The admiral clenched her hands together and shook her head. "Well, that's that. They've attacked the Army and the ROKs. Time to bring the ROK military leadership into the game and tell them that both our forces are under attack."

She looked at the screen. "Y'all have anything else? How's the commander doing?"

"She's more comfortable," Doc Pearson said. "Too early to tell if the tecoviri-mat is having any effect."

"Thanks," the admiral said. "Keep us posted."

She turned to Eric and Mark. "Let's get cracking. Bad news does not get better with age."

Twenty minutes later, Vice Admiral Louise Lassiter, Commander US Seventh Fleet, along with her intelligence and operations officers, walked into a secure room to brief General Cleavon Alexander, triple-hatted as Commander United Nations Command Korea (UNC), Commander US/ROK Combined Forces Command (CFC), and Commander US Forces Korea (USFK). In a few words, Lassiter described the apparent smallpox attack on the Seventh Fleet, USFK, the ROK army, and perhaps the Greater Seoul Metropolitan Area and the east coast of South Korea around Donghae—if not the entire peninsula.

At General Alexander's direction, General Choo Hyeong-Jin, the ROK deputy commander of Combined Forces Command, soon joined them.

Less than an hour later, the combined military forces went to full operational alert. The US and ROK chains of command ordered bases locked down, ships kept at sea, and non-secure communications with the outside world severed. This was all done under the guise of "a planned bilateral exercise to test CFC's rapid response plan."

Through Top Secret channels, the military and civilian leaders of both countries received briefs on the crisis. By early afternoon, the two nations' presidents conferred with each other. Understanding that the greatest threat to both health and public confidence existed on the Korean Peninsula, the crisis leaders concentrated their efforts there. This strategy would allow the US military to maintain its command-and-control function over the US naval forces. The combined US and ROK offshore forces could become the vital deterrent to the now elevated risk of North Korean aggression and serious incapacitation of the Combined Forces Command's ground combat power.

"This could be the precursor to a major attack," General Alexander said. "Weaken our ability to respond by deterring force movement on the peninsula because of this threat and cause panic among the citizens of South Korea. They can't do that to ships at sea."

"Assuming *Shenandoah* is the only one hit," said Vice Admiral Lassiter.

The National Command Authority (NCA)—the US President and the Secretary of Defense—agreed. As quietly as possible, they ordered an additional carrier battle group and other maritime resources, including the hospital ship USNS *Mercy*, to the East and West Seas off both coasts of the Korean Peninsula.

The doctors on board the flagship had requested *Mercy* as the ideal offshore quarantine platform should the disease spread on the Korean peninsula, *Shenandoah,* or other ships. Fortunately, the hospital ship was already in the Western Pacific conducting its biannual Pacific Partnership humanitarian and nation-building mission. All nonessential and non-US military personnel from non-governmental organizations and other nations' military units were off-loaded from *Mercy*'s current location in Vietnam, to be returned from there to the United States. The remaining military personnel would prepare the hospital ship to receive known or highly suspected smallpox victims from either the Korean Peninsula or other US ships.

Supplies of smallpox vaccine from the US Strategic National Stockpile and other sources were rushed to the area. A plan to procure and distribute tecovirimat soon followed.

Thwarted in their efforts to enter the limelight in Guam, the US civilian and military medical and transport teams that had arrived there in vain attempted to redirect themselves to Osan Air Base south of Seoul, to join forces with the US Air Force Fifty-First Medical Group to form rapid response and containment teams should any additional cases affect US or ROK military on the peninsula. The USFK commander rejected that idea as adding no discernible value to the response plan already in place and rehearsed many times throughout the years.

"No reason to reinvent a well-oiled machine," the crusty general said.

For his part, Captain Eric Mikleson, under a direct order from the Seventh Fleet commander, engaged with ROK and US military and civilian intelligence and law enforcement authorities to find the suspected human vector who had infected Cricket Squire. Adapting with fierce efficiency to his new role as both intelligence officer and detective, Eric acquired from the flagship a scanned image of the photo of Lee Yeong Nae in Cricket's stateroom. He reproduced and sent it out for wide dissemination.

"This is not the woman we seek," he said, "but it would be a woman of similar appearance, a half-sister. This premeditated attack targeted a specific victim, Commander Squire. We believe the vector to be Korean."

Eric thought about the woman who had walked past Nick Juel and him as they hurried to find Cricket in the ladies' room at the hotel. In retrospect, she resembled the woman in the photo.

If only we'd come for Cricket a few minutes sooner...

***

The hunt began in Donghae, at the Meridian Hotel, where local law enforcement showed the photo to employees and guests. A desk clerk and bartender had seen a woman who looked like the photo. The clerk confirmed she had registered as a guest the day before the US/ROK dinner as Min Kyung-Soon, a Seoul business-woman. She had departed during the night of the dinner, without checking out or paying her bill. She had left the room empty save for a black leather dress on the bed.

The woman we saw wore a black leather dress.

"What happened to the dress?" Eric asked the investigator who had called him with this information.

"They had it in the lost-and-found area," the investigator said. "We have procured it as potential evidence."

Eric's heart sank. "Did anyone touch it? Did anyone touch the actual dress?"

"Yes, I put it into an evidence bag myself."

"It may be contaminated. You need to find out who else touched that dress. Anyone who touched that dress is at risk and must isolate. You should get a smallpox vaccination as well."

The silence at the end of the phone showed the depth to which this news penetrated, and how naïve the investigative forces might be.

"It will be done," the man said. "We will keep the dress in the bag and await further instructions."

A search of hotel registries and local addresses in Seoul failed to come up with anyone named Min Kyung-Soon.

"She has to be here in Seoul under a different name," Eric said to the investigative task force. "She would target the headquarters here, starting with the KATUSA."

"We can't be sure the KATUSA officer has smallpox," someone said.

"Either way, we need to talk to him," Eric said.

Lying on the bed in the isolation room in the Brian Algood Hospital on Yongsan Garrison, surrounded by individuals in bioprotective suits, the young ROK Army officer looked terrified.

"I have the flu. What is all this?"

"You might not have the flu," Eric said. He held out the photo of Lee Yeong Nae. "Do you know any woman who resembles this one?"

The soldier's face went pale, and he turned away.

"No."

"He lies," Eric said to the ROK investigator who had accompanied him. "I know he speaks good English, but please tell him in his native language the consequences of not telling us the truth."

The man spoke to the soldier in harsh Korean. When he finished, tears streaked the young officer's face.

"Her name is Yo Ji-Min," he said.

"How do you know her?" Eric said.

The man shook his head. He spoke in a whisper. "We sometimes sleep together."

"Where does she live?"

The young man gave them an address in Yongsan-Gu.

"Fifteen minutes from here," the Korean investigator said.

"Let's go," Eric said.

Chapter 61

C RICKET RELISHED THE PRE-REVEILLE darkness and silence of her state-room. She cherished this alone time without the constant intrusion of corpsmen and doctors and their silly measurements and inscrutable jargon. Now that she'd committed to live, Cricket became impatient to get on with it. She understood that recovery would be slow and incomplete, but she yearned to be back in battery, taking the fight to the enemy and destroying him. Now she had her own personal enemy, not some generic regime or foreign army. Cricket knew whom to blame for her misery and for making her a threat to her own people. That man must pay the ultimate price.

Jessica Squire guaranteed it.

The ringing telephone startled her. The corpsmen had brought in a longer cord to perch the phone on a ledge in the bulkhead next to her rack. Cricket fought off the pain as she turned to reach the receiver.

"Hello?" Speaking no longer caused pain in her throat.

"Good morning, ma'am. This is Petty Officer Jones in main comms. Can you take a satellite call from a Rear Admiral Mahoney?"

Stunned, Cricket hesitated.

Kate Mahoney, calling me now? Am I dying after all?

In a few seconds, she recovered and said, "Yes."

"If you'll hang up the phone, ma'am, I'll patch the admiral through."

She hung up and pushed herself to a sitting position in the bed. Ten seconds later, the phone rang again.

"Hello?"

"Cricket, it's Kate." Her former mentor's voice sounded strained. "I hope I didn't wake you."

"Uh, good morning, ma'am. I was awake." She didn't know what else to say. Surprise, anger, and relief all bundled into one tongue-locking emotion.

"Are you well enough to talk?" Kate asked.

"Uh-huh."

"It's lame of me to ask, but...how are you feeling?"

"Like Satan himself fucked me. Ma'am."

"I'm sorry to hear that," Kate said. A tremor in her voice betrayed deep emotion. "I'm sorry about a lot of things, Cricket."

"Me too."

"I apologize for calling so early in your time zone, but it's my only chance today. I wanted to hear your voice, and assure you that the entire US Navy supports you in this fight. I lead that effort."

She paused, and Cricket sensed that Kate was fighting her own tears.

"I owe you that, Cricket. I owe you a hell of a lot more than that. We all do."

Cricket sighed. "No one owes me, Kate, least of all you. I put myself here."

"We will get you through this."

"You rescued me from hell once," Cricket said. "You don't have to do it again. I need docs now, not a fighter jock."

"You've got the best docs in the world supporting your medical team on the flagship. I know about the experimental drug, and I understand there's cause for optimism."

"Yeah, sure."

"Look, shipmate," Kate said, "I'm talking to you as a friend. I care what happens to you. No one wants you to get better more than I do."

"For what reason? Guilt for letting me come back to the flagship?"

Kate's voice turned edgy. "Has that bug invaded your brain? Is that why you think I called? To salve my own conscience?" After a long pause, Kate spoke in a flat voice. "Maybe it was a mistake to call. I'm sorry."

"Wait," Cricket said. "I'm sorry, Kate. I know better."

After another pause, Kate said, "You're not all wrong either. I keep thinking that if I had blocked your return to the fleet, you'd be well today."

"No one was going to stop me from coming back, and no one could predict this shit. It's not anyone's fault."

"I believe that." Kate gulped. "I called to tell you I care about you, and I love you as a friend."

Second shipmate to declare love for me.

"I know." Without warning, Cricket sobbed. "You should see me, Kate. Ugly boils cover my whole body. My joints ache. I have crappy vision. Even if I live, I won't ever recover. I'll be crippled and covered with scars. I'll never fly again, never make love again, never feel whole."

"I get it," Kate said. "I intended to visit you in person, but the docs and higher command forbade it. If I were with you, I'd hold your hand and talk about your inner strength and beauty that no one knows better than I do. I would tell you to believe, that strength and courage can get you through anything."

Cricket chortled through her tears. "I would tell you to fuck yourself. Ma'am."

Kate laughed, then turned serious. "Don't give up on us, Cricket. Don't give up on yourself."

"That's what Eric said."

"Take that to heart. You are loved. Whatever happens, whatever your physical condition when this is done, you have friends who will stand by you. Always."

"I have one good reason to live," Cricket said. "To snuff out the monster who did this."

"You'll get plenty of support on that front, not only from Eric and me, but from the entire chain of command. Count on it."

"That's my drive to live. I appreciate everything you've said, Kate." She paused. "I love you back, by the way. But the fire in my belly right now is to see that bastard rot in the same hell as me."

"Whatever it takes, my friend."

A knock on the door heralded the two corpsmen who would tend to Cricket's morning care. She waved them away. "I'll be another minute."

"Sounds like you have company," Kate said.

"It's just the medics to administer the morning torture. I told them to wait."

Kate sighed. "Hang in there, Jess. Remember what I said. We all love you, and we will nail that asshole."

"Thanks...friend."

"Always," Kate said.

The call disconnected. Cricket lay back on her rack and stared into the middle space.

I can do this. One moment at a time.

She called for the corpsmen to enter the room.

Chapter 62

Seoul, Republic of Korea

E RIC AND THE INVESTIGATIVE team stopped in front of the locked apartment door to don bioprotective suits. Once dressed, Eric nodded to the two Koreans and two other Americans.

The ROK police officer unlocked the door and pushed it open. The fetid stench of decaying flesh drove the party away from the opening. By agreement, the ROK Army investigator and local Seoul police officer entered first, followed by the US Army official, the US embassy representative, and finally Eric.

As a senior Navy captain and intelligence officer, Eric didn't need to be there. But he wanted to see the scene for himself, to help him understand the course of events, and maybe to recognize the woman he'd seen in Donghae.

In the dimly lit one-room apartment, they traced the foul odor to the bed. There they viewed the woman's body, her skin pocked from head to toe with scabs and old pustules. A Type 70 pistol lay on her upper chest. Black and gray viscous goo saturated the pillow beneath her shattered cranium.

The ROK police officer guessed the time since death and articulated the obvious cause. "Gunshot to head. Self-inflicted. Maybe two days ago." He spoke into a radio, no doubt reporting the discovery and requesting support.

Fighting nausea, Eric studied the dead woman's frozen face. He held the original photo of Lee Young next to the corpse's head, but the extensive disfigurement from both the pox, gunshot wound and death mask made exact comparison impossible.

"Has to be her," he said to no one in particular. "This woman is the human vector who infected Commander Squire and the KATUSA officer with smallpox."

Who is she, and from where?

A polite but intense discussion ensued about which agency of which nation would assume custody of the body and take the lead on the case. The ROKs argued that the woman was a Korean who had died on South Korean soil, so she belonged to the ROK authorities. The Americans declared her as the primary suspect in a biological attack on US forces in Korea, and therefore ROK authorities should turn the body over to US authorities as a deceased enemy combatant.

Just as the conversation escalated from cordial to tense, two other men in bioprotective gear entered the room and demanded silence, one in Korean and the other in English.

The Korean man addressed his countrymen in sharp tones. He showed them credentials and an official document.

The American pulled Eric and his colleagues aside. First, he displayed his own credentials as a senior CIA agent, and then a document, signed by the US ambassador and the president of the Republic of Korea, remanding custody of the body and crime scene to the joint authority of the ROK National Intelligence Service and the US Central Intelligence Agency.

"You all can leave the scene," the CIA man said. His tone made it not an invitation, but an ultimatum. The ROKs who had come with Eric received a similar command. They were already heading out the door.

Eric stood his ground. "This is a matter of grave import to the mission of the combined military forces, not only in South Korea but throughout the Western Pacific. This woman is an enemy combatant. At the very least, we must take part in the investigation."

Even through the visor of the bioprotective suite, the CIA man's steel-gray eyes pierced Eric. "Leave now, or I will arrest you."

Eric stared back at him for a few seconds and then moved toward the door. "This is not the end of it."

Chapter 63
USS Shenandoah (LCC 19). Underway, Philippine Sea

WHEN THE CORPSMEN HAD finished Cricket's morning care, Doc Pearson came in to administer the second dose of tecovirimat.

"You look maybe a bit better today," he said.

"Could you be any more ambiguous, Doc?"

He ignored the rebuke. "How do you feel?"

She shrugged. "Throat not sore. Head hurts again. Blurred vision, unchanged. Joints still hurt. Skin still burns. One better, one worse. Guess that's a standoff, eh, Doc?"

"We'll take a standoff for now. Let me examine you before we do the pills."

When he shone a penlight in her eyes, he frowned. She didn't actually see him frown, but she sensed it. Cricket blinked, trying to clear what she thought was mucus film from her eyes. The doctor and the rest of the scene in front of her appeared foggy.

Pearson stepped back and held up his hand. "How many fingers do you see?"

Cricket squinted. "Three."

"Now."

"One."

"Now."

"Five."

"Now."

"None."

"You get a hundred percent on gross vision," he said. "Let's see if you can read."

He took a card from his pocket and held it in front of her. Through the blur,

Cricket recognized an eye chart. "What's the best line you can read?" the doctor asked.

Cricket shook her head. "None. Maybe the big E on top, but that could be my Navy pilot memory. I've seen a few of those charts in my time."

Pearson turned to the corpsman. "Call down to medical for fluorescein strips and a Wood's lamp." He turned back to Cricket. "Let's get the pills into you." He handed her the tecovirimat tablets, one at a time. She swallowed each with a chaser of water.

"Throat does feel better," she said.

When the requested supplies arrived, Pearson wet two thin strips of orange-dyed paper with saline and then applied drops of the resulting liquid into the corner of each of Cricket's eyes.

"Blink," he said. The corpsman turned off the stateroom light. In the darkness, Pearson shone a purple light into her eyes, grunted, and then asked the corpsman to switch the room light back on.

"You have early ulcerations on each cornea," he said.

She squinted at him. "What's that mean?"

"Pockmarks and scratches on the surface of your eyeballs, indicative that the virus has invaded there."

"Will it blind me?"

He shook his head. "Not necessarily. The drug will help, even though the corneas get less blood supply than other parts of the body. They should heal. Like with everything else right now, we'll just have to wait and see."

"Cute pun, Doc," Cricket said. Through the haze in her vision, she sensed his chagrin.

"I didn't mean..."

"Lighten up, Doc. I was yanking your chain."

"Nice to see the sarcastic wit again," he said in a smiling voice. "A positive sign."

Once assured she was comfortable, the medical team left Cricket alone with her thoughts. The ballooning pain in her head had worsened through the course of Doc Pearson's exam. She had trouble thinking through the pain, so she pumped morphine into her IV and lay back.

Cricket tried to focus her mind on the recent conversations with Kate Mahoney and Eric Mikleson.

I am loved; they say. How do I deserve such friends? How do I...

The half-formed thought hovered in Cricket's mind as the warm waves of morphine salved the ache in her head. She raised a heavy arm as if reaching for a coherent thought, but the arm dropped to the mattress. Her body weight seemed to double, and she slept.

Sometime later—minutes or hours?—Cricket awoke to a basketball inflating inside her skull. She groaned and opened her eyes, but saw only shadows. Was someone in the room? She could not make her head turn to look, and her arms and legs did not respond to her mind's commands. The pressure inside her head worsened, and the room seemed to close in and crush her.

Just as she felt her head would explode, she pushed hard on the trigger for the morphine drip.

Within seconds, the narcotic flushed the pain from her brain, and she drifted into a deep coma. Her mind, rendered defenseless by drug and disease, succumbed to unfettered visions.

Five-year-old Jessica Squire looked with terror on her father's agonized death mask the night he succumbed to a cancer that had slowly, relentlessly defeated his body. Then Cricket Squire stared at her own death mask, grotesque, scabbed, contorted in agony as the malignant virus squeezed out her life, one millimeter at a time. Finally, she was just Jess, banishing the dark shadows with a light that brightened within her.

Seconds later, the subconscious images disappeared.

All that remained was a deep, eternal void.

Chapter 64

ONE DECK BELOW IN the JWICS compartment, Troy and Rose Deckert discussed the latest news from the Korean peninsula via VTC with Eric Mikleson and Mark Gunderson.

"Now that we know the immediate attack vector," Troy said, "we have to stop investigating? We can't trace back to the origin? How stupid is that? The entire world could be at risk."

"Way above our pay grades," Mikleson said. "Above both admirals' pay grades, too."

"What do we do now?" Deckert asked.

Mark Gunderson replied. "You take care of your patient and you prepare to execute your contingency plan if anyone else gets sick."

"That includes strategic communications and managing the message," Eric said.

"That's asinine," Rose said. Troy had never seen her more agitated. "This is a public health emergency of potentially massive proportions. We have an entire army of infectious disease experts, clinical epidemiologists, and preventive medicine specialists at our disposal to find the source and mitigate the effect, if not actually eradicate the threat."

"According to higher authority," Eric said, "You have an isolated case of illness resembling smallpox, which you will continue to manage as you have done so far."

Now Troy waxed livid. "What about the KATUSA soldier in Seoul? What about the dead Korean woman?"

"What KATUSA?" Eric said. "The ROK Army remains responsible for KA-
TUSAs, just as the ROK authorities manage local deaths of Korean citizens, from
whatever cause."

"Whitewash and sellout," Rose said. "I can't believe you support it. Don't they
see it's war?"

"We don't support it," Eric said. "Did I mention way above our pay grades?
Our most important mission now—your most important mission—is to get
Cricket Squire healthy. Lose her and we lose the war."

"Meanwhile, we'll keep pushing the noodle uphill here," Mark said.

The VTC ended, leaving Troy and Rose to stare at each other, not believing
what they'd just heard.

An enlisted cryptologist entered the room. "Excuse me, Doctors," she said.
"There's a corpsman outside asking for you. He says it's urgent."

They rushed out of the JWICS. In the passageway, they found an ashen,
wide-eyed corpsman.

"Commander Squire is unresponsive."

Minutes later, both doctors in bioprotective gear hovered over Commander
Squire. She seemed asleep, but did not awaken to their voices or to vigorous
shaking. Troy pressed his thumb into the small space between her eyebrows.
Nothing. He twisted two of her fingers around each other. Nothing.

"Not responding to deep pain," he said.

Deckert moved him aside. "No time to be bashful, Troy." She reached under
the hospital gown, pinched Squire's right nipple between thumb and forefinger,
and twisted it hard. The patient's face grimaced, and she made a weak effort to
turn away from the stimulus.

"Responds to actual deep pain," Deckert said. "If this were a male patient, you
wouldn't hesitate to squeeze his balls."

Troy ignored the rebuke. "Someone's still home inside that head." He shone a
penlight into his patient's eyes. "Pupils react, sluggish." He turned to the corpsman. "Show me the medication record."

The young man did as ordered. "If anything," Troy told Rose, "she's under-medicated, given her high tolerance. So it's not from the morphine."

The doctors raised each of Squire's arms and legs above the bed and then let go. Each extremity dropped to the surface, with no effort by the patient to stop them. Troy held the commander's right arm about a foot over her face and then let go. The arm fell, and the hand smacked her forehead.

"Motor function absent," Troy said. "Flaccid."

"So," Deckert said, "normal vitals and respiratory rate, unresponsive except to deep pain, pupils react, no signs of cranial nerve dysfunction, flaccid paralysis with no lateralizing signs. Generalized coma, but why?"

The corpsman interjected. "Sir, ma'am, she had a temperature spike an hour before she went unconscious. I gave her some liquid Tylenol, which seemed to handle it."

Troy scratched the mask over his face. "I'm thinking viral encephalitis."

"Most likely," Rose said in a hollow voice.

"Her chances of recovery just plunged below fifty percent," Troy said.

Rose sighed. "Yep. Now what?"

"Best possible supportive care and hope her body cures itself. All we have left."

Troy looked at the mechanical ventilator they had on standby in case their patient developed respiratory difficulty. He turned to Rose with hope in his eyes. "Let's see if we can get in touch with an intensivist on the secure phone. Consider putting her completely out, general anesthesia, where we control all her vital functions."

"Do we have that skill?"

"We have nothing else. If it is smallpox encephalitis, it will compromise her breathing. She already sounds stertorous, like she's snoring. If her respiratory drive gives out, she'll become hypoxic and either die or suffer permanent brain damage. Best hope we can give her is to keep her brain cells oxygenated."

"I agree," Rose said. "No other choice, except the 'transport from Guam to NIH' idea." The weather storm had passed east of the island, without adverse effect. The medical team from the United States stood by at Anderson Air Force Base, hoping the plan would change again.

Troy glared at Rose with a look that could have caused her to dissolve into random molecules.

"No way."

Two hours later, they returned to the commander's room, frustrated and angry. With considerable effort and loss of valuable time, they had initiated a secure phone call with an intensive care specialist at Tripler Army Medical Center in Hawaii. Without listening to the entire clinical scenario, the haughty colonel had interrupted Troy's case presentation to rebuke him for considering "heroic" measures on a Navy ship; with a low likelihood of success.

"You need to get her to a proper care environment."

Troy had held his ground, insisted on recommendations for ventilator settings, medication dosages, and the like, and then politely thanked the man for his service and dedication to his nation.

Cricket's condition had worsened in the interim. Before beginning treatment, Troy spoke to the small group he'd crowded into the room: Captain Deckert and four trusted corpsmen.

"This room is now an intensive care unit, and our patient is critical. Captain Deckert and I will spend as much time here as we can, given our other responsibilities." He focused on the four corpsmen. "Two of you will remain in the room at all times to provide constant monitoring and attention. Twelve-hour shifts."

He gestured toward Commander Squire. "Please keep this one thought foremost. Here lies an American hero fighting for survival against a ruthless invader. We can and will help her win. We may not be taking enemy fire in here, but make no mistake, we are at war. This is the pivotal battle in that war. Defeat is not an option. Do you understand me?"

All nodded, including Rose Deckert.

Troy addressed the corpsmen. "We're going to put the commander into a coma so that her body can fight the encephalitis while we support her vital functions. We must keep her blood pressure, pulse, respirations, and—most important—oxygenation as close to normal as possible. That will require constant vigilance. In short, her life-or-death outcome depends on us and the quality of our care."

He looked at each corpsman in turn. "Questions?"

None.

Troy planned a rapid sequence intubation to secure Commander Squire's airway. The procedure began with a corpsman strapping a mask over her face to administer one hundred percent oxygen for three minutes. Then Troy ordered a sedative to relax her pain response, followed by the same ketamine dose that he'd given before, and then an anesthetic agent called propofol.

The next part would be the most dangerous and tricky. Holding a laryngeal mask airway, or LMA, at the ready, Troy gave the order to paralyze the patient with succinylcholine. The corpsman pushed the requested drug, and Troy watched the fine tremors of quivering muscles course through Commander Squire's body.

When the tremors stopped and she became flaccid again, he asked a corpsman to hold pressure over the cricoid cartilage just below the larynx ("Adam's apple") while he slid the elliptical mask end of the LMA into her throat and past the hard palate, pushing gently until the mask came to rest just above the larynx, plugging the esophagus. He inflated the cuff through a small inflation tube and then hooked the protruding end of the LMA to the ventilator. They now had a closed passageway to pump oxygen-enriched air from the ventilator directly into the patient's lungs. The oxygen would cross the alveoli of her lungs into the bloodstream and go straight to her brain cells.

As he stepped back to allow the corpsmen to tape the airway in place, Troy felt the sweat drench him beneath the bioprotective suit. He was terrified.

What the hell am I doing?

With trembling fingers, Troy started the propofol drip and went over the orders for the ventilator settings, anesthetic drip, and physiologic monitoring with the corpsmen and Captain Deckert. Since the commander could initiate her own respirations, the ventilator would assist rather than control her breathing. Confident that all understood the game plan, Troy sat down with the two corpsmen who would take the first shift to watch and wait. The other two corpsmen went off to get some sleep. Captain Deckert headed to the flag spaces to brief the COS and then contact Captain Mikleson in Seoul.

Alone with their patient, neither Troy nor the two corpsmen spoke. All three stared at the commander and the rise and fall of her chest in rhythm with the ventilator's audible cycling between inspiration and expiration. She looked more at peace than she had since first taking ill.

Lord only knows what's happening in her head.

Chapter 65
Seoul, Republic of Korea

E RIC ATTRIBUTED THE HEADACHE and back pain to his generalized fatigue and frustration. The digital clock on the wall of the SCIF read 0300 local in South Korea, 1600 in Washington, D.C.

As the operational tempo intensified after the definitive diagnosis of smallpox in Cricket Squire, Vice Admiral Lassiter seemed to hold up better than Eric and Mark Gunderson.

The admiral switched off the TV monitor. "They have for sure weaned us off the cow. Not even a hind teat for us."

"Not surprised," Eric said.

They had just finished a secure VTC with the Secretary of Defense himself, along with the Combined Forces Command and Pacific Command leaders. The secretary had told them without rancor or equivocation that support for the ROK authorities' investigation of the smallpox outbreak in South Korea now rested with the Department of State and the CIA. The Department of Defense and US Navy would stand down any attempts to gather information, investigate the infections on the peninsula, or communicate with the ROKs.

The CDC had also been called off, deferring all medical support to the World Health Organization.

As for Seventh Fleet, the National Command Authority required absolute containment of the solitary infection on USS *Shenandoah*, resumption of maritime command and control in the Seventh Fleet area of responsibility, and continued lifesaving care of the ill commander.

"We look forward to reports every six hours, forwarded via your chain of command," said the career politician, whose sole military experience was a single tour as an Air Force enlisted man who never left the United States.

"Aye, aye, sir," Vice Admiral Lassiter had said. Eric reckoned the SecDef had caught the rancor in her voice, even over the secure telecommunications link.

The three officers seemed too exhausted to get up, leave the SCIF, and make their way back to the Dragon Hill Lodge for only a few hours of rest before they had to return to USFK headquarters to begin a "normal" day.

"What's our next move, ma'am?" Eric said.

"You heard the SecDef," the admiral said in a flat voice.

Eric pondered in the silence that followed. "Ma'am, you and I both know who's responsible for this."

"Duh," she said. "But how?"

"Does it matter? It's an act of war, for which the United States must retaliate."

"Not if we can't prove it." The admiral smirked. "You think those weenies in DC will take military action against North Korea based on, 'We know KJU did it 'cause he's a real bad man'?"

Eric spoke the foremost thought in his mind. "If Cricket dies..."

"Then KJU would be guilty of murder, but only if proven beyond doubt to an 'unbiased' international court."

The throbbing headache made Eric's vision fuzzy. "We can't let him get away with that!"

Louise Lassiter's eyes penetrated his. "Who do you mean by 'we,' Captain?"

He didn't respond. Deep inside, he knew the answer.

***

Four hours later, they were back in the SCIF. Eric watched the faces of the *Shenandoah* medical team appear on the secure VTC screen.

"Where's the chief of staff?" the admiral asked.

"He was up very late and not feeling well this morning," Captain Deckert said. "I advised him to get some sleep. We can back-brief him later."

"Y'all two docs should take your own advice," the admiral said. "You look like sun-dried cow pies."

"We're okay, ma'am," Deckert said.

Eric needed to cut through the small talk. "How's our patient?"

Doc Pearson answered. "Her vital signs and physiologic parameters are normal. We can't assess her level of consciousness while she's under anesthesia. We'll continue this course until midday, give her as much brain protection as we can. If she still looks stable, we may attempt to wake her up."

"Attempt?" the admiral asked. "You mean she might not?"

"Sorry, ma'am," Troy said. "Poor choice of words. We would lighten the anesthesia to assess her neurological status. We'll need to decide whether to put her back down for another twenty-four hours or accept that she's as good as she'll get."

"You mean give up?" Eric said, hot with anger.

"More like accept reality," Deckert said.

Eric blasted back. "You don't give up. Not as long as there's any chance she'll recover."

"We have no intention of quitting, sir," Pearson said. "We want her to survive as much as anyone does."

The admiral broke in before Eric could continue his rant. "You got anything else for us today?"

Captain Deckert responded. "Yes. Our CDC consultant, Doctor Menon, attempted to contact an acquaintance at the Vector Institute in Russia, a Doctor Nikolai Orlov. It gets strange. Someone at the institute told him that Doctor Orlov is away dealing with an unknown family issue. This morning, Doctor Menon learned from his sources that the wife and daughter are in Boston. The daughter is under treatment at Boston Children's Hospital for a brain tumor." She paused. "Doctor Orlov is not with them. The wife doesn't know where he is."

"What does your consultant know about this doctor?" Eric asked. "You said he's an 'acquaintance'?"

"He met the Russian doctor and his wife at an international virology symposium some years ago. Doctor Orlov is the most renowned virologist in Russia. I found an extensive professional history on Google. He's famous, or he was when Russia was part of the Soviet Union. He may have been prominent in the USSR's biological weapons development program at Vector."

"Sonofabitch," the admiral said.

Remembering again the *Eastern Dream* ferry in Donghae, Eric said, "Who else knows this information?" The admiral gave him a curious look.

"I'm not sure," Captain Deckert said. "I can try to find out."

Eric looked at the admiral, who gave him a barely perceptible nod. "You do that, Captain. See if your consultant can talk to the wife—off the record, as an acquaintance, not an official inquiry."

The fleet surgeon looked puzzled. "Will do, sir. I'll try to reach him before bedtime in the States."

As soon as the VTC ended, Vice Admiral Lassiter turned to Eric. "You know we should pass that information to State."

"What information?" Eric said. "There's no credible intel there."

Lassiter rendered a sad, sardonic smile. "If you get me court-martialed, I'll take you down with me. Feel me, Captain?"

Eric shrugged. "Moderation in the face of crisis is no virtue, ma'am." His eyes moistened. "This is for Cricket."

"I get it," she said. "You've got forty-eight hours."

Ten minutes later, Eric vomited into the toilet in the men's head outside the SCIF. He put the back of his hand to his forehead. The skin felt hot to the touch.

I *hope I have forty-eight hours.*

Chapter 66

USS Shenandoah (LCC 21). Philippine Sea, Underway to Guam

A FTER THE VTC, TROY returned to his office to study and prepare for the trial awakening of Commander Squire. Chief Martinez stepped in and closed the door behind him. The surgical mask that medical personnel were required to wear when seeing patients hung loose around his neck.

"Doc," the chief said. "We have a problem."

Troy looked up from his computer. The look on the chief's face triggered an alarm in Troy's brain.

"I need you to look at a suspicious throat rash in a patient I've put in the isolation room."

Troy hurried from his office, arriving in the isolation room ahead of Chief Martinez. He stopped at the door to don a surgical mask, gown, and gloves, then stepped inside. A female third class petty officer sat on the edge of the bed, her posture and facial expression communicating terror. She wore the standard Navy aquaflage uniform, with the name "Espiritu" over the right pocket.

"I'm Doctor Pearson," Troy said. "First, tell me how long you've been ill."

The young woman appeared to be in her mid-twenties. She spoke in a high-pitched, frightened voice, but barely above a whisper. "Almost a week." She swallowed hard.

"With what symptoms?"

The woman shook her head and pointed to her throat. "Can't talk."

Chief Martinez filled in the history to Troy. "We saw her a few days ago with headache, backache, low-grade fever. Kept her under observation for twenty-four hours per protocol, and she seemed to get better. We released her yesterday morning. Today she came back complaining of sore throat." He handed Troy a light. "You need to look at it, sir."

Troy looked in the petty officer's throat. Red blotches covered her palate. Most contained the telltale fluid-filled blisters. Troy reached out his hand. "Specimen tube."

The chief had it ready. Troy swabbed the sailor's throat, which made her gag.

"Sorry." He turned to the chief. "Get that into the LightCycler right away. And send another corpsman in here, please."

The chief left. The young woman caught her breath, then looked at Troy with wide eyes. "Is it...?"

Troy touched her arm. "Don't know until we get that test back. But we need to act like it is, just to be safe."

A corpsman entered the room, gowned, masked, and gloved, the same as Troy and the chief.

Troy said, "Draw the usual blood work, start an IV, give her Tylenol for discomfort, and keep her isolated in here. No one comes in or out but you, Chief Martinez, or me. Double up on the protective gear. Do not relax any precautions. Got it?"

The corpsman nodded.

Troy turned to the patient. "It will get pretty scary for the next few hours, okay? But we'll take good care of you, and we'll let you know the diagnosis as soon as we have it. Try to relax and let Petty Officer Campos here do all the work."

The ill sailor nodded, the fear in her eyes not the least assuaged. Troy started toward the door, then turned back. "One more question, Petty Officer Espiritu. What's your rate and where do you work?"

The sailor struggled to speak against the pain. "I'm an MS, mess specialist. For the last month, I've been assigned to female officers' berthing."

An icicle as large as a tree root stabbed Troy's gut. "Including Commander Squire's stateroom?"

The MS nodded.

"Did you have any interaction with her in the last week or so?"

"Once. I picked up her laundry."

The ice mass in Troy's gut exploded, shooting frozen shards throughout his body. "What did you do with Commander Squire's laundry?"

"Washed it," the sailor said. "In the ship's laundry room."

Troy bolted from the room, threw off his mask, gloves, and gown, and hurried from the medical department, up the ladder to the flag level, and down the passageway to the fleet surgeon's office.

A startled Captain Rose Deckert looked up from her desk. Troy grabbed her arm and half dragged her out of the chair. "We need to see the chief of staff now. I'll explain on the way."

"In the early days of our country," Troy told the chief of staff a few minutes later, "during the siege of Fort Pitt, the British gifted the Native Americans with blankets from a smallpox hospital. That caused an epidemic that weakened the natives and enabled the British to conquer the fort."

COS Santiago looked at Troy and Rose with sunken eyes, his gaze weary and pained. "You think that...?"

"We don't have the PCR results yet, but, sir, this woman has smallpox. She got it from handling Commander Squire's bedding."

"Which means...?"

Troy and Rose exchanged glances. "Which means," Deckert said, "that the ship's laundry is contaminated and that MS3 Espiritu may not be the only new infection."

The COS rubbed his eyes. He looked like he might faint.

"We need to quarantine the ship's laundry and any sailors who have used it," Rose said.

"We need to vaccinate anyone possibly exposed," Troy added.

The chief of staff waved them off with a dismissive gesture. "Just do it, docs. Whatever you need."

Troy rose from his chair, walked around the chief of staff's desk, and felt his pulse. He turned to Rose Deckert. "Weak and thready."

She winced. "Got it. I'll take care of the laundry issues."

Troy turned to the chief of staff. "COS, I need you to come down to medical with me. Right now."

"No way."

"Then I'll bring medical to you." He picked up the desk phone and dialed his department. "I need a corpsman with IV materials, normal saline, blood draw equipment, specimen swabs, and bioprotective gear in the chief of staff's office. Now."

When he hung up the phone, he felt as if the ship had plunged into the sea and that torrents of water rushed in from all sides.

Chapter 67

B Y DUSK, MEDICAL TEAMS had quarantined the ship's laundry and begun identifying and vaccinating sailors who had had contact with MS3 Espiritu. As expected, the petty officer tested positive for smallpox in the PCR results. They moved her to a stateroom across the passageway from Commander Squire's. They informed the admiral and Eric Mikleson in South Korea. Per Vice Admiral Lassiter's instructions, the ship released another OPREP PINNACLE message notifying the military hierarchy that the flagship now had a second confirmed case of smallpox.

No one suggested it would be the last.

With the admiral's concurrence, the doctors put the chief of staff on sick-in-quarter (SIQ) status and confined him to his bedroom, which was already ideal for isolation. Troy's examination revealed profound dehydration, mid-grade fever, and generalized symptoms of weakness. At best, the COS had allowed his workload to render him exhausted, undernourished, and fluid-depleted. More likely, he'd contracted a flu-like illness that had compounded the effects of work-related sleep deprivation and meal skipping.

At worst...

But Troy had found no rash for PCR analysis, and no other telltale signs of the smallpox virus.

Yet.

Night had fallen over the flagship by the time Troy, Rose, and the four corpsmen mustered in Commander Squire's stateroom for her trial off anesthesia. Six hours later than planned.

"Maybe we should wait till tomorrow," Rose said. "We'll all be fresher."

Troy thought about it. He'd made it his practice not to undertake any new therapeutic maneuvers after nightfall, except in emergencies.

Is this an emergency?

He reviewed Squire's clinical record since he'd last seen her. Her temperature remained normal, but her pulse rate and blood pressure had increased in increments to the upper limits of normal. Could this mean that she was trying to wake up, trying to fight off the anesthesia? He watched her ventilator-assisted breathing. She made her own respiratory efforts, not driven by the machine. He shone a light into her eyes, checking for pupillary reaction, but couldn't see any response.

Anesthetic effect?

"She's breathing on her own," he said, "and she's been under anesthesia for over twenty-four hours. We can't keep this up indefinitely. Her pupils don't react, so we may have her over-sedated. Let's lighten her up to where we can do a decent neuro assessment."

He looked around the room. No one, including Rose Deckert, dissented.

Troy reduced the intravenous propofol drip and noted a steady increase in Squire's respiratory rate. Her blood pressure and pulse remained steady. Checking her pupils again, he saw no response. A nipple twist met with no reaction to the pain. He reduced the IV drip rate further and waited.

No change. Once again, he reduced it.

"She's moving," a corpsman said.

Indeed, her hands and feet twitched.

Moving, or...?

Suddenly, Squire's body lurched as if to rise off the bed. The alarm on the ventilator blared as her rapid respiratory rate exceeded the safe value. Her body fell back to the bed and twitched all over in the typical jerks of a major motor seizure.

"She's seizing," Troy said. "Watch that airway, watch the IV." He increased the drip rate of the anesthetic, to no avail.

He shouted. "Midazolam, two milligrams IV push now. Watch that airway."

"Pulse ox is down to eighty," the corpsman said. That meant Squire was oxygenating her blood to only eighty percent saturation, as opposed to the desired ninety-four percent or better.

The seizure stopped, but Squire coughed and bucked against the LMA. Thick, white mucus filled the tube.

"Suction," Troy said.

He unhooked the LMA tube from the ventilator just as a corpsman handed him a flexible plastic catheter connected to a suction machine. Troy thrust the catheter tip down the tube and snaked it as far down as it could go. Then he closed his thumb over the side vent to activate the suction. Mucus rose into the catheter and spewed into the reservoir on the suction machine.

Troy repeated the procedure several times, stopping in between to reattach the ventilator and pump 100% oxygen into Squire's lungs. Once he'd cleared her airway of the mucus, he reassembled the ventilator connection and secured it.

"Pulse ox coming up," the corpsman said.

Troy would accept the ninety-four percent reading for now. But how long had she been hypoxic, starved for oxygen? Would her already compromised brain survive that insult?

As the sedative took hold, the patient settled down and her respiratory effort stabilized. Blood pressure and pulse had risen during the episode but seemed to stabilize as well.

"BP one-forty over ninety, pulse seventy, respirations eighteen," the corpsman said.

"Repeat every two minutes," Troy said.

"Pupils?" Rose asked.

Troy had been avoiding that assessment. With a penlight in his right hand, he raised both eyelids with the thumb and forefinger of his left hand. Squire's pupils were about four millimeters in diameter, which would be mid-position, and equal. Troy thought he saw a slight constriction in each when he shined the light into them.

He stepped back, let out a deep sigh, then took in a deeper breath. "That was close."

Troy explained to the corpsmen that a mucus plug, no doubt the result of the patient's continuous supine position, had blocked the tip of the LMA, causing respiratory distress and hypoxia. "To prevent that from happening again, you need to suction her often and roll her from side to back to side every couple of hours."

"BP one-fifty over ninety-eight, pulse sixty, respirations fourteen," a corpsman said.

"Sir, she's moving again," said the other corpsman.

Squire's limbs did not twitch or jerk as before, but moved with a semblance of purpose.

"Midazolam wearing off?" Deckert said.

"Probably," Troy said. "Let's watch for a minute or two, see if she's waking up."

"BP one-seventy over one-ten, pulse forty, respirations twelve," the corpsman said.

As if on cue, Commander Squire's body went into writhing movements, all four extremities twisting and reaching out into full extension, hands and feet curling outward. Then her back arched like an exaggerated yoga posture and her neck bent backward to where she seemed to look behind her.

Troy's heart froze.

Opisthotonos.

The body going into full, exaggerated extension was not purposeful movement. It signaled a brain in severe, life-threatening distress. Troy looked into her pupils; both were fully dilated with no light reaction.

"She's herniating."

Squire continued to writhe into rhythmic episodes of full extension as the swelling in her brain squeezed the putty-like cerebrum—or upper brain—down through the rigid shelf inside her skull known as the tentorium. As the upper brain crowded through the hole, the tentorium mashed her brain stem, the repository of vital physiology and life itself.

"Hyperventilate her." Troy dialed up the anesthetic drip rate. "Another dose of midazolam. Turn the respirations up as high as they go. Blowing off CO2 will reduce the swelling. Give her one-hundred percent O2."

He shouted at the others. "C'mon, people, she's dying here."

The scene became chaotic, everyone in hyper motion. Within minutes, the drugs took effect and the patient's abnormal movements stopped. She lay flaccid and unresponsive on the bed.

The room went deathly silent, save for the rhythmic clicking and whooshing of the ventilator. Despite the coolness in the room, Troy and his colleagues dripped with sweat.

"Okay," he said. "Let's do a careful reassessment. Start with vitals."

"BP ninety over fifty, pulse forty-eight, respirations..." The corpsman stopped and looked at the ventilator. "Ventilator reset to eighteen, but she's not tripping the machine, sir. Not breathing on her own."

Troy went through the motions of eliciting a deep pain response and got none, as he'd expected. Squire's limbs remained flaccid, with no discernible muscle tone.

"You have to look at her pupils, Troy," Rose said in a quiet, kind voice.

He took up the penlight and repeated the previous maneuver. He flipped it off within seconds.

"Dilated and fixed."

For the second time that evening, a gloomy silence descended upon the medical team, broken after a minute by the corpsman's monotone voice.

"BP eighty over fifty, pulse sixty, respirations still eighteen by the machine."

Troy glared at Rose Deckert. "We're not done. We don't quit."

He turned to a corpsman. "Get norepinephrine from the crash cart. We'll mix up a drip to elevate her blood pressure and pulse. Turn the respiratory rate up to twenty-four. We'll continue to hyperventilate, continue the propofol drip, maintain her blood pressure and pulse as close to normal as we can. Give her some time."

He looked across the room at no one in particular, a teary film over his eyes. "And then we'll see how she does."

Chapter 68
Seoul, Republic of Korea

E RIC MIKLESON STARED INTO the video camera in the USFK secure conference room. "You had this under control. How did she deteriorate?"

On the large LCD monitor, the faces of Doctors Troy Pearson and Rosalie
Deckert appeared larger than life-size. They exchanged looks, each expecting the
other to respond. Captain Deckert, the fleet surgeon and senior physician, took
the lead. "She experienced an acute insult last night as we weaned her off the
anesthetic drip."

Eric scowled. "Details, please. In English."

Doc Pearson found his voice. "Perhaps it will help if we summarize the events
of the last sixty hours, some of which you know. Early on, Commander Squire
appeared to improve after the first two doses of the antiviral medication, tecovirimat. Thirty-six hours ago, she developed altered mental status, meaning she
became unresponsive except to deep, painful stimuli. The most likely cause under
the circumstances would be viral encephalitis. The smallpox virus had invaded
her brain and posed a serious threat to her life or to useful recovery.

"We judged that her best chance of survival would require putting her brain at
total rest under light general anesthesia, also known as 'twilight sleep' or 'con-
scious sedation.' In short, we put her into a ventilator-assisted coma to allow her
body complete rest to divert all available energy to fight off the brain infection.
We intended to continue that treatment for twenty-four hours and then try to
wake her up so that we could assess progress."

"We know all that, Doc," Eric said, frustrated at the physician's long-winded
treatise. "Cut to the chase, please."

Doc Pearson frowned. "We had intended to wean her off the anesthetic yesterday afternoon, but the COS and the other new smallpox patient took priority. We didn't get back to Commander Squire until late evening. Her blood pressure and pulse rate increased, which might have meant she was recovering and trying to wake up. We gave her that chance, and gradually decreased the anesthetic drip, the propofol."

His voice broke. "As soon as we did that, she had a major motor seizure."

"Why?" Vice Admiral Lassiter said.

"We don't know, ma'am," Pearson said. "There are several possibilities, internal or external."

"Meaning you might have caused it?" Eric said.

Captain Deckert rose to her junior colleague's defense. "Or the virus, or the brain swelling, or hypoxia. We can't speculate about causation. It happened." She paused. "That's not the worst." She nodded to Doc Pearson to continue.

The younger physician gulped. "After the seizure, the commander showed signs of increased pressure on the brain."

He demonstrated with shaky hands. "The cranial vault is like a wooden box, divided in the middle on three sides by a shelf, called the tentorium, or tent. That 'tent' divides the upper brain from the midbrain and brain stem where the body's vital function centers live. The tentorium is rigid, whereas the brain has the consistency of putty. When pressure on the brain increases, it pushes the putty through the tentorium, a process called 'herniation.' If enough of the upper brain contents get squeezed through the tent, the brain stem gets compressed and its vital function compromised. Death or permanent brain damage often results."

The room had turned deathly silent during the doctor's explanation.

Vice Admiral Lassiter spoke the question on everyone's mind. "What are her no-bullshit chances for survival now?"

Doc Pearson hesitated. Captain Deckert spoke. "Less than fifty percent, ma'am."

"But not zero?" Eric said.

"Not zero," Deckert said, "but not good, sir. Her chances for a useful quality of life are very poor. We don't know how much brain damage she suffered."

Eric stood and leaned into the camera. He spoke through gritted teeth. "You do not give up on her!"

Louise Lassiter touched Eric's arm and gave him a look at once withering and empathetic. He sat. To the screen, the admiral said, "What are your plans, docs?"

Visibly upset, Doc Pearson answered. "We won't give up, ma'am. As long as there's a sliver of a chance that she'll recover a useful life, we will do all we can to save her."

Eric regained his composure. "Thank you, Doc. I apologize for my outburst. You all know how much Commander Squire means to us, to the fleet, to the nation."

Pearson nodded. "Yes, sir. We put her back on the propofol drip. We're controlling her respirations with the vent and maintaining her blood pressure with an IV norepinephrine drip. We hope to keep her in the optimal physiologic milieu for her body to reverse the insult. We plan to hold this course for another twenty-four hours."

"What are your options after that?" Lassiter said.

Deckert responded, "Only Commander Squire can tell us that, ma'am."

As the doctors relinquished their seats to the operations staff for the next portion of the morning brief, Eric excused himself. Filled with anger, grief, and nausea, he rushed out of the JWICS and down the passageway to the nearest men's head. In the first stall, he kneeled over the commode and vomited.

An enlisted sailor appeared by the stall. "Are you okay, sir? Should I call medical?"

Eric raised his head from the toilet, embarrassed. His head pounded. "I'm okay. Must have gotten some bad bulgogi last night. It will pass."

"You should go to the hospital and get checked, sir."

"Thank you, Petty Officer. I'll do that." Eric stood and pushed past the sailor. "Soon as I get the chance."

At the sink, he rinsed out his mouth and washed his face. The pounding in his head felt mild compared with the fire in his soul.

Cricket cannot die. That North Korean asshole cannot win.

Not a religious man by history, Eric bowed and prayed aloud. "God, if you are there, if you hear me, please, please let her live. This woman deserves to live. More than anyone. More than I do."

The words seemed empty. Eric stood and glared at himself in the mirror.

As God is my witness, if she dies...

Chapter 69

USS Shenandoah (LCC 21). Philippine Sea. Underway Towards Guam.

WHEN THEY LEFT THE JWICS, Rose Deckert turned to Troy. "Let's get coffee." Her tone reflected an order, not a request.

Troy followed her down the passageway and up the ladder to the flag mess. Breakfast hours had ended, and the mess crew had cleared the tables. Rose and Troy had the room to themselves. They sat across from each other at the end of a long table.

"I suppose this is not a social coffee," Troy said.

"We need to talk, About Commander Squire."

Troy pursed his lips. "How so?"

"You may have lost your clinical objectivity."

Too annoyed to answer, Troy stared into the middle distance.

"Look, Troy." He turned to her. Her face and body language seemed compassionate yet firm. "What's your therapeutic endpoint?"

"I'm not ready to quit."

"The right question is whether Commander Squire is ready to quit."

"Well, she's not talking to us, is she, Captain?" Troy fumed. "We must give her every chance."

"For what?"

"To live, dammit."

"Live for what, Troy?"

"We don't get to decide that."

Deckert took a long sip of coffee. "Okay, not for us to decide; but if she could talk, what would she want?"

"How the hell do I know?"

"Let's discuss her realistic chances for full recovery. What are they?"

Troy thought about it for almost a full minute. "Nil, if by 'full recovery' you mean continued service as a naval aviator. But is that the only way she would define her life?"

Deckert shook her head. "You need a heavy dose of reality, Troy. First, her odds of recovering from the latest insult are slim. We don't know how long she was hypoxic, but we do know she suffered some degree of irreversible brain damage. Second, we don't know what the virus itself has done to her brain, what cognitive ability she has left, if any. Third, before she lost consciousness, she had corneal impairment. That won't get better without a transplant. Fourth, the pox will leave her disfigured for life, and if her joints are involved, she'll be a cripple."

Rose pursed her lips and leaned forward toward Troy. "Now, can you tell me in good faith that Commander 'Cricket' Squire would choose that quality of life for herself?"

Tory folded his arms. "No matter the odds, we can't choose for her."

Rose shook her head. "You already have, Troy. By keeping her anesthetized on life support, you choose to not let her decide."

Troy did not respond.

"Consider your own motives," Rose said. "Are you keeping her on life support because you think she may recover, or because you refuse to accept defeat? Are you doing the 'macho' thing to show up that arrogant Army colonel at Tripler?"

Troy wanted to storm out of the room, but the sense that the senior physician spoke the truth quenched the fire as soon as it ignited.

Rose allowed him as much silence as he needed.

Finally, he spoke. "When she first came into medical, I blew her off. I thought she was seeking drugs."

"So?" Deckert said. "She had that history."

"I prejudiced the corpsmen against her."

"So?"

"I thought she had chickenpox."

"So?"

"If only I'd recognized the actual cause a day earlier…"

"If only you were God." Rose reached across the table and touched his hand. "Troy, you did not give her smallpox. You're not responsible for that."

Troy jerked his hand away. "I'm responsible for her current clinical state."

"You are not. Or did I miss the part where you made the virus invade her brain?"

Again, Troy stared into the middle distance. A feeling of doom flooded through him. He looked back at Rose with moist eyes. "It's not fair. Commander Squire, more than anyone, doesn't deserve this."

"I agree. But it's not for you or me to decide that."

"I thought we'd turned the corner with the tecovirimat, but then the encephalitis…"

"You thought *she* had turned the corner."

Troy sighed. "You're right. I'm too emotionally involved."

"Beats apathetic."

Troy swallowed the rest of the coffee. "We need to stop the propofol."

"Sadly, I concur." Rose looked at him with sympathetic eyes. "Maybe she'll wake up."

Troy smiled. "Wouldn't put it past her. She's surprised me at every step so far." The moisture in his eyes belied the smile.

Chapter 70

WEARING BIOPROTECTIVE SUITS BACK in the cluttered makeshift ICU that had once been Commander Squire's stateroom, the two doctors assessed no change in her condition since the pivotal downturn twelve hours earlier. Her vital signs, sustained by the ventilator and IV drip, hovered near normal. Her pupils remained large and nonreactive to light.

"The pupils could be from the anesthetic," Troy said.

"Might be," Rose said.

With the eyes of a plaintive puppy, Troy said, "Twenty-four more hours on life support after we stop the propofol?"

"Then we involve our favorite Army intensivist in the final decision."

Troy grimaced at that suggestion.

"You'll be glad you did," Rose said. "Share the decision. Spread the responsibility."

Troy understood. Whether Commander Squire lived or died, the post-event scrutiny would be intense. He nodded in assent as he reached for the pump controlling the intravenous propofol drip, double-checked to be sure he had the right one (the other controlled the IV solution maintaining her blood pressure), and with a final shrug of capitulation, shut it off.

Both doctors and the corpsman watched their patient as if they expected her to sit up and ask for breakfast.

Nothing happened. Fifteen minutes passed. Twenty. Twenty-five.

Troy examined her again. She remained unresponsive, even to a sternal rub and nipple twist. Her limbs were flaccid, with no hint of muscle tone. Her pupils remained dilated and did not react to light.

He turned to the corpsman. "Continue the vent, same settings, and titrate the norepi drip to maintain her blood pressure. Call me if you see even a hint of change."

The medic nodded.

Troy and Rose turned to leave. At the door, he took another look. Commander Squire lay still, the only movement the rise and fall of her chest as the ventilator cycled air into her lungs.

Fighting tears, Troy left the room.

After changing into fresh bioprotective gear, Troy and Rose checked on Petty Officer Espiritu. The young sailor sat up in bed, sucking on ice chips. The telltale red rash of early smallpox blossomed on her skin.

The corpsman in attendance gave a brief report. "She slept most of the night. This morning her vitals are normal, and she says that her throat hurts less. I just gave her the second dose of the teco, which she swallowed with only minor discomfort."

"How do you feel?" Troy asked Espiritu.

"Scared." A plaintive pause. "I don't want to die."

"Don't worry about that," Troy said. "The medicine is working. We expect you to recover."

"What about this rash?"

"You have smallpox," Troy said. "Your PCR test confirmed that. The rash will progress from red bumps to blisters to scabs. The medication should keep it to a minimum, but you will have discomfort. We'll try to diminish that. For now, it's important that you stay positive. We have every reason to believe you'll get better."

"Will the rash cause scars?"

"Too early to worry about that," Troy said. "Just keep holding good thoughts."

Troy and Rose left the petty officer's room, disposed of their bioprotective gear, and stepped through the watertight door that formed the barrier between the quarantine area and the rest of the ship.

A corpsman awaited them. "Sir," he said to Troy. "We have two more mess specialists in medical with the same presentation as Petty Officer Espiritu."

Troy looked at Rose. "Well, here we go. If you would check on COS, I'll see these new ones." He shook his head. "We'll see more before this is done."

Rose nodded. "I'll let you know about COS. Then I've got some fleet stuff to do. After that, I can help you out in medical."

They parted ways without another word.

Chapter 71

T HE TWO MESS SPECIALISTS Troy saw in the medical department had the same early findings of smallpox infection that Petty Officer Espiritu had shown the previous day. No surprise to him, since both also worked in the ship's laundry. He collected specimens for PCR testing and moved the two sailors to the quarantine area. He now had four patients with smallpox—five, if the chief of staff had the disease.

"There will be more," he told his corpsmen in an impromptu all-hands call in the treatment room. "Plus a horde of worried well. Continue to follow the protocol. Not everyone who presents with influenza-like symptoms will have smallpox, so you'll need to triage, contain, and isolate as we've outlined. So far, we have only two known sources of infection: Commander Squire and the ship's laundry. If we've been successful in containing those sources, and in protecting their contacts with the vaccine, we may still hold off a ship wide epidemic."

A voice at the door interrupted. "Sorry, sir, " a corpsman said. "Captain Deckert needs you STAT in the chief of staff's stateroom."

When Troy entered Captain Santiago's bedroom, he found Rose Deckert and two corpsmen hovering over the prostrate form in the bed. One corpsman was attempting an IV, while the other positioned a face mask attached to a tube from a portable oxygen cylinder. A blotchy purple rash spread over Santiago's arms, very different from what they had seen on Commander Squire or the two sailors in medical.

More frightening to Troy, the COS labored to breathe.

"He looks toxic," Rose said. "BP 90 over 50, pulse 110, respirations 24. Awake but lapsing in and out of awareness. And then there's this." She lifted the sheet. Large patches of the same deep purple rash covered the chief of staff's chest, abdomen, and legs.

Troy's heart sank. "I checked his PCR results before I came up here. Positive for smallpox. This must be..."

"The severe hemorrhagic form of smallpox," Deckert said. "One hundred percent fatal."

"But how? Why him?"

She shook her head. "He was run down and malnourished before he got infected. Maybe his immune system became too compromised to fight it."

"What do you suggest?" Troy asked.

"Full supportive care as best we can for now. You should get on the horn to Vish Menon. See if he has anything to offer, especially regarding tecovirimat." She paused. "And we need to tell the admiral."

Troy agreed. "Once we get the COS squared away here, can you call her while I talk to Vish?"

"Of course."

Troy looked at his watch. Only 1300, and already a day full of challenges. He pursed his lips. Just under twenty hours for Commander Squire to turn her own tide.

When Troy looked back at the COS, he saw a man already dead.

Troy walked through sick call on the way to his office to call the CDC. Sailors and officers waiting for exams lined both sides of the passageway. Most appeared healthy, at least on the surface.

The biggest drain on resources is always the worried well. But any of them could have the virus.

By the time he got through to Vish Menon, Troy felt exhausted in body and mind. To his dismay, the trusted consultant had nothing good to offer.

"The FDA just approved clinical safety trials for an IV form of tecovirimat," Vish said. "But we can't get any there in time to help your patient. Your only option is to crush the pills, make a slurry, and put it down a nasogastric tube directly to his stomach. Given his physiologic state, you may not get good absorption."

The silent pause said more than his words. When he continued, his voice sounded weary. "You must consider how to best manage your limited supply of tecovirimat. Your two recent cases probably represent another wave of the disease. Expect to see more new infections over the next few days."

Another long, disturbing pause. "Given the fatal nature of the hemorrhagic form, and that it's already progressed to this stage, I cannot advise you to treat your chief of staff with tecovirimat. You may later wish you had those pills to treat a new patient with better odds of survival."

"I get it," Troy said.

***

Troy donned bioprotective gear and reconvened with Rose Deckert in the chief of staff's bedroom.

Santiago's condition had deteriorated. Many of the purple patches had coalesced and turned black. He breathed in rapid but labored grunts. His eyes seemed to recognize the physicians, but any efforts to speak resulted in muted gibberish. Vital signs had not improved, despite a generous volume of IV fluids and 100 percent oxygen by mask.

Troy thought of Commander Squire's limbo state one deck below. He looked at Rose, his eyes almost pleading, and pulled her out of earshot.

"Decision time," he said.

She pointed toward the deck below. "His odds of survival are less than Squire's."

"He's the chief of staff," Troy said. "Any direction from the admiral?"

Rose scoffed. "This admiral knows better than to practice medicine. She said to use our best judgment."

"What's your call?" Troy paused. "The COS is your boss."

Rose stroked her chin. "In his place, I'd tell you to keep me comfortable and let me go."

"That's what I would want."

"Well, then," she said. "We have consensus."

Troy returned to the bedside, bent over, and spoke into Captain Santiago's ear, disregarding the usual protocol for addressing senior officers.

"José, you're very sick with the hemorrhagic form of smallpox." He looked for any sign of recognition. He saw none, except perhaps a slight increase in the man's respiratory rate.

Troy continued, "We'll do our best to keep you comfortable, but we have no cure. I don't know if you can hear or understand me, but I suggest you make peace within yourself and with whatever higher power you may have."

Rose spoke from behind Troy. "He's Catholic. We should call the priest."

The Seventh Fleet chaplain, a Catholic priest wearing full bioprotective gear, administered the last rites of his church to the stricken chief of staff. Three hours later, Captain José Santiago, United States Navy, succumbed to his disease and became the first fatality of the heinous biological attack on the US Seventh Fleet.

Troy Pearson made the formal pronouncement of death at 1713.

Less than sixteen hours left for Commander Squire to show signs of improvement, or she becomes our second fatality.

Chapter 72

WITH THE CHIEF OF Staff deceased, and the admiral and deputy chief of staff Mark Gunderson both in Seoul, the reality of who would assume operational control for the Seventh Fleet staff on board the flagship became problematic. By naval tradition, authority passed to the next most senior officer eligible for command at sea: Captain Cyrill Dusenburg, the N5 (Director, Future Plans and Operations), an arrogant submariner neither liked nor respected by his colleagues.

Both Troy and Kim understood he was no fan of Navy medicine.

For his first order of business, the new acting chief of staff demanded a complete accounting from the two physicians. This included an extensive inquiry—to a level of detail only an obsessive-compulsive nuclear submariner would require—into the entire history of smallpox and its potential use as a biological weapon, the diagnostic tools and rationale for treatment, the current status of Commander Squire and the other known infected personnel, the process for surveillance and containment, and finally—after two hours of discussion—the immediate issue of disposition of the chief of staff's body.

"We must consider the remains contaminated and contagious," Rose Deckert told her acting boss.

"Can't you dump it into the sea?"

Troy bristled. "Human remains, contaminated or not, deserve respect. We don't dump him like garbage."

Captain Dusenburg's eyes narrowed. "José Santiago is gone, Doc. The safety of this staff and crew is paramount. We don't have the luxury of empathy."

"We have a plan," Rose said, "consistent with existing protocol for deaths on board Navy ships. The galley staff will clear out one of the refrigerated storage lockers on the fourth deck. We can store the body there until we know when the ship will make port."

"Won't you contaminate the route from the second to the fourth decks, not to mention the reefer itself?"

"We have a protocol for that," Rose said. "We'll wrap the body in a plastic disaster bag, seal it with impermeable tape, and then enclose it in a second body bag. We'll take the most direct route from the stateroom to the reefer, and everyone involved in transport will wear bioprotective gear."

"Can't wait to see that on CNN," the acting chief of staff said.

"The plan is sound, sir," Troy said. "We can assure the safety of the staff and crew."

Captain Dusenburg waved his hand. "Fine. After I clear it with the admiral. If she concurs, you're good to go."

"Time is of the essence, sir," Rose said.

The captain glared at her. "I'll call the admiral right now. I hope that's soon enough for you, Doc."

He picked up the phone and then stared at the two physicians. They assumed they would take part in the conversation with the admiral, as they had been throughout the crisis.

"I'll let you know her decision," Dusenburg said in a curt voice. "You two have other things to do."

In the passageway after their summary dismissal, Troy and Rose faced each other. "If he expects to throw anyone's remains over the side like trash, he'll have to include me in the package," Troy said.

"And me," Rose said.

Fifteen minutes later, they were summoned back to Captain Dusenburg's office. The acting COS spoke with noticeably less arrogance. "The admiral concurs with your plan, and further authorizes you to manage the medical situation without need for her concurrence." He scoffed. "Or mine."

"Very well, sir." Rose did not quite hide her smile.

"Thank you, sir." Troy did not try to conceal his contempt for the man in front of him.

"For your information," the acting COS said, "the admiral ordered us to come about and return to MOD LOC off Okinawa, pending further direction from higher authority."

Troy and Rose exchanged quizzical looks. "Thank you, sir," Rose said. The physicians turned to leave.

"One more thing," Dusenburg said. "You're not to take Commander Squire off life support unless first cleared directly by the admiral." He raised an eyebrow. "Those are her orders, not mine."

"Understood, sir," Troy said.

Back in the passageway, Troy checked his watch. The time was 2100. Twelve hours until their self-imposed decision time for Commander Squire.

Unless the admiral has other thoughts.

Chapter 73

I T TOOK UNTIL 2300 for the medical team to clear out the last of the sailors seeking attention in sick call. About three hundred sailors, a third of the ship's total complement, had passed through the medical department. As Troy had predicted, most were not sick, but worried or frightened. Of the rest, the majority had symptoms not associated with smallpox. Some had gastrointestinal complaints, while others had common colds or similar minor ailments, wherein the index of suspicion for smallpox infection was low.

After Troy, Rose, and the sick-call corpsmen closed up shop for the night, they counted a dozen sailors in the inpatient ward with influenza-like symptoms awaiting further development or completion of PCR testing. Most would be returned to duty or confined to sick-in-quarters.

They had triaged two additional mess specialists to the quarantine area, making five known smallpox victims, plus Commander Squire, whom Troy insisted on counting separately. And the COS.

Seven victims, one dead, one clinging to life. No new sites of contamination on the ship. Maybe our containment strategy worked.

Together, Troy and Rose entered the quarantine area and donned bioprotective suits. First, they checked on Petty Officer Espiritu and her shipmates from the laundry. Espiritu looked improved since that morning. The rash had progressed some, but remained in the flat red macular stage, without signs of blisters or pustules. The other two sailors showed signs of early red papular bumps, but their rashes had not progressed as rapidly as the doctors had observed in Commander Squire.

"Either they have the less aggressive form, or the tecovirimat is making a difference," Troy said.

"Too early to tell," Rose said, "but it looks hopeful."

Five minutes later, they entered Commander Squire's room. Other than a different corpsman standing the watch, the room and its primary occupant looked the same as they had that morning.

"Any change?" Troy asked.

The corpsman shook his head. "Negative, sir."

Troy conducted a quick neurological exam. No improvement since the morning. On Squire's arms and legs, the pox had all scabbed over; no more pustules.

"She's in the last phase of the skin lesions," he said. "But for the encephalitis and all that happened after that, she'd be home free by now."

"We can still hope," Rose said.

"You think she has a chance?"

She grimaced. "I hope."

Troy looked at his watch. Midnight. "She has nine hours to turn the tide. Maybe more, depending on what the admiral has in mind."

After leaving the commander's room, disposing of the bioprotective suit, and bidding good night to Rose Deckert, Troy retired to the stateroom he shared with a junior chaplain and crashed on the rack.

He fell asleep in two minutes.

Chapter 74
Seoul, Republic of Korea

E RIC MIKLESON AWOKE AT 0530, shivering in a bath of stale sweat. For an instant, he thought he was in his rack on the flagship, but he opened his eyes to the now familiar surroundings of the VIP room at the Dragon Hill Lodge. He rolled onto his back, the oblivion of deep sleep giving way to harsh reality.

Smallpox attack. Cricket in coma. COS dead. Cover-up. Admiral and N3 back to Shenandoah.

Without willing it, Eric ignored his own condition, despite the sweat-soaked sheets and raging sore throat.

He got out of bed and went straight to the shower, deferring a look in the bathroom mirror until he had to shave and brush his teeth. Reflected in the glass, his face looked drawn, his skin sallow. When he rinsed his mouth after brushing, the water caused searing pain in the back of his throat; as if he'd rinsed with pure alcohol. Eric shook off the pain, donned a clean working uniform, and headed out for the short walk to USFK/CFC headquarters for the 0700 brief with the flagship.

He skipped breakfast.

"Where's the ship's doc?" Eric asked the fleet surgeon on the secure video teleconference.

"He's tied up in the medical department," Captain Deckert said. "We've seen a constant stream of sick sailors, and even more who are not sick but frightened."

"What's Cricket's status?" Eric said.

"No change when I checked on her first thing this morning," Deckert said. "Doc Pearson and I plan to see her together around 0900. We'll make a determination then about whether to continue life support." She paused. "To be honest, sir, I think she's brain dead."

Eric exploded. "You and the other doc are not authorized to pull the plug on her. Is that clear?"

The surgeon looked perplexed. "We got that word from the acting COS yesterday."

Eric composed himself. "Right. It will be a command decision. The admiral and the N3 are on their way back to the flagship now. They took an overnight jet to Okinawa, where the *Shenandoah* helo picked them up for transit to the flagship. The admiral will consult with you both as soon as she arrives."

"But—"

Eric raised his hand. Deep fatigue and hopelessness flowed through him. "She does not intend to make a medical decision. She will be there to support whatever you recommend. You should understand why that's important."

The surgeon nodded. "Yes, sir. Makes sense."

Eric paused. "The other news does not directly affect you, but I need to share it for your situational awareness. Late yesterday, we received word from our embassy that the ROKs believe they have neutralized the threat to their homeland."

"Seems premature," Deckert said.

"I don't know that we can trust it," Eric said. "But they claim their citizens are immune to the disease because of their comprehensive vaccination program, and that their rapid public health response thwarted the spread of the disease to their citizens."

"What about the sick KATUSA?" Deckert said.

"Getting better. The Army docs gave him that drug you're using. He's already improved. No one else in that command has gotten sick."

Deckert paused for a bit, contemplating. "Here on the ship we've had this steady stream of influenza-like illnesses and worried well. Has the same not happened there?"

"Not at all," Eric said. "The general populace is oblivious to any of this, because the government put a tight lid on it. Handcuffed our own news media too. It's become a closely guarded secret known only to a select few. In essence, they activated River City across the entire country."

"Wow." Deckert's attention diverted for a moment. "They just called flight quarters. Would that be the admiral on approach?"

"Must be," Eric said.

"One other question," Deckert said. "What about the dead Korean woman? Who was she, and how did they dispose of her body?"

"No information on that," Eric said. "The CIA and its ROK equivalent took over, and they are sharing nothing."

"So on the peninsula it's business as usual?"

"Yep," Eric said. "Except for fewer than a dozen people read into it, the rest of the country and our own forces know nothing about this attack. Nor will they, ever."

"That's not right."

"Tell it to the commander-in-chief."

"They just bonged the admiral aboard," Deckert said.

"She'll want to see you and the ship's doc right away," Eric said. "Please keep me in the loop. I'm in a communications bubble here."

"Will do."

Before the fleet surgeon could switch off, Eric interjected. "I want to know the instant there's any change in Cricket's status."

"Of course," Captain Deckert said.

Chapter 75

USS Shenandoah (LCC 21), Underway Near Okinawa, Japan.

T ROY SLEPT THROUGH THE night without dreaming or moving, oblivious to the noise and movement of the ship's rapid transit toward Okinawa.

He awakened to the sound of the 1MC. "Flight quarters, flight quarters. The ship is at flight quarters. All designated personnel, man your flight quarters stations. Wear no covers topside; throw no items over the side. All hands not involved in flight quarters remain forward of the superstructure. The smoking lamp is out. Now flight quarters."

A blaring test of the ship's collision and fire alarms confirmed a helicopter inbound to land on the flagship.

Based on what the acting COS had said, Troy figured it to be a logistics flight from Okinawa. He wondered why no one had asked if he needed any medical supplies or equipment.

He looked at his watch. 0710. He had slept through reveille and morning muster in medical. Why had his staff let him oversleep? Troy was already ten minutes late for the morning VTC brief with the admiral. Why hadn't Captain Deckert called him?

As if on cue, the phone rang. A corpsman from the medical department. "Sir, we need you in the treatment room. The place is filling up again."

"I'm already late for the brief with the admiral. I'll come down after that."

"Captain Deckert called at 0700," the corpsman said. "She said to let you sleep and that she would handle the brief."

"Okay," Troy said. "On my way."

He bounced out of his bottom bunk, noting that his junior chaplain room-mate had already left the room. At the shared sink, he hurried through washing his face, shaving, combing his hair, and trying to look as professional as he could under the circumstances. He put on the same aquaflage uniform he'd worn the day before, laced up his boots, and rushed out the door to make a brief head stop before moving on to his department. He planned to check in with his staff before joining up with Rose Deckert to visit Commander Squire.

Although he hoped for the best, he dreaded what he expected to see there.

When he entered the medical department, Troy saw a fresh gaggle of sailors waiting to be seen in sick call. He quickly estimated that they numbered more than at the same time yesterday.

When will it end?

Eight bells and a new 1MC announcement stopped Troy's stride toward the treatment room.

"Seventh Fleet, arriving."

"What the...?"

Troy hurried to the treatment room, where the corpsmen had already tuned the television to the closed-circuit channel focused on the flight deck.

Troy and his medics watched the familiar olive-green HH-60 helicopter descend through the morning mist. The words "Commander, US Seventh Fleet" along the fuselage and the three white stars on the door confirmed the occupant as Vice Admiral Louise Lassiter. The helo set down lightly on the deck, and the crew crouched forward to chock the tires.

The rotors continued to turn as the passenger door opened and Admiral Lassiter, recognizable by her short stature and the three stars on the shoulders of her flight suit, disembarked. Behind her, the tall figure of Captain Mark Gunderson, N3 and deputy chief of staff, also disembarked.

No signs of Captain Eric Mikleson. Perhaps the N2 had stayed behind as the admiral's representative in Seoul.

A final attenuated ding on the bell, called the "stinger," announced the admiral's entry into the ship. The flight deck crew hustled to remove the chocks from the helo's tires. As soon as they cleared the arc of the rotors, the engine revved up, the aircraft lifted off the flight deck, and turned back to the northwest as it departed. The TV screen now showed just the empty flight deck, as if the arrival drama had never occurred.

Troy surveyed the treatment room, where corpsmen had already returned to seeing the first wave of sailors looking for reassurance that they would not die from the deadly disease that had killed the Seventh Fleet chief of staff. He began a quick round to assure that none represented a fresh case of the disease.

A corpsman approached him. "Sir, the admiral wants to see you and the fleet surgeon in her office, asap."

Chapter 76

TROY AND KIM SAT on the plush couch in Vice Admiral Lassiter's spacious, parlor-like office. The admiral sat in a soft side chair of the same upholstery. Her hair still tousled from the flight helmet she'd worn on the helo from Okinawa, she looked tired; thinner than Troy had remembered her. He had just finished briefing her on the chain of events since their last video conference, highlighting the chief of staff's death and the decision to take Commander Squire off the anesthetic and give her another twenty-four hours on life support before deciding to stop treatment.

"What's magic about twenty-four hours?" the admiral asked.

"Nothing," Troy said. "It's an arbitrary decision point. We can keep her on life support for months if we choose, but..."

"If she can't breathe on her own," Rose said, "her quality of life will be nil. She'll end up ventilator-dependent with a permanent tracheotomy. 'Persistent vegetative state,' it's called. Not life."

Vice Admiral Lassiter leaned forward. "Forget about quality of life for a moment. Forget about the Cricket Squire we all know and respect. Does your patient have any reasonable chance of recovery?"

Troy sighed. "What's reasonable? Her chances of survival are somewhere between zero and ten percent. For anything beyond a vegetative state, maybe between zero and five percent." He glanced at Rose, who nodded in agreement.

"Well, those are shitty odds," the admiral said. "Why have you kept the life support going so long?"

Unable to form his words, Troy looked at Rose.

"We're having trouble letting go, ma'am," his colleague said.

Troy found his voice. "I feel responsible for her. I don't want to lose her."

"None of us want to lose her, Doc," the admiral said, her voice empathetic. "But cutting to the chase, y'all don't think she's gone yet?"

"She may be," Troy said. "That's why we decided on a trial off of life support. If she can't breathe and maintain circulation on her own..."

He choked up.

The admiral looked over their heads, as if scrutinizing the knickknacks and mementos in the étagère behind them. When she reengaged, her eyes became soft, maternal.

"You got anyone you can consult?"

"We talked to an intensivist at Tripler," Troy said. "To be frank, he's a jerk. He inasmuch said she's already dead and we're just trying to be heroes."

"Shit-can the Army asshole," the admiral said. "You got any Navy docs you trust?"

"The PACOM surgeon, Rear Admiral Matteson, has been very supportive," Rose said. "He took on the surgeon general and got him off our backs."

"That's a point in his favor," the admiral said. "About time someone shot down that pompous SG character. Can you trust the PACOM surgeon's medical judgment?"

"He's an emergency physician," Troy said. "Has considerable familiarity with life-and-death situations. And yes, I trust his judgment, and his compassion."

"Call him. Report straight back to me when you're done."

***

It took over an hour to set up the secure VTC consultation with the PACOM surgeon. After summarizing their case, Troy and Rose listened intently for the response.

"How long was she hypoxic?" Admiral Matteson asked.

"Probably five minutes," Troy said.

After a pause, the surgeon said, "You want my frank opinion, right?"

"Yes, sir," Troy said.

"Your patient is brain dead. Even if she regains spontaneous breathing, between the encephalitis and the hypoxic episode, she's suffered irreversible brain damage. Her odds of any useful quality of life are zilch."

Spoken with such simple yet kind authority, the words seemed straightforward and obvious. "So we should proceed with the trial off life support," Troy said. It was not a question.

"What I would do," the surgeon said. "I see no value in prolonging inevitability, leastwise under your current circumstances."

Troy looked at Rose. She nodded.

"We are all in agreement then," Troy said. His voice shook and his hands trembled. "Thank you for your time, sir."

"Happy to help." Rear Admiral Matteson stared into the camera. "One more thing, Troy."

"Sir?"

"It's not your fault."

Troy's eyes moistened. He couldn't speak.

"Do not forget it," the admiral said. "It's not your fault."

"Thank you, sir. That means a lot."

Chapter 77

B ACK IN THE ADMIRAL'S office, Troy stood by as Rose Deckert gave her boss the news. "PACOM surgeon believes she's brain dead, or at best has severe irreversible brain damage. Doc Pearson and I agree. We should withdraw life support."

"I want to see her first," the admiral said.

"Ma'am, that's not a good idea," Troy said. "You shouldn't risk infection."

Vice Admiral Lassiter's steely stare transfixed him. "Not a request, Doc. I will see her. I don't give a bat's behind about the risk."

"Yes, ma'am," Troy said.

Vice Admiral Lassiter stood. "Let's get to it."

Twenty minutes later, after donning bioprotective gear, they all crowded into Commander Squire's stateroom, silent except for the rhythmic whoosh of the ventilator. If Louise Lassiter experienced any emotional response to Squire's miserable state, she hid it well.

"Can she hear us?" the admiral asked.

Troy shrugged. "No way to tell for sure. Assume she can."

Lassiter moved to the head of the bed and kneeled beside it so she could talk through her face mask directly into the commander's ear. She held Squire's hand in her own gloved hand.

"Cricket, it's Louise Lassiter. I hope you can hear me, because I have something important to say to you." She paused and looked at Squire's face, perusing it for any sign of recognition.

Nothing.

"I know you've suffered, darlin'," Lassiter said, "but you've got one more flight to make, and then you won't suffer ever again. Before you launch, I want you to know that you are a genuine hero, not only to the Navy and the nation, but to me and anyone who's had the honor of being your shipmate."

Another search for any sign of recognition.

Nothing.

The admiral squeezed the commander's hand. "You are a most courageous and honorable naval officer." She chuckled. "That sound like bullshit? It's true, you are. And so much more."

She paused, as if collecting herself. "You, Jessica Squire, are the most inspiring woman I've ever known. A model for us all. You've shown how a woman can be true to herself, damn anyone who takes offense, and live an honest, committed life no matter the obstacles. You, dear Cricket, are our hero. You leave behind a horde of women who strive to be just like you." She stroked Squire's arm. "That's your legacy, sweetheart."

Lassiter took Squire's hand in both of hers and held them tightly to her forehead. "Fair winds and following seas, shipmate. I am honored to serve with you." Her voice cracked at the end of the sentence. All eyes in the room filled with tears.

The admiral stood and stepped back to allow Troy to approach the bed.

His vision fogged with regret. He flipped off the switch on the IV pump to stop the flow of blood-pressure-sustaining norepinephrine. Then he moved to the ventilator, which brought him close to the commander's head. He stopped in mid-reach, paused, and leaned over to speak into Commander Squire's ear.

"I'm so sorry, ma'am." He sobbed and stepped back to compose himself.

Rose Deckert spoke. "Do you want me to..."

Troy held up his hand. "I have to do it." He stepped to the ventilator and flipped the switch to the *off* position.

The rhythmic swooshing stopped, and the room went silent except for the all the sobs. Troy disconnected the ventilator hose from the LMA and scrutinized the tube for any slight mist of air movement. He stared at Squire's chest, hoping to see a rise.

Nothing.

Troy stood next to the admiral and Rose Deckert, watching the commander and the cardiac monitor.

Over a few minutes, the cardiac rhythm progressed from a normal morphology at a regular rate to a slow, irregular tracing.The spikes representing ventricular activity widened.

Heart dying.

All at once, Squire's chest rose, and her quick breath transfixed the room's occupants. After several seconds, another breath, followed ten seconds later by another one.

Troy saw no air movement in the LMA tube. He glanced at the cardiac monitor. The heart rate had slowed to forty, and the tracing had widened to an inverted U.

"Those are not respirations," he said to the admiral, his voice surprisingly calm and matter-of-fact. "It's a reflex. We call it 'agonal.' The same term applies to her electrocardiogram. See how it's becoming slower and widening out? With her brain already dead, her heart and lungs are dying without the benefit of our support. It won't be long now."

As if on cue, Commander Squire took another agonal breath that moved no air. Then her EKG complex became a solitary line that meandered across the screen.

"She's flatlined," Troy said.

He moved to his patient and rubbed her sternum. No response. He looked at her pupils. Fully dilated without response to the penlight. He moved close to the LMA tube, stared at it, and discerned no air movement. Finally, he put an electronic stethoscope to her chest and cranked up the volume.

No air movement, no *lub-dub* of a heart beating.

Just cold, inexorable, absolute silence.

Troy stepped back, turned off the monitor, and looked at his watch. "Time of death, 1018."

He choked back the sob in his throat.

Seeming to sense Troy's immediate need, the admiral and Rose Deckert left the room. The corpsman looked at Troy, seeking direction.

"Wait outside, please."

Troy was alone with her, the woman who had been both his nemesis and his inspiration. He kneeled by the bed, grasped her hand, and wept.

"I am so sorry. I should have treated you better."

He looked at her face, free of pain and agony. A peaceful countenance almost smiled through the pox scabs. For a long time, Troy Pearson gazed at that face, more serene in death than he'd ever seen it in life.

His own life had changed forever.

Chapter 78

B ACK IN HIS HOTEL room waiting for news about Cricket, Eric scrolled through international news sources. A *Washington Post* article caught his eye.

Noted Russian Scientist Confirmed Missing

Russian authorities confirmed today that noted virologist Dr. Nikolai Orlov, 63, former head of the Vector Institute in Koltsovo, Novosibirsk, has been missing since early last month and is feared dead. Sources at the Vector Institute confirmed that the scientist left work early because of illness on the day of his disappearance, but never returned to his home. His whereabouts remain unknown.

Orlov's wife, Svetlana Orlov, 41, was contacted in the United States, where their daughter, 9, is undergoing treatment for brain cancer at Boston Children's Hospital. Speaking through an interpreter, Svetlana Orlov said her husband had been despondent over their child's illness and their inability to get in Russia what he considered proper care. Without his wife's knowledge, he apparently made arrangements through an unknown professional contact to have the girl and her mother transported to the United States for treatment. The unknown benefactor paid all the expenses. When pressed, Svetlana Orlov maintained that she had no knowledge of Dr. Orlov's whereabouts, and that she had not heard from him since the night before he disappeared.

Nikolai Orlov rose to prominence in the former USSR as the head of the Vector Institute's biological weapons development program. After the fall of the Soviet Union, he remained in Novosibirsk Oblast to oversee one of the world's two remaining stores of smallpox virus and to teach at Novosibirsk State University. The other remaining smallpox store is contained at the Centers for Disease Control in Atlanta.

Russian authorities stopped short of declaring Dr. Orlov dead and said that the search for him continues on a multinational scale.

Eric spent the next forty-five minutes scouring the Internet for any information on Dr. Orlov, the Vector Institute, the former USSR biological weapons program, smallpox (although he'd already made himself an expert on that disease), and finally, childhood brain cancers and their treatment.

A Russian scientist, no matter how prominent or well connected, could not afford to send a child to Harvard for brain cancer treatment. Where did he get the money?

In a flash, Eric knew the answer.

He sells smallpox virus to an international criminal. But how?

He thought about the little girl with the brain tumor, and then about his own family and his young daughter.

How far will a desperate man go to save the life of his child? As far as he must.

Eric returned to the Internet and pored again over the known information about smallpox and its transmission between humans. All at once, he pounded his forehead in a blinding flash of the obvious. The woman who attacked Cricket in Donghae, whose body they found in Seoul, must have acquired smallpox from Russia and then transmitted it to Cricket. Like a suicide bomber, she had either chosen or been forced to sacrifice her life for the mission.

Nikolai Orlov was the first vector! He made the choice, but for the sake of his family, not his government.

Eric reflected on the *Eastern Dream* ferry moored in Donghae. He reasoned that Orlov, self-infected by the virus, had traveled there from Vladivostok, met up with the Korean woman, who was probably a KPA agent, and transmitted the infection to her. When *Shenandoah* arrived in Donghae, the woman had waited for them! No doubt the KPA had killed Orlov and disposed of his body.

No chance of finding those remains.

"No way to prove any of this," Eric said aloud.

Let alone persuade the powers-that-be to retaliate. Meanwhile, Cricket...

He looked at his watch. Two hours since Vice Admiral Lassiter had landed on the flagship.

What the hell is going on?

A wave of nausea forced him into the bathroom. His head ached and his throat burned.

I should look at my throat.

As he searched for a flashlight, the phone on his desk rang and he hurried to answer it, anticipating news about Cricket.

"Captain Mikleson," he said in a rushed voice.

The reply came in a thick Korean accent Eric recognized as his clandestine contact with the ROK intelligence agency.

"Off the record. We identified the dead woman as Lee Myung Suk, a KPA agent. Her DNA is a half match with Lee Yeong Nae. They were half sisters. You never got this phone call."

The caller clicked off, leaving Eric staring at the dead receiver.

If Cricket survives to hear this...

He sat on the edge of the bed, holding his head in his hands. The entire chain of events burst into his mind.

KJU's revenge, as masterful as it is evil.

Waves of anger boiled within him, and his head felt as if it would explode.

The phone rang.

Eric calmed himself before picking it up. "Yes."

Louise Lassiter's voice was subdued, tender, yet firm. "I'm sorry, Eric. Cricket died."

Chapter 79

USS Shenandoah (LCC 21). Underway, Philippine Sea.

B Y MID-AFTERNOON, THE MEDICAL team had transferred both bodies to the large walk-in refrigerator that had become the flagship's morgue. The process included an abundance of measures to thwart even the slightest risk of contamination.

Troy locked the door, pocketed the key, and turned to the corpsmen who had moved the bodies.

"Station an honor guard at this door twenty-four-seven. No one enters without my permission. And I do mean *honor* guard. Parade rest, no slouching, no chitchat. We treat these fallen warriors with the respect they've earned."

"I wish we could've saved her," Petty Officer Campos said.

"We all wish that," Troy said.

"It's not fair, sir. Whoever did this should pay."

"He would pay if you and I could get our hands on him, right?"

The corpsman's voice seethed. "Damn right."

"I doubt we'll get the chance, Campos, but I hope someone does."

After a shower and a change of uniform, Troy met up with Rose Deckert outside the door to the quarantine area.

"You okay?" she said.

"No. But it doesn't matter."

"We can talk."

"No time. We still have work to do."

Without further words, the two physicians donned their bioprotective gear and passed through the watertight door to visit their remaining patients. The number had grown to six, all of them mess specialists from the ship's laundry.

An hour and a half later, the doctors emerged back through the barrier door. As they disposed of the bioprotective suits, Rose said, "What do you think?"

Troy rubbed his chin. "As gun-shy as I am, I think we may have turned a corner. They all look stable." He thought of Commander Squire and Captain Santiago. "Considering the alternatives."

"I agree," Rose said. "Either the tecovirimat is working or they all have the milder form of the disease."

"Or both," Troy said.

"Or both."

"Or neither. Let's see what the next twenty-four hours bring before we get optimistic."

With that, they went their separate ways, Troy to check out the scene in sick call, Rose Deckert to brief the admiral and the acting chief of staff.

***

Just before dinnertime, Troy retired to his office to catch up on paperwork after conducting sick call with the corpsmen. The familiar routine of seeing and treating patients had a calming, therapeutic effect on him. Life would go on. The constant ache in his gut and fog in his brain would eventually resolve. The urge to break into tears without warning would also go away.

This will all end.

The apparent downturn of both volume and illness in sick call encouraged Troy. They had seen fewer patients than the days before, and although they sent four to the observation area, Troy's index of suspicion for smallpox was low.

Maybe we have seen the worst of it.

Death certificates for Captain José Santiago and Commander Jessica Squire sat atop the pile of papers on his desk for signature. Troy stared at both for a long time, fighting the turmoil in the pit of his gut. Finally, he signed them.

Petty Officer Campos is right. The bastard should pay.

Halfway through the paperwork, Troy answered a phone call from Rose Deckert.

"Admiral wants burial at sea for both the COS and the commander," she said. "To be more accurate, higher authority directed that. We're to make the arrangements, along with the personnel staff. The ship is turning back toward Guam, but won't make port. We'll receive whoever comes aboard for the funerals by helo, then put out to sea for the burial."

"What about the other patients?" Troy asked.

"We're to keep treating them. If they get better, we coordinate with higher authority on repatriation."

"They will get better." Another thought struck Troy. "What about next of kin for the burial?"

Rose sighed. "We're still on communications lockdown. So far as anyone outside the inner circle knows, *Shenandoah* is conducting routine maritime security ops in the Western Pacific, and the comms blackout is an exercise. The point is moot, because next of kin are not authorized to attend burials at sea. At the right time, when this is all over, the admiral will notify them."

Troy's mind shifted to Jessica "Cricket" Squire, returning alone to the sea. Forever.

Chapter 80
Seoul, Republic of Korea

H OURS HAD PASSED SINCE the phone call from Louise Lassiter, but Eric's head still pounded and his eyes remained crimson. The initial soul-wrenching grief now yielded to an all-consuming rage.

He could not hold still sitting in the secure conference room at USFK, waiting for Vice Admiral Lassiter, Rear Admiral Kate Mahoney, Captain Mark Gunderson, and the Pacific Fleet chief of staff to join the video teleconference from *Shenandoah* and Hawaii, respectively. The meeting's purpose was to plan for the burials at sea for Captain Santiago and Commander Squire, and to determine the future direction for the flagship and its occupants.

Eric had another agenda, for which he had elicited Admiral Lassiter's cooperation. When she had described for him the gruesome details of Cricket's death, he could no longer ignore his own symptoms, no more deceive himself about his own fate. He had looked into his throat and recognized the telltale red rash.

I am already dead. I can never go home, never again see Melody and the kids. Only one choice left for me.

A technology delay enabled Eric to crystalize his thoughts and feelings. When the meeting began, the conferees labored under the cloud of realization that a notorious despot had murdered two of their shipmates. Their despair worsened with disappointment that higher leadership had turned cheek.

The plan came together quickly. *Shenandoah* would continue to Guam, where it would linger within helicopter distance to receive whatever dignitaries would attend the ceremony. That would include both the PACOM commander and the Pacific Fleet commander.

"Cricket was my shipmate and friend," Kate Mahoney said. "I will attend." She was not asking for concurrence, but stating a fact.

Once all attendees arrived on board, *Shenandoah* would sail to deep water, where the burial at sea would occur. The flagship would then return to helo distance from Guam and transfer the remaining smallpox victims to the US medical team that had stood by in Guam since the original plan for Commander Squire's transfer to NIH. The ill sailors continued to improve and expected to survive.

Once all smallpox victims had left the ship, *Shenandoah* would remain at sea for two weeks to confirm no fresh cases of smallpox emerged. When cleared, she would rendezvous with USS *Ronald Reagan*, the Navy's forward-deployed aircraft carrier in the Western Pacific. The admiral and her remaining staff, confirmed clear of any risk of smallpox, would transfer to the *Reagan*, which would become the temporary Seventh Fleet flagship.

Shenandoah would proceed to Pearl Harbor, Hawaii for inspection by personnel from the Navy's Environmental and Preventive Medicine Unit, OSHA, and other government environmental watchdogs. After that, higher authority in the national capital area would decide whether to return the stolid gray lady to the Western Pacific as the Seventh Fleet flagship or scuttle her.

Eric squirmed in his seat during the latter discussion. No one seemed at all interested in talking about retaliation or ongoing force protection following the dramatic attack on the forward-deployed naval force, engineered by one of the nation's worst enemies.

Did Eric's nausea stem from illness or disgust?

Finally, all plans were complete and documented, and the conversation was about to end. Vice Admiral Lassiter asked Eric and Kate Mahoney to stay on the line, then dismissed everyone else.

Eric keyed the microphone in front of him. "Ma'am, I recommend we all sign off now and then establish a new connection for your follow-up." He wanted to be sure no one remained surreptitiously plugged in to hear the next discussion.

"Sounds good," the admiral said. "We'll reconnect in ten minutes. Gives me time for a head call."

When they reconnected and Eric assured himself that no one else was listening, he nodded into the camera. "Ma'am."

Vice Admiral Lassiter took the cue. "Kate, we need a favor from you."

"Of course," Kate Mahoney said, her voice and face curious. "If it's doable."

"Actually," the admiral said, "we need a favor from your boss, Admiral Lewis."

Kate rubbed her chin. "Yes?"

"We need him to talk to his bubba in the White House. I'll let Eric fill you in."

When Eric finished talking, Kate Mahoney stared stone-faced into the camera, speechless.

Vice Admiral Lassiter broke the silence. "We need to do this. For Cricket."

"For Cricket," Eric said.

Kate's face remained impassive. "I'll set it up."

Chapter 81

USS Shenandoah (LCC 21). Underway. Philippine Sea Near Guam.

SHENANDOAH HAD MADE EXCELLENT time traversing the distance between Okinawa and Guam, arriving near the US territorial island by early morning of the third day. Troy had suffered through anguish-torn, sleepless nights. Despite his concerted efforts to clear his mind and get needed rest, the events surrounding Commander Squire's sudden downturn and death played in an endless loop inside his brain. He found himself second-guessing every decision that he had made.

Maybe the intensivist was correct. Maybe I was trying to be a hero. Maybe if I'd paid closer attention when she first got sick. Maybe...

Around midnight of the third day, he had ambled down to the medical department, opened the pharmacy, and taken an Ambien sleeping pill. He thought about Commander Squire and his steadfast efforts to get her off the sedatives and narcotics. Now he had a new understanding, however slight, of the psychic pain she had suffered. Her need for medication made sense.

By the time Troy returned to his stateroom, the combination of exhaustion and the sedative had made him groggy. At last he slept, only for his alarm clock to awaken him a few hours later. He forced himself out of the rack. Troy had promised to meet Rose Deckert in the flag mess for breakfast at 0600 before they made their rounds on the remaining smallpox patients.

"You look like two-day-old dog shit," Rose said over her omelet and bacon.

"Feel worse."

"Want to talk about it?"

"No."

"You made the best decisions you could under the circumstances," she said. "I supported you with all of them."

"I said I don't want to talk about it."

"Fine. Don't talk. Listen."

Troy put down his fork and glared at her. "I don't need your therapy." He looked around the room as other staff officers entered. "Even if I did, this is not the right place."

"Not therapy. I'm talking to you as a colleague and friend who understands what might go on inside your head."

"You don't understand crap."

Troy threw down his napkin and left the room.

A half hour later, Troy was donning his bioprotective suit when Rose entered the anteroom. Before putting on the headpiece, he gave her an earnest look.

"Sorry for the outburst. I was unprofessional, Captain, ma'am."

Rose smiled. "I get it, Troy. I may not know all that you're thinking, or what's turning in your head, but I know one thing. You are not to blame for Cricket Squire's death."

"In my head, I know you're right. Especially on that last day. By then she was already in extremis. But I wonder if we should have followed the original plan to move her off the ship in Guam."

"That would never happen," Rose said. "The storm, remember?"

"Then it would be the storm's fault."

An announcement over the 1MC calling the ship to flight quarters interrupted their conversation. Rose looked up at the speaker box.

"Taking on dignitaries for the burial. I believe the PACOM surgeon is coming with Admirals Mahoney and Lewis."

"Then we'd better get on with these rounds so we have updated information for him."

Without waiting for her to respond, Troy donned his headgear and passed through the watertight door into the quarantine area.

The remaining smallpox patients continued to improve, and there had been no fresh cases for three days. Troy and Rose found Petty Officer Espiritu sitting up in her bed. The skin rash had progressed to the scab phase. It did not cover her entire body.

"I'm hungry," she said.

"If you continue to improve," Troy said, "we can feed you soon. The good news, we think you're out of the woods." He smiled. "You're going to make it, Petty Officer Espiritu. You may end up with some residual scarring from that rash, but you should be back to normal otherwise in a couple of weeks."

The young sailor clasped her hands together in a gesture of adoration and looked above her. "Salamat sa Diyos!"

Her eyes filled with tears, and she reached out to touch Troy's hand. "I thank God, and I thank you, doctors. Thank you for saving my life."

Troy's heart jumped into his throat. He could not speak, but squeezed her hand and nodded; thankful that she could not see through the bioprotective suit that his own eyes had filled with tears. Then he left the room, passed through the watertight door, doffed his gear, and hurried down the passageway to his stateroom.

He didn't want Rose Deckert to see him bawling like a scolded child.

Ten minutes later, as he washed and dried his face, he heard the announcement on the 1MC, "Pacific Command, arriving." Admiral Lewis and his entourage would soon embark by helo to the flagship.

Troy was changing into his dress white uniform with medals and ribbons for the burial ceremony when his phone rang.

"Sir, the PACOM surgeon is here in medical looking for you," a petty officer said.

"Thank you, Petty Officer. Tell him I'll be right down."

In his office, Troy found Rear Admiral Miles Matteson sitting with Rose Deckert. Both wore dress white uniforms. Troy noted the five rows of medals adorning the left side of the admiral's chest. Besides various service medals from past and present combat zones around the world, the two-star medical admiral sported seven personal awards, including two Legions of Merit and a Bronze Star.

A man whose wisdom and experience Troy could trust.

After the initial pleasantries, the admiral spoke. "Foremost, I want to thank and commend both of you for the outstanding jobs you've done in meeting this challenge; not only dealing with severe circumstances, but for success in containing and mitigating this threat to our operational forces."

"Thank you, sir," Troy said. He looked at Rose. "It's been a team effort."

"I recognize that," the admiral said. "But I also know that the two of you, and especially you, Troy, as the physician of record, had to make hard decisions under extreme duress."

Alarmed at the serious undertone in the admiral's voice, Troy shifted in his chair.

"If it were up to only Rear Admiral Mahoney, Admiral Lewis, and me, you would both receive the highest commendations with commensurate medals."

"But?" Rose said.

"It's not up to just us. Commander Squire's death sent shock waves through-out the Beltway, including the office of the Navy surgeon general. Some people question what happened to her here."

"What people?" Troy said.

"The organizers and proponents of the original plan to transfer her to NIH, for one. A certain intensivist at Tripler Army Medical Center for another. The Pacific Fleet surgeon for yet another."

The admiral blew out a breath. "These people suggest that treatment in a shipboard environment under the care of physicians inexperienced with critical care was not the correct choice. The Army colonel claims that your decision, against his advice, to treat her with general anesthesia amounted to a kiss of death."

Troy felt as if his entire body would implode, yet he feared it would not. He looked at the admiral, terrified at what he might hear next.

Rear Admiral Matteson leaned toward Troy. "The surgeon general has ordered an independent investigation into the entire history of the medical care rendered to both Commander Squire and Captain Santiago. In the interim, he's put your clinical privileges in abeyance, Troy. As of today, you may no longer provide clinical care to any patients on this ship or anywhere in Navy medicine."

Troy recoiled, as if attacked by a bear but unable to run.

"After the burial ceremony," the admiral continued, "when we rendezvous with the helo to return to Guam, one of the family physicians from the naval hospital will be on board to assume your clinical duties. You may remain on the flagship in an administrative capacity only."

Matteson reached inside the jacket of his uniform and produced an envelope. "You will find everything I just said documented in this letter from the surgeon general."

Rose Deckert raged. "That is fucking bullshit, sir." She gestured at Troy. "This man is a medical hero. Navy medicine should treat him as such, not make him a stepping stone for other people's personal gain."

Rear Admiral Matteson raised his hand. "I know that. So does Admiral Lewis. Vice Admiral Lassiter will agree. But the surgeon general of the Navy holds ultimate authority over matters of credentials and clinical privileges."

He turned back to Troy. "By Navy instruction, this period of abeyance ends in thirty days. Then the SG must choose to either restore your full clinical privileges or revoke them. That gives us thirty days to assure he makes the right decision."

"If he revokes my clinical privileges," Troy said in a quivering voice, "it will haunt the rest of my career. I'll be flagged in the National Practitioner Data Bank. I may not be allowed to practice anywhere, military or civilian."

Rear Admiral Matteson clapped Troy on the shoulder. "That won't happen, Troy. I'll put both my two stars on the table before I let it. For now, you need to hold your head high, understand that you did the best you could, and that you made the right decisions. What happened to those two officers was not your fault. We all know whose fault it was, and I hope we haven't heard the end of that."

Troy pursed his lips. "Thank you, sir. I appreciate your support."

As soon as the admiral left, the 1MC sounded overhead. "All hands, bury the dead."

"It's time," Rose Deckert said. She put her arm around Troy's shoulder. "Let's go out together."

Chapter 82

W HEN TROY AND ROSE walked out onto the ship's main deck, the late summer heat and humidity hit them like a furnace blast.

"I thought the ship would go farther out to sea," Troy said. "We may still be in helo range of Guam."

"Easier for the dignitaries." Rose's voice edged with sarcasm. She stopped him at the doorway, place her hand on his shoulder. "I'm telling you now, Troy Pearson, whatever happens next, today or any future day, you are not alone."

Troy smiled. "Thanks, shipmate. We'll take it one step at a time. Right now, we have to say goodbye to two former patients."

Rose nodded, and the two walked together across the forward deck of the ship to take their places in the honor platoon on the starboard side, across from the bugler and the seven-man firing party on the port side. Rose lined up with her Seventh Fleet staff senior officers at the front of the formation while Troy took a spot at the end of the fourth row. He sweated in his white polyester dress uniform with the "choker" collar and long sleeves.

He pulled the brim of his combination cover down to shade his eyes, which were concealed behind dark sunglasses.

The honor platoon included all the officers and chiefs of the Seventh Fleet staff and USS *Shenandoah*'s ship's company. Captain Mark Gunderson stood in front of them, acting as adjutant. When they had fully assembled, Gunderson called out, "Honor Platoon, attention."

All complied. With the ambient heat and humidity intensified by radiant heat from the steel deck, Troy worried he might faint before the ceremony ended.

The door to the ship's superstructure opened to admit a master-at-arms, followed by eight enlisted body bearers in dress white uniforms carrying the flag-draped casket of Captain José Santiago, USN, deceased. Behind them, six body bearers emerged with the identically covered casket of Commander Jessica "Cricket" Squire, USN, deceased.

Each of the latter body bearers was a hospital corpsman who had cared for Commander Squire during her battle against the disease. Troy had passed over the offered opportunity to be one of the body bearers, choosing to enable his corpsmen to perform this final honorable act.

At the first sight of Squire's casket, Troy's eyes filled with tears, and a heavy lump rose in his throat. His body shook. A single, mournful sob escaped before he could control himself.

The body bearers brought both caskets forward, and the adjutant called, "Honor Platoon, hand, salute."

In unison, Troy and the others in the platoon snapped hands to hat brims. As the cortege moved past the honor formation, Troy realized he was not the only officer struggling with emotion. Stifled sobs, sniffles, and choked gasps echoed all around him.

The body bearers placed the draped caskets on sturdy stands on the port side, the ends of which extended over the railing. They positioned each casket with feet toward the ship's side and the union segment of the national ensign at the heads and over the left shoulders.

Captain Gunderson called, "Honor Platoon, parade rest." Everyone assumed that position, feet spread, arms bent, hands clasped behind their backs, all eyes forward.

Then nothing happened. They all stood and waited.

"Why are we waiting, and where are the flag officers?" the lieutenant next to Troy whispered.

"Beats me." Sweat mixed with the tears trickled on his face.

The distant sound of a helicopter from the direction of Guam caught every-one's attention. As the noise crescendoed, an HH-60 helicopter painted olive

green with a white top emerged in the distance. At the same time, an announcement boomed over the 1MC.

"United States, arriving."

The helicopter circled the ship for landing. Troy and everyone else noted the
American flag painted on the engine mounts and the white wording on the
fuselage: "United States of America."

"Marine One," Troy said in a soft voice filled with awe.

"He's supposed to be golfing in Hawaii," the lieutenant said.

Only then did Troy notice the podium bearing the seal of the President of the
United States, the white-covered chairs set up aft of the caskets, and the video
cameras aimed at the podium. Glancing back toward the ship's superstructure,
he spotted the Seventh Fleet band ready to play.

As soon as the noise of the helicopter landing on the flight deck behind the
superstructure stopped, they heard the "stinger," and the adjutant called, "Honor
Platoon, attention."

From the side of the superstructure, a formation emerged, led by the captain of
USS *Shenandoah*, followed by Rear Admiral Kate Mahoney; Rear Admiral Miles
Matteson; Vice Admiral Louise Lassiter; Admiral Victor Amaya, the commander
of US Pacific Fleet; General Cleavon Alexander, commander, US Forces Korea;
and finally Admiral Darnell Lewis, commander, US Pacific Command.

Those dignitaries formed into two lines, acting as side boys in front of the
superstructure.

The band struck up "Ruffles and Flourishes," followed by "Hail to the Chief."

All present rendered a hand salute as the President of the United States, clad
in a black business suit, white shirt, and dark blue tie, returned the salute, passed
through the side boys, and proceeded to the center seat. The other dignitaries
quickly took their places on either side of the commander-in-chief. Like everyone
else, the president wore dark glasses against the harsh afternoon sun.

The adjutant called, "Honor Platoon, parade rest."

The Seventh Fleet chaplain stepped to the podium. As all heads bowed, he read
from Scripture.

"Out of the depths I cry to You, O Lord, hear my voice! Let Your ears be attentive to my voice and supplication. If You, O Lord, mark iniquities, Lord, who can stand? But with You is forgiveness, that You may be revered. I trust in the Lord; my soul trusts in His word. My soul waits for the Lord. More than sentinels wait for the dawn, let Israel wait for the Lord, for with the Lord is kindness and with Him is plenteous redemption; and He will redeem Israel from their iniquities.

"O God, the Creator and Redeemer of all the faithful, hear our supplication and through Your infinite love and mercy graciously grant to the souls of Your servants departed, José and Jessica, the remission of all their sins, and grant to them everlasting rest and happiness through the infinite merits of Jesus Christ. Amen."

The chaplain then looked toward the president and dignitaries and swept his gaze across the deck to the gathered assembly. "Please pray together with me as our Lord taught us. Our Father, who art in heaven..."

At the conclusion of the Lord's Prayer, the adjutant called, "Honor Platoon, attention!"

Everyone followed the commander-in-chief's lead in standing at attention. Both sets of body bearers moved forward to the boards holding the caskets. They grasped each national ensign by the edges.

"Firing Detail, present arms," the adjutant said.

The seven men and women of the firing detail snapped to and held rifles directly in front of themselves.

"Hand, salute," Captain Gunderson announced. All military members snapped salutes and held them as the chaplain continued. The president also rendered a salute.

"O Lord, we commend to You the soul of Your servant José, that having departed from this world, he may live with and by the grace of Your merciful life. Through Christ our Lord..."

The body bearers attending the remains of Captain José Santiago tipped the board toward its foot, and the casket slid out from under the national ensign and plunged into the sea.

"Amen," the chaplain said.

The body bearers returned the board to the horizontal position and held fast, clutching the national ensign.

The chaplain sighed and paused as everyone's attention turned to the casket bearing the remains of Cricket Squire. His voice cracked as he read the identical passage that he had just completed for the deceased chief of staff, and he had to stop and compose himself before he said, "Through Christ our Lord..."

The six corpsmen tilted the board toward the sea, and the casket holding the remains of their former patient slid into the water. Even from four rows behind her, Troy heard Rose Deckert crying aloud in synchrony with his own sobs.

"Amen," the chaplain said.

As if everyone wanted time to stand still, the entire entourage stood in silence, broken after a few moments only by Captain Gunderson's command, "Firing detail, order arms. Parade rest."

The assemblage stood at parade rest with bowed heads, and the fleet chaplain pronounced the benediction in a solemn voice. "Eternal rest grant to them, O Lord, and let perpetual light shine upon them. May they rest in peace. Amen. May their souls and the souls of all the faithful departed, through the mercy of God rest in peace. Amen."

"Firing Detail, attention," the adjutant commanded. "Company, attention. Hand, salute."

Everyone on deck came to attention and rendered the hand salute.

"Fire three volleys. Ready, aim, fire." The simultaneous crack of seven rifles firing into the sea struck Troy's chest like a hammer, and he almost dropped his salute.

"Ready, aim, fire." The second volley almost caused him to double over.

"Ready, aim, fire." The last volley seemed to split his brain in two.

With the sound of the volleys still resounding in the distance, the bugler played a soulful rendition of Taps as everyone remained at attention and held the hand salutes. Behind the dark glasses worn by most of those present, not a single dry eye remained, least of all the commander-in-chief's.

At the conclusion of Taps, the adjutant commanded, "Firing Detail, order arms. Parade rest."

The body bearers folded each of the national ensigns into the traditional triangular shape. They presented them to the master-at-arms, who carried both to the commander-in-chief.

"On behalf of a grateful nation…"

The president accepted the flags with a bow. He passed them to Admiral Lewis and then stepped up to the podium. He spoke without notes.

"Honored warriors, there is no place else in the universe where I need to be right now except with you to mourn the passing and to honor the service of these two great Americans whom we commended to the sea today. A sad day, not only for the United States Seventh Fleet and its flagship, not only for the Pacific Fleet, the United States Navy, Pacific Command, and the Department of Defense. This is a sad day for all Americans, because we have lost two courageous warriors at the hands of an evil foreign regime.

"Cut down at the peak of his promising career, Captain José Santiago leaves behind not only a fleet staff that depended on his guidance of wisdom and experience, but also a growing and loving family. The Navy, robbed of his military and executive prowess, will sorely miss his leadership and inspiration. His family will forever mourn his premature departure from their bosom.

"Commander Jessica "Cricket" Squire was already a national hero before she volunteered to return to the tip of the spear with the Seventh Fleet. She understood better than any of us the risk that she embraced. Yet she took up arms again, because she knew the battle was not done and the evildoers who had tortured and abused her, but failed to take away her dignity and honor, would not rest. They would continue to seek the demise of freedom and to destroy the individual liberties of their own people and everyone around the globe."

He paused and looked around the assemblage on the deck of the Seventh Fleet flagship. "Cricket Squire will always be a hero in the hearts of Americans and anyone who values freedom above life. That is why I am recommending to the United States Congress that they award her posthumously her grateful nation's highest military award, the Medal of Honor."

The entire assemblage broke into applause. The president nodded and raised his hand. "A medal, no matter how prestigious or well deserved, does not repay Jessica Squire for her sacrifices on behalf of this nation and its people."

The president looked directly into the television camera that was recording his speech. "We have incontrovertible evidence that the illness that took the lives of José Santiago and Cricket Squire resulted from a deliberate, premeditated, diabolically executed biological attack targeting Cricket Squire, the United States Seventh Fleet, and the people of the Republic of Korea. The person ultimately responsible for this heinous act is none other than the so-called 'Dear Leader' of the Democratic People's Republic of Korea."

He pointed at the video camera. "The United States of America cannot and will not allow this act to go without response. Therefore, I have ordered retaliatory action, in kind. That mission will take place at a time and in a manner of our choosing. But it will happen."

What the hell?

"We bear no ill will toward the innocent citizens who eke out their lives in North Korea, and we will not stoop to the same depths of depravity and unconscionable evil to which their leadership has subscribed. Our response will be swift and complete, yet commensurate with the attack on one of our nation's most honored military officers and her colleagues."

The president gestured toward Admiral Lewis, who was holding the two national ensigns. "When I return home, it will be my sad duty and honor to present these national ensigns to the families of Captain Santiago and Commander Squire. I shall do so with a heavy heart, but also with the reassurance that the deaths of the Santiago family's son, husband, and father, and the Squire family's daughter and sister, have not been in vain.

"Let the world know that this nation, under God, will always stand for freedom, ready and willing to fight any threat to our liberty or that of our citizens. God bless Captain José Santiago. God bless Commander Jessica Squire. God bless the United States Seventh Fleet and the United States Navy. And God bless America."

Immediately upon the conclusion of the president's speech, Marine One's rotors turned, and he walked from the podium to the waiting aircraft, accompanied only by Admiral Lewis and General Alexander. The assembled sailors on the flagship's deck saluted in respect. In less than five minutes, the helicopter lifted off, made one full circle over the flagship, then flew away toward Guam.

The adjutant released the participants and spectators, all of whom left the deck in relative silence, whispering among themselves. As the working party moved to disassemble the podium, chairs, and platforms, the flagship picked up speed and turned toward Guam.

Two officers remained on the deck: Troy Pearson and Rose Deckert. They stood together by the railing where the caskets had plunged into the sea.

"She would've been proud," Rose said.

Troy snorted. "She wouldn't have given a crap."

Chapter 83
Seoul, Republic of Korea

AT THE DRAGON HILL Lodge, Eric had set his alarm for 0200. 3:00 PM in Falls Church, Virginia. His wife Melody, fourteen-year-old son John, and twelve-year-old daughter Melissa, were spending the summer with family there while Eric deployed.

He awoke on sweat-dampened sheets with a pounding headache, gut-twisting nausea, and a raging sore throat.

Time running short.

Eric sat up and switched on the bedside lamp. With trembling hands, he fumbled with the phone. The receiver dropped to the floor. Leaning over the bed to retrieve it, he stopped in mid-reach. Tears filled his eyes, and he fell back onto the bed, overcome with the enormity of the day, or days, ahead.

He sat on the edge of the bed and tried to ignore the pain in his head and throat. Fingers trembling, he punched in the international number sequence to Melody's mobile phone.

She answered on the second ring.

"It's Eric."

A brief pause before she replied. "Why are you calling? Is something wrong?"

"I'm fine." He had expected Melody's surprise, because he seldom called her while deployed. "I'm in Korea."

"What time is it there?"

"Just after two in the morning."

"But nothing's wrong? Why would you call me in the middle of your night?"

The pain in his throat made it difficult to speak. "I wanted to talk to you and the kids. I'll be out of pocket for a while."

"What's going on, Eric? You sound stressed. What's with your voice?"

"A touch of flu," he said. "Sore throat. Nothing serious."

"Why are you in Korea, and what do you mean 'out of pocket'?"

"Seventh Fleet stuff. North Koreans acting out again. Admiral has me doing deep intel."

He heard the sigh over the phone. "Fine. You can't tell me. But you sound awkward."

"It's an important mission. All I can say."

"I figured something was up when Seventh Fleet canceled the Hong Kong port visit."

"It will end soon. Then we'll resume normal operations. Have to deal with the jerk up north first."

"Whatever."

Eric had heard that sarcastic tone of voice from his wife many times in the past.

"Are the kids there? I'd like to talk to them."

"Sure." Melody's tone became more concerned. "I'll get them."

"Daddy!" Melissa's voice chimed with delight.

"How are you, sweetheart?" He forced cheerfulness into his voice.

"We are having the best time," his daughter said. "I love my cousins. Can you please, please get your next assignment here?"

"I can try. I'm glad you're happy and having fun."

"When will you be home, Daddy?"

He choked on the words. "I don't know, honey. Soon, I hope."

"I miss you."

"I miss you too." He gulped. "You're my angel. After Mommy, of course. I dream you will grow up to be just like her."

"I want to grow up to be me."

An image of Cricket flashed across Eric's brain. "Of course you do, and you will. Just like Mommy." They both laughed. The effort sent electric slivers through Eric's throat.

"Enjoy the rest of your summer," he said. "Never forget, you are my angel."

"I love you, Daddy."

"I love you too, Missy. Now let me talk to Johnny."

"Hi, Dad," the young man's tone was more serious than his sister's. Eric's son's voice had deepened since last they'd spoken.

"How goes it?" Eric said.

"This place is okay, but I'd rather be in Japan." John had become an ardent Japanophile during their two tours in that country.

He may never see Japan again.

"I understand," Eric said. "It's a wonderful place. At least you can get your anime and manga in the US."

"Not the same," John said. "What's up with you, Dad? Why the call?"

"Had the chance, so I took it. Checking up on you guys. Is everyone all right?"

"Duh. The most boring family in America. Nothing ever happens with us."

"Except you got to live in Japan and other cool places," Eric said.

"There is that," John said.

Eric's voice was about to fail. He needed to get to the point. "You know I rely on you to take care of your mom and sister, right?"

"Duh. Like either of them needs it."

"Someday they might. Especially when I'm away. I count on you for that."

"Of course." John's voice turned edgy. "Why did you say that?"

"Just thought about it. I know I can count on you."

"Okay, Dad. No need to drive it into the ground. Sheesh."

"Sorry," Eric said. "I'm proud of you, son, and I love you."

"This is getting weird, Dad."

"Can't a dad be proud of his son and love him?"

"Yeah, sure, but you don't have to, like, say it. I know that already."

"And?"

"And I love you too, Dad. Okay?"

"Thank you," Eric said. "Have a great summer. Now put your mom back on the phone."

"Why are you freaking out the kids?" Melody's voice sounded strained and tinged with anger. "Missy just asked me if you're going to die."

"Didn't mean to freak anyone out. Least of all you."

Her silence shouted.

Eric struggled to articulate his feelings. "You know I love you more than life itself. You have always been the light of my life, and our children have been my greatest joy."

"What's going on, Eric? What the actual fuck?"

"Nothing that I can tell you. But it'll be all right."

Melody's voice trembled. "Are you having an affair on that ship? Is that what this is about? Is this you leading up to leaving us?"

Eric's heart sank. "Oh my God, no. Nothing remotely like that. You are my one true love, and I've always been faithful to you."

A long pause before Melody answered. "What is it then?"

"I cannot tell you. It's top-secret national security business, nothing more. And sure as hell, it's not an affair. Believe me."

"Then reassure me you didn't call to say goodbye; that you are not leaving us."

Eric remained silent. His head felt as if it would explode, his throat was ablaze, and his body limp. He spoke in a calm, determined voice.

"No matter what happens, I will always be with you."

He hung up the phone before she could respond.

Chapter 84

E ARLY IN HIS NAVY career, Eric Mikleson had learned to sleep whenever he got the opportunity, no matter the conditions or his personal stress level. After the phone call with his family, he dozed in fits.

When his alarm sounded at 0700, he awoke in a sweat; the bedding wrapped around him mummy-style. The causative nightmare retreated into his subconscious, leaving only a snippet in his mind. Eric and Cricket on the deck of *Shenandoah,* gazing at the sunlit sea. She leaned close and spoke into his ear.

What?

Eric shook it off. He had less than an hour to get ready.

He showered and shaved, more from habit than need for the day. He used the light on his smartphone to examine his throat in the mirror. The red spots on his palate hadn't changed, but they would, maybe soon. He considered his chances of survival under the various scenarios he'd already rehearsed in his head and staved off the second thoughts. He had just one course of action left.

"For Cricket," he said aloud. Then the fleeting sound of her voice in his ear. Unintelligible.

Eric dressed in casual civilian clothes—slacks and a short-sleeved collared shirt. He placed his military ID card and passport in the shirt pocket. Then he donned a surgical face mask that he'd bought the night before in the hotel's mini-store. Since it was a common habit among Asian people to wear face masks to protect themselves and surrounding people from infectious diseases such as influenza, he would not stand out as he would in the United States.

He needed the mask to avoid exposing the wrong people. Especially since he was about to go rogue against higher authority's refusal to approve his revenge plan against Cricket's killers.

Ten minutes later, Eric walked through the Dragon Hill lobby and out into the sultry late-August air. A temperature inversion had worsened the air pollution. He coughed into the face mask as he took his place in the line waiting to board the bus for the organized tour of the Demilitarized Zone (DMZ) and Joint Security Area (JSA) in Panmunjon, South Korea.

No one paid him any heed, least of all the Asian-American woman and her husband standing in front of him, and the young off-duty soldier who'd taken the spot behind him. Those accomplices also wore face masks.

During the hour-long ride north from Seoul, Eric feigned dozing, as he had no desire to talk to anyone. He opened his eyes when the bus slowed for the first stop, the Dora Observatory, from which the tourists looked into North Korea to see the Kaesong Industrial Complex six miles away. The complex was a failed attempt at collaborative economic development between the governments of North and South Korea. Eric's sole interest in the site was the enormous flag of the Democratic People's Republic of Korea flying defiantly from a North Korean tower near the complex. He glared through powerful binoculars at the ostentatious flapping cloth, with its royal-blue top and bottom borders and the central red field with a single red star superimposed over a white circle. He thought about all that he and his Seventh Fleet colleagues and friends had endured, and lost, from the regime that cloth represented.

Eric wished he could spit across the distance onto the flag. Perhaps later he would get a chance.

Cricket's voice whispered in his ear. Something about "martyr."

After several minutes back on the bus, Eric felt the mounting tension, not only within himself but in his fellow passengers, as the vehicle entered Camp Bonifas, the gateway to the Joint Security Area. The tour group departed the bus through a phalanx of US and ROK Army security forces, through an ID checkpoint where Eric showed his personal passport instead of his military ID, and into a small auditorium.

Eric took a seat and fought off a wave of nausea and dizziness. He broke into a sweat.

A US Army soldier, fit and serious in his olive-green service uniform, stood tall in front of the group. "I am Staff Sergeant Bruce Spencer," he said with clipped military inflection. "I will be your guide for this portion of the tour. We begin with a brief slide show, after which I will provide you with important details of your visit to the JSA."

The slide show depicted the history of the Korean War, the armistice signed in 1953 to "insure a complete cessation of hostilities and of all acts of armed force in Korea until a final peaceful settlement is achieved," and the reality that the divided nation remained technically at war because no settlement had occurred.

The show then described the history of the DMZ and the Military Demarcation Line (MDL) dividing the once united nation, and iterated the series of incidents that had occurred there since the armistice. These included the three North Korean incursion tunnels, various skirmishes across the MDL, and the infamous 1976 "axe murder incident" wherein North Korean soldiers had killed two US Army soldiers, including Captain Arthur Bonifas, for whom the camp was named.

When the slide show ended, Staff Sergeant Spencer resumed his place in front of the group. "I will now brief your visit to the JSA and the Military Armistice Commission Conference Room, or MAC. It is imperative that everyone pays strict attention to these instructions, for your own safety and those around you.

"Foremost, keep in mind that North and South Korea are still technically at war. Once we leave this building, you will be in direct view of armed North Korean soldiers who will scrutinize you. Remain respectful. Do not stare at the North Korean soldiers. Avoid any provocative actions, hand gestures, or sudden movements. Do not take photographs in restricted areas. Do not leave the group for any reason. Follow my instructions at all times. Is that clear?"

Nervous nods responded to his question.

"We will now proceed out of this building and down the stairs to the MDL and the MAC. I will stop at the foot of the stairs to explain the next phase of the tour."

Eric walked in the middle of the group of about a dozen tourists, many of whom engaged in nervous chatter as the sergeant led them out of the conference room, across a vast lobby, and through the glass doors to the outside. Eric did not acknowledge the same couple and US soldier who had stood with him in the bus line at Dragon Hill Lodge. When he emerged into the sultry air, he felt he might faint.

Cricket's voice in his ear. "Life goes on." He had said those same words to her, what seemed a lifetime ago, on the *Shenandoah* deck. Before...

Te tourists slowed their pace at the sight in front of them. Three single-story low buildings, painted in the same sky-blue tone as the NATO flag, stood in a row, each building about sixty feet long by twenty feet wide. They straddled a concrete curb, the actual MDL that divided North from South Korea. In the near distance, on the North Korean side beyond the blue buildings, a four-story gray stone-and-brick building overlooked the area.

On the south side of each blue building, uniformed ROK Army soldiers wearing helmets and sunglasses stood in tae kwon do ready stances, some partially shielded by the buildings, fists clenched, staring into North Korea. Similarly attired and very serious ROK Army soldiers marched back and forth across the fronts of the buildings, stopping abruptly to stare at something in North Korea.

Three well-armed North Korean soldiers in dark brown uniforms marched from the gray building up to the MDL and stood at attention, glaring back at the ROK soldiers. A tense air of confrontation permeated the entire scene, as if it could erupt into violence at any second.

Sergeant Spencer stood in front of the tour group. "The MDL runs through the middle of these Military Armistice Commission buildings. Today we see soldiers of the Korean People's Army, or KPA, guarding their side north of the line. That's an unusually provocative posture, but they choose to be unpredictable. From the gray building on the North Korean side, you are being watched with binoculars, and you are being filmed. I repeat, you must avoid any challenging gestures or sudden movements for the rest of this portion of your tour."

Nods of assent greeted his words.

"We will now enter the MAC, where ROK Army soldiers will guard you. Ladies and gentlemen, you are about to step into North Korea."

Eric thought of Melody and their children as he followed the others into the building.

Inside the MAC, the tourists crowded on the south side of the conference table that straddled a four-inch-wide white line that transected the building. Eric stood to the right side of the table, flanked on his right by the Asian-American woman and her husband, and on his left by the American soldier. At the opposite end of the table, an ROK Army sentry in service uniform, helmet, and dark glasses stood in the ready position with fists clenched, eyes staring straight ahead. Another sentry, identically attired, assumed the same position in front of the north door of the building, the portal to North Korea.

Glancing at the window on the north side across from him, Eric saw KPA soldiers peering into the building. Over his right shoulder, he spotted another North Korean soldier at the window just behind and to his right.

Sergeant Spencer stood across the table from his tour group. "This building, and the other two like it, were built at the time of the armistice, to support ongoing peace talks between the two sides. Once every week, ROK negotiators sit on your side of the table, ready to continue those talks. To this date, no North Korean negotiators have appeared."

He pointed at the white line. "This line that divides the building is the de facto MDL that divides North from South Korea. You cross that line, you are standing in North Korea."

He gestured toward the two ROK soldiers. "These ROK Army sentries are here for your protection and to secure the integrity of the building." He pointed at the sentry guarding the north door. "The door behind this sentry remains locked and guarded at all times. One time, North Korean soldiers stormed through that door and pulled an ROK soldier into North Korea. Despite intense diplomatic efforts, he was never seen again."

He paused. "You are now invited to cross the line and enter North Korea—safely."

Eric's pulse quickened, and he involuntarily looked at his feet as he crossed the line behind the couple, followed by the American soldier. He moved back closer to the sentry and the door, to allow his accomplices to stand in front of him.

"Please keep moving," Sergeant Spencer said. He'd repositioned to the south side of the building, standing next to the other sentry.

Cricket's voice came again to Eric's ear, this time crystal clear. "Don't martyr yourself for me. Life goes on."

Eric coughed hard into his mask to attract attention, then looked at his accomplices, the couple and the soldier. He gave them a slight shake of his head. Each returned an almost imperceptible nod. Eric followed them around the room and crossed back over to the South Korean side. When he crossed the white line, he slumped to his knees.

"Please," he said to Sergeant Spencer, "I am very ill. I need help."

Chapter 85

Three Days Later. US Naval Hospital. Yokosuka, Japan.

E{RIC WAS DROWNING.}

Filthy water ran up his nose and mouth, choked him, and robbed him of vital air. On impulse, he tried to flap his arms and kick his legs to get to the surface of the water, but they were bound so tightly, he could not move them. He stood in a vat of filthy water that just covered his mouth and nostrils, forcing him to rise on tiptoes or tilt his head back to breathe. He had received intel about this common North Korea torture routine, but never imagined he would suffer it himself. How had ended up in the hands of those he'd meant to serve vengeance?

Voices echoed around him. "Suction," one said in clear English.

Not Korean?

An assailant rammed a tube down his throat, forcing an immediate gag. He bucked and flailed. The assailants held him down, and one applied suction to the tube, seeming to rip out his lungs.

And so I die.

A woman's voice. "Morphine. Now."

Eric lapsed into unconsciousness.

Horrific images invaded his mind. The assailants pulled him from the torture vat and dropped him to the floor. He writhed in agony.

Another woman's voice. Familiar. "Eric."

He awoke with a start to the wretched, pocked face of the Korean woman, Myung, the diabolical vector who had delivered the fatal virus to Cricket Squire and the Seventh Fleet. The woman snarled and spat in his face.

Eric wrenched away, turning his back to his attacker.

A gentle hand caressed his neck. "Eric, it's me."

He forced himself into full consciousness, opened his eyes, and turned. His wife, Melody, gazed at him with mixed emotions of fear and love.

"Welcome back," she said.

"Where?"

"Safe. The Navy hospital in Yokosuka."

"How?"

"For reasons no one will tell me, you collapsed during a DMZ tour. They took you to a hospital in Seoul, but they refused to keep you. Something about a contagious disease. So the Army medevaced you here. You've been unconscious for days."

Eric squeezed his eyes, remembering. He looked at Melody. "I initiated the abort plan. At the last minute, when Cricket..."

Melody's face tightened into a half-frown, then relaxed. "Whatever. I'm just happy you're back. The medical people here wouldn't let me see you until today. They say you're 'safe' now, but they won't tell me why or what from." She raised her eyebrows.

He looked back at her with a blank expression. He could never tell her he had designated himself as the human vector to exact vengeance on Kim Jong Un.

"It was a stupid plan," he said.

"Not the first you've ever done."

As Eric's mind cleared, a dread struck him. "*Shenandoah?* Seventh Fleet?"

"On their way to Pearl Harbor. That 'whatever' mission is over, but no one can board the flagship until it's 'cleared.'" She gave him a sly look. "I'm guessing from whatever it was they had to clear you from."

Eric laid his head back on the pillow and covered his eyes with his arm. *So KJU and his thugs get away with it. Damn.*

He forced himself to look at Melody and smile. "It is so good to see you again, love." A pause. "I didn't know that I would."

She stroked his forehead. "Get some rest."

"The kids?"

"Back in CONUS, enjoying time with their cousins. Eager to see you again." She shot him another quizzical look.

At once, he understood what he must do. "Soon." He looked away, then back at her. "I'm done, Mel. Really done."

She patted his shoulder. "Plenty of time for that discussion later. Get some rest now." She left the room.

Eric laid back and closed his eyes. A single tear ran down his cheek. "For Cricket."

***

Sometime later (hours or days?), Eric awoke when someone entered the room. No sign of Melody. Two corpsmen pushed a wheelchair next to his bed.

"Captain, if you're up for it, we need to take you to the SCIF. You have a secure call from the USS *Shenandoah*."

Eric practically leaped out of the bed.

Ten minutes later, he was on a secure conference call with Vice Admiral Lassiter, Captain Deckert, and Doc Pearson.

The admiral spoke first. "How are you doing, Eric?"

"Physically, I'm fine. Some gaping holes in my memory for why I ended up here in Yoko." He blew out a breath. "And what happens next."

The admiral chuckled. "Not for nothing, we all did some serious boot licking up the chain of command to cover your ass."

"Sorry. I assessed the danger too great once I appreciated the whole battle space."

"Right decision," the admiral said. "Wasn't hard to convince higher authority, including the commander-in-chief. For a guy who never served, he has a keen sense of letting the commanders in the field call the shots vice him micromanaging from thousands of miles away. Can't say the same for the pompous four-stars around his table, but in the end, everyone concurred. So, no harm, no foul."

"Thank you, ma'am." He paused, but the line went silent. "So, uh, what happens next?"

"I'll let Dr. Deckert explain that to you."

Rose Deckert summarized Eric's plight since he aborted the mission at the DMZ. "You didn't have smallpox. You had a severe upper respiratory infection that included a non-specific throat rash. Exhaustion and dehydration exacerbated the symptoms and contributed to your collapse at the DMZ. You just needed good supportive care and rest. You should be better by now. In another week, a full-up round."

She paused. "Doc Pearson and I have already discussed with the admiral and senior staff the imperative of making a definitive, data-based diagnosis of a major communicable disease before embarking on some, uh, rogue plan to use it against an enemy."

Admiral Lassiter cut in. "Duly chastised, we're glad you came to your senses. Even if you had hit the target, the bomb would have been a dud." She snorted. "Not calling you a dud, of course."

"Thank you, ma'am," Eric said. "That's great news." He paused. "I suppose an apology would sound hollow at this point?"

"You suppose right, but apology accepted. We'll deal with the consequences for you later. Right now, you just need to get well."

The admiral continued in a lighter tone. "The flagship is two days out from Pearl. We know your wife is with you there. So I've authorized a week of liberty before you rejoin the staff. Up to you whether you spend it in Japan or in Hawaii."

Eric smiled. "Ma'am, that's the toughest choice you've given me since you took command. Would it be possible to split the time between both?"

"Of course," she said. "Make it ten days of liberty. Five each in Japan and Hawaii."

"Thank you again, ma'am."

"No problem, Captain. You've earned it."

Eric took a deep breath. "Uh, ma'am, might I speak to the docs alone? Private medical stuff."

"Of course. You get well now, hear?"

As soon as the admiral left the call, Captain Deckert spoke. "What's up, Eric?" He hesitated, then spoke in a trembling voice. "I, uh, aborted the mission because... Because Cricket told me to."

"You heard Commander Squire speak to you?"

Eric's breathing quickened. "Yeah. Her voice in my ear."

"What did she say?"

Eric told her.

Doc Pearson broke the ensuing silence. "You and Commander Squire were close friends, right?"

"Yes."

Captain Deckert spoke in a gentle voice. "Do you believe in ghosts, Eric? Do you believe dead people can whisper in your ear?"

"Of course not. That's why I wanted to talk to you docs about it." He pursed his lips. "Am I going crazy?"

"Certainly not," Deckert said.

"Cricket's death traumatized all of us," Doc Pearson said. "We're all suffering it in our own ways."

"It was your subconscious mind, Eric," Deckert said. "A combination of grief, probably some PTSD, and your deep-down realization that your battle plan made no logical sense. Those realities broke through your all-consuming obsession with vengeance. Just in time, as we often say in the Navy."

Eric thanked the doctors for their support. Upon returning to his room, he sank into his bed and entered his first sound sleep since his decision at the DMZ.

Chapter 86

Two Weeks Later. Joint Base Pearl Harbor–Hickam, Honolulu, Hawaii

WHEN TROY PEARSON RETURNED in late afternoon from PACOM Headquarters at Camp Smith to the Gateway Inn on the US Navy side of Joint Base Pearl Harbor–Hickam, he reacted with mixed surprise and pleasure to see Rose Dekcert in the lobby. Troy wore his summer white uniform, an uncomfortable contrast to her khaki shorts, pale blue blouse, and sandals.

When they hugged, she smelled of sunblock, a welcome scent to Troy.

"I thought you were on leave back home," Troy said.

"I was." She sighed. "Not for pleasure. I had to finalize my divorce."

"I'm sorry," Troy said. "I had no idea."

"You had no need to know." She shrugged. "Something I had to do. I'm all the better for it. On my way back to Japan to rejoin the fleet staff on the *Reagan*. I booked a layover here to get some beach time."

Rose looked Troy in the eye and smiled. "And I thought I might run into you. We have unfinished business from the flagship. If you're up for it, I'd like to buy you a drink and maybe dinner."

"Regarding unfinished business," he said, "I've just met with Rear Admiral Matteson. Navy medicine restored my full clinical privileges, thanks to his support and that of Vish Menon." He smiled at her. "I understand you played a prominent role in that as well."

"I simply told the investigators the truth, as I saw it firsthand."

"In that case," Troy said, "I owe you a drink, and most definitely dinner."

A few hours later, they lingered over after-dinner drinks at the Il Lupino Trattoria and Wine Bar on Waikiki Beach. Troy had changed into shorts, a Hawaiian shirt, and sandals. He felt mellow and relaxed for the first time since Commander Squire had appeared in his sick call with the early signs of her fatal illness.

He thought about this bit of "unfinished business."

"I've come to accept," he said, "that there are no wrong clinical decisions when your patient is *in extremis*. If we did nothing, she was going to die, so whatever we did to try to save her life was right."

He looked at Rose, hesitant to move forward but reassured by the empathy in her eyes. "What still bothers me is not considering the diagnosis when she first presented with the illness."

"Would that have mattered?"

"Earlier diagnosis might have meant earlier treatment with tecovirimat. She might have survived."

"You give that drug too much credit," Rose said. "Our two fatalities had one thing in common. They were both immune compromised. Their bodies were not as fit to fight the disease as Espiritu and the others. That's why she died, Troy."

"Perhaps."

Rose reached across the table and touched his hand. "I'll tell you for the last time. You didn't kill her. The devil who did has not appeared in public for almost a month now. Now, you can either shit-can the 'woe is me' attitude and buy us another drink or I'll call Louise Lassiter to whup your ass."

Troy laughed and gestured to the server. "Aye, aye, ma'am."

After the drinks arrived, Rose asked him, "Now that you have clinical privileges again, what's your plan? I assume *Shenandoah* won't return to sea soon."

"If ever. I'm still a part of the ship's company, but they've closed the medical department. *Reagan* has its own medical department, including a surgeon. They don't need me out there. My only choice is to see patients at the Navy clinic here in Honolulu."

"That doesn't sound rewarding."

"To be honest," he said, "I'm thinking of getting out of the Navy. My current commitment ends in six months."

Rose did not hide her surprise. "Why would you do that? What makes you think you could get the same satisfaction in civilian practice?"

"I love the clinical side of Navy medicine," he said. "I truly believe in the mission of supporting Sailors and Marines and their families. But the bullshit and bureaucracy that we endured, and the threat to my professional reputation on account of prejudice and jealousy, leaves a bitter taste. I don't know if I can accept that anymore."

"Then don't." She squeezed his hand. "Change it, Troy. You can do that."

Troy smirked. "I don't think so."

"If not you, who?" She gave him an earnest look. "I don't know anyone in Navy medicine who better embodies the core values, especially commitment to the operational forces. We need you, Troy Pearson. The nation needs you in uniform."

"You certainly know how to boost a person's self-confidence, Captain Deckert. Thank you for that."

"I speak the truth."

She smiled. "Just promise me this: no quick decisions. You don't need to decide anything right now. Keep your options open. And give those of us with better sense the chance to help you make the right decision."

"Deal." He returned the smile. "Thanks for being my friend tonight."

"Friends always."

Troy blinked. "Do you get dreams? About..."

"Nearly every night. You and I are in her room and she's dying."

"Me too. I watch her die again every night—the whole thing, including when she convulsed and herniated. I'll bet I've looked at those pupils a thousand times. They never change."

Rose took his hand again. "Sounds like we two docs have a touch of PTSD."

"In spades." He grimaced. "Know any wonderful cure for that?"

"Afraid not, shipmate."

They talked for another hour before Troy looked at his watch. "I'd better look for a cab to get me back to the inn."

"You could do that." Rose hesitated for a second, then gazed at him with soft eyes. "Or, you could walk me down the beach to my hotel."

Troy met her gaze. "I would like that."

THE END

***

If you enjoyed this final book of the Mahoney & Squire series, you might try Mike's medical conspiracy thriller series (just click on the embedded link below):

Dr. Zack Winston Medical Conspiracy Thrillers

DEAD ALREADY, Book 1

A drug-laced conspiracy. A former Navy surgeon with a harrowing history. Will a covert frame job end his career... and his life?

***

If you are so inclined, I would very much appreciate a review on Amazon, Barnes and Noble, Goodreads, BookBub, and/or other retail platforms.

Glossary

1MC: THE LOUDSPEAKER system for making announcements throughout a Navy ship.

ACOS: Assistant Chief of Staff. Another name for Department Head or Director on an admiral's staff.

ADM: Admiral

Aiguilette: A ceremonial braided silk cord or cords worn off the left shoulder by US Navy officers who serve as chief of staff, executive assistant, or similar office to support an admiral. The number of cords corresponds to the number of stars worn by the respective admiral.

Alveoli: Tiny air sacs in the lungs where the exchange of oxygen and carbon dioxide occurs in the blood.

Amidships: The center of the ship.

Article 32 Hearing: A proceeding under the United States Uniform Code of Military Justice, similar to that of a preliminary hearing in civilian law, to determine whether sufficient evidence exists to proceed to a formal court-martial.

ASEAN: Association of Southeast Asian Nations. Includes Brunei, Cambodia, Indonesia, Lao PDR, Malaysia, Myanmar, Philippines, Singapore, Thailand, and Viet Nam.

ASW: Anti-Submarine Warfare

ASUW: Anti-Surface Warfare

BDA: Battle Damage Assessment

Biosafety Safety Level 4 (BSL 4): The highest level of biological safety used in work with dangerous and exotic microbes that pose a high risk of infection.

Bravo Zulu or BZ: The combination of the Bravo and Zulu nautical signal flags, i.e., Bravo Zulu, typically conveyed by flag hoist or voice radio, meaning "Well Done" regarding actions, operations or performance.

Bulbar Palsy: Bilateral dysfunction of the lower cranial nerves, associated with lesions in the brain stem.

BUMED: US Navy Bureau of Medicine and Surgery, the highest command in Navy medicine. Headquarters of the Navy Surgeon General.

BUPERS: Navy Bureau of Personnel, headquarters in Millington, TN.

C-2: The Grumman C-2 Greyhound prop aircraft capable of landing on an aircraft carrier. Used to transport personnel and supplies between shore and ship. Also referred to as *COD*, for Carrier Onboard Delivery.

C-40: A military transport jet, modified Boeing 737.

CAG: Commander of the carrier air wing aboard a US Navy aircraft carrier.

CFC: Combined Forces Command, US and ROK military.

Chaps: Navy slang for chaplain.

Chicoms: Derogatory term for People's Republic of China, "Chinese communists."

Chit: A one-page document that transmits information. E.g., an "up chit" from a Navy flight surgeon certifies that a naval aviator is physically fit to fly.

CNFJ: Commander Naval Forces Japan, headquarters in Yokosuka, Japan

CNFK: Commander Naval Forces Korea, headquarters in Busan, South Korea

COD: Carrier Onboard Delivery. See C-2.

CONOPS: Concept of operations

CONUS: Continental United States

Corvette: The smallest class of warship.

COS: Chief of Staff, pronounced as one word, "cahz."

Cricoid: The ring-shaped cartilage of the larynx.

DHHS: US Department of Health and Human Services

DMZ: The Demilitarized Zone across the Korean Peninsula that divides North from South Korea.

DoD: US Department of Defense

DPRK: Democratic People's Republic of Korea (North Korea)

East Sea: Korean name for the Sea of Japan

EEZ: Economic Exclusion Zone or Exclusive Economic Zone. An area of the sea in which a sovereign state has exclusive rights for exploration and use of maritime resources.

ELINT: Electronic Intelligence. Covert intelligence gathering by electronic means.

Enanthem: A rash (small spots) occurring on the mucous membranes. E.g., the throat. Often caused by viral illness.

EP-3: An electronic signals reconnaissance variant of the P-3 Orion. Used by the US Navy for ELINT purposes.

ETA: Estimated time of arrival.

Exanthem: A widespread rash or eruption on the skin, often caused by viral infection.

FCR: Flag Conference Room. The main auditorium on board the flagship.

FINEX: The ending of a military exercise.

FLAGSEC: Acronym for Flag Secretary, the naval officer who serves as administrative assistant to the fleet admiral and chief of staff.

FLIR: Forward Looking Infrared Camera

Fresnel Lens: Also called the "meatball." An optical landing system that provides glide slope information to Navy pilots approaching an aircraft carrier.

FONOPS: Freedom of navigation operation

Flag Deck: The deck on a flagship that houses the fleet admiral, staff, offices, conference rooms, and mess facilities. Typically the first deck below the open main deck.

Frag: Destroy by combat action.

GSMA: Greater Seoul Metropolitan Area.

Guillan-Barre Syndrome: An autoimmune disorder characterized by ascending paralysis of peripheral nerves. Potentially fatal if brain stem affected.

Gundeck: A Navy slang term for falsifying or fabricating an official record or report.

Head: Navy slang for bathroom or restroom.

HM: US Navy hospital corpsman. Further defined by rank: **HM3** – Third Class, **HM2** – Second Class, **HM1** – First Class, **HMC** – Chief, **HMCS** – Senior Chief, **HMCM** – Master Chief

HUMINT: Human Intelligence. Intelligence gathered through interpersonal contact, a category of intelligence derived from information collected and provided by human sources.

ILI: Influenza-like illness.

J2: Designation for the director of intelligence at a joint command, such as US Pacific Command.

J3: Designation for the director of operations at a joint command, such as US Pacific Command.

JAG: Judge Advocate General, or colloquial reference to a Navy lawyer

JASDF: Japanese Air Self-Defense Force. The Japanese air force equivalent.

JG: Junior Grade, as in LTJG for Lieutenant, Junior Grade

JIC: Joint Intelligence Center. Secure compartment in the ship for processing/reading classified materials and communications.

JMSDF: Japanese Maritime Self-Defense Force. The Japanese navy equivalent.

JSA: The Joint Security Area in Panmunjon, South Korea, that guards the border between North and South Korea.

JSDF: Japanese Self-Defense Force. The unified military forces of Japan.

JWICS: Joint Worldwide Intelligence Communications System. A secure top secret classified system or process.

KATUSA: "Korean Augmentation to the United States Army." English-fluent ROK Army members assigned to support the US Army staff in Korea.

Ketamine: A dissociative anesthetic that may have hallucinogenic effects on some patients.

KJU: Acronym for Kim Jong Un, ruler of the DPRK, North Korea.

KPA: Korean People's Army of the Democratic People's Republic of Korea (North Korea)

LightCycler: Brand name for a certain PCR analyzer (See below).

LIMDU: Limited duty status, often based on medical conditions expected to resolve.

LMA: Laryngeal Mask Airway. A device that keeps a patient's airway open while unconscious, or as a life-saving measure against a difficult airway.

LNO: Liaison Officer

Macular Rash: A skin condition consisting of flat, discolored areas.

Maculopapular Rash: A skin condition consisting of flat, discolored areas (macules) and small raised bumps (papules).

MAST: Medical Anti-Shock Trousers. Similar to aviator G-suit, intended to compress the legs and force blood into the body's core or head. Not to be confused with "captain's mast," a US Navy procedure for non-judicial punishment.

Medulloblastoma: An aggressive cancerous brain tumor that invades the lower back part of the brain. Often occurs in children.

Midazolam: A short acting sedative drug with rapid onset of action, commonly used in seizure treatment, anesthesia, and treatment of anxiety disorders.

MODLOC: A term often used for keeping a naval asset within a confined sea space, pending further orders or operations.

MP: Military police.

MPRA: Maritime Patrol and Reconnaissance Aircraft Program in the US Navy

N00: The Fleet Commander

N1: ACOS for Personnel

N2: ACOS for Intelligence

N3: ACOS for Operations

N4: ACOS for Logistics

N5: ACOS for Planning

N6: ACOS for Combat Systems/Information Systems

N7: ACOS for Theater Security

N8: ACOS for Resources Integration

National Command Authorities or National Command Authority (NCA): Informal reference to the President and Secretary of Defense, the ultimate source of military orders.

NCIS: Naval Criminal Investigative Service

NIH: National Institutes of Health, based in Bethesda, MD.

NLL: Northern Limit Line. An imaginary line that divides the seas around the Korean peninsula between North Korea's and South Korea's authority.

NLSO: Naval Legal Services Office.

Norepinephrine: A chemical stimulant with various medical uses, including raising blood pressure.

Nugget: Navy slang for a neophyte or rookie.

O-1 to O-10: Officer rank designations. **O-1:** Ensign, **O-2:** Lieutenant JG, **O-3:** Lieutenant, **O-4:** Lieutenant Commander, **O-5:** Commander, **O-6:** Captain, O-7: Rear Admiral Lower Half, **O-8:** Rear Admiral Upper Half, **O-9:** Vice Admiral, **O-10:** Admiral

OOD: Officer of the Deck.

Opisthotonos: Spasm of the muscles causing backward arching of the head, neck, and spine.

OPREP: An operations report.

OPREP PINNACLE: An operations report of a highest priority threat to national security.

OPSEC: Operational Security

Orthopox: A genus of viruses that includes smallpox virus.

OSHA: US Occupational Safety and Health Administration.

P-3 Orion: Four-engine, turboprop anti-submarine and maritime surveillance aircraft developed for the United States Navy

P-8 Poseidon: Multi-Mission Maritime Aircraft (MMA) offering surveillance and reconnaissance, long-range anti-submarine warfare capabilities. Replaced the P-3 Orion.

PacFleet: US Navy Pacific Fleet, based in Honolulu, HI. Responsible for naval operations throughout the Pacific. Subordinate commands are US 3rd Fleet, based in San Diego, CA; and US 7th Fleet, based in Yokosuka, JP.

PACOM or USPACOM: US Pacific Command, one of the US Joint Service combatant commands. (Renamed in 2018 to USINDOPACOM for US Indo-Pacific Command)

PAO: Public Affairs Officer

Papular Rash: A skin condition consisting of small raised bumps (papules). See: maculopapular rash above.

Pathognomonic: A medical term that means "characteristic for a particular disease." A pathognomonic sign is a particular sign whose presence means that a specified disease is present beyond any doubt.

PAUSEX: An operational pause in a military exercise.

PC: Politically Correct

PCR Analyzer: A medical instrument that analyzes and amplifies DNA or RNA sequences to diagnose diseases, screen for genetic abnormalities, and such. "PCR" = "Polymerase Chain Reaction."

PLA: People's Liberation Army of the People's Republic of China

PLAN: People's Liberation Army Navy of the People's Republic of China

Pohang Class: Variant of the Corvette class of naval warships, deployed by the Republic of Korea (South Korea)

POTUS: President of the United States

Prodrome: A medical term for the early signs or symptoms of an illness or health problem that appear before the more obvious symptoms

Propofol: An intravenous anesthetic and sedative used to help patients relax or sleep during medical procedures and surgery.

PRC: People's Republic of China

PTSD: Post-traumatic stress syndrome.

Pustular: A skin condition that includes pustules, i.e. pus-filled blebs.

Quarterdeck: The main security check point aboard a vessel when it is in port or anchored. The area of the ship where the gangway is rigged and the watch is posted. Overseen by the officer of the deck.

RADM: Rear Admiral (Upper Half)

RDML: Rear Admiral (Lower Half)

Recon: Reconnaissance

River City: Navy code name for the operational security process of shutting off all non-secure communications from or two a ship. Includes Internet and email capabilities.

RHIB: Rigid hull inflatable boat often used by operational special forces.

ROK: Republic of Korea, i.e., South Korea. Also, an informal term for a citizen thereof.

ROK Fleet: Headquarters for the ROK Navy fleet in South Korea.

ROKN: Republic of Korea (South Korea) Navy

ROKS: Colloquial term for South Korean people

RTB: Return to Base

SAG: Surface Action Group

SCIF: Sensitive Compartmented Information Facility. A secure facility to support classified communications.

Sariwon Class: Variant of the Corvette class of naval warships, deployed by the Korean People's Army (North Korea)

Semper Fidelis or Semper Fi: Latin for "always faithful" or "always loyal." The motto of the United States Marine Corps.

Seppuku: The Japanese ritual of suicide by self-inflicted evisceration.

Sinpo: A class of North Korean submarine, capable of launching ballistic missiles from underwater.

SIQ: Sick in quarters.

SNS: Strategic National Stockpile

Songun Politics: Military-first politics.

STARTEX: The start of a military exercise.

Stockholm Syndrome: A psychological response to captivity, wherein the prisoner forms a psychological connection to their captors and sympathize with them.

Suboccipital Craniotomy: A neurosurgical procedure that involves removing a section of bone at the base of the skull to access the brain beneath it.

Succinylcholine: A skeletal muscle relaxant, paralytic agent. It is used to relax muscles during surgery or while on a breathing machine.

SWO: Surface Warfare Officer (compared to aviator or submariners.)

TACCO: Tactical Coordinator. US Navy aircrew who coordinates the activities of the crew responsible for the tactical operation of the aircraft and its systems.

TAD: Temporary Active Duty

Tecoviromat: An antiviral drug that treats infections caused by orthopoxviruses, including smallpox, monkeypox, and cowpox.

Torp: Torpedo

Type 70 Pistol: North Korean-made version of the Russian Makarov semiautomatic pistol.

Type 88 Rifle: Chinese-made semi-automatic version of the AK-47 assault rifle.

UFG: *Ulchi Freedom Guardian*, a former annual joint US and ROK military exercise conducted over a two-week period in August.

UNC: United Nations Command in South Korea

UNCLOS: United Nations Convention on the Law of the Sea. Establishes a legal framework for all maritime activities.

USFJ: United States Forces Japan, headquarters in Tokyo, Japan

USFK: United States Forces Korea, headquarters in Seoul, South Korea.

VADM: Vice Admiral

Vesicular: A skin condition consisting of fluid-filled blisters.

WestPac: Western Pacific

West Sea: Korean name for the Yellow Sea between China and Korea.

WMD: Weapons of Mass Destruction. Typically nuclear, chemical or biological weapons.

FREE BOOKS and OTHER PRIZES

S IGN UP TO RECEIVE Mike's regular newsletter that offers insights into military and emergency medicine, news about Mike's books, and a monthly contest for gift cards, novellas, free audiobook downloads, and signed paperback books. No spam ever.

Join Mike's newsletter mailing list here:
https://mikejkrentz.com/newsletter

All Books by Mike Krentz

Dr. Zack Winston Medical Conspiracy Thrillers

DEAD ALREADY

A drug-laced conspiracy. A former Navy surgeon with a harrowing history. Will a covert frame job end his career... and his life?

WARM AND DEAD

He flourishes in the heart of a hectic ER, but the threatened loss of family becomes his greatest fear. Can an intrepid doctor protect his own from a twisted mind?

DEATH AGENT

They threatened his life. They hurt his kid. Can this gifted ER doctor deliver payback without becoming addicted to revenge?

Mahoney & Squire Women's Military Adventure Fiction

HER SHOW OF FORCE

She can stand her ground with the best of them. But she'll need all her strength to keep her family and her sailors afloat...

HER PACIFIC SHOWDOWN

Enemies attacking from all sides. Can she counter the offensive long enough to claim victory?

POINTS OF ATTACK

She's flanked by enemies, inside and out. Can this dedicated officer execute a strategy to save a colleague's life before they're both MIA?

VECTORS OF VENGEANCE

She killed her treacherous lover before she escaped from the prison camp. Safely home, will she discover what goes around comes around?

Standalone

ANGELS FALLING

The lives of an ex-seminarian turned criminal profiler, an ex-priest turned cult leader, and the former nun they both loved collide in the aftermath of a heinous, ritualistic murder. Must two die for one to live?

About the Author

MIKE KRENTZ WRITES MEDICAL suspense, psychological thrillers, and military fiction based on his experiences as an emergency physician and US Navy medical officer and flight surgeon.

Born and raised in Arizona, Mike earned a classical degree in English from the University of San Francisco, a Doctor of Medicine degree from the Medical College of Wisconsin, and a Master of Public Health Degree from The Johns Hopkins University.

Following a stellar civilian career in emergency medicine, Mike rededicated his professional life to serve the men and women of America's Navy and Marine Corps and their families. He served in both land-based clinical settings and in afloat warships. His last active-duty assignment was as Seventh Fleet Surgeon on board the flagship, USS *Blue Ridge*.

After retiring from the Navy, Mike continued his service as a consultant to the Navy and Marine Corps Public Health Center, Health Analysis Department. Upon completion of that mission, he returned to his earliest life passion as a full-time writer. DEATH AGENT is his seventh published novel. He has others in various stages of production.

Mike serves as Vice-Chairman of the Board of Directors of The Muse Writers Center, where he also teaches fiction writing and leads an advanced fiction studio.

Mike, his wife Kathryn, and miniature schnauzer Yoshi live in Norfolk, VA.

Follow Mike on social media: Facebook, Instagram, YouTube

Bravo Zulus

MY WIFE, KATHRYN; SON, Matthew; older children, Jewls, Lisa, Debi, and Michael; stepchildren, Kate and James. You've endured more than a fair share of your imperfect dad's life wanderings, yet remained loving through it all. You are each special in your own way, and will always have my constant and unconditional love and gratitude.

Jayne Ann Krentz, cherished cousin-in-law, for your encouragement, support, gentle nudges, and solid counsel. Your confidence helped me to believe in myself as a writer.

A sad but honorific salute to my cousin, the late Frank Krentz. You were my boyhood hero, closest I ever had to a biological brother.

My colleagues at The Muse Writers Center whose cogent commentaries and enthusiastic support elevated the quality of my writing: Kelly Sokol, the late John Cameron, Susan Paxton, John Aguiar, David Cascio, Lea Ann Douglas, Jim Hodges, Christine Braig, and Tamako Takamatsu. You all are fabulous writers whose works deserve publication. A huge thanks to Michael Khandelwal, founder and guiding light of The Muse for establishing a world-class writers' community in our hometown, and a salute to Shawn Gervin who keeps the ship sailing north.

To fellow canine enthusiasts and daily dog walking "buddies" for your encouragement and support of my writing. Thanks to Bill Caruso, Margaret Herr, and Dave John for your review and comments on an early draft of this novel. Last but not least, to canines Arlo, Chester, Grace, Lazlo, Daisy, Maxine, Stella, Chewie, Chloe, Carli, Bruno, Ellie, the late Damoo, and most especially to our own miniature schnauzer, Yoshi, for daily examples on how to love life no matter what.

Fellow former military officers, Captain (retired) Elwood "Hoppy" Hopkins, US Navy Medical Corps; and Colonel (retired) Bill Caruso, US Army, for continued inspiration and your generous reviews and blurbs.

Captain (retired) Chris Herr, USN, and quintessential Navy brat, spouse, and mom, Margaret Herr, for camaraderie and inspiration during our morning neighborhood dog-walks and shared experiences of military life in Japan and the Seventh Fleet. As individuals and as a couple, you both epitomize the true meaning of honor, courage, commitment.

A warm salute to the men, and especially the women, of The World's Finest Staff — the officers, Sailors, Marines, and civilians who serve the Seventh Fleet commander in winning the peace over a vast region ever teetering on the verge of conflict. Your consummate professionalism and selfless commitment to commander and mission represent the finest tradition of naval service. Few Americans will ever know or understand your sacrifices for our nation and its ideals. However unsung, you are all my heroes, and I am forever honored to have served with you aboard the flagship.

Most of all, thanks to my readers. I appreciate your investment in my novels, in both time and money. I hope you enjoyed reading this story as much as I did writing it.

If you are so inclined, I would very much appreciate a review on Amazon, Barnes and Noble, Goodreads, BookBub, and/or other retail platforms.

VECTORS OF VENGEANCE (Mahoney and Squire Military Series, Book 4)

By Mike Krentz

Published by Purple Papaya

ISBN: 9781621812272 (paperback); 9781621812265 (e-Book)

Cover Design: GetCovers.com

Editor: Ignatius Stuart

Revised, Second Edition

First edition published as VECTORS, by Mike J. Krentz, Copyright © 2016 by Mike J. Krentz

Connect with Mike Krentz online: mikejkrentz.com

Printed in the United States of America.

www.ingramcontent.com/pod-product-compliance
Lightning Source LLC
Chambersburg PA
CBHW022033120726
47899CB00001BB/150